A Pack of Two

Jacky Russell

LYRICAL PRESS
Kensington Publishing Corp.
www.kensingtonbooks.com

Lyrical Press books are published by
Kensington Publishing Corp. 119 West 40th Street New York, NY 10018

Copyright © 2012 by Jacky Russell

All Kensington titles, imprints, and distributed lines are available at special quantity discounts for bulk purchases for sales promotion, premiums, fundraising, and educational or institutional use.

Special book excerpts or customized printings can also be created to fit specific needs. For details, write or phone the office of the Kensington Special Sales Manager:
Kensington Publishing Corp.
119 West 40th Street
New York, NY 10018
Attn. Special Sales Department. Phone: 1-800-221-2647.

Kensington and the K logo Reg. U.S. Pat. & TM Off.
Lyrical Press and the L logo are trademarks of Kensington Publishing Corp.

First Electronic Edition: November 2012
eISBN-13: 978-1-61650-423-6
eISBN-10: 1-61650-423-4

First Print Edition: November 2012
ISBN-13: 978-1-61650-903-3
ISBN-10: 1-61650-903-1

Printed in the United States of America

A witch and a werewolf. A pack of two.

Master Sergeant Breanna Welker loves hockey games, cheesy fries, and being second in command of the U.S. Army's Bravo Company. The fact that her commanding officer is a vampire and most of her fellow soldiers are werewolves doesn't slow her down a bit. Her colorful vocabulary and uncompromising loyalty have endeared her to her unit, who don't give a damn she's a shape-shifting witch.

Lucas Benelli can't boast the same loyalty from the people close to him. His father is the Alpha of the largest known werewolf pack in the world–a pack Lucas is expected to be the leader of. But Lucas has spent most of his life avoiding contact with his father's pack and they don't seem to like him much either.

Together, they forge a connection not even Lucas's dysfunctional pack or Breanna's meddling unit can break–and come face-to-face with the hardest choice either of them has ever had to make.

Books by Jacky Russell

A Pack of Two

Published by Kensington Publishing Corporation

For Corey

Acknowledgements

My sincerest gratitude to the people who helped more than they know. To my husband for his unshakable faith in me, especially on the days when things weren't going so well and to Wendy G for always listening and being brave enough to read it first. You guys rock. Couldn't have done it without you!

Many thanks to Lyrical Press and most especially Dianne B for patience, diligence, and belief in this novel and me.

And a special thanks to dogs for understanding when I had the computer on my lap instead of them.

Chapter 1

Breanna

Spend five minutes in the woods and it's easy to understand why rabbits are on the bottom of the food chain. Reconnaissance duty meant lots of down time and with no activity on my assigned stretch of road, the rabbit had become my target. It really should have noticed my owl form perched in the tree less than fifteen feet above its fuzzy brown head. That grass must have been good.

The distant roar of a motorcycle meant Flopsy wouldn't be dinner. Damn.

The headlight of a Ducati sliced through the fog, the rider hunching forward to guide it along the winding mountain road. As he approached a turn, the rider reined in his bike, man and machine in perfect harmony. The moon glinted off his black helmet. The black-and-red leather riding suit contoured to his body. The bike roared as he released it into the curve.

I'd returned to my musings of Flopsy with a dollop of mustard when more headlights appeared. Through the fog I could barely make out a sedan rushing forward, tagging the back wheel of the Ducati.

How the hell had I missed that car?

The rider fought to remain upright but the bike skidded on its side before careening off the road. The rider disappeared over the edge, his bike crying out for pavement.

So much for a quiet night of recon.

A fireball blinded me as the Ducati exploded into a fountain of flames, the remnants of the motorcycle consumed.

Precious seconds ticked away while the flames died and my eyesight returned. The rabbit dashed into the leaves. The sounds of raspy breathing drifted from the brush, the gurgle of blood-drenched lungs struggling for air. The rider, thrown clear of the explosion, lay deathly still within the thick undergrowth.

The clipped voice of my commanding officer, Major Simon DuChard, resounded clearly in my head. *Do not engage anyone or anything. Recon only. Call if you have something to report but do not, I repeat, do not engage.*

Partially shielded by the bushes, the rider's battered body looked human, but he wasn't. A human would have been dead.

The slam of a car door broke the stillness, followed by a flashlight beam sweeping across the burning remains of the Ducati. A muted groan escaped the rider's lips and the beam turned urgently in his direction. Gravel rolled freely as a cloaked figure slid down the incline and landed with inhuman grace in the clearing. The air in the clearing vibrated with a chaotic evil. Suffering and death surrounded the cloaked figures.

Had to love being able to read auras. Hooray. One for the witch.

"He's breathing," the cloaked freak yelled to his counterpart at the top of the hill.

A cloak? Really? Who the hell wore a cloak? That was wrong on so many levels.

A second cloaked figure leaped gracefully into the clearing and sneered. "Good. The others would be disappointed if he was already dead."

The rider grunted when jerked onto his back. He couldn't fight them even if he tried. He was badly injured and at their mercy.

Recon only, Welker. Do not to engage.

Sitting by, pruning my feathers, was not an option. I needed to protect him. He was helpless. Vulnerable.

And I was under orders, but oh well.

I needed a plan. If I flew out of hearing range and called for backup, the cloak brothers would be gone. If I flew along behind the car, I'd lose them. There was only one choice. My beak chattered as my plan began to take shape. I would engage.

Plan? This wasn't a plan. This was crazy female witch insanity.

Tendrils of black magic surged around my body as I screeched and dove. My chest constricted, the magic choking air from my lungs. My owl form was not nearly as resistant to the power of dark witchcraft as my human form, but for now dive-bombing was the best plan of attack I had.

Dive-bombing? Really, Welker? That was the best a seventeen-year veteran of the US Army Bravo Company could come up with? Bird brain.

The first figure slapped at me like I was a giant mosquito. The second chanted in a language I didn't understand. Definitely not an invitation to a Tupperware party. The magnitude of the situation hit me as I circled for a second approach. These were Malandanti, powerful Italian witches known for ritual killings. Great, these guys were so old they were around when Hell formed. Unless I stopped them, the groaning rider would be their next sacrifice to who only knew what. I would be dinner.

Simon was gonna kill me.

Magic crackled in the air as I landed in a pile of leaves. The two Malandanti chanted in unison. I summoned my own magic and shifted seamlessly to human form.

The black magic surrounded me like a smothering blanket of evil. Without opening my eyes, I repeated the protection spell my grandmother had taught me. As the last words left my mouth, the cool sensation of my own protective magic enveloped me.

Now whatcha gonna do, Welker? Exchange recipes? Brilliant plan, Sergeant.

The Malandanti stood between me and the rider. If I could breach their magic, I could take them down. The Malandanti had powerful magic, but their hand-to-hand skills sucked. Mine, however, did not.

"Have some of this, boys."

Wave after wave of spells slammed into me as I dashed kamikaze-style through the moonlit clearing. My protective cast was holding, though it felt more and more tattered as the Malandanti increased their fervor. With one great lunge, I knocked both witches to the ground, their hoods falling away from their faces. Their inky black eyes glistened as I glided over their heads. My loud whoops made me sound a bit on the crazy side. That was fine. Whatever worked.

Landing on my feet, I peeked at the downed rider. Life slowly drained from his body with each labored breath. I should have helped him, but healing spells were not my forte. Hell, I'd probably turn him into a frog. The cloak-wearing scary-faced uglies in front of me climbed to their feet.

"You guys have serious fashion issues."

The Malandanti hissed as I took a step toward them. Together, with enough effort, they could overwhelm my arcane protective spells, but maybe they didn't know that. Earth witches weren't common and hopefully these guys wouldn't know the limits of my magic.

Great. I had hope. They had skills.

I traced a sign of protection in the air and stepped around it. The blue-gray glow increased until it bathed the dying rider. The Malandanti snarled, their black teeth obviously never having seen fluoride. Their pasty faces had a greenish, rather ghoulish glow. Damn, they were some kind of ugly.

"Guess you guys don't floss, huh?"

"*Strega*," the taller Malandanti snarled, his eyes wide as he stared at my protection symbol.

Hmm, *strega*? That was much cooler than witch. I liked it. Breanna Welker, Earth *Strega*.

For now, the Malandanti magic fell from me as if I were Teflon-coated, but one more step away from the glow and my Teflon would be gone.

This was not looking good for the home team. Oh well, game on.

"Leave or die," I demanded, smiling in satisfaction at using one of my favorite movie lines. With a flick of my finger, a blue-green fireball landed at the feet of the closest Malandanti. He yelped and jumped sideways to avoid the bouncing flame.

"Simon is so gonna kill me."

I ducked as the remaining Malandanti hurled a bolt of lightning in my direction. The bolt whizzed past my head and embedded in a tree. The ground shook with the force of the impact, the tree shuddering before thudding to the ground. Guess my fireballs weren't all that intimidating.

"Damn," I grumbled, diving toward the rider. The protection sign faded. I needed a diversion.

"Hey, look over there," I yelled, pointing to the top of the cliff. The idiots fell for it.

I straddled the rider and called upon the ancient magic of my people. My mind reached out to the forest, beckoning an ally from its depths. The connection clicked into the place as the protection symbol flickered its last moments of life. The Malandanti, no longer staring into the wild blue yonder, advanced.

"We do not wish to kill you, *strega*. We only seek the werewolf."

"Uh huh, whatever."

The Malandanti danced as my curtain of flames touched off tiny fires within the hems of their robes. Their predicament gave me just enough time to cast another protection spell over the rider. The acidic smell of black magic tormented my nose and brought tears to my eyes. My magic tank was almost empty. The ugliest Malandanti sputtered a mean-sounding curse and the ground began to shake.

"Yeah, not happening, Dumb and Dumber. You can't sic the earth on an earth witch."

My final vapors of magic quieted Mother Earth. The Malandanti screamed and threw another energy bolt. I tucked and rolled but not quickly enough. The voltage sizzled along my nerves, searing my insides to a charcoal-y well-done.

The second Malandanti attacked my protection spell, shredding the rider's only defense. I tried to cast another spell, but with no magic and burned-out circuits, all I managed were a few tough-sounding words that held no power.

Muttering a string of profanity my fellow soldiers would have been proud of, I clambered to my feet. The Malandanti ignored me. That was insulting.

"Yoohoo!"

Both witches glared at me.

"I wasn't done yet. Why don't you guys go make some brew or something? Or, I've got it--go fly a kite in a thunderstorm. A visit to the spa could really help with those wrinkles."

Their lips moved but I couldn't hear the words. They were casting and I was receiving, or something like that. Earth witches have the ability to absorb black magic and if I didn't deflect their magic, my internal organs would cease to exist. No magic in my tanks meant no deflector shields. This was gonna hurt.

The slashing of my guts increased as the Malandanti chanted louder. I pulled a knife from my boot and side-armed it, but the freak ducked before the blade reached its target. My liver bubbled and my spleen baked as the magic swirled inside me. I was almost witch fricassee when a bellowing bear burst from the forest. The Malandanti screamed and ran from the clearing with the bear in hot pursuit.

"Damn well took you long enough."

Bears didn't get in a hurry to answer a summons from an earth witch. He was probably on his nightly constitutional when I called and a wild bear in the woods would not rush.

The bear roared as tires squealed from the cliff above. The Malandanti were so busy trying to run away they hadn't bothered to cast any spells. That was good. If the bear had been hurt, Mother Earth would not have been pleased with me and I didn't want the big bad Mama angry.

I pulled my radio from my pocket and made a note to thank the manufacturer since the thing worked even through my shape-changes and the Malandanti fireworks.

"Ordy, this is Welker. You out there?"

The radio crackled to life. "Gotcha loud and clear, Bre. What's up?" Theodore Ordison answered in his slow Louisiana drawl.

"I need the Humvee over here. Got a wolf down, civilian."

A long pause followed before the Cajun answered. "Uh, we weren't supposed to engage anybody. What did you do to him?"

"It wasn't me, Ordy. The Malandanti attacked him. Now get your ass over here with the Humvee ASAP."

"Be there in fifteen minutes."

"Make it ten. This guy's hurt pretty bad."

My body trembled and my legs felt encased in concrete as I crawled toward the rider. A tiny carpenter was building cabinets in my head. Blood dripped from my nose. Damn black magic. This was supposed to be an easy recon mission, just watch the road and report anything odd. Nobody had said anything about Malandanti sightings and why was a lone werewolf out here this time of night, anyway? Werewolves were pack creatures. Hell, they didn't even go to the bathroom by themselves.

The rider wasn't moving but there was air whooshing into his lungs. He was alive, barely. He lay on his back, his face hidden by the dark mask of his helmet. I knelt beside him and shook off my coat. He groaned softly, his boots scratching against the dirt as I unzipped his black leather jacket and ran my hands along the hardened muscles of his chest. Gritting my teeth and trying to be gentle, I pulled the helmet from his head.

"I'm sorry," I whispered when he moaned. Waves of chestnut curls spilled around the most handsome face I'd ever seen. Sinfully dark lashes rested against perfect olive skin. With high, chiseled cheekbones and deliciously full lips, he was traffic-stopping gorgeous. An unruly lock of hair fell across his forehead, giving him a heart-stealing mischievous look even as he lay unconscious and bleeding. The smell of musk and leather was intoxicating. A sense of coiled power and pure masculine sexuality surrounded him.

Yum.

I scooted closer, actually checking his injuries this time. He was losing blood rapidly through his leg, the jagged femur jutting through a rip in his pants. He had at least four broken ribs beneath a set of washboard abs that made me seriously want to do laundry, a nasty bump on the back of his head and a constant stream of blood flowing from his mouth. The injuries would have been enough to kill most beings but werewolves were tough.

After pulling my radio from my fatigues, I couldn't resist running my fingers through the rebellious chestnut hair on his forehead.

"You're going to be all right, Wolf. Just hang on, okay?" The bristly stubble along his jaw tickled my fingers.

My radio beeped. Simon answered immediately.

"Breanna, where have you been? You were supposed to report in a half hour ago."

"I found a couple of Malandanti."

"Are you all right?"

"Uh, yeah, I'm fine but I'm with a werewolf who's been hurt. He needs medical attention."

"Which one? Aaron?"

"No, not a Bravo wolf. I think he's one of the Italian Pack wolves." The line buzzed long enough I thought the call had dropped. "Hey, Simon?"

"Why are you with an injured werewolf? " He sounded calm but he was P.O.'d in a very big way. Simon's accent was always much stronger when he was angry and right now my vampire commanding officer sounded very Frenchy.

"He was attacked by Malandanti. They wrecked his bike and he's here beside the road with a bunch of broken bones and a hell of a lot of blood on the ground. Can you send a Medivac Transport for him?"

Simon ignored my request. "Are you sure these were Malandanti?"

"Got the sizzle marks to prove it. Now will you please send help? I tied a tourniquet on his leg but he's losing a lot of blood."

"He's a civilian and since we are under orders not to engage, I can't very well send an American military aircraft to land in the middle of the road," Simon bellowed. He was ready to strangle me for disobeying orders.

After a French cursing tirade, Simon agreed to call for a chopper. "You need to get away from that wolf now. Injured wolves are dangerous and this one doesn't know you."

Simon was right but I couldn't walk away from this wolf. His head was now on my lap and his fingers firmly clamped around my hand. He hadn't spoken, but he knew he wasn't alone. He might believe I was someone else, his mate or girlfriend, someone to comfort him as he lay dying. If that was what he needed from me, so be it.

"Does that wolf have any idea what you did to get rid of the Malandanti?"

"No, he hasn't regained consciousness."

"Good, at least we won't have to try to explain that. By the way, how did you get rid of them?"

"I called a friend." The back of my fingers brushed along the wolf's bruised cheek. He moaned softly and licked his lips.

"Breanna, you need to let the Bravo wolves deal with this. The Italian Alpha is one of the most powerful werewolves in Europe and could easily believe you attacked this pack wolf."

"I'll be careful." I signed off and looked down at the injured werewolf. His grip, even in his weakened condition, was substantial enough my bones ached. I pulled a cloth from my fatigue pocket and dabbed at the blood trickling from his mouth.

His eyes fluttered opened, pure silver boring into me. The werewolf, his wolf fully ascended, watched me warily. He was human in body but wolf in mind and that made him very unpredictable. He was injured, but had enough strength that he could easily snap my neck if he felt I was a threat.

"I mean no harm," I said.

The silver eyes never wavered from mine. In wolf language, direct eye contact was a display of dominance, a solicitation for a fight, a demand for submission, but oddly there was no threat in his stare. Somewhere deep inside me, something snapped to attention, as if my soul had awakened for the first time.

He squeezed my hand harder. My bones threatened to crunch. He held his breath and clenched his teeth until I placed a hand on his forehead.

"Shhh, easy, Wolf. Shhh, easy." I stroked his forehead while his breathing resumed and his jaw relaxed. "Easy, Wolf, I'm here to help."

He swallowed hard and closed his eyes, his grip loosening a little. My heart beat wildly as his thumb rubbed tiny circles on the back of my hand. My body reacted to his touch, yearning for more, wanting to caress his lips, his chest, his…

"Thank you." He sounded like he'd gargled with glass.

"You're welcome."

He opened his eyes, now tinged with brown, and smiled weakly. "What happened?"

"You ran off the road. Your bike's over there. Pretty much totaled, I'd guess."

He turned his head and groaned at the sight of the charred Ducati. I chuckled and the brown eyes captured me.

"Why are you helping me?"

I wiped the blood from his face and shrugged. "You had a cool bike."

He reached for my face, gloved fingers softly caressing my cheek. I was lost in his eyes, helpless as a mouse with no hope of escape as his fingers travelled along my jaw toward my chin.

"What's your name?"

"Breanna."

"Breanna. A beautiful name for a beautiful woman."

"You must have hit your head when you crashed."

He clenched his eyes and gritted his teeth, a semblance of a laugh rumbling in his chest. "Ow," he choked, coughing up fresh blood.

"Sorry," I said, wiping his pain-twisted face.

He smiled but it didn't touch his eyes. I wished I could do more to help him. My grandmother would have known how, but his injuries were beyond my magical abilities.

"Some other wolves are on their way to help get you to the hospital."

I expected him to look relieved but he didn't. He hacked up more blood. I eased him farther onto my lap and held his head until the coughing fit passed.

"You need to save your strength, Wolf." I wiped the blood from his face, my fingers lingering along his jawline.

Silver tinged his espresso eyes. "Will they hurt you for being here?"

What an odd question.

I brushed back his hair. "No, they are soldiers in my unit. They won't harm anybody unless I tell them to."

He smiled and my heart thundered loudly enough every living thing in the forest could have heard it. He had the most beautiful, perfect white teeth. "I'd kill them if they hurt you."

"Brave words for a wolf in your condition," I muttered before finding myself lost in a sea of brown.

"I'm Lucas." His voice was weak, his eyes dulled with pain, but there was an aura about him, unrelenting dominance. "Lucas Benelli."

The man was too hot for words. It really had to be illegal to look that good in a leather riding suit.

Holy cannoli.

Before I could formally introduce myself, the bright glow of headlights shone over the cliff above us. Tires squealed to a stop, followed by voices yelling for me.

"Sounds like the cavalry is here," I said as the voices grew closer. "Down here, fellas."

Rocks rolled and I shielded Lucas's head with my body as Ordy and two other werewolves plunked into the clearing. They were all empty-handed.

"Did you forget something?" I asked as they got closer.

The soldiers looked at one another like I had asked for the top speed of a charging wildebeest.

"You guys plan to kiss him and make him better? Where the hell are the backboard and the first aid kit?"

Lucas tightened his grip on my hand. Alpha-like dominance filled the air.

"It's okay, Lucas. They're friends." I laid my hand against his cheek and urged him to look at me. "I give my word they mean no harm."

Desperation flickered to fear before the silver took over his eyes. His wolf surged, trying to force a change, but a change in this condition would kill him.

"Lucas, can you hear me?" I motioned for the approaching wolves to stop. They did.

Nothing but wolf looked back at me.

"Wolf, listen to me." The silver eyes watched apprehensively. "If you force the change, you will both die. Let me help and you will both live. I swear no one will harm you."

His gaze flickered from me to the waiting werewolves. "Stay."

I nodded and the silver slowly receded. He sighed heavily.

"Thank you."

I motioned for my wolves to come forward but their eyeballs were bugging out of their heads. The impatient snap of my fingers made them resume their approach. Lucas death-gripped my hand.

"They're going to help lift you and slide the board under your back, all right?"

His entire body tensed but he nodded. As the soldiers neared, Lucas fought with his wolf for control. I laid my free hand against his cheek and his wolf settled. "Easy, Wolf. You have to trust me."

Lucas blinked and for a fleeting second he reminded me of a scared little boy. Yeah, a scared little boy who could rip my throat out if his wolf surged at the wrong time. Of course Ordy and the others would immediately kill him, but that would be a waste.

We got him loaded onto the chopper and I sent the boys back to the Humvee. They argued, saying Simon told them to ride with the injured werewolf. I wasn't about to leave him--not that Ordy or the others would hurt him, but Lucas wasn't comfortable around them.

"Breanna?"

I looked down into his handsome face. "Uh huh?"

"Are you an angel? I mean, I must be dead or something, right?"

Being a witch and a woman in the military, I'd been called many things, but never an angel. "I'm not an angel and you most certainly are not dead."

His face softened. "I think you're an angel."

He thinks I'm an angel? Damn, how hard did he hit his head?

The chopper ride took fifteen minutes. We needed to go to a hospital equipped to tend injured werewolves. The human pilots looked a little surprised when I ordered them to fly to a hospital farther away than their normal flight pattern, but one look at the stripes on my shoulder garnered me a curt "yes, ma'am" and the chopper took flight. They had no clue their injured cargo was a supernatural.

The hospital helipad was on the roof and a team of medical staff, all Elvin folk, were milling about. Naturally gifted healers of the supernatural world, the peaceful blue-eyed, blond-haired elves were always the ones who took care of injured werewolves, vampires, or whatever other non-human came through the doors.

The humans thought supernaturals were of a religious faith that did not believe in any type of blood testing or transfusions. It wouldn't be cool for some third-year medical student to come across the undead blood of a vampire or the ramped-up metabolism of a werewolf. It took keeping the right people in the right places. The Divine Council, the ruling body of the supernatural world, did a great job of managing all the details.

We hadn't talked during the ride to the hospital, our hands locked together. His wolf was quiet. His breathing was soft. His heart had calmed. As the elves circled the chopper, I softly kissed his forehead.

"We're here, handsome."

The lost little boy look was back. "Can't you come in?"

It felt good to be wanted, even if it was by a werewolf delirious with pain. "Probably not a good idea," I answered, hoping my voice didn't crack.

"Okay," he said, "but can I see you again?"

Brown eyes swallowed me.

"Take care of yourself, Lucas Benelli." I brushed another kiss on his forehead as the nurses wheeled him away. His fingers slipped from mine as he disappeared behind the enormous double glass doors of the hospital. It took every ounce of strength I had to climb into the waiting chopper.

He's gone. Suck it up, buttercup, and move on.

"To the base, ma'am?"

"Yeah."

He thought I was an angel?

Every instinct in my body said I should go in the hospital and make sure Lucas was all right. He was injured. He was vulnerable.

He needs me.

I banged my fist against the chopper door. An unknown witch among supernaturals would cause nothing but trouble and Simon would wring my neck if I got all of Italy in a tizzy.

I was under orders not to engage. Going in the hospital would be further engagement. Damn.

As the chopper lifted, I slipped on my headset. Simon would be furious and I needed to get a hold on myself before we landed at Camp Ederle. He would blast me for disobeying orders and doing something plain damn stupid like riding to the hospital without any backup. He would be right, of course. Simon was always right.

I settled into the back seat and rubbed my hand. Lucas had held on so tightly he'd left bruises. Holding werewolves' hands as they were transported for medical treatment wasn't new, but with Lucas, there was something that ate at me. The sadness and fear in his eyes made my chest hurt.

I should not have left him.

An invisible rope tugged me to go through the double doors of the hospital. I could wait with him for a little while. Hold his hand while the doctors checked his injuries.

Too bad I didn't have an invisibility spell. Wonder if they'd have noticed an owl?

With muscles bunched, I was ready to leap from the chopper when a wave of power swept across the helipad. An Alpha werewolf, probably the Italian Alpha, was in the building. Anger--no, make that rage--coursed through the air. One very pissed-off Alpha was on the premises and a lone witch was not what he needed to see.

Chapter 2

Lucas

The sharp smell of antiseptic assaulted my nose and bright light needled my eyes. My mouth tasted like cotton and what the hell was wrong with my leg? Had a train hit me?

"Lucas? Can you hear me?" The worried words of my father rattled in my head. Why didn't painkillers work on wolves?

"Turn the lights down, Josef. They're blinding him," my mother chimed in her feathery soft voice. "Lucas, you're in the hospital. Your father and I are here."

The fuzzy figures of my parents standing over me came into focus.

"Tell us what happened."

"Oh, Josef, please let the boy wake up before you interrogate him," my mother snapped. Only she could get away with talking to the Alpha of the Italian Pack in such a manner.

"Gemma, I am only trying to determine what course of action I should take."

"Hey, Mom."

My mother leaned down and smiled. "Oh, honey, we were so worried."

"What happened?" my father demanded as he moved to the foot of my bed.

"I crashed my bike."

Josef Benelli slammed his hands on the bed railing. "Why were you on the mountain road?"

And here we go.

"I'd been to see Tristyn."

Not what he wanted to hear.

My father snorted and rubbed his temples. "Why were you not with your mate?"

I tried to sit up but stopped abruptly as sharp pain slashed across my side. "Tessa is not my mate."

"You are to be joined at the next full moon," Mom said as she perched on the chair beside my bed. "The Alpha has declared as such."

I lolled my head in the pillow. "I can't have a conversation with Tessa without it ending in a fight. How could I possibly take her as my wife?" I meant the question rhetorically but my father answered.

"You do not need to talk to her. You need to bed her and produce offspring for the life of the pack."

Now I knew why he and Mom fought all the time. My father wasn't exactly up on modern thinking.

"Is that why you went to see Tristyn, because you're worried about your impending mating?" My mother's brows knitted, her gaze darting from me to my father.

"No, I went to watch the hockey game."

My father crossed his arms and frowned. "Lucas, it is time you took a greater role in this pack and spent more time with your own kind. I have tried to indulge your desire to maintain a friendship with Tristyn, but it is time you dedicated yourself to your pack."

"This isn't my pack." Was there a jackhammer in my head?

Silver flakes appeared in his blue eyes. "You are the son of the Alpha. It is your role in this pack."

"Josef," my mother interrupted. "Please don't do this now. We almost lost Lucas tonight."

My father bowed his head, slowly calming his wolf. "We will discuss this when your injuries have healed. I will post a guard outside your room tonight. The doctors said you should be able to go home tomorrow. Your mother will prepare your room and you will stay with us."

I ran my fingers through my hair. Every conversation with him ended in a fight. "I'll be fine at my house."

"It was not a suggestion, Lucas," he replied as he turned to the door. "Your mate is waiting to speak with you."

My wolf stirred at the sharp words of my father. We'd done nothing but fight since I returned over a year ago. At the time, coming back to Italy had seemed like the right thing. Now, not so much.

Mom watched quietly as my father left the room. "He is worried. You could have been killed tonight."

"But I wasn't."

She pursed her lips. "Lucas, you need to try harder to work things out with your father. He loves you but he doesn't understand why you stay so far from your pack."

"You know why I don't go around the pack."

She handed me a cup of water. "You are an adult now. Stephano forgave you years ago. It is time to let go of your deranged childhood notions and take your place in the pack."

The ghosts of long-buried memories strained against walls that kept them confined in a rarely visited part of my mind. I'd worked hard to lock them away and now my mom was coaxing them to escape.

Thanks for being on my side, Mom.

"They weren't notions." I put the cup back onto the tray and watched her face. She didn't believe me now any more than when I was ten years old.

"You were confused about your…your…desires."

The walls quivered but the memories stayed inside. Even twenty years later her disregard for what had happened sent shockwaves through my stomach. How could a mother not believe her son?

"What happened had nothing to do with my desires."

She crossed her arms. "Stephano has scars yet he has worked hard to remain a part of his pack."

I had scars, too.

She crossed the room to the window. "Stephano could have asked the Alpha for your life, but he chose to forgive your indiscretions."

"Just leave me alone, Mom. I don't want to talk about this."

Her shoulders heaved. "Your father deserves more from his son." Tiny flickers of silver appeared in her eyes. "It is up to you to right the wrongs of the past with your father and your pack. Any other Alpha would have killed you for what happened, but Josef saw fit to let you live. You have no idea how trying that time was for him and the pack."

She stormed out, leaving me with an even bigger headache. I should have kept my job with the Divine Council and stayed away from this place. Trying to rebuild the relationship with my father was not worth all this. It didn't matter what I did. I was not my brother.

Tessa Del Vigglio burst through the door, practically knocking it from its hinges. The statuesque blond bombshell turned her wicked blue eyes in my direction.

"I thought you were working late and now I find out you were at that freak vampire's house. What the hell is wrong with you?" she demanded, shaking a perfectly manicured red nail at my face.

"I'm doing fine, thanks for asking."

"You're an idiot. You were supposed to be with me, helping plan our mating ceremony. I've had it with you. My father is on his way to speak with the Alpha about your behavior. Do you have any idea how many wolves wanted me as their mate and your father declared I was chosen for you, to bear children for the future Alpha?" She threw her hands into the air in true drama queen fashion.

I gritted my teeth and looked out the barred window, so tired of this conversation. "I am not going to be the next Alpha."

She wrinkled her nose. "Of course you aren't. You don't have the balls to lead and nobody would listen to you, anyway. I deserve so much better than a pathetic loser like you. If your father wasn't the Alpha, I wouldn't have given you a second glance and you would have been dead the day you returned to pack territory."

And now that I had stepped foot back into pack territory, I was stuck. The son of an Alpha was not generally welcome in other pack territories. My mother had already lost one son and didn't deserve to lose another.

"Tessa, we both know we are not mates, regardless of what my father may have said. If you wish to mate with another, I will gladly relinquish a challenge for you."

She'd never looked at me with anything but disdain and money signs in her eyes. Now there were silver flecks in the icy blue depths. "You are too much of a coward to fight for the privilege of being with me."

"Would you fight to be with me?"

She cackled. "I don't have to fight for anyone."

The bedside phone interrupted my "go to hell" response. Tessa snatched the receiver off its cradle and out of the grasp of my outstretched hand.

"Ciao," she answered in feigned sweetness.

My werewolf ears picked up the voice of an American woman. "May I speak with Lucas, please?"

"Who is this?" Tessa snarled. The heavy scent of rage filled my room.

"Um, just a friend calling to make sure he's all right."

Tessa slammed the phone hard enough the bell cried.

I cursed and tried to grab the phone. My broken ribs voiced their disagreement and I fell back into the bed, gasping for breath.

"Who was that?" Tessa demanded.

"The most beautiful woman I've ever met. Her name is Breanna."

All the color drained from her face. "You are a bastard. I wish you had died on that mountain road."

"Sorry to disappoint you."

Tessa threw the water pitcher across the room and slammed the door on the way out. My wolf rumbled. He'd always hated her.

With a lot of effort and discomfort, I managed to reach the phone.

My nurse, Anira, quietly entered the room and knelt to clean up the spilled water pitcher. "I'll bring more water for you, Mr. Benelli. How are you feeling?"

"Better since she left."

Anira laughed softly as she placed another pillow behind my head. "Are your stitches pulling? They may be ready to come out." With my werewolf metabolism, even deep gashes like the one on my leg would heal within hours if properly attended.

"Whoever tied the tourniquet around your leg saved your life. When the femur broke, it ripped your femoral artery. With all the internal injuries you sustained and the blood loss from the artery, you would have bled to death before your body could heal itself."

"Her name was Breanna."

Anira looked over her shoulder at me. "The one in the helicopter?"

"Yes. I hoped she would come in."

Anira snorted. "Of course she wouldn't come in. She's a witch."

"So?"

"The Alpha would have killed her on sight. You know how everyone feels about witches."

I folded the cover back so she could get to the sutures. "Not all witches are evil. The dark witches are, but the white witches are very peaceful."

"She didn't look or feel peaceful to me. We were all rather shocked someone like her was helping you."

I barely felt anything as she removed the sutures. I asked if there was any way to track the number that had just called my room and Anira shook her head. "Sorry, the switchboard has no computer backup. However, you are in a cellphone-safe zone if you would like to use your own phone."

After she checked my vitals, Anira fished my phone out of my jacket pocket. I stared at the scratched screen, ridiculously hoping Brenna would call. Even if she had managed to find this number, why would she call after what Tessa had done?

The phone came alive in my hand. Without thinking, I answered it. "Breanna?"

The familiar laugh of my best friend, Tristyn Ziccardi, came through loud and clear. "Sorry, buddy, it's just me. I heard about a motorcycle wreck on the mountain road. You okay?"

I spent the next hour trying desperately to remember the details. What I remembered most was Breanna. Incredible amber eyes, beautiful auburn hair, the gentleness of her fingers along my face. She was an angel.

"How's your mom?" Tristyn asked.

"She's doing all right. Tired, but all right."

"And your dad?"

"Humph, don't ask."

"How much did he yell?"

"Only a little. I'll hear it tomorrow when I leave the hospital. He expects me to stay with them for a few days."

"That's a good idea, Luc. If you don't really remember what happened, there could be a lot more going on than you know."

"Yeah, you're right. I'll call you when I get back home."

"All right. I'll do some checking and see what I can find about this witch you met."

Sleeping with broken ribs and a broken leg was almost impossible. Anira tried her magic but my werewolf blood would have none of it. My body was healing itself and with that healing came pain.

Somehow I had to find Breanna. My wolf always bristled when anyone, werewolf or not, came near, but he craved her. We both did. I wanted to smell that intoxicating blend of strawberries and honey so uniquely Breanna.

She had been gentle and my wolf listened to her. Hell, he didn't listen to me most of the time. For her, my wolf had settled.

I slid off the side of the bed and limped toward the adjoining bathroom. My ribs and leg were mending. My head still thumped, but now it felt like it was a small car rather than a train that hit me.

A soft rap at the door preceded a tentative, "Lucas?"

Vinnie Petrazzini's blond head appeared around the corner. The subordinate wolf had stayed at my door all night. "A vamp came by last night asking about you." Vinnie stuffed his hands deep into the pockets of his khaki pants.

"A vampire?"

Vinnie stared at the floor. "Dark hair, French accent, wearing camouflage."

That didn't sound like any vampires I knew. "Did he give his name or leave a number?"

Vinnie shook his head and chewed his bottom lip. My wolf stirred at the scent of apprehension.

"He asked if you were all right, if your injuries had been attended, and if you remembered what happened."

I waited for him to continue but Vinnie was fascinated with the linoleum. "And what did you say to him?"

"Um, I told him you were doing well, your injuries were healing and you didn't really remember what happened." Vinnie looked around, shifting his weight foot to foot. "I probably shouldn't have said anything."

My wolf hated his meekness. "It's all right," I mumbled, limping toward the bathroom.

Vinnie slipped out the door without another word. He was the lowest ranking wolf in the pack and the only one my wolf didn't want to kill just for breathing. A part of me wanted to be nice to Vinnie but nobody treated a subordinate wolf with respect and if I did, it would only confuse him.

Chapter 3

Breanna

"I cannot believe you asked me to do that," Lieutenant Christopher LeCavalier fumed as he paced outside my cell. His eyes sparkled as he spun to face me. The fluorescent lights gave his coal black hair an eerie glow.

"I needed to know he was all right." The telephone call I had placed to the hospital before reporting to the brig at Camp Ederle had not gone well. A woman answered and promptly slammed the receiver in my ear. Bitch.

"You could have called the front desk." The vampire's thick French-Canadian accent made his irritated words sound angrier than he was.

"Yeah, I'm sure it was a terrible experience since you love elf girls in nurses' uniforms."

Chris sneered at me. "Will I need to go check on him later tonight to be sure he is tucked in properly?"

"Check on whom?" Simon asked, stepping onto the long narrow hall and glancing in my direction.

"Chris went to the hospital to check on Lucas."

Two blond eyebrows shot up. "Lucas?" he asked, drawing out the name.

"Yeah, you know, the wolf the Malandanti were after." I flopped onto the pitiful cot. A spider skittered from his hiding place beneath the mattress.

Simon glared at me.

"What? I tried to call but didn't get much info so Chris stopped by."

"That wolf is dangerous. That pack is dangerous. Stay away from him and that's an order, Sergeant." Simon pointed a finger at Chris. "And you should have known better than to fall for this."

Chris lowered his eyes and I stormed to the front of the cell. "I just wanted to know Lucas was all right. Is that a bad thing?"

Simon pinched the bridge of his nose. "Had you asked, I would have given you a full report regarding the injured werewolf."

Oops. "You checked on him?"

Simon looked insulted. "I phoned the hospital. If you would bother to check, you would see I had indeed left two messages for you."

I was dog shit on a boot heel. "Is he okay?"

Simon walked to the front of the cell. "The doctors said your tourniquet saved his life. He would have bled to death had you not intervened."

There was a "but" sure to follow.

"But you disobeyed my orders to not engage. You went after the Malandanti without permission or backup."

"They were going to kill him, Sime. I had to engage."

He shook his head. "You chose to engage."

I stomped my foot. "Yeah, to save Lucas. They were going to sacrifice him for some stupid ritual."

"But you chose to ignore my order and handle things yourself, did you not?"

My breath was the only sound in the room. "Yes, sir."

Simon looked over his shoulder. "Lieutenant LeCavalier, you may go."

Chris tossed a sympathetic shrug my way before slipping down the hall. Simon reached for the keys and unlocked the brig door. I moved to the far corner and sat quietly on the cot. Simon would never hurt me, but his lectures were enough to make me throw myself into traffic.

"Breanna, my dear, you are one of the finest reconnaissance soldiers I have ever known, but your petulance and impatience worry me greatly."

There was a bridge over the main road coming into base. Lots of traffic. If I was lucky, a tractor trailer would hit me first.

"I contacted the hospital tonight to not only verify the condition of the injured wolf but to ascertain if any ill will was directed toward you since you had so brazenly drawn attention to yourself at the hospital."

I stared at the cracks in the floor. "I couldn't leave him, Sime. He was upset and his wolf kept trying to force a change."

Simon snorted. "Ah, yes, and there is that. Theodore was babbling about you talking to the injured wolf and stopping an imminent change. Would you care to share your secret?"

"My secret?"

"You were able to have a conversation with the wolf side of a werewolf?"

"Oh, yeah, guess I did talk to his wolf but if I hadn't, Lucas would have died."

"And?"

I jumped from the cot. "And it would have been my fault."

"No, it would not have been your fault. It would have been his fault for being on the mountain road alone at that time of night. By the way, there is absolutely no evidence to support your claim the Malandanti were there."

"You think I'm lying?"

"I do not. However, most supernaturals are not quite so willing to accept the word of a witch."

He didn't mean it to hurt but it did. I might have been able to change shapes and fly around like an owl, but bottom line, I was a witch and nobody liked witches.

"You're on duty tonight," Simon said as he rose fluidly from the cot.

"I'm not. I'm in the brig per your orders."

"You and Lieutenant Miller have the river. Lieutenant LeCavalier and Sergeant Ordison will take the road." Simon was inches from my face before I could blink. "Please follow orders tonight, Master Sergeant Welker. No engagement without calling first." Cool fingers startled away my foot-stomping response. "Breanna, my dear, I am thinking of your safety." He released my arm and backed away. "We will discuss the injured werewolf when you return."

Ninety minutes later I landed on the bank of the Brenta River. It was a dark night with only a sliver of moon occasionally peeking between the clouds. My owl form easily slipped between the overhanging branches as I glided toward my werewolf partner for the night.

The river was loud, the water lapping over the edges of the banks. The forest knew we were there and kept her animals hidden in the darkness. Lieutenant Aaron Miller was sitting cross-legged on a rock.

"Hey, Bre," he called as I landed. Apparently he didn't mind talking to a bird. In a flash I changed, my form flowing from owl to human. It was times like this I was thankful my touch of magic always included my human form re-emerging fully clothed. The werewolves didn't have that luxury.

"What's up, Aaron? What'd you do to tick off the old man?"

Aaron grinned, giving him a boyish charm. "I asked for duty when I heard you were on deck."

"Yeah, right." Nobody requested duty with me.

Aaron moved closer, slowly running a finger up my arm. "Ah, now, Bre, you know I think you're the sexiest witch in our unit."

I met his eyes. "I'm the only witch in your unit."

Aaron was one of the sixteen werewolves in my recon unit and was by far the sultriest of the lot. There were also five vampires and one very important civilian elf in our midst.

A twig snapped in the distance and we both dropped to the ground. Movement along the far river bank attracted our attention. "I'll fly around behind," I whispered. "You take the point."

Aaron glowered. He was charming in a naughty boy kind of way. "There might be more than one. We shouldn't split up."

"Move it, Miller. That's an order."

He gave me a playful snarl before slipping into the darkness.

I shifted, my owl form giving me greater eyesight and much more maneuverability among the trees. As I flew deeper into the darkness, the sounds of the night called to me. Rabbits shrieked in alarm, mice dove into the leaves, and footsteps moved along the forest floor.

You're lucky I ate dinner, Flopsy.

Staying high in the trees and avoiding the revealing snippets of moonlight, I circled to hone in on the faint sucking noises of two pairs of shoes in the mud.

My orders were not to engage.

The heavy limbs of a giant spruce gave good cover. The footsteps along the bank stopped, but another set of shoes was approaching from Aaron's side. It wasn't Aaron, the footsteps much too loud for a recon soldier, but they were soft and light, perhaps a woman?

Across the river Aaron stalked through the underbrush less than fifty yards behind a shadowy figure. I flew to another spruce and peered between the branches. The footsteps on my side of the river had not resumed. Were they planning an ambush?

The lone figure Aaron was trailing stopped at the riverbank. She looked around, nervously pulling a scarf tightly around her head. If she'd turn just a little more, she'd reveal her face.

Maybe I should squawk or something to make her look in this direction.

Two cloaked figures, most certainly Malandanti judging by their outdated robes, appeared directly across the water from her.

Squawk aborted. Shut up and watch.

I waited, hoping to catch at least a glimpse of the woman's face, but she kept her head down while stepping gingerly onto the rocks. The gurgling water drowned out any words exchanged between the Malandanti and the woman as she passed a manila envelope to one of the cloaked figures.

Gotta have that envelope. That is not engaging. That is acquiring evidence.

Soundlessly diving and carefully avoiding the dapples of moonlight, I ripped the envelope from the bony fingers and flapped with all my might to push my owl body as far from the Malandanti as possible.

I had just reached the other side of the riverbank when the first wave of Malandanti magic swept over me. The magic wasn't comfortable, but no damage done.

"Bre!" Aaron yelling for help made me drop the envelope and rush toward him.

Trapped in a binding spell, struggling to keep his head above the water, Aaron flailed like a stickman in a windstorm.

The woman disappeared, but the Malandanti were standing firm, their spell dragging Aaron closer to a watery grave. I landed on a rock and shifted to human. The Malandanti dashed into the forest. The binding spell broke, leaving Aaron to flounder in the roaring current. I tried to grab his outstretched hand but the frothy water snatched him.

"Hang on, Aaron, I'm coming!" Geez, I hated cold water. I tossed my heavy jacket to the side and dove into the dark depths, promptly slamming headfirst into a boulder. The current was a monster, sucking me farther under and pinballing me along the jagged rocks.

I hated those damn cloaked asshole witch bitch freaks.

I bounced to the surface, gasping for air. Only a few feet away, Aaron surfaced in a swirling rapid of white water and logs. I ducked under the water and swam to him.

"Gotcha." I had a good grip on his wet fatigues. "Come on and we'll get out of this water."

"I can't swim," he rasped as he clung to a floating chunk of oak.

Werewolves and water. Damn.

"Can't stay here, Miller," I shouted. "Trust me, I'll get you out."

Bobbing against the log, the cold water leaching my strength, I managed to pull Aaron's back against my chest in the survival swimmer position.

"Don't fight or you'll drown us both."

He was heavy as a tank and the going was slow, but we made it to the shore. We climbed through the mud and collapsed side by side on the shore. It was so damn cold a penguin would have been miserable and now I was soaked to the bone. My muscles were on strike. Beside me, Aaron's breathing calmed. Every werewolf I'd ever met was deathly afraid of water, something about the density of their bodies making it impossible for them to swim.

Warm fingers closed around mine as Aaron rose to an elbow. "Bre, you okay?"

"Yeah, just give me a minute."

Aaron leaned over me, brushing strands of hair out of my face. "Do you need mouth-to-mouth?"

"Don't make me kill you after all that."

Aaron chuckled and helped me sit up. "What happened back there? I tracked the female werewolf to the edge of the river and the next thing I know, I can't move and I'm drowning."

"She was a werewolf? Are you sure?"

"Positive."

"That was Malandanti magic. They caught you in a binding spell."

"Malandanti? Seriously? I didn't see anybody but her."

I banged my fist against my forehead. "We need to find that envelope she gave them. I grabbed it, but dropped it upstream a ways."

He snorted in disgust. "Why did you drop it?"

Damn arrogant werewolf. "To save your scrawny hide." I climbed to my feet. "Let's go. I'm cold."

His arms snaked around my waist. "I know how to warm you up."

I kicked him in the groin and he crumpled.

"I guess I deserved that," he grunted.

Thankfully I'd left the radio in my jacket pocket. "I'm getting backup."

"Bonjour, my dear," Simon answered. "Please tell me you have not disobeyed another order."

"Maybe a little, but it was to save Aaron."

"Explain."

I filled him in on the Malandanti, Aaron's ordeal, and the envelope.

"I'm almost there," Simon replied, abruptly ending the conversation.

"Find it?" Aaron asked as I stomped up the muddy bank.

"No, they must have circled around and got it." I kicked a rock and it rolled toward spit-shined black boots.

Major Ezekiel Trenton, the werewolf commander of the Combat Unit of Bravo, curled his lip in disdain as I drew closer. Aaron and I stood to full attention.

"Sergeant Welker," the enormous man muttered as if he would vomit from saying my name.

"Major Trenton, sir. I was not aware the Combat Unit was in the area."

He snorted. "That proves what kind of Recon Unit a vampire runs. A pathetic one."

Simon emerged from the darkness. "Greetings, Ezekiel. Have you lost your wolves again?"

A chuckle stuck in my throat and Trenton glared at me. "Major DuChard," the werewolf answered coolly. "It seems your recon soldiers have been playing in the water."

"We aren't playing," Aaron said. "We were looking for the envelope the Malandanti dropped."

Trenton's eyebrows shot up. "Malandanti? There haven't been Malandanti sightings in over two hundred years."

"Just because nobody saw them doesn't mean they aren't here," I responded before really thinking.

Trenton ignored me. Typical.

"My soldiers have seen no signs of Malandanti. Where's your evidence?" he asked Simon.

"Bre saw them," Aaron piped in, meaning to be helpful, but Trenton took advantage.

"You're taking the word of a witch there are witches here?" Trenton rolled his head back and laughed. "DuChard, you have lost your mind."

"Major Trenton, you will address all members of my unit with respect or you will answer to me," Simon responded with no hint of emotion.

For a moment I thought--at least hoped--Trenton would make a move. Simon would wipe the floor with him. Apparently Trenton knew it because he stepped back and reined in his wolf. With one last sneer in my direction, he turned on his heel and tromped through the forest.

I never realized how much crap Simon got for having me in his unit. It was tough being the only vampire commanding officer of a primarily werewolf company, but knowing he had to deal with shit like this gave me even more respect for my commanding officer.

"Thanks."

Simon nodded suavely. "I am sorry you had to hear that exchange, my dear."

"I'm sorry they give you a hard time about me." I thought back to all the things I'd done in the last ten years and clenched my fists. I'd do better from now on. No more disobeying orders.

"So, you engaged the Malandanti again?"

Damn.

Aaron bumped my shoulder. "She had to, Major DuChard. Bre pulled me out of the water."

"Ah, that would explain the poor appearance of your uniforms."

Aaron, Simon and I slopped along the muddy riverbank, searching for footprints or something to support our story. Simon and Aaron picked up the faint scent of a female werewolf. I got the residual black magic from the spell casting, but nothing concrete we could share with the command post.

"Thanks for looking," I said as we made our way back toward the road. "I'm sure they were Malandanti. I think they were the same ones from last night."

"I wish I could've gotten a better look at the werewolf," Aaron muttered. "I got nothing but scent."

"Could you identify that scent again?" Simon asked.

Aaron crinkled his nose. "Not sure. It was so faint. I know it was a woman and she wasn't in heat."

All righty, more info than I needed to know.

We piled into Simon's Humvee and rode to Camp Ederle. Aaron headed to the showers and I followed Simon into his makeshift office. Celeste, his elf mate and the designated healer of the unit, was waiting. She leaped into his arms and I tried not to watch. The two were so in love they were painful to be around.

"So, Simon, got any ideas why a werewolf might be meeting with the Malandanti?"

He put his arm around Celeste. "Not really."

The reappearance of Malandanti after so many years bothered me. All the data we had suggested the cloaked witches had been annihilated in the nineteenth century. So why were they running around Italy, and more specifically, why were they after Lucas?

"Aren't Malandanti considered opportunistic?" I asked.

Simon nodded. "They are not known for elaborate schemes such as what was carried out the night the werewolf was injured."

"They were there. I saw them."

He tilted his head. "I believe you, Breanna, but once again you see the problem. No evidence."

Sometimes it really sucked to be a witch.

Chapter 4

Lucas

My room hadn't been mine in a very long time. I'd spent most of my childhood at boarding school, holidays at Tristyn's house, and all of my adult life away from the headquarters of the Italian Pack. Even after so many years, the thought of this room being pitch black at night sent a shiver up my spine.

The door swung open. "Lucas, are you hungry?" my mother asked for the third time in twenty minutes.

"I'm fine but thanks anyway."

Mom perched on the edge of my bed. My leg and ribs had healed, but movement was uncomfortable. "Honey, can we talk about Tessa?"

"There's nothing to talk about."

"Tessa is a beautiful woman and dedicated to the pack. She was to be your brother's mate. Nicolli's disappearance devastated her."

"Did Father pick her for Nic, too?"

"No. Tessa and Nic had been together for over two years." A single tear rolled down her face. My mother was much too beautiful to be crying.

My brother's disappearance had been particularly hard on her. Nicolli had been the golden boy of the pack, the future Alpha. Mom loved me, but she adored Nicolli. Everyone did.

Mom fidgeted with the edge of the sheet. "You are the future Alpha. Your father must ensure your mate is appropriate to stand in a position of power within the pack."

Was my entire family stone deaf? "I will not be the Alpha. I've told him that at least a hundred times. I came home to help with the company, that's it. He needs to find someone else to run this pack."

"Lucas, you are all he has left. When Nicolli disappeared it almost killed him."

"Nicolli's life was this pack. I'm not him."

She started to cry and I felt like a total ass.

"Mom, I'm sorry, please don't cry."

She dabbed at her cheeks. "I don't know what we'll do if you don't help your father. He spends all his time trying to manage the pack and run Benelli Enterprises. I'm worried he'll work himself into an early grave."

I doubted that. My father was strong and young in werewolf years. He was a great Alpha, though we didn't see eye-to-eye on pack politics.

"I don't want to take Nic's place. There are lots of wolves who would gladly step up and lead this pack. I'll help him with the company, but I'm not getting involved with the pack."

She stood abruptly. "You are his only remaining son and it is your job to follow in his footsteps. Put aside what you want for the good of your pack." She said the words with so much bitterness, I looked up. The faintest flecks of silver shone in her eyes.

I argued with my father all the time and made my mom cry. What a great son.

"Tessa is downstairs. Would you like me to send her up?"

"Send her home."

"Lucas," my mother chastised, "that is no way to treat your future mate." She hurried from the room but left the door ajar.

I managed to scoot up in my bed far enough to see the orange and pink hues of the setting sun. My window looked out into the edge of thick underbrush. It was quiet, peaceful.

My father had gone into town on pack business and the other pack wolves were standing around the front door. Not wanting to run into any of them, I found my cane and limped along the wall to the glass patio door. It had been a long time since I'd been hurt, not since Tristyn and I had run into a very angry demon. That had been worse and no beautiful witch had held my hand on the way to the hospital.

"Breanna, where are you?" I asked the wind. Meeting her had been the only good thing to happen since I returned to Italy.

I had come home with the best of intentions, to work out things with my father. Nicolli handled most of the work for Benelli Enterprises. His disappearance had left a gaping hole in the company and in my father.

Mom had convinced me to come home, saying my father needed me though he would never ask. Mom had been sure this was a way for us to mend the differences between us.

She'd been wrong.

And I was stuck here. My old agent job had reopened a few months ago and I sent in my application without speaking to my father. He'd been livid when the Divine Council called him about releasing me from my pack ties so I could take the job. Mom had intervened to keep us from coming to blows. She knew how hard it was for me to control my wolf around my father.

The smell of female musk interrupted my thoughts. There was nowhere to go so I eased onto the wooden bench.

"Why are you out here?" Tessa snapped, her steps shaking the patio.

"Leave me alone."

She wrinkled her nose and sniffed the air. "I want to go over the mating vows."

"No."

She stomped her foot. "What did you say?"

I'd always tried to be polite to Tessa. Within three days of my return to Italy, my father had told the pack I would be taking Tessa as a mate and replacing Nicolli as the future Alpha. That had gone over real well, since every wolf in the pack hated my guts.

"I will not take you as my mate."

I thought she'd be upset--instead, she laughed. "Like you have the balls to disobey your father."

I rose to my feet and placed my cane against the wall. "Call your father and have him come over."

"Why?" She crossed her arms.

"So I can tell them the mating is not going to take place."

She laughed again, the sound grating on my nerves. "And what reason are you going to give my father for refusing me as your mate?"

Any kindness I'd ever felt for her was gone. "I don't want you."

"You don't want me? Do you know how many wolves want me?"

My wolf rumbled. He hated her.

She curled her lip disdainfully. "Stephano said you begged him."

I lunged, but she leaped out of reach. "Go to hell," I roared, my wolf dangerously close to taking control. If he succeeded, Tessa would never make it to the house.

She narrowed her eyes. "I've heard the stories. Your father was so disgusted, he sent you away so you wouldn't bring shame to this pack."

Wood splinters flew when I slammed my fist into the patio. The support pole cracked from the impact. Tessa shrieked and ran for the house.

My control was slipping. My hands trembled as I fell back on the bench. My wolf wanted blood. Tessa's blood.

Tessa stopped halfway between the gazebo and the house. "You killed him, didn't you? You killed Nicolli!"

My wolf surged as she dashed the last few meters into the house. I hadn't killed my brother. My life would have been much better if he was alive. At least I wouldn't be here.

My father's car wheeled into the drive. "Lucas!" he yelled, stepping from his car.

There was no way I could deal with him now. He'd rant about what a disgrace I was, about how much better Nicolli had done with the company, and about how many mistakes I had made throughout my life.

My wolf wanted to fight the Alpha. Our wolves hated one another with an unnatural passion, but the human side of me didn't want to fight. The human side of me loved my father in spite of everything that had happened.

A change was coming, my wolf seizing control. Needing time alone, I limped toward the trees. If my father pushed me today, we would fight and one of us would die.

My transition from human to wolf was painfully slow. The injuries affecting my human body resonated within my wolf form but it was worth the pain. My wolf needed to taste blood. Better a rabbit than my father.

The smell of rotting leaves and dampness calmed my wolf. For hours, the soft crunch of the forest floor beneath my paws was the only sound. It was cool, the animals preferring the warmth of their dens and nests to the open night air.

Breanna. Where are you?

Wanting to get to know someone was an odd feeling. Tristyn had known me since we were kids, but I'd never been close to anyone else.

Wonder what her favorite color is? What kind of music does she like?

The stars twinkled as I walked along an old deer trail. Maybe Breanna was out there staring up at the same stars. Doubtful. A woman as beautiful as she surely didn't have to spend her nights alone.

In the distance, limbs snapped. The thrum of Alpha power rushed through the forest.

Get away from here now.

My wolf bristled for attack.

Go. Deeper into the forest. Go. Now.

My wolf fought for total control. He wanted the blood of my Alpha, the blood of my father.

What the hell is wrong with me? Sons don't kill their fathers.

I dove farther into the brush. My wolf demanded his due.

Alpha compulsion pushed through the darkness, my father commanding me to stop.

Wolves should bow to the dominance of their Alphas. Wolves wanted to be with their packs. Why didn't I feel pack bonds? Why didn't I feel compelled to obey my Alpha?

The crashing of limbs was closer. If we fought, one of us would die.

Fine. Let it be me.

I crouched in the clearing and waited. The Alpha stopped. It seemed like an eternity before the soft footsteps of my father in human form tracked closer. My wolf sensed victory, my father no match for me in wolf form.

"Lucas?" he called. "We need to talk."

I couldn't see him yet, but his dominance was choking. And enraging.

"Are you hurt?" he asked.

He would have felt the pain or anger or fear of a pack wolf. With me, there was nothing. He stepped into the clearing. I met his glare with my own and forced my wolf to take a step back. I had never bowed to his dominance, but I would acknowledge his status.

"If you feel so strongly about not taking Tessa, I will entertain other choices for your mate."

If I'd been in human form, I would have smiled. My father was trying to work with me. That was a first.

"There are women who would help create an alliance between the French and Italian Packs. I will speak with Alpha LaPierre regarding his niece, Morganza."

My heart sank. This had nothing to do with me.

"She is not an attractive woman and I understand she is difficult. However, the mating would greatly strengthen our ties with the French. With the Croatian wolves becoming more aggressive, it would be in our best interest to bolster our defenses."

The mark of a great Alpha, always thinking of the safety of his pack.

"I intend to host a pack run Friday night for out-of-town guests. I expect you to be here."

My father nodded before disappearing into the darkness. My wolf wanted to follow, to stalk him and end it all tonight, but I held onto the slimmest thread of control. Sons did not kill their fathers.

By the time I trudged home, the sun was cresting the horizon. My house was twenty kilometers from my father's estate and the walk left my leg thrumming. I ducked into the heavy brush and changed to human form. Naked and starving, I punched the key code and slipped through the gate onto my property.

I tossed on a clean shirt and jeans and headed into the kitchen. Alpha power rushed into the room. My father would be arriving any moment and he never bothered to knock. Too tired to avoid him, I scavenged for food. Sustenance would appease my wolf while I dealt with my father's demands.

Josef burst in the door as I finished my third sandwich.

He dropped my phone onto the bar. "I have spoken to Alpha LaPierre. Morganza is not interested in meeting you." The sheer disappointment in his voice was like a gut punch. "However, I expect you to be at the pack run. We will have guests and you need to make an appearance."

There was no time for me to protest, not that it would have mattered. He never listened. He knew I didn't do pack runs, no matter how much he snarled and grumbled. Too many werewolves. Too much contact. Too many memories.

Chapter 5

Breanna

The windows of the training hall of Camp Ederle shook as the obnoxiously loud sounds of American rock music filled the air. I delivered kick after punishing kick to the heavy sand bag hanging helplessly before me. The bag hadn't done anything wrong, but was still taking the full brunt of my frustration. I couldn't stop thinking about the warm brown eyes of a certain werewolf.

"Stupid, stupid, stupid," I grunted as I landed three consecutive roundhouse kicks onto the bag. "Not your wolf," I panted, punching the bag with a vengeance.

"Hey, Bre, you all right?" Celeste asked as she padded into the room.

"Yep." The bag shook from my spinning whip kick.

"Uh, okay. Have you seen Simon?"

Combination punch. Left, right, left, right, followed by a heel kick. "Nope."

"I can't find him anywhere." She sat daintily in a chair nearby. "I thought he was with you."

Front kick left, front kick right, punch, punch, punch. "Nope."

I had a great sweat going when I realized she was watching me with puppy-dog eyes. "Do you want me to look for him, Cee?"

She leaped up and threw her arms around me. "Yes, please!"

I toweled off and headed to the double doors, Celeste trotting beside me. She chatted about the stars in the sky, the crickets chirping, whatever crossed her abnormally happy mind. I'd learned to ignore the chatter or I'd have strangled her.

We stepped into the orange glow of the sodium lights surrounding the parking lot. Musk and a faint whiff of vampire tickled my nose, but it was the unusual energy in the air that made my hair stand on end.

"Bre? What's wrong?"

"Something weird's going on around here," I answered, scanning the flat expanse of asphalt.

Celeste peered into the dim light. Typical elf, she hated any type of negative energy and there was plenty to be felt tonight. Not really black magic, just a strange vibe. The wind whipped the angry clouds, adding to the already spooky atmosphere.

"I'm going to look around. Why don't you go back to the barracks?"

Celeste shook her head. "I'm not leaving you."

It would be hard to sneak across an open parking lot and harder with an elf hanging onto your arm. How could someone so small make so much noise?

Someone stormed around the corner and mowed into both of us. Celeste shrieked and I went into attack mode until I realized it was Simon.

"What the hell are the two of you doing out?" he demanded as he helped Celeste to her feet.

"Looking for you," I replied, brushing the dust from my pants.

"I asked Bre to find you," Celeste said. "I was worried about you."

Simon didn't bother to hide how much her concern meant to him. "I am sorry to have worried you, my love. An unexpected situation required my attention."

He pulled her into an embrace while I stood to the side, feeling as out of place as a condom machine in a convent.

"Why did you uncloak your power?" I asked when the two finally separated.

Simon delicately kissed Celeste's forehead. "I must accompany my mate to our quarters and then will speak with you regarding the events of this evening. Would you meet me in the briefing room at twenty-one hundred?"

I checked my watch. Thirty minutes. Time for a shower.

When I made it to the briefing room, Simon had his arms crossed and was staring out the window. He didn't turn around as I rushed in.

"My apologies for addressing you so rudely earlier, Breanna. I was not expecting you to be out."

"No biggie. What's up?"

He motioned to a chair and pulled out another for himself. "The Italian Alpha was at the security gate earlier tonight. He was not happy one of his wolves was transported to the hospital without his permission or knowledge."

WTF? "Well, that's stupid. Lucas was hurt and needed medical attention. I had the list of approved supernatural hospitals and that's where we took him. What's the issue? Would he have preferred I wait for permission and let Lucas bleed to death?"

"Actually, yes. Alpha wolves are very much about control of their pack."

I slammed my hands on the table. "He was going to die!"

"I know, Breanna, but you need to understand the ways of the wolves."

"Galen would have expected me to take one of his wolves to the hospital."

"Yes, but Galen is an American Alpha and is much more open-minded than other Alpha werewolves."

"So the Italian Alpha was mad because a witch brought one of his wolves to the hospital?"

"No, he was angry because I did not call him."

Damn. I'd gotten Simon in trouble again.

"I'm sorry, Simon. I didn't mean to cause trouble. I just wanted to help Lucas."

Simon smiled sadly. "I know you meant well, Breanna, but these are the things I've been talking about. There are repercussions for any and all actions."

I snorted. "He's just doing that 'cause you're a vampire."

"Perhaps, but it matters not what his motivation is. There are protocols in place for dealing with situations such as these and one of us should have consulted the Alpha before transporting the injured wolf."

"Couldn't you have called him when you called the chopper?"

Simon pretended to ponder my question. "Ah, yes, I could have and then a livid Alpha werewolf would have been waiting as you disembarked the Medivac. Since you saw fit to travel without any Bravo soldiers as backup, what would you have done had he attacked?"

I was an idiot.

"Damn, Sime. I'm sorry. I only wanted to help Lucas. He was holding my hand and his wolf kept pushing for a change and I didn't know what to do. I should have called you but I couldn't leave him. I just couldn't."

I met Simon's eyes and then looked away. That excuse was pathetic but it was the truth.

"You felt something for this wolf?"

I shrugged since I was nothing but a slug. "I didn't want to leave him alone."

"You attacked two Malandanti in order to save a werewolf you didn't know. You hopped willingly and alone into a Medivac to accompany this same unknown werewolf to a hospital where you could have easily been in danger. I would say you felt something for this wolf, my dear."

I sucked in a breath before answering. "He said I was an angel."

I braced for Simon's laughter but none came. "And what did you say?"

"That he must have hit his head really hard when he crashed the bike."

Simon chuckled. "I assume a simple 'thank you' would have been too much for you?"

Not a response I'd even considered.

After a never-ending pause, Simon continued. "The injured wolf was asleep when Lieutenant LeCavalier visited. Apparently the Alpha took exception with Christopher's presence as well."

Damn. Chris had gone to the hospital for me. I wasn't a slug anymore. I was the trail the slug left behind.

"The Alpha also said the injured wolf mumbled the name Breanna."

My heart stopped. Lucas remembered me?

I glanced up at Simon before quickly regaining my composure. It didn't matter if he did remember me. Lucas was an Italian Pack wolf who could have anyone on the continent. We'd be leaving in a few days and I'd never see him again. Tell that to my heart that was threatening to beat out of my chest.

"Did you tell the Alpha about the Malandanti?" I asked, taking a deep breath and trying to calm my heart.

"Yes, but Ezekiel had already phoned him. The Alpha's reaction was very much the same as Ezekiel's."

"He didn't believe you?"

Simon shrugged. "No proof."

Damn.

"Breanna, about this wolf. Do you wish to speak with him before we leave Italy?"

Yeah, sure, I'll just call him right up and tell his girlfriend to put him on the line. "Nah, he's got a mate."

"How do you know?"

"A woman answered when I called the hospital."

Simon tented his hands and stared at me for several moments. "As you wish, my dear. The Alpha, while perturbed with my breach of protocol, was indeed grateful for our intervention. He invited the wolves of Bravo to a pack run on his property Friday night."

That was classic. Werewolves invited. Witch and vampires, not.

"What are you doing?" I asked.

"Celeste and I are going to find a quiet place for dinner. The other vampires are planning an evening trip into the city as well. You are welcome to join us."

"I think I'll hang out, maybe go see a movie or something."

Simon nodded thoughtfully. "Whatever you would like, my dear. We will leave for Wisconsin when the next transport is available."

A few hours later, a quick check on the internet gave me a list of movie theatres in the area. Nothing grabbed me so I opted for a walk. It was nice to have some time to myself. I loved the soldiers in Bravo but after three weeks with them twenty-four-seven, a little me-time was good.

I found a nice walking path and dodged the abundance of handholding couples. There was a low vibe of a vampire somewhere nearby but no worries. It wasn't a master vampire and a little fire zap would scare a young one.

The path led me into the business district of the city central. Most offices were dark, their hardworking occupants either at home or out on the town. The buildings were older but stately. The brick facades watched over weathered cement sidewalks teeming with humans.

I ordered a pasta plate to go and found a single bench in a tiny park near the center of the city. It was a little oasis, complete with oak trees, grass, and a reflecting pool. I settled onto the bench, opened the Styrofoam plate, and inhaled the incredible smell of lobster ravioli. Chasing a string of cheese into my mouth, I noticed the sign across the street.

BENELLI ENTERPRISES

A single office light burned on the second floor, but the foyer was dark. I took a bite of ravioli and watched the window. Too far away to smell or feel anything, but how common was the name Benelli?

I finished my ravioli and never saw any movement from the office. Maybe someone had just left the light on.

"You're being stupid, Welker," I mumbled around my last bite of ravioli. Even if it was the same Benelli, Lucas wouldn't be in the building. He would be at the pack run.

I tossed the plate in the trash and headed deeper into the park. Shifting to owl form, I flew into the tree nearest the office building. If my talons weren't so strong, I would have fallen out of the damn tree.

I'd recognize those shoulders anywhere.

A huge stack of paperwork had Lucas working late into the night. I scratched my feathers. Why was he here? The Bravo wolves never missed a chance to run amok through the woods chasing rabbits and deer.

Eventually exhausted, they would flop in a pile, curled up next to one another, and sleep.

Lucas ran his hand through his hair and rolled his head on his shoulders. He looked stressed, shoulders tight, fists clenched.

I could work those kinks out of his neck.

He stood and crossed the room toward a fax machine, giving me a firsthand look at him from behind. I was not disappointed. His black dress pants perfectly fitted what was without a doubt the shapeliest ass I had ever seen. He wasn't overly tall, probably standing around six foot. He could have been a living stone statue. My beak chattered at the thought of those rock-hard abs and that chest, oh, that chest.

I'd like to rip the buttons off his shirt.

The light on the fax was blinking and he pulled open all the doors and drawers. He reached into the machine and bared his teeth. The thought of those perfect teeth nipping along my flesh made me overheat.

Owls don't sweat, idiot. Calm down before you fog up the window.

Maybe I could show up at his office door and help fix the fax machine. If I was a better witch, I could have cast a spell through the window to help him. That was too risky. A wayward spell might hurt him.

Lucas had looked really good when I found him beside the road but now, in that dress shirt and those dress pants, oh my.

Drop-dead fall-off-the-limb gorgeous.

Even through the window, there was wildness about him. A shiver shook my feathers as he whirled away from the fax machine and stormed toward his desk. Flakes of silver sparkled in his eyes as he glanced out the window and looked straight at me. I closed my beak and stared back at him. Did he know?

With a heavy sigh and slumping shoulders, Lucas glanced at his watch, grabbed his jacket, and headed toward the door. After one last look over his shoulder, he flipped off the light and disappeared into the darkness.

I swooped closer to the bustling street. My bird heart was pounding.

I needed to calm down before I pooped on his head.

The vibration of a master vampire slid across my feathers. The power was strong, but it wasn't Simon. My vampire commanding officer cloaked his power to make his strength unreadable. This vampire wanted others to know he was here.

Chapter 6

Lucas

If I didn't get out of the office, the fax machine would end up out the window. Four hours on contracts, bids, purchase orders and capital expenditures made me hungry. My client meeting was in an hour and that gave me time to get real food before eating a "normal" dinner with the human.

The pack wolves were out tonight so I'd have the local restaurants to myself. A big juicy steak sounded good and the musings of the local human population would be a nice change from the ill-tempered werewolves I'd been dealing with for the last few days. I stepped onto the sidewalk and got a nose full of car exhaust, human and food scents.

An odd tingle was in the air tonight, a familiar yet foreign magical vibration. With the full moon, lots of supernaturals would be out. The wolves hunting, the vampires stalking and, by a fire somewhere, naked elves danced.

None of that interested me anymore. When I was an agent for the Divine Council, I loved to see the full moon nights because it meant we were going to be out patrolling for those who didn't abide by the laws of the supernatural world. Now full moon nights were nothing special. Calculating the amount of drywall needed to finish a three-story office building dominated my days. Yeah, life was grand. Going to meet a client not pleased with the progress on his project. This should be a great dinner.

I checked my phone and saw three voicemails and two texts, all from my father, who insisted I be at the pack run tonight. I sent a text that I was stuck at work. He'd be angry, but by now he was in the forest leading the run. Oh well. He stayed angry with me. Why should tonight have been any different?

The unusual tingle increased as I walked the three blocks to Danton's. With no scent in the air, the tingle meant a vampire in the area.

"Ciao, Lucas." I knew that voice.

"Ciao, Istagio." His eyes were black as midnight and as usual, he wore the most expensive Armani suit money could buy.

"May we speak for a moment?" Istagio asked, falling into step beside me.

"Sure, just on my way to grab a steak."

He wrinkled his nose in obvious disdain for my meal choice. "One of our young ladies has gone missing. Giovanna disappeared three nights ago."

I stopped. "Do you have any leads?"

Istagio looked into the darkness. "None. It is like your brother. She simply vanished into thin air." He paused, shoving his hands deep into his pockets. "I have consulted a local oracle, who proclaimed Giovanna was taken to be used as a sacrifice."

"Sacrifice for what?"

"The oracle could not see," he answered as we continued walking. "I fear she is dead. A youngling, only four summers old, would not have known to stay away from the darkness of black magic."

"You created her?"

He bowed his head. "Yes. I turned her. I stumbled upon her as she lay dying in the wreckage of a dreadful auto accident. She was so beautiful and her aura pure. I felt she would do well amongst my kind."

"I'm sorry, Istagio."

"Your father has no news of your brother?" he asked.

I shrugged. "Not that I've heard."

Istagio's forehead wrinkled. "There are rumors of dark magic."

"I'll put in a call to Tristyn and see if he's heard anything." My best buddy, an ambassador for the Divine Council, knew the happenings within the supernatural world.

Istagio nodded and bowed his head. "I appreciate your concern for my lost young one. I am afraid we are too late for her, but I do not wish to lose any others."

To have people you care about disappear was, in some ways, worse than knowing they were dead. Lack of closure was hard on those left behind. I'd seen what it had done to my father and mother. No one deserved that type of torment.

I offered my hand and the cool skin of the vampire brushed against mine. "I'll let you know what I find out."

He pumped my hand once. "Thank you, Lucas. If there is any way I can be of assistance, please do not hesitate to ask."

"Thanks, Istagio. Call if anything comes up."

The vampire dipped his head and disappeared into the darkness. We had strayed from the main thoroughfare as we talked and my stomach demanded food. I loosened my tie and broke into a jog to follow the aroma of steak.

The odd vibration in the air remained long after Istagio and I parted ways.

Chapter 7

Breanna

Lucas never came out the front door. In human form, I waited across from the office building, but he must have taken a side exit. What the hell kind of recon soldier couldn't keep up with one civilian werewolf in a sea of humans? My tracking skills definitely needed work.

I decided against shifting to owl form and looking for him from the air. The sidewalks were much too crowded and he probably wasn't alone. This was stupid anyway. Why would he want to talk to me?

After one last long look through the milling humans, I ducked into a bustling sports bar. They had hockey. In jeans and t-shirt, I didn't look anything like the scantily dressed women scattered along the bar, but that was okay. There were no supernaturals inside and all I wanted was to relax with a cold beer, a basket of nachos, and an obnoxious group of fellow hockey fans.

Melting into the crowd, I joined in with the drunken cheering and ridiculous singing. A tall, thin blond human climbed onto the bar stool beside me. I ignored him until he tapped my arm.

"Are you tired?" he asked in perfect English.

"Uh, no, not really, why?"

"Because you've been walking in my dreams all night and I can't get enough of the way your ass looks in those jeans."

I took a big gulp of beer and leveled the coldest look I had. "That is a terrible pick-up line."

The human wrinkled his forehead before slithering off the stool and back into the crowd. A fresh beer appeared in front of me.

"On the house. You deserve it after that come-on," the female bartender said.

We laughed and I spun on the stool, hoping for a better seat near a window. I liked to watch people. Humans were interesting, with their lovey-dovey ways and emotional melodramas. Romance was lost on me. You didn't make it as far as I had in the military by living with your head in the clouds and waiting for a white knight to show up. Hell, if I saw someone in chainmail, he was going down.

A booth in the far corner of the bar finally opened, the googly-eyed couple leaving for more private surroundings. I sprinted to the open table, just beating a giggling group of bimbos. Leaning against the window and stretching out my legs on the bench would ward off any more pathetic pick-up lines.

Not.

Another human man slid onto the bench across from me. He seemed nice enough, but my Italian wasn't so good and his English was terrible. The conversation lasted all of forty-five seconds before he smiled politely and excused himself. Poor guy took a bunch of ribbing from his buddies. Sorry. No speaka da Italiano.

It was a good hockey game, several goals and lots of fights. The nachos were hot and crispy, the salsa spicy. It was a great evening until the scent of musk ruined it.

Where the hell were the exits?

The musk grew stronger and so did the power associated with whatever werewolf was coming. There was no guarantee the werewolf coming in was hostile--heck, maybe he was just looking for a cold beer. It wasn't unusual for werewolf guys to hook up with human women for a wild night of sex. Female werewolves didn't generally hook up with humans. Human men couldn't satisfy the needs of a werewolf.

However, it was odd since there was a pack run tonight. Lone wolves in Italian Pack territory weren't likely and there was only one werewolf I knew wasn't at the run. The musk was definitely male.

I licked my lips and tried to pinpoint the musk. Luckily I was sitting when I saw him, otherwise I may have become a puddle on the floor. Smoldering brown eyes made me weak. Broad shoulders tapering to a slim waist made me bite my tongue. A quiver started in my belly. My heart threatened to stop beating at any moment.

He's really here.

Lucas smiled as the crowd parted. Every human woman turned to stare as he strode through the bar with the power and grace of a predator. His eyes locked onto mine and I smiled like an idiot.

"Breanna?" he asked as he stopped at the end of my table. His eyes sparkled and my body tightened at the thought of those powerful arms surrounding me.

"Hi, Lucas," I replied, moving my legs so he could sit down.

His smile widened as he settled next to me, trapping me against the glass. I'd just willingly given up my only escape route. What the hell was wrong with me? God, he smelled good.

He was what was wrong with me. I was a pile of goo whenever he looked at me. Lucas oozed masculinity in a way that made me want to rip off his shirt and kiss him senseless.

"Do you mind if I join you?"

Oh dear God, he was polite, too? "No, please, be my guest."

"I'm surprised you're here by yourself."

I laughed like a nervous teenager. "Pack run."

He nodded but didn't elaborate.

"I'm surprised you're here by yourself," I countered.

His forehead crinkled. "I was working late."

Hmm, wonder where the phone bitch was.

"You are even more beautiful than I remembered."

Beer went up my nose and a nacho wedged in my throat. My face was getting hot, but at least the nacho slid on down.

"I was across the street and saw you through the window."

Well, wasn't this embarrassing. I was the recon specialist and he'd spotted me. Maybe I was losing my edge.

Lucas cleared his throat. "I'm sorry, Breanna. I'm being extremely forward here. I really wasn't stalking you, I swear. I have a client dinner meeting at Danton's."

Him stalking me? I was the one who had flown up and peeped in his window. "Did you leave your client?"

He nodded before pulling his phone from his jacket pocket. His conversation was in Italian and I didn't have a clue, but he hung up and smiled at me.

"Client meeting is over," he said. "Would you like something more substantial than nachos?" His smile was contagious and I was turning to mush. Damn, he was gorgeous.

"Sure, cheesy fries are always good. Do you like hockey?"

"Love it."

"For real? I've never met a wolf who liked any kind of sports."

He motioned for the waitress and ordered a large basket of fries. "I played a little in college."

My jaw dropped. "No way! Where did you go to college?"

He ducked his head and fidgeted with his beer. "Dartmouth."

An Italian wolf educated at a private university in New Hampshire? Not what I'd expected.

"I had to be careful and not hit the puck too hard. A few panes of glass broke my freshman year when I missed the net."

I grinned at him. "Bet you were the fastest skater."

He beamed. "Hands down."

The waitress arrived with the fries and we dug in. We talked about the hockey game and he explained the differences between European and NHL hockey.

"Would you like to go to a game? There's one tomorrow night. I could get tickets." The pink color in his cheeks was adorable. Damn, he was gorgeous and sweet.

My heart rate tripled. I almost choked on a fry. He was going to think I had some type of eating disorder if I kept choking.

"That sounds like a lot of fun. I don't think we've got anything on schedule for tomorrow night."

We cheered and jeered along with the human crowd as the hockey game wound down. He asked lots of questions about Bravo and exactly what I did. I'd never spent so much time talking about myself.

"I wanted to thank you again for saving my life." Our eyes locked, our conversation stopping but our souls continuing to communicate. Our bodies touched, our fingers inching together on top of the table.

That little door inside me that had clicked the night I met him was standing wide open now. The warmth of his body soaked into mine. My hand acted on its own, reaching for the shadowy beard on his chin. The stubble tickled my fingers, his lips parting as I leaned closer.

His fingers brushed my jaw as he tucked a stray piece of hair behind my ear. "You are so beautiful," he whispered.

His eyes were like pools of chocolate and I was drowning. It was a good way to die.

Our booth shook. We had company. Damn.

"Bre, why didn't you answer your phone? Who the hell are you?" Aaron growled at Lucas.

Lucas's eyes went silver.

"Aaron Miller, this is Lucas Benelli." I hoped a neutral tone would rattle them out of their eyeball battle. It didn't. "What do you want, Aaron?"

He ignored me and continued the staring contest with Lucas. The scent and feel of the air was changing. The humans felt the disturbance and turned to look. Not good.

"Lieutenant Miller, what is your business here? And don't play the selective deafness card because I know you heard me."

Lucas leaned back from the table and wrapped my hand in his. He was giving Aaron a chance to back out of this stupid dominance game all the werewolves played. Aaron didn't take the hint. He leaned forward.

"Aaron. Stop. Now."

There was a slight tremor in his eyes but he would not disengage. Lucas, the more dominant, let out a breath before turning to me. His eyes were almost completely silver.

Lucas ground his teeth while staring into my eyes. I was eyeball-to-eyeball with his wolf.

"Thank you," I said.

Lucas dipped his head and closed his eyes. The air around us calmed as he took both my hands in his. The power coursing through him was incredible. Rage, dominance, strength.

"Hey, Bre!" Ordy shouted over the milling humans. He strolled over and stopped abruptly beside Aaron. "Take it down a notch, Miller. You don't want none of him." Ordy nodded toward Lucas while waving a hand in front in Aaron.

Aaron's eyes flitted to me. Lucas eased forward. The air was stuffy again, dominance flowing freely.

"Lucas?" I squeezed his fingers.

A muscle ticked in his jaw. I glanced at Ordy and inclined my head to Aaron. "Ordy, can you take him out and find a fire hydrant to keep him entertained?"

Ordy gave me a sly grin before grabbing Aaron by the arm. Aaron tried to snatch away but there was no getting away from Ordy's meat hooks. "We're supposed to bring you back to base, Bre. DuChard recalled us from the run. Something about a new sighting we have to check out."

Damn. Damn. Damn.

Ordy yanked Aaron from the bench. "We'll wait outside."

"Thanks, Ordy. I'll be out in a minute."

Lucas squeezed my fingers again, bowed his head, and closed his eyes. After several moments, he looked up, his eyes mostly brown, a crooked smile on his face. "Sorry about that." His cheeks flushed an adorable shade of pink. "My wolf really likes you."

His wolf liked me? What the hell did that mean?

Aaron tapped on the window and pointed to his watch. I rolled my eyes and motioned for him to go away.

"I gotta go before they start peeing on the light poles."

Lucas smiled and shook his head. I wanted to grab him by the ears and kiss the breath out of him.

Aaron rapped on the window again and Ordy grabbed him. Three more werewolves from my unit came inside and waved for me. Damn it.

"It might be best if you wait here until I get them away."

Lucas glared at the pacing wolves and then back to me. His face softened. "May I call you?"

My hands shook as we exchanged numbers. I didn't want to leave, but this time there was no choice. I had to go or there would be a dogfight, literally.

His shoulders heaved as he slid off the bench. "Be careful," he said without releasing my hand.

"You too."

He pressed his lips to the back of my hand and my knees jellified. "Good night, my angel."

Chapter 8

Lucas

"Trist, I'm telling you, she's amazing. I've never met anybody like her."

The phone conversation with my best friend of over twenty years had gone on for almost half an hour as he listened to me go on about Breanna.

"Did she say what kind of witch she was?"

"An earth witch."

"Bet your wolf liked her."

I swallowed hard, remembering the way my wolf had reacted to her. "Yeah, he did." It should be a great thing, my wolf liking her, but it scared the shit out of me. My wolf didn't like anybody.

"Luc? You there, buddy?"

"Call her, Lucas. Call her tonight," a woman called from the background.

Tristyn laughed. "You hear that? My witch wants you to get your own witch so we can double date."

When we were agents for the Divine Council, before Tristyn met his mate, we would often double date with human girls. Truthfully, I went along because he felt bad about leaving me at home alone. "Wolves need companionship," he would say before always adding, "and I promised this girl you would go out with her friend."

"So, when are you going to tell your dad?" Tristyn asked.

"Not now."

"No, but it's only a matter of time and you'll be head over heels in love with her."

In love with her? My chest was so tight I could barely breathe.

"Luc? Are you all right?"

"I don't know. I'll deal with him when I have to. Do you think Alex could help me with some info on earth witches?"

Tristyn's mate, Alexandria, was a powerful white witch and the Witch Representative to the Divine Council. She took her job very seriously, especially considering the negative attitude the supernatural world had against her kind. Most supernaturals, werewolves included, didn't bother to find out if witches were peaceful or evil. They killed them all, usually without repercussion.

In the background Tristyn spoke to his mate before returning to the phone. "Alex said she'd have to make a few inquiries and see what she could find out for you."

We hung up a few moments later and I headed back to the office to renew my battle with the fax machine. The sidewalks were busy but I did my best to avoid the crowds. I glanced around, hoping Breanna might appear from the darkness, but no such luck. She was gone.

I entered the office building without bothering with the lights. The carpet crunched softly under my shoes as I approached the open door to my office. A surge of adrenaline shot through me, my body tensing at the knowledge someone had been here. There was no strange musk, no vibration of vampire, but there was something different.

Strawberries.

I clicked the light, my heart hammering at the idea Breanna might be here, in my office. The strawberry scent lingered strongest near my nemesis, the fax machine. When I left, the fax machine had demanded paper and had been strangling on the jam I couldn't reach. Now it was calm and quiet, all red lights off and the paper tray fully loaded. Three incoming faxes waited patiently in the stacker.

I had to see her again. I grabbed my coat on the way out the door.

* * * *

Ten gun-wielding guards watched warily as I approached the brightly lit gate of Camp Ederle. The American base was located near Vicenza and housed soldiers stationed in the United States Army Africa Division and the 173rd Airborne Brigade. According to Breanna, Bravo Company utilized the base anytime it deployed to Europe.

"I must be out of my mind," I muttered, rolling down the window as the guards approached. The soldiers at the bar had made it clear they didn't want me talking to Breanna, yet here I was, asking for her like I was her new best friend.

The human guards agreed to call her. Endless seconds stretched into minutes before the echo of boot stomps made my breath catch. Stepping out of my car, I waited as the heavy steel door beside the gate opened.

The smell of musk rolled over me and my wolf took notice of the humans scurrying inside and the flood of werewolves pouring out.

"What the hell do you want?" one of the wolves asked.

Ten of them burst through the door and surrounded me. My wolf surged, demanding control, as I fought to push down the rising bile in my throat. I gave over to the beast within, my own dominance flowing forth. The soldiers backed away a few steps, giving me much-needed breathing room. My wolf wanted total control, to kill these who threatened me.

"I'm here to see Breanna," I said between gritted teeth.

The blond wolf from the bar marched forward. His fist connected with my chin before I could react. I dropped my head and charged him, catching him in the stomach and slamming him into the iron gates. He pummeled the back of my head, but the pain barely registered as I landed blow after blow to his midsection.

Hands grabbed at me and I reacted, raining blows upon anyone within striking distance. The scent of blood, musk, and rage filled the night air. I was an animal, acting on sheer instinct, the need to survive taking over all rational thought. There was yelling, but nothing came through as words until she spoke my name.

"Lucas."

I didn't throw another punch, though a few more landed on me. I didn't feel anything or see anything except Breanna.

Time stood still as she walked toward me. She was dressed in black fatigues and a US Army sweatshirt. Her brows were raised, a splatter of blood on her cheek, as she reached for my hand. Her lips moved but there was a deafening roaring in my ears now, my wolf furious at the attack.

Her eyes locked onto mine, her lips continuing to move as she stood mere inches from my face. I was gasping for air, desperate to calm my wolf, but unwilling to let go of the power he gave me. She came closer, until the warmth of her body pressed against mine.

She touched my jaw and my wolf retreated, leaving a trail of pain from the beating I had taken. For the first time I noticed the other wolves, now watching me warily, some on the ground while the others were leaning against the gate. One sprawled on the hood of my truck.

"Lucas, can you hear me?"

I nodded, not yet trusting my voice to stay steady. My body trembled under her fingers and I did what I could to pull myself together. This was not at all what I wanted her to see.

"C'mon in and I'll get you cleaned up," Breanna said softly as she turned my hands over to examine bloody knuckles.

"I'm not sure that's a good idea," I rasped. The others were watching us, their eyes swirling with silver.

"Fuck them," she snarled, leading me past two wolves who were holding their ribs. "I'll deal with them later. Right now, I need to get you taken care of."

We passed the human guards and she told them to pull my truck inside the gates. They saluted her and dashed toward the front entrance.

"I'm sorry about all that," she said as she led me into a room filled with medical supplies. She nodded toward a small examining bed and I pulled myself onto the paper-covered mattress.

"Seems every time you get around me, you end up getting hurt," she said with a smile.

I ducked my head, my face getting hot. I must have looked like a weakling to her. I pushed off the bed, no longer willing to buy into the fantasy I had created. A woman like this didn't want damaged goods like me.

"Hey, where you going?" She stood between me and the door.

The genuine pain on her face sucked the life from my soul. None of the kicks or punches hurt nearly as much as the way she was looking at me right now.

"I shouldn't have come here," I said lamely.

"Why did you come?" she asked. There was no accusation or anger in her voice, only concern.

"I wanted to thank you for fixing the fax."

She took a deep breath, the rise and fall of her breasts making my own breath catch. She turned her back, busying herself with bandages.

"You could have called," she said before spinning around to face me.

My hand that was resting on the door handle fell limply by my side. As much as I knew how this would turn out, I didn't want to leave her.

"I wanted to see you again," I answered, giving her the opportunity to call me on my ridiculous obsession.

"I wanted to see you, too."

I gulped for air like a fish out of water.

She stepped toward me, taking my hand in hers. "Now that we are both equally uncomfortable, can I clean you up a bit?"

Her smile was friendly, so sincere it turned me to mush. The way I kept losing my ability to talk, Breanna would probably think I had some type of speech impediment.

She apologized over and over for the actions of the werewolves at the gate as she wiped the blood from my knuckles and face. She insisted on bandaging my ribs and holding ice to the blossoming bruises around my eye.

The powerful vibration of a master vampire preceded a vigorous knock at the door.

"Sergeant Welker?"

"Come on in, Sime."

A tall, blond vampire marched into the room. Breanna didn't flinch as she maintained the icepack against my cheek. Nothing in her scent suggested she was afraid of the vampire now scrutinizing us.

"Lucas Benelli, this is Major Simon DuChard, my CO."

The vampire nodded eloquently. "Are you injured, Mr. Benelli?" He sounded French.

"Yes, he's injured," Breanna snapped. "Ten against one isn't exactly fair."

The fact she was defending me made me warm inside. Not a lot of people defended me.

"Nothing vital, Major DuChard. It was a misunderstanding," I answered.

Breanna's eyes lit up. "Misunderstanding, my ass. Aaron and them were being shithead bullies and they got their asses kicked." She paused to adjust the ice bag. "And they'll get them kicked again when I'm done."

The vampire scowled. "Sergeant Welker, may I speak with you outside?"

"Not now."

The vampire's shoulders slumped, his irritation flooding the room. I'd already caused enough trouble and didn't need to add to it.

"I'm okay," I said, forcing a smile. "Go ahead and talk to him."

She took my hand and placed it against the ice pack. "Hold this. I'll be right back." She snorted before walking past the vampire and out the door. God, she was beautiful when she was angry.

Breanna brooded over my scrapes and bruises for almost an hour before she walked me to my truck. Her unit was departing in a few hours and rather than getting rest, she was fussing over me. Major DuChard assured me Breanna was in no danger of retaliation from the soldiers I had fought. Actually, he'd insisted he would be protecting the werewolves from her.

I made it to work on time and was putting the final touches on the new estimates when Alpha power shook the building. Bull-like breathing announced my father's presence on the hall.

"Lucas!"

I was rolling up the blueprint and placing the estimates in the folder as the door flew open. Josef should have been pleased. We were coming in under budget.

"Alpha," I answered, his power threatening to suffocate me.

"Why did you cut short the meeting with Burlesconi? I spoke to him this morning and he said you left your dinner meeting without an agreement."

My wolf bristled at the accusatory tone. "Something came up. I called and rescheduled the meeting. He didn't sound upset."

Josef turned and stalked to the door, his body shaking. "What came up?"

I opened my mouth to answer as he turned back and stormed to my desk.

"And why were you on the military base? You have no business there." The desk shook with the force of his rage. "Is that what happened to your face? A human teach you a lesson for being with his whore since you seem incapable of satisfying a woman of your own kind?" And then he delivered the dagger to my heart. "You were with a woman, I hope."

Why was I doing this? Nothing I said would be the right answer. "I think it's time I leave Italy. This isn't working and we both know it isn't going to get any better."

He stared out the window. "You can't run from everything, Lucas. It is time you took your role in this pack. I have neither the time nor the desire to fight you every step of the way. I gave you the most desirable woman in the pack as your mate, yet refuse her. I offered you a place as my second-in-command and you parade your disrespect by not bothering to attend any pack functions."

"Not going to pack functions has nothing to do with disrespect for you. I don't want to be a part of this pack. I don't know how many times I have to say it for you to understand. I only came home to help you with Benelli Enterprises, period."

He didn't bother to turn around. "I hope whatever was so important last night was worth it, because you cost this company a twenty-million-dollar contract. Your brother would have never done something so selfish and irresponsible."

He walked out the door and I grabbed the edges of my desk to keep from chasing him. Why did I keep doing this? I should throw my clothes in a bag and catch a plane to somewhere, anywhere but here.

When I was working as an agent for the Divine Council, I had the legal right to move freely from pack territory to pack territory. Now, because

I lived in Italy, I was a member of the Italian Pack and not welcome on other pack territory. My father wouldn't release me to join another pack and the life expectancy of a lone wolf was less than a year.

Maybe lone wolf wasn't a bad idea after all. I'd be a target for other Alphas angry with my father and he had plenty of enemies. At least I'd be away from here. The way my mom had been acting, she wouldn't miss me either.

Pent-up rage bubbled to the surface as I flipped the desk, sending papers and pens flying. My phone slid across the floor to safety but my laptop wasn't so lucky. I sank into my chair and buried my head in my hands, the desk flipping incident not making me feel any better.

"Mr. Benelli?" Clara asked, peeking around the corner. "Are you all right?"

She frowned at me like a kid who had broken a window. She leaned down and retrieved the blueprint. Maybe she didn't see the silver flakes in my eyes but she knew I had lost control again.

"I'm sorry, Clara."

"Mr. Benelli, I may be out of line and you may certainly fire me if you so choose, but I think you should go back to your Divine Council job. This business is not for you. You are not happy and no matter what you do, your father will never be satisfied."

Her words crashed on my head like a brick wall. "I was stupid to come back."

Cloth rustled as Clara crossed the room toward me. "Not stupid, just not in your best interest. You've never been a pack wolf, Mr. Benelli. Why did you think things would be any different this time?"

I couldn't look at her face. "I didn't think things would be different. I only came back to help with Benelli Enterprises. I wasn't exactly a joy as a child, so I thought I owed it to my parents to help."

She stood to the full height of her five-foot-one frame. "You owe them nothing, particularly your mother." Tiny flickers of silver flecked her eyes as she swiped a handful of pens from the floor. Clara patted me on the shoulder and I did my best not to flinch. My wolf did not approve of her touch, even in kindness.

"You will never be happy in Italy."

She was right but I couldn't walk away. I didn't care about the pack, but I did wish my father and I could get along. We'd never be as close as he and Nic had been, but I'd hoped we could at least eat dinner together without arguing. So far, that had not happened and it didn't look good.

I grudgingly returned my desk to its upright position and gathered the broken laptop.

"I'll take care of this, Mr. Benelli. You should take the blueprints to your father. He's meeting the client at Coraleon's."

My wolf rumbled at the thought of being in the same room with my father. Clara held out the roll of blueprints and I took them gingerly. Coraleon's was only a ten-minute walk and fresh air would be good. Clara was gathering up my mess as I flashed out the door.

"Mr. Benelli?" she called before I rounded the corner.

I glanced over my shoulder.

"Be sure to check your messages."

"Thanks, Clara. Will do."

After dropping off the prints to my surprised father, I drove out to my house for lunch and a run. My wolf needed to kill something other than my father.

Almost forgetting Clara's advice, I quickly checked my messages and found several. Only one mattered. Breanna had called. Bravo Company pulled out early this morning and she'd called to say goodbye.

Now I really needed to kill something.

Chapter 9

Breanna

The flight to wherever the hell we were going was terrible. The turbulence bounced us like boobs on a treadmill and the monotonous droning of the motors made me want to stab my eardrums. Without warning, the plane took a sickening drop.

"Where are we?" All I could see were clouds and trees. Lots and lots of trees.

"Paraguay," Simon replied without opening his eyes. I hated takeoffs and he hated landings.

"South freakin' America?" Aaron asked in disbelief.

"That would be correct," Simon answered.

Great. Mosquitoes and snakes. Whoopee.

"What the hell are we doing in bumfuckin' Paragum?" Aaron grumbled.

"It's Paraguay and you'll be briefed when we land," Simon said.

Aaron took the hint and didn't say anything else. Simon wasn't normally grumpy, but when he was, everyone left him alone.

We all sat in silence as the big plane lumbered along the landing strip. The werewolves stirred first, gathering their belongings as the rolling slowed. The vampires and lone elf always waited until the plane was completely still before moving.

I waited as well, not because the movement bothered me but because I was usually sitting with Celeste and Simon and it seemed rude to hop up while they sat rigid in their spaces.

Once the plane stopped, the familiar weight of an intense gaze began. "I'm fine, Simon."

He placed a hand on my shoulder. "You have strong feelings for this Italian wolf, do you not, Breanna?"

I shrugged, preferring not to go there right now.

"When there is time, I wish to speak with you regarding your wolf. There are things I believe you should know."

Oh hell.

There was no way he was going to walk away and leave me hanging like that. "What does that mean?" My words came out harsher than I intended.

Simon gave me a puzzled look before switching to the "apologize or I'll not say another word" look.

"Sorry, Sime. I'm tired."

He gave me a long, hard look.

"Yeah, I know, not your fault. I had no reason to snap at you."

He bowed his head in a graceful vampire acknowledgement. "We will speak of this matter when we have privacy."

I was dying. "Is it bad?"

"Not particularly."

I argued with Simon until he disappeared into the darkness. What did he know about Lucas? I knew next to nothing, other than his name and he worked in a big brick building in downtown Vicenza. Just thinking about how hard his chest had looked in that dress shirt was enough to make me need a very cold shower.

"Hey, Bre," Aaron called as he wandered into the dirty barracks we were using for the next few nights. He dropped his sleeping bag onto a bunk and a cloud of dust appeared. Bedbugs. Yuck.

Unrolling my sleeping bag and ignoring the itchy sensation on my leg, I noticed a cockroach scurrying along the wall. Ug, I hate bugs.

Earth witches should embrace all Mother Nature's creatures. Yeah, well, I ain't making friends with a freaking roach.

The other werewolves trickled into the cat-puke-green barracks. Scientists could have discovered new strains of mold and mildew in this place.

Simon entered, followed closely by the other vampire members of Bravo. Celeste quickly scooted past the vampire parade and hurried to me.

"Come with me," she said. "Simon wants to talk to you."

I followed her outside and into a dank, dreary office space several hundred feet away. Within moments, Simon was directly behind us, closing the door and making sure we were alone.

"Okay, Sime. Talk to me."

The vampire motioned for me to sit and I plopped, very unladylike, into a chair. Celeste perched on the arm of the chair Simon had chosen.

"Your wolf is the son of the Italian Alpha."

My guts bubbled.

"The Alpha announced several months ago his son was to be mated to a woman within the pack."

So the telephone bitch was his girlfriend. Should have known he was too good to be true. Double damn.

"Your wolf has declared he will not take the woman chosen for him. He is defying his father and for that there is turmoil within the pack."

Turmoil within his pack? Pack turmoil was not a happy thing for werewolves. There was something about the pack bond thing that made them more open to each other than non-pack wolves and other supernaturals. I didn't fully understand it, but the wolves seemed to love being in a pack.

"He is not highly regarded within his pack, but none of my sources know exactly why. There are many rumors regarding his lifestyle choices, but the vampires of Italy hold him in the highest regard. He was at one time an agent for the Divine Council, but resigned his position to return to Italy and help with the family business."

He left the Divine Council to return to a pack that didn't like him? What was up with that? But something else Simon had said bothered me more.

"What do you mean by lifestyle choices?"

Simon arched his platinum eyebrows, his crystal blue eyes hooded. "My sources did not go into details."

"You are not telling me he's gay, are you?"

"I am merely repeating the information I was given."

"He is not gay."

Celeste hopped from the chair arm and flitted toward a window. "Perhaps he likes both. Would you be okay with that?" she asked with her arms crossed.

"I, um, I, well, I don't really know."

Simon watched me curiously before speaking. "Have you spoken with your wolf?"

I shrugged. "I left a message before we flew out but--oh shit, I haven't turned my phone on since we landed." I dashed out the door and to the barracks for my bag. There was no service inside the dilapidated building so I took off up the hill. The wolves yelled at me, but I kept running.

Finally, at the top of the hill, my phone registered a single bar of service. The message icon wasn't on. Lucas hadn't called. I plunked onto a rock and looked up at the stars. Of course he hadn't called. Every time he talked to me, something bad happened.

The phone suddenly lit up in my hand, the message icon flashing like a beacon. I fumbled with the keys before finding the right buttons to play the message.

The computerized lady announced I had two messages. The first was a hang-up and my heart sank a little. The next began with a long pause and I almost deleted it until his rough, heavily accented voice came through the speaker.

"Hello, Breanna, this is Lucas, Lucas Benelli." A heavy sigh followed by what sounded like rustling clothes. "I hope your trip goes well." Another uncomfortable pause, followed by a grunt. "So, uh, if you have a chance, give me a call, any time. I'll have my phone on." Heavy breathing like he wasn't sure what to say. "Be careful out there."

I replayed his message three times. His accent and the roughness in his voice, geez, sexy as hell. Damn, what was wrong with me? Sitting on a rock in the dark playing a voicemail over and over? Really? You'd think I'd never had a guy call me before.

So, yeah, it had been a long time since I'd had a date. Even longer since I had a date with someone I wanted to get to know. I didn't date the guys in Bravo and, with my work schedule, meeting someone wasn't exactly easy. I'd dated a vampire once, but my dates were usually humans just because they were no threat and their intentions were so completely obvious. Even a witch liked to feel wanted sometimes. Of course the humans had no idea I was anything other than a female soldier serving in a rather obscure military unit. It was easier that way. No strings attached.

But Lucas was different. With him I liked the thought of strings--hell, I'd even consider ropes and chains if that was what he liked. He knew what I was and never batted an eye. I'd heard the Europeans weren't exactly keen on witches and the werewolves were particularly negative, but Lucas wasn't like that.

He'd said he was friends with a white witch. I didn't know any white witches, but had heard they were all beautiful and could cast spells to heal. Hell, I couldn't do much more than toss fireballs, ask the animals for help, and call up water-thin protection spells.

I listened to his message a couple more times before working up the nerve to call him. He answered on the second ring.

"Ciao."

"Hi, Lucas. It's Breanna."

"Hey!" He sounded happy. "How are you?"

The small talk chit-chat took over for a couple of minutes. I told him about the plane ride, and a little about our mission. I left out the potential bed bug issue and anything else a civilian shouldn't know.

"So, when are you going home?" he asked.

"We're on for two weeks here. Could be more or less, depending on what we are looking for." Finding a specific supernatural in a South American rainforest was not an easy task. We could look for three months and never find a trace.

"I'd like to come visit you in America when you get back," he said softly. I almost fell off the rock as he continued. "Would that be all right?"

I didn't need a mirror to know I had a stupid grin on my face. "Yeah, that'd be great."

I could hear him smiling. "*Magnifico!* Just let me know when you'll be back."

We talked for almost an hour. My cell bill would be scary, but it was worth it to hear his voice, to imagine his smile as he laughed at my stories. Was it possible to miss someone you barely knew? The idea of seeing him again made me all tingly. He was willing to spend good money to fly to America to see me? Me?

When we hung up my heart whimpered. This was all so strange. The way I responded to him was unnerving, like he had some kind of control over me. I was acting like a lovestruck teenager and it would have been embarrassing if it hadn't been so real.

A slight vibration in the air told me I wasn't alone. The vampires were near.

"Breanna? Everything okay?" Christopher asked as he stepped into the moonlight.

"Hi, Chris, yeah, everything's all right. I was talking to Lucas."

He raised an eyebrow. "The Italian werewolf?"

I nodded, the stupid teen-in-love grin slipping into place. "He called me."

Chris hopped onto the boulder effortlessly. "You really do like him, don't you?"

I tried to play off the question, but Chris kept me pinned with a droll stare. "I guess I do. He wants to come to America for a visit."

"Do the wolves know?"

"I haven't talked to them. Why?"

"Lucas will need to gain permission to be in another pack's territory."

That was the way of the werewolves, but I didn't think Galen McGregor, the Wisconsin Alpha, would have a problem with Lucas.

"For what it's worth, Breanna, we vampires like Lucas Benelli. He is good friends with Tristyn Ziccardi, the Vampire Representative to the Divine Council."

"He said he was friends with a white witch also."

Chris smiled knowingly. "Ah, yes, that would be Alexandria."

I did not like the familiarity in his voice. "You know her, too?"

I dropped to the ground and Chris landed soundlessly beside me.

"She is Tristyn's mate."

"A vampire mated to a witch?"

Chris clasped his hands behind his back and walked with me toward the barracks. "Tristyn is no ordinary vampire. He is a born vampire, the *viata sange*. According to the prophecy of the Divine Council, the *viata sange* would help bring peace and stability to the supernatural world. For many years Lucas Benelli served as his bodyguard. Lucas risked his life many times for the *viata sange* and even fought a demon to protect Tristyn's mate."

I tripped on a rock and Chris's cool hand grabbed my arm. "Lucas fought a demon?"

"He was injured and took several weeks to heal. Tristyn and Alexandria delayed their mating ceremony until Lucas was well enough to attend."

I paid more attention to where I was walking as we hit a particularly rough patch of ground. Funny, the terrain had not been an issue on my run up the hill. "How did a werewolf end up guarding a vampire?"

"They were best friends from childhood. I'm not sure how they met, but Lucas never left Tristyn's side until Alexandria came along."

White witches were decent in the magic department, drawing on their bloodlines for their magical abilities. If she was any good, she could take care of Tristyn without Lucas's help.

And then there were earth witches calling out brown bears and tossing fireballs. Whoopee. Somehow that just didn't seem fair, but it was what it was. No need to whine about it.

Chris's wicked pace slowed as the barracks came into view. "I hope this works out for you, Breanna. You deserve to be happy." The vampire pecked me politely on the cheek. "Sleep well, *ma cherie*."

Chris disappeared into the darkness and it dawned on me he hadn't been out on a stroll when he happened upon me sitting on a rock. He had purposefully made the climb to make sure I was all right. I'd saved his life almost a year ago when a group of very angry sorcerers had captured him, planning to cut him into bits and feed him to their cats. The sorcerers had been hoping the vampire's body would give their cats immortality.

The cats didn't get immortality but they did get rehomed into a cat rescue group I found in Green Bay. The sorcerers ended up in a special supernatural prison in Bulgaria and Chris had been one of my closest allies ever since.

* * * *

It was zero four hundred and we assembled for our briefing. Simon hadn't talked much about our mission and we were all anxious to know what exactly we were hunting.

Simon stepped to the front and the room fell silent. "There have been reports of a rogue werewolf in this area. The closest pack is four hundred miles away and that pack reports no loss in its numbers. Our mission is to find this rogue wolf, kill him, and dispose of the body in an appropriate manner."

An eerie quiet filled the room. The werewolves were never completely comfortable hunting one of their own. Interestingly, the vampires didn't have that issue.

Simon allowed time for his words to settle before continuing. "This wolf is reportedly black, medium build, and has been sighted twice near the Bermejo River. We will conduct our search as four units. Sergeant Welker will fly ahead and recon." Intense blue eyes turned in my direction. "And she will report her intel and will not engage."

"Got that?" Aaron whispered as he bumped my shoulder.

"Shut up and get away from me."

"Do the two of you have something to share, Sergeant Welker or Lieutenant Miller?"

"No, sir," we answered in unison. A couple chuckles broke out around us but Simon's glare quieted every sound.

"Ready your gear for a three-day trip. Sergeant Welker, Celeste will see to your pack."

"Yes, sir."

Simon dismissed us and we headed toward the barracks. Aaron loped along beside me. "So, Bre, what's up with you and that Italian?"

"I'd appreciate it if you and your boys didn't try to beat the shit out of a guy who wants to talk to me."

"You shouldn't be talking to him."

"Excuse me?"

"His pack doesn't like him and I got a bad feeling about him at that bar."

"You were being a territorial asshole in the bar, Aaron."

He shrugged, holding the door open for me. "Maybe, but when a pack doesn't like a pack wolf, there's something wrong. They said he tried to kill another pack wolf when he was younger because that wolf threatened to tell everyone what he liked to do."

"What he liked to do? What the hell does that mean?"

"They said he liked men."

My blood pressure shot up fifty points. "Oh, you are so full of shit. You're just saying this because I like him."

Several other wolves walked up. I'd been ignoring them all, but it looked like that was about to end.

"I'm going to say this once. Leave. Lucas. Alone."

Aaron picked up my sleeping bag. "He likes vampires."

"So do I."

Aaron growled, tossing the bag into my duffel. "No, I mean he really likes vampires. Guy vampires."

Oh hell, here we go again.

"Bullshit."

"I'm serious, Bre. You need to stay away from that guy."

"I like him, Aaron, and he wants to come to Wisconsin to see me. If he liked guy vampires, why would he want to do that?"

Aaron looked puzzled for a second before looking around to see who was listening to our conversation. Everyone looked preoccupied with packing but they were listening to every word we said.

"Maybe he wants to see LeCavalier. I've always wondered about that vamp anyway. He looks at me funny."

Oh, for God's sake. "Christopher is not gay and neither is Lucas, now will you please go pack your bag and leave me alone?"

Aaron mumbled something more worth ignoring but then opened his trap again. "His pack hates him, Bre. That should tell you something."

I threw a dusty pillow at Aaron's head. "How do you know so much about Lucas?"

He grabbed the pillow and tossed it to the side. "I talked to some of the Italian Pack before we left. He's damaged goods, Bre. You need to stay away from him. He's fucked up."

"Shut up, Aaron. When we get back home, Lucas is going to come see me and you'd better leave him alone."

"You deserve better than him."

My fingers twitched, fire arcing along my nails. "There is nothing wrong with Lucas. Leave him alone, Aaron. I mean it."

I was in his face, nose to nose, when a wave of happiness swept through the room, Celeste trotting in. "Hey, Bre! Got your stuff packed?"

With one last glare at Aaron, I shoved another sweatshirt into my bag and handed it to the waiting elf. She took it with a big smile and grabbed my hand. "Simon wants to see you."

Great. Probably a lecture about following orders, protocol, etcetera, etcetera, etcetera.

The tiny elf wrapped her arm around mine. "Did you talk to Lucas?"

I told her about my conversation as we entered the shanty office building. She leaped for joy when I mentioned Lucas wanted to come for a visit. At least she didn't tell me he was gay.

We entered the office and I snapped to attention as Major Trenton scowled at me. Damned protocol.

"Thank you for coming, Sergeant Welker," Simon said as he disrupted Trenton's line of sight. "Major Trenton's Combat Unit will be acting as backup on this mission."

Trenton moved to stand shoulder to shoulder with Simon. The werewolf major was a little taller than Simon and much broader through the shoulders, but everyone knew Simon was the best fighter in Bravo.

"We are not acting as backup, DuChard. We are completing the kill and disposal. I don't know why your unit is here other than to get you out of the general's hair."

Simon's spine went rigid. "We are here because it is our job to find the wolf and your soldiers will stay out of our way until we complete our mission."

Trenton's eyes flashed silver. "And you would do best to remember, DuChard, we are here to make sure the mission is completed."

Simon's power filled the room. My back hurt from standing at attention for so long.

"Major Trenton, I will contact you when the wolf has been captured. Sergeant Welker will be forward of the unit, relaying her intel. We will capture the target and transport him back here. Your unit will then take custody of the target and my soldiers will return home." Simon looked over at me and frowned. "Sergeant Welker, you are dismissed."

I saluted and got out the door as quickly as possible, Celeste close behind.

"Sorry, Bre. I didn't know Major Trenton was there."

"That's okay. Do you know what Simon wanted to talk to me about?"

Celeste twirled her golden blond hair around her finger. "Not really."

I touched base with the unit leaders, double-checked my radio was in my pocket, and took to the air. No need to waste time waiting to see what Trenton was up to, and I'd had about as much werewolf crap as I could take. Simon would handle him and the quicker I found the target, the quicker I could see Lucas.

It was dark and I'd flown almost twelve miles when a big black wolf came into view. Lying in the shallow pools beside a stream, he was huge, much too large to be one of the native mane wolves, but only a medium wolf by werewolf standards.

I circled for a suitable landing place. The wolf, intelligence glowing in his silver eyes, watched me curiously, but made no attempt to leave or come closer. The wolf pawed at the water and lolled his tongue like a puppy. He yipped and playfully splashed the cool water in my direction.

He wriggled his hips and splashed the water again. I snapped my beak and he yipped happily. This must have been a lonely wolf if he was trying to play with an owl. I hopped two rocks away and shifted to human. The wolf immediately bared his teeth, all signs of playfulness disappearing.

"Easy, big fella. I'm not here to hurt you."

Shiny white teeth said hello.

"Hungry?" I asked. He responded with a low warning growl and even more teeth.

I pulled a pack of jerky from my pocket and tore into the crinkly wrapper. I took a bite and tossed a piece toward the wolf. He ignored it. From the look on his face, he would have ignored a bloody rump roast.

"Fine, don't eat it. That just means more for me."

The wolf turned tail and ran, disappearing into the darkness. I dug into my pocket for my radio. The GPS would give the coordinates I could forward to Simon.

Two minutes later, Simon radioed.

"Good work, Master Sergeant," he said when I answered. Trenton must have been nearby for him to address me so formally.

"Thanks, Major DuChard."

We discussed the logistics of setting a trap for the rogue and decided something involving female scent would work best given the wolf's apparent lack of food motivation. Trenton mumbled in the background and then a door slammed.

"May I speak to you in private, Major DuChard?" I asked.

"Trenton's gone."

"That wolf didn't try to attack." He should have charged rather than wiggling his butt in an invitation to play.

"Our duty is to capture him, Breanna, not to pass judgment on his actions."

"What if he isn't a rogue? What if he's confused?"

Simon drew in a sharp breath, obviously in irritation because as a vampire, he didn't have to breathe. "You did your duty, Breanna. Return to base and we'll finalize the plans to complete this mission."

"Yes, sir." Damn it.

Chapter 10

Lucas

"Lucas, did you speak with the clients regarding the office building in Florence?"

"Yes, they were happy with the prints I had couriered yesterday."

My father shook his head. "Couriered? I asked you to hand-deliver those prints."

"I couldn't deliver those prints to Florence and meet with the subcontractors in Verona. The courier service guaranteed delivery and the subcontractors needed my signature on their work orders."

"You need to learn how to budget your time better. Niccoli would never have used a courier service." My father turned on his heel and slammed my office door closed behind him.

The phone rang. I hated that phone.

"Lucas Benelli."

A client, unhappy with our crew's work on a site in Tolmezzo. Great. I tried to appease him, but sometimes humans couldn't be satisfied.

"I'll be there in the morning, Mr. Franconetti."

The human babbled angrily.

"No, sir, Nicolli isn't available. He no longer works here."

Franconetti slammed the phone in my ear and I returned the favor. Problem was, my phone burst into a hundred pieces and he had already hung up.

The fax machine beeped, demanding more paper. I rushed to its aid since my father was expecting three contracts. The paper didn't make it into the drawer in time and the sending fax disconnected abruptly.

The heavy oak desk cracked as I slammed my fists into the top. Why had I come back here?

Clara stuck her head in my door. "Lucas, you have a visitor."

I shot her a questioning look and she mouthed "Tessa" I shook my head and put my hands together in a mock prayer. She nodded and pulled the door closed.

My personal phone vibrated.

"Hey, Trist."

"Hey, Luc, got some news on your girl. Want to meet for dinner tonight? Alex and I can meet you in Vicenza."

I checked my calendar and rubbed my eyes. I was supposed to have a dinner meeting with a client at six.

"Could we make it late?"

"Sure, whatever works. Alex and I can stop by your house after we eat. We'll bring dessert."

"Yeah, that would probably be best. My meeting might run a little long. You know the code to get in if I'm not there. You guys can stay the night if you want. There's a hockey game on at midnight."

My meeting dragged on forever before Ms. Menetti would agree to the terms of our contract. She smiled and flirted over cocktails. She talked about her art collection and how much she would love to show me her favorite pieces. I couldn't get out of the restaurant fast enough when she finally signed the papers.

Tristyn's car was in the drive when I got home. Alexandria laughed as Tristyn and I exchanged shoulder punches. Tristyn was more my brother than Nicolli ever had been.

"Master Sergeant Breanna Welker is in Bravo Company," Alex chirped as we settled onto my overstuffed couch. "I didn't find anything about her background except she joined the military at seventeen. Bravo is American-based. She's the only witch and I think the only woman."

And the most beautiful woman I've ever laid eyes on.

The cute brunette who had been Tristyn's mate for a little over two years rifled through a stack of papers. "I didn't find much on earth witches. From what I can tell, they are very rare. Do you know anything about her parents?"

"She didn't talk much about her past except how it related to her work with Bravo." Breanna had looked uncomfortable when I asked about her family.

Alex screwed up her face like she always did when she was thinking. "Did she feel more grounded than I am?"

"Yeah, you could say that."

"Did you see any of her magic?"

"No."

"Why was she there, anyway?"

"She was on reconnaissance duty and had been assigned that stretch of road. I haven't had a chance to talk with her much about that night. I still don't know why I crashed my bike and don't remember much except waking up and seeing her."

Tristyn poured three glasses of wine. "Didn't you say she talked to your wolf?"

"If she hadn't, I wouldn't be here. My wolf wanted to change after the accident, but with the injuries, I would have bled to death before the change was complete. She talked my wolf down. I couldn't stop the change but she did. My father can't control my wolf the way she did."

An Alpha werewolf was able to control every wolf in his pack. Usually the amount of dominance an Alpha displayed was enough to deal with even the most unruly wolves, but the touch of magic associated with being an Alpha was always enough. Well, always except in my case. My wolf felt no compulsion to obey the Alpha.

"Earth witches can usually shapeshift. Did you see any of her forms?"

All I really remembered was the way Breanna had looked at me. "No. I didn't see anything but the face of an angel."

Tristyn strolled in with a plate full of chicken wings. "Your dad's gonna flip."

"You really like her?" Alex asked, nibbling on a wing.

Just thinking about Breanna made me smile. "I do. I talked to her about going to visit when her unit gets back from South America."

An odd look passed between Tristyn and Alex. They were as close as two people could get and sometimes I swear they could read each other's minds. Wonder if Breanna and I could ever be that way?

Alexandria fell asleep before the end of the second period of the midnight hockey game. Tristyn carried her gently into the guest bedroom and settled her in for the night.

"So, what's the plan?" he asked as he kicked out the recliner.

"She said she'd call when her unit was going back to America. I'm going to take some time and go see her."

"Do you know the Alpha in that territory?"

I didn't but I would soon. I'd have to contact him before entering his territory. Ideally, my Alpha would contact him for me, but in this case that wouldn't happen.

"I'll check into it," I said, grabbing a wing.

"Let me know when we leave."

"We?"

Tristyn nodded as he plucked a chicken wing from the plate. As a living vampire, he ate regular food like the rest of us. "You'll need someone to watch your back."

"I wasn't expecting you to go."

My friend tilted his head. "You've already had problems with these wolves and now you are about to go into their territory. You need backup and if the situation was reversed, you'd be there for me."

"It won't be safe for Alex. If things get bad for me with the Wisconsin Pack, she could be in danger. I've heard the American Alphas are more tolerant of witches, but Alexandria will be a stranger in the territory."

"Alex is going to visit her grandmother," Tristyn answered. "She and I have already talked and she expects us to have the trip planned by the time she wakes up."

I didn't know what to say. Trist and I had been through so much and I trusted him with my life, but he had a mate now and didn't need to be risking his life for me.

Tristyn finished his glass of wine and reached for the remote. "No need to argue with me on this, little brother. I'm going with you."

"I appreciate the offer but you shouldn't."

Tristyn cocked a blond eyebrow. "Like I said, Luc, no need to discuss this any further. I'm going with you." Tristyn crossed his arms and leaned back on the couch. The look on his face was one I knew well. He was coming with me.

"As soon as I know anything, I'll call you," I mumbled around a mouthful of chicken.

"Sounds good," Tristyn replied as he snatched the last wing off the plate. "How are things with your mom?"

"She's been acting a little strange, but there's so much tension between Josef and me, she's probably just afraid we'll kill one another."

Tristyn stopped eating. "Is it that bad?"

I nodded, not at all proud that my father and I did not get along.

"He won't let you leave?" Tristyn asked. "Release you from your pack ties?"

"Won't even talk to me about it."

Tristyn leaned forward. "I'm sorry, Luc. Is there anything I can do?"

"Find me a way out of the Italian Pack that doesn't involve me killing my father."

Chapter 11

Breanna

We set the trap, but it took five days before the rogue wolf finally caught the scent of the girls and followed his nose into a four-sided cage. Poor guy never saw it coming. I went out to visit the wolf before Trenton gave the order to put him down. It was sad, a young wolf like this destroyed without having done anything wrong. It was all about protecting the species and a werewolf who was fully wolf was a danger. If the wolf died and a group of scientists found his body, the supernatural world would stand on its head.

"Hey, big fella," I called. The wolf was lying in the far corner of his cage, his silver eyes filled with rage and perhaps a tiny bit of fear. There had to be fear in there. Wolves didn't go Rambo unless something bad happened.

The big black wolf rumbled as I eased onto the ground outside the cage. I tossed a piece of jerky in his direction but he looked at it like it was dirt.

"You don't know what you're missing. I love this stuff."

He lifted his lip and showed off his pearly whites.

"Fine, your loss." I munched on a strip of chewy meat.

The wolf whined and laid his head on his paws.

"You don't have to die, you know." The wolf sighed but didn't open his eyes. "If you'll let your human side come back, they won't execute you."

The wolf stood, circled three times before settling, his back to me, onto the hard wooden cage floor. He wanted the conversation to be over. Too bad.

"So, what's a big tough wolf like you afraid of? You could take humans with no problem, I'd wager you could hold you own against most werewolves and a vampire would be mighty stupid to mess with you." He raised his head and looked over his shoulder at me. Progress? Maybe, if he understood English.

"We don't want to hurt you but can't let you run around in the jungle like this. Don't you have a pack somewhere?"

The black wolf tipped his head as if mulling over my words. The werewolves said their wolf forms did understand language though the comprehension wasn't nearly that of the human form. I kept the conversation simple.

"Look. Let your human side come back and I swear no one will hurt you. If you stay in this form, you're a dead wolf walking."

Rising to his feet, the wolf stared at me. I met his eyes. He looked at the floor.

The wolf edged closer to the cage bars as I held a piece of jerky for him. He sniffed the meat and my hand. His jaws had enough strength to rip tendons and break bones, but I needed to show a little faith. Maybe if he saw I trusted him, he'd do the same by me.

His teeth grazed my finger and I resisted the urge to snatch my hand out of the cage. His cold nose brushed along my thumb as his tongue slowly licked the four-inch piece of jerky. He took the jerky between his teeth and swallowed it.

"Will you keep your teeth to yourself if I come in?"

I stood and summoned my magic. As an owl, I hopped through the cage bars. The wolf didn't come closer or try to snap me like a Scooby Snack. I shifted to human and sat cross-legged on the cage floor.

The big black wolf tensed but did not attack. I started talking about whatever came to mind. Of course the topic always on my mind was Lucas. I chattered to the wolf until the sun sank below the horizon. As darkness enveloped the cage, he laid his head on my leg and whined.

Carefully, as not to startle him, I touched the soft fur behind his ears. His body jerked and for a moment I thought he would attack. Instead he let out a low rumble that sounded remarkably like a sigh of contentment.

"I give my word we will help if you will allow your human form to come back."

The wolf looked up at me, his eyes so full of sadness and pain it made my heart hurt. He wasn't a rogue. He was scared.

His change started slowly, his body twisting and contorting from wolf form to human. He cried out many times but I didn't touch him. Changes for werewolves were painful under normal conditions, but this wolf hadn't changed in a very long time and that meant his change would be even worse.

Over an hour later, a naked young man, curled in the fetal position, lay shivering beside me. I pulled off my jacket and draped it over his shoulders. His body was crisscrossed with deep scars, most jagged but others were straight and long, the telltale sign of a whip. His tanned skin stretched tautly over a much-too-thin body.

As the moon ascended, the teenager sat up and covered his privates with my jacket. His coal black hair was long and unkempt and he smelled much more strongly of musk than a normal werewolf. His hands trembled as he pulled at the buttons of the jacket.

"I'm Breanna."

He looked at me shyly and quickly averted his eyes. "I'm Levi."

He sounded American. "Where you from?"

"Arizona."

What the hell was an Arizona werewolf doing in Paraguay?

"Where am I?"

"South America."

The shock on his face was real. He had no idea where he was and, I bet, not much of a clue what had happened. He looked to be about sixteen and hadn't been a werewolf very long. In the younger ones, the wolf was always much stronger. The newly turned wolves needed mentors to help them learn to control their instincts. Without guidance the youngsters were a menace.

"Thank you for helping me," he whispered. I gingerly put my arm around his shoulders. He melted into me like a small child.

The soft crunching of grass was the only clue I had of Simon's approach. Levi raised his head as the vampire came into view. Silver flakes appeared in the youngster's eyes.

"He won't hurt you," I said loudly enough Simon would hear.

The silver-flaked gaze turned toward me. His wolf wanted to retake control but his human was fighting.

"I swear he will not hurt you."

Levi ground his teeth and even my nose could smell his fear.

Simon stopped short and gave me a dirty look. I probably should have told him I was planning to crawl into the cage but I really hadn't planned to do anything but come out and say goodbye. Oops.

"Master Sergeant Welker?"

Levi's teeth chattered. I pulled him closer. "I'm not leaving him, Sime."

Simon crossed his arms and stared at the frightened teenager. "This is not our decision, Breanna."

"I will not leave him."

Simon let out an exasperated sigh. "Major Trenton is on his way here."

Levi buried his head in my shoulder.

"Then I most definitely am not leaving him."

Footsteps scuffled through the woods behind us. It was a relief to see the faces of my unit. They crowded the front of the cage, trying to get a closer look at the werewolf youngster.

"He speak English?" Aaron asked.

"He's from Arizona," I answered. Startled looks passed between the wolves. The vampires watched curiously as Levi clung to me like a terrified child.

The Bravo Combat Unit arrived from the opposite direction. The all-werewolf unit was always louder than my recon guys. They couldn't sneak up on a dead human.

Major Trenton pulled up short when he saw me inside the cage. He turned to Simon. "DuChard! Get your witch away from my target."

Simon gave me a pained look before releasing some of his power. "Major Trenton, I will contact headquarters regarding the change in status of the target."

The werewolf commanding officer was not impressed. He strode nonchalantly to the front of the cage. Levi kept his head buried and trembled. This poor kid was so scared he couldn't move.

"Or let the witch stay. Perhaps one of our bullets will miss its target."

The air around the cage exploded as my unit charged. The werewolves exchanged punches but it was the vampires who pulled open the bars and formed a circle around Levi and me.

Master vampire power slammed into everyone as Simon regained control of his unit. "Stand down, Bravo," he ordered, his voice resonating with authority. The fighting immediately stopped, though the snarling continued unabated.

I couldn't see anything past the legs and butts of the vampires. They had formed a tight circle to keep Levi and me hidden from view. Simon and Trenton shouted at one another. Trenton wanted to kill Levi and Simon was doing his best to save the kid and me. Christopher looked over his shoulder and winked.

"Trenton will have to come through us, Bre."

"Thanks, Chris."

He nodded and said something to the other vampires in French. The air around us vibrated, some sort of vampire magic helping to keep us invisible.

Simon managed to place a call to headquarters and convinced his superiors to spare Levi's life. Trenton was livid, storming back to the barracks, cursing the whole way. Power crackled around Simon as he gave the order for his unit to return to the base. I didn't move.

"We will take the wolf to the base with us tomorrow," Simon said, his voice rough from anger. "We will speak of this later."

He turned on his heel and disappeared into the darkness. The vampires passed through the bars and followed Simon. The werewolves were reluctant to follow Simon's order, but knew they should.

"Thanks, guys," I called as they meandered near the cage.

"He gonna be all right, Bre?" Ordy asked, nodding toward Levi, who had yet to lift his head from my shoulder.

"Yeah, he'll be fine once somebody helps him understand all that wolf shit you guys do."

The wolves laughed away some of the tension of the evening.

Christopher reappeared with a pair of sweats. "I think these will fit the young one," he said as he placed the pants and shirt onto the floor inside the bars. "I'll bring your sleeping bag and pillow as soon as I find Celeste."

"Thanks, Chris."

Aaron leaned against the bars. "Hey, kid, you want something to eat?"

Levi didn't move. He might not have been hungry but I was starving.

"Would you get us something, Aaron? Levi has to be hungry."

Aaron's blond eyebrows shot up. "You know his name?"

"His first name is Levi, not sure about the rest. After he gets some sleep, he'll probably feel more like talking."

Aaron agreed and left to find something for us to eat. Christopher kept his word and deposited my pack into the cage a few minutes later. I opened the sleeping bag and spread it out.

"You're staying with me tonight?" Levi asked when everyone had gone.

"Would you rather I leave?"

His green eyes got very wide. "No, I didn't mean it like that. I guess I just thought you'd want to go somewhere it was comfortable."

Anything was better than bedbugs and obnoxious werewolves. "Compared to the barracks, this isn't so bad and, besides, one werewolf isn't nearly as hot as a whole bunch of them."

Levi had no idea what I meant.

"Werewolves have higher body temperatures than other beings," I explained.

He looked more confused. "Oh, I didn't know that."

The poor kid had no clue what it meant to be a werewolf. He needed to spend some time with a wolf who could tell him about being a wolf. Aaron was a good guy when he wasn't tending my business, but he wouldn't have the patience to explain things to a newly turned wolf. Ordy wasn't exactly mentor material. Maybe tomorrow I could talk to Johnny Reed. Johnny was friendly and smart, a good guy.

Levi and I settled under the blanket and he curled into a ball. In the morning my muscles would regret sleeping on the wooden floor, but it was the right thing to do. Trenton's group wouldn't violate orders and hurt Levi, but they would harass him. The kid was already scared and confused. He didn't need a bunch of werewolves bullying him. His wolf might take over again if he was scared enough.

By zero one hundred Levi was softly snoring in my ear. In the distance a twig snapped and my eyelids popped open. Levi mumbled and rolled over, but didn't wake.

My nose began to burn and my eyes watered as I walked to the front of the cage. Black magic was nearby. I radioed Simon and waited for his response.

Hooray for me, following orders.

Another twig snapped and I cast a sensing spell. If there were black witches in the area, it would feel it like a fish on the line. It might be a tiny tug or a big yank, but if they were there, I'd know.

Something tugged on my sensing spell. Catching only residual spell-casting magic, I couldn't tell what specific kind of witches, only that their magic was dark. They hadn't sent anything our way or my body would be absorbing it. If the witches launched an attack, it would be hard for me to counterattack if I was imitating SpongeBob.

"Breanna?" Simon's ice blue eyes sparkled as he remained in the shadows.

"Black magic," I mouthed.

He nodded and motioned for me to take to the air.

I'd only been airborne a few minutes when movement in the eastern quadrant of the base caught my eye. A group of six women were doing a pitiful job of sneaking along the base walls. They were much too close together, their pathetic green camo jackets standing out vividly against the wooden fence. *Some people shouldn't try to be sneaky.*

These were definitely not Malandanti. Their magic, even combined, wasn't nearly as strong as what I'd felt in Italy. Nonetheless, they could have been dangerous to my unit, so I flew down to intercept.

Soundlessly landing behind the group, I shifted to human. The women turned, one letting out a shriek of alarm. They were in their early thirties, not exactly the outdoorsy types, and absolutely terrified of me. Good.

"*Habla ingles*?" I asked. One of the women stepped forward as the leader of the rag tag group.

"Yes," the dark-haired woman answered. "We are here for our wolf."

"What wolf?" I asked, taking a step toward her. She shuffled backward.

"The big black one. He belongs to us."

I looked down the line at the other fidgety witches. "That wolf does not belong to you. Wolves belong to no one but their packs."

The leader hissed. I called up a big breeze and blew her stupid-looking hat off her head.

"Please do not harm us," several of the witches begged. Holy hell, they were pathetic.

I calmed the wind and waited for them to stand from their huddle. "Why did you have that wolf?"

"He was payment for a debt of another werewolf. We wanted our own wolf from which we could collect blood and conduct rituals. We were using him to summon a lesser demon when he escaped."

Demon rituals involved blood and suffering. That explained the whipping marks on Levi's back. Stupid as this coven appeared, they probably had underestimated the strength of Levi's wolf. Most likely they had used some sort of binding spell to keep him from changing, but his wolf was strong enough to overcome the spell and escape. Idiots.

The leader looked me up and down. "Surely you understand the convenience of having a sacrifice so readily available."

No, she did not just say that to me.

I pointed to myself. "Earth witch here, chick. I don't do sacrifices."

"Earth witch? Those aren't real."

"Well, pardon me for being a figment of your imagination. Now, what wolf turned him and then gave him to a group of dark witches?"

The leader bowed her head, refusing to answer. I tossed a fireball at her friends and it was amazing how quickly she began babbling about a wolf with an Italian accent who wanted to know about Malandanti magic. I radioed Simon. He asked a few questions and she answered quickly, only hesitating once and another fireball took care of that.

Simon contacted the Alpha of the Wisconsin pack and he agreed to take in the youngster. If Levi couldn't learn to control his wolf, Galen would put him down during a one-way trip into the woods.

I texted Lucas and let him know we would be back in Wisconsin on Thursday. He replied he was going to visit over the weekend. I hadn't fully decided about speaking to Galen before Lucas arrived. If I talked to Galen and Lucas didn't show up, I'd look like a total idiot. Galen seemed like a reasonable kinda guy even if he was over a hundred years old. He didn't look it, of course--like all the other werewolves, he was the picture of vitality and youth, with his body locked in its prime. The wolves weren't immortal but they were hard to kill, lived hundreds of years, and I'd never met an ugly one.

I'd also never met one who took my breath away until I found Lucas. He was mouthwatering, but there was much more to him, so much more I wanted to know. He had a vulnerability in his eyes that made me want to wrap my arms around him and protect him from the world. There was strength about him also, so powerful I wanted to climb into his arms and let him hide me.

His lack of involvement with the pack wolves made no more sense than why he was interested in me. Aaron's comments about Lucas had gotten under my skin. Pack wolves always supported one another. Did Lucas's pack really not like him or was Aaron making that up just to piss me off? I'd never known Aaron to lie, but what was there to not like about Lucas?

We finally made it back to America, our lumbering C-47 circling the base like a buzzard over a carcass. A lump of lead settled in my stomach. Levi was doing his best to be brave, but the kid was terrified. Johnny had been a good choice as a mentor. He was soft-spoken and thorough as he explained how Levi should act when first meeting the Alpha. Levi's wolf was strong, but hopefully he would succumb to the power of the Alpha. Levi had made no effort to challenge any of the wolves of Bravo and that was a good sign. If he went after the Alpha, he wouldn't make it to dinner tonight.

As the plane rolled to a stop, I stepped through the rigid vampires and grabbed my bag. It was time for the kid to meet his future. I waited by the door as Levi followed Johnny like a puppy.

"Galen is a good man," I said as Levi looked around nervously. "Do what Johnny told you and you'll be fine."

Levi swallowed hard and took a deep breath. Tiny flickers of silver tinged his eyes but that was to be expected. He had never met a true Alpha.

"Sergeant Welker?" he called softly.

I smiled at him. "Yeah?"

"Thank you."

I took his hand and squeezed it. "I'll see you soon."

Levi walked alongside Johnny. I stayed on the ramp and watched as the two disappeared into the night. Johnny was taking Levi to Galen's house for the formal introduction. Hopefully Mother Earth would answer my prayer to help the kid do the right thing. Galen would be fair, but ultimately he would do whatever was necessary to ensure the safety of his pack. If that meant Levi must die, so be it.

Aaron tromped down the ramp. "That kid owes you his life, Bre."

Maybe, if he lived through this. "You think he'll be all right?" I asked, momentarily forgetting I was not a member of Aaron's fan club.

Aaron slung his bag over his shoulder. "He didn't go after any of us and he damn sure didn't want to do anything to disappoint you, so he'll probably be fine. Galen knows how to handle newly turned wolves."

It was hard to watch Levi walk away knowing he was either going toward his new life or certain death.

We disembarked and headed to the debriefing room. Simon kept the meetings short, particularly when we'd been gone for weeks.

Thirty minutes later Simon dismissed us to head our separate ways. My house, about ten minutes off base, was close enough for me to walk or fly to work. Tonight the stars were twinkling and the moon was shining bright--a stroll sounded good. I waved goodbye to the guys, promised to call Celeste later, and headed down the sidewalk toward the quiet neighborhood I called home.

Lucas hadn't said he'd call again, but I thought, or at least hoped, he would. The phone didn't beep and after three minutes, no new messages showed up. A little more lead plopped into my stomach. Maybe none of this with him was real after all. He could have been stringing me along, toying with me for whatever reason. It didn't make any sense why he liked me anyway. I was a witch and not exactly the belle of the ball. I spent more time polishing my boots than brushing my hair.

"He's not coming," I muttered, rounding the block onto my street. I could have kicked myself for being disappointed.

"Stop feeling sorry for yourself," I fumed, passing the last two houses before my little cottage. I had a solid career, worked with good folks, and made a difference in this world. The humans didn't have a clue how close the monsters of their nightmares actually were and Bravo made sure they never found out. Yep, life was good. Who needed smoldering brown eyes for company at night? I had the NHL Network and a gallon of cookie dough ice cream waiting for me.

My house looked the same as it had twenty-two days earlier. I'd bought the two-bedroom one-bath bungalow fixer-upper for a song. Simon had scowled and told me it was in need of razing, not fixing up, but I bought it anyway. It had taken all my savings to buy the house and its two-acre lot, but I loved it and it was mine. I knew its faults as well as my own, right down to the squeaky boards on the porch and the closet doors that scuffed.

There was something out of place on my front porch. As I got closer, the odd thing on my porch took the shape of a vase of flowers. Okay, not just a vase of flowers but a vase full of every flower the local florist must have had in stock. The display of wild flowers was breathtaking in the moonlight and wider than my front door.

The card danced in the evening breeze, announcing the florist just off base had delivered the flowers. I plucked the card and read the message.

Welcome Home. Can't wait to see you again. Lucas.

Someone at the florist had written the words, but they had come from him. The flowers fluttered like they were waving at me and I stood dumbstruck for several minutes. These flowers were for me. These flowers were from him. He had sent me flowers.

Nobody sent me flowers. I wasn't a flower kinda girl. I was dressed in camo with my hair in a scrunchie and dirt under my nails. I hadn't showered in two days and smelled as musky as the damn werewolves.

It was ten in the morning in Italy and Lucas would be at work. I called him anyway.

"Good morning, *il mio angelo*," he answered. Geez, his accent was sexy as hell. I wanted to reach through the phone and rip his shirt off.

"Good morning, Wolf. I just got home and there was a big vase of flowers on my porch."

"Oh?"

"Thank you," I said, praying my voice didn't tremble.

"Did you like them?"

"They're beautiful."

"As are you."

My face got hot and I was glad he couldn't see how much he affected me.

"Did you find what you were looking for?" he asked.

Thank you for the change of subject. "We got him. We brought him back with us. He's a kid, newly turned wolf, and Galen's gonna help him."

Jacky Russell

"You make a career out of saving damaged werewolves, Sergeant Welker?"

"Just doing my job, sir."

He planned to fly to Wisconsin in a few days and promised to call as soon as he could. I never asked if he wanted me to talk to Galen. The werewolves could be funny about chain of command and territorial permission crap.

I carried the flowers inside.

Kitchen counter or bar?

They ended up on the nightstand beside my bed where I could stare at them while I fell asleep. A part of me was so excited that somebody like Lucas was even interested. Another part of me was scared to death because, realistically, how could this work out between us? Would he expect me to give up my career to be with him? I loved my job and, for the most part, the guys I worked with. Would Lucas understand that?

"Getting ahead of yourself, aren't you?" I mumbled around my last spoonful of ice cream. I hadn't had a single date with the guy and already had us breaking up because of my career.

Talk about negativity. Way to go, ray o' sunshine.

The phone danced to life on the nightstand. I was comfortable and warm, all tucked in with my Pluto pillow and Dumbo blanket, a stomach full of cookie dough ice cream, and very tempted to let the call go to voicemail. I was tired of talking.

Except this call was from Lucas and I almost fell out of the bed to grab the phone.

"Hey, Lucas! What's up?"

Chapter 12

Lucas

"What did your dad say?" Tristyn asked as the plane rolled down the runway.

"Not much. I told him I'd be back Tuesday and I was going with you."

Tristyn unfolded his newspaper. "Ah, he thinks we're on one of our special trips, huh?"

Tristyn knew my father didn't approve of our friendship and the pack had long whispered the two of us were more than friends. Tristyn and I had met when my father sent me away to boarding school in France. Tristyn's father had sent him to the same school, though for a totally different reason. We both graduated from L'Ermitage in France and then Dartmouth College in America.

"He didn't ask, just grumbled about me taking time off from work and how Nicolli would have never done something so irresponsible."

Tristyn shook his head and pulled out the sports section. "I don't know how you deal with him. You can't do anything right."

I shrugged off his comment. "He's a hardass."

"Have you guys ever talked about what happened?"

"No."

"Is Stephano still around?"

The mention of my cousin's name put my wolf on edge. "He's in Naples. Josef sent him there to oversee the southern offices of Benelli Enterprises."

"Is that the only reason he sent him away? Maybe after all these years your dad has come around to your side of the story."

"Doubt it."

I leaned back, hoping to take at least a short nap during the double-digit-hour plane flight. Between the layovers and weather delays, it would be almost twenty-four hours before we stepped into Green Bay, Wisconsin.

Tristyn drifted off to sleep, but my mind would not settle. What did I have to offer Breanna? Her kind wasn't welcome in my father's territory and I couldn't leave.

"This will never work," I mumbled out loud.

"Yes it will," Tristyn answered sleepily.

"I thought you were asleep."

"I was," he groused, "until you started with the Poor Pitiful Lucas routine."

"Pardon?"

Tristyn elbowed my arm off the shared armrest. "Everything will be fine. We'll find her, she'll be crazy about you, and the two of you will live happily ever after. Quit worrying," Tristyn huffed as tried to sleep again.

"You think I'm worried?"

"Uh huh."

"You're wrong. I'm not concerned."

"Yes, you are," he replied without opening his eyes.

I tried to stare a hole through his head. He finally looked at me.

"You've been chewing on your lip nonstop and if you'd stop bouncing your knee I might get some rest."

I looked at my knee. "Sorry."

"Do you remember how nervous I was around Alex when I first met her?"

He had been a nervous wreck and Tristyn had dates all the time.

"You're worse."

That was a sobering thought. Nerves weren't good. The Wisconsin Pack wolves would smell my insecurity. I had no idea how they would react to me coming into their territory. I had opted not to contact the Alpha beforehand, not willing to chance him saying no to my request.

Tristyn bumped my elbow again. "I've never seen you so worked up over a girl before. This one must really be special."

"I've never met anybody like her. It was the way she looked at me, like the two of us were the only people on earth."

"Hey, maybe you guys can start your own pack." Tristyn laughed. "And you can get the hell away from your dad."

That really didn't sound too bad. "Our own pack of two."

I closed my eyes. God, I hoped she liked me as much as I liked her. We hadn't really spent a lot of time together, but when she was near, my world was quiet. Her presence brought a calm I'd never felt. It was like our souls had known each other long before we met.

"It's fate, Luc. Fate brought you to her. Stop second guessing and enjoy it," Tristyn said, leaning against the headrest. "We'll deal with the hard stuff later. Right now, think about what you want to say the first time you see her."

When the plane finally landed, I found a quiet place and called the Alpha of the Wisconsin pack. This was the first step to seeing Breanna. Pack protocol dictated the Alpha must give his permission for me to be in his territory.

We drove three hours to the Wisconsin Pack's public meeting place, the local Shoney's. Tristyn and I had secured a table in the corner before the Alpha and his wolves arrived. It was tradition for the Alpha to bring his second-in-command to any meeting. The Wisconsin Alpha had his second and six more wolves.

Galen McGregor was exactly as I had pictured, only taller. At six-foot-five and over two hundred fifty pounds of solid muscle, the man was an imposing figure. Salt and pepper hair, weathered skin, and sharp green eyes that saw everything without looking, this werewolf was over a hundred years old but could easily pass for mid-thirties.

"Bet there's more in the parking lot," Tristyn said quietly as the group moved toward us.

Tristyn and I kept our eyes down as the wolves fanned out and filled the booths around us.

"You boys eat yet?" Galen called from the breakfast bar.

"No, sir," I answered without looking.

"Well, get some food. No sense talking on empty stomachs."

Tristyn shot me a questioning look before heading toward the stacks of plates. I stayed close behind him, not trusting the wolves at his back.

With plates full of food, we returned to our booth. The Alpha motioned for us to join him.

"Tristyn, it is an honor to meet you." The Alpha extended his hand. "How is that beautiful mate of yours?"

"She's well, Alpha McGregor, thank you for asking," Tristyn answered politely as the two shook hands. Everybody knew Tristyn. That was what happened when you were the subject of a prophecy.

"Call me Galen."

Tristyn nodded in acknowledgement.

"So, Lucas, what brings you to Wisconsin?" the Alpha asked as he gulped a glass of milk.

"Personal business, sir."

"Hmm."

I tried to swallow my steak but it stuck in my throat. "My business does not involve any of your wolves, sir."

Green eyes twinkled across the table. "You sure about that?"

I looked up at him and quickly lowered my eyes. I didn't want to do anything he might misread as a challenge. I only wanted permission to be in his territory.

No one spoke for several minutes. The chatter of hungry humans was deafening.

"So why are you looking for Breanna?"

I dropped my fork. If the Alpha knew her by name, that meant she was of interest to his wolves.

"Lucas?" He waited for an answer.

"I only wish to speak to her, sir." That came out much weaker than I intended.

He cocked his head and smiled. "How badly do you wish to speak with her?"

I glanced at Tristyn, who looked as perplexed as I felt. "I'm not sure what you mean, Alpha McGregor."

The Alpha had not offered me the use of his first name.

"Would you accept a challenge from my wolves?"

"Yes."

The Alpha cocked an eyebrow. "More than one?"

"Yes."

"Multiple challenges have been formally filed regarding your presence in my territory. If you defeat these challengers, I will grant your request to be in Wisconsin Pack territory for up to a week. If you do not win the challenges, your request will be denied. You will leave immediately. Failure to do so will be considered a direct threat to pack security."

That meant if I lost but stayed anyway, the wolves would kill me.

"I understand." I was no stranger to challenges but never multiples.

The Alpha bantered politics with Tristyn for several minutes before turning his attention to me.

"Change your mind?"

"No, sir."

The big man laughed and took another gulp of milk. "Your father isn't pleased about you being here."

"You talked to my father?" Maybe Josef had called on my behalf.

The Alpha didn't answer until I looked away. "Yes. I called him. He was surprised you were in America."

There were probably multiple enraged voicemails on my phone.

"Why are your wolves challenging Lucas? Non-pack wolves come here all the time." Tristyn asked.

The big Alpha leaned back in the booth. "Well, it's complicated. They think Lucas might hurt Breanna and as much grief as they like to give her, every wolf in this pack is protective of that witch."

"I won't hurt her."

Alpha McGregor twirled his glass. "She'd probably kick every one of their asses if she knew they challenged you for the right to talk to her." He shook his head. "She's a spirited one, that's for sure. Eat your fill, Lucas. We'll handle the challenges in a few hours at my house. I have a training room in the basement. My wolves will not bother either of you while you are under my roof. We'll finish our meal and the two of you will ride with me. One of my wolves will drive your rental."

"Yes, sir." For the first time in my life, I didn't finish all the food on my plate.

Chapter 13

Breanna

Saturday morning dawned clear and bright. I had visited the hardware store and was ready to work on my house. My plan to fix the porch boards, sand the cabinet doors, and lay the tile in the guest bathroom would take most of the day.

Lucas hadn't called. Sitting around twiddling my thumbs waiting for what might happen was stupid. Hell, he might not show up. Why waste time? Wisconsin winters were unpredictable and today was a surprisingly mild forty-five degrees.

My iPod and I were in our own world when the smell of musk interrupted my porch repair. My heart did a skip, then resumed normal operation. Johnny Reed's long, lean form stood on my steps.

"What's up, Breanna?"

I held up the hammer and nails.

He looked surprised. "On your day off?"

"Why are you here?"

I liked Johnny, but this was weird. He sank onto the step as though I had invited him to stay. I hadn't. "Whatcha doing tonight?"

He leaned back on his elbows to watch me hammer nails. He looked very handsome in his khaki pants and baby blue pinstriped shirt. With sandy blond hair and eyes so blue you'd swear you were looking at the ocean, Johnny was easy on the eyes.

"Grouting."

"What?"

Guess he wasn't a home improvement kind of guy. "Working on the floor in my bathroom. Why?"

"I was wondering if you want to see a movie or something."

I missed the nail and slammed my thumb. Damn.

Johnny grabbed my hand and rubbed it gently. "Geez, Breanna. Why don't you hire someone to do this before you hurt yourself?"

"Because I enjoy doing it myself," I snapped, snatching my injured hand from his.

"So, about tonight?"

"Johnny, you know I don't date within the unit."

His forehead wrinkled. "Why not?"

"It's not a good idea, you know the whole code of ethics thing."

"Dang, Breanna, it's just dinner and a movie. I thought you'd appreciate going out since you don't ever date."

The next nail went in with one hit. "I'm busy."

"Doing what?"

"Grout."

"What the hell is grout?"

I wanted to bang my head against the wall. Better yet, bang Johnny's head against the wall. "Why don't you call Shelly? She wants to go out with you."

"She does?" Johnny looked genuinely surprised the newest lady werewolf in their pack would be interested in him. Most women were interested. Johnny was a decent guy and, like most werewolves, he was a stud muffin.

"Go ask her." I turned on my music and went back to nailing. Johnny watched me for a couple minutes and his mouth moved, but my music was too loud to hear him. Darn.

By mid-afternoon, all the boards were secure except for a single aggravating one on the corner. I ate a sandwich and started sanding. The cruddy yellow paint didn't want to let go, but the sandpaper's bite slowly won out and the natural glow of oak began to show.

Two sandwiches later I was tackling the bathroom. I had already pulled up the disco era linoleum a few weeks earlier and prepared the surface. Stacks of warm brown tiles were nestled in the corner. When I bought the tiles, they reminded me of melted chocolate. Now all I saw was the same color as Lucas's eyes.

"Hey, Bre? You home?" Bates Sorenson yelled from the front porch. Why had I bothered to install a doorbell and a knocker? Damn werewolves had no manners.

"No, I've left for the day," I yelled as he opened the door and let himself in.

Dressed in black dress pants and a turquoise shirt that molded to every muscle in his chest, Bates was quite the head-turner. The man loved women, particularly the scantily dressed human ones who drooled when he walked by.

"*What* are you doing?" Bates asked, staring wide-eyed at my trowel.

"Grouting."

"What the hell is a grout?"

Damn, did none of these guys know anything about home improvement? "It's tile for the floor. Why are you here? You look like you're going clubbing."

"I'm going to the Meridian later. Do you want to go?"

I dropped my carpenter's square. "What?"

He picked up the square as though it was a deadly weapon. "I thought you might like to go dancing, play pool, you know, do something fun."

This was weird. First Johnny and now Bates? Was I that pathetic? "Uh, I'll pass, but thanks anyway. I really want to get this floor finished."

He knelt beside me and picked up one of the tiles. "I could stay and help you."

I plucked the tile from his fingers. "Go find a hoochie in black lace and heels. I'll be fine."

He gave my saw a distrustful look. "You sure you should be doing this by yourself?"

I tossed a blob of adhesive onto the surface and began to smooth it. "I'm pretty sure I can handle it. Go drive the women crazy."

He backed away as the adhesive began splattering. "Well, if you change your mind, come on to the club. I'll find somebody to dance with you."

"Gee, thanks." I really must have been pathetic.

Chapter 14

Lucas

Galen kept his word and his wolves stayed away from Trist and me, though their dislike was evident. Tristyn and the Alpha bantered for several hours about Divine Council policies, the state of the economy, and other assorted things. I focused on not hyperventilating at the scent of so much musk.

I stumbled upon a quiet, though well-used, walking path around the property. The muted winter sounds of nature helped calm my nerves. The cool wind cleared my head. My wolf wanted out, but a change was energy I could not afford to use. Everything I had needed to be conserved for the challenges. Many a wolf had met death while fighting in a circle like the one I was about to face.

I debated calling Breanna, just to let her know I was nearby, but decided against it. There was no guarantee things would go well for me tonight. Galen had given his word to protect Tristyn, no matter the outcome of the challenges, and there was no need to drag Breanna into werewolf affairs.

As I made my way back to the house, Galen was sitting on the deck.

"You sure about this, Lucas? I can call it off, no problem."

My wolf normally rumbled at the close proximity of an Alpha. Today he was unnervingly quiet.

"I'm sure I will fight the challenges, Alpha, though I do appreciate your concern."

Galen nodded, watching me over tented hands. "Have you spoken with Breanna?"

"Not yet." When the Alpha cocked an eyebrow, I continued, "I didn't want to create any more issues between her and the others."

Galen squinted like he was watching some sort of circus freak. I couldn't help but squirm under his gaze.

"Does your father know about Breanna?"

"No, sir."

"So if his son doesn't come home, Josef Benelli won't know it was because of a witch?"

I choked on a growl. "If I do not return to Italy, it will not be because of her. It will be because I was not strong enough to win."

Galen nodded, but his expression changed. "Hopefully it will not come to that. You are strong, your wolf is powerful, and you fight for something other than yourself. Such combinations are hard to defeat."

It was a small, almost tiny affirmation of belief in me, but it meant the world. Galen maintained his guarded expression, his eyes swirling with silver. "I'll leave you to gather your thoughts. We'll be downstairs whenever you are ready."

Tristyn and I descended the stairs to the basement training room. The floor was covered in thick mats and heavy punching bags hung ready for use. The room smelled of musk and sweat and tonight the musk was overwhelming. The wolves had been arriving for well over an hour and now the Wisconsin Pack anxiously awaited the fights.

Keep it together, Benelli.

My wolf was ready to explode, the suffocating proximity of so many male werewolves enough to send us both into spasms. Breanna was worth enduring whatever I faced. It was the only way to see her. Deal with this pack. Win these challenges.

Breathe, Benelli. Get a hold of yourself. You know how to fight.

I was dressed in a loose-fitting pair of sweats and no shirt. My muscles were warm and stretched. It was time to fight. The first wolf stepped forward. He was a big man, dressed in military fatigues, short brown hair in a traditional crew cut and a cocky bounce in his step.

Stay away from the crowd.

The Alpha quieted the group of fifty-plus werewolves standing three deep along the walls. "Tim? You ready?"

The big man nodded, his eyes locked onto mine.

"Lucas? You ready?"

I nodded. I'd need to take down this guy fast. If he got me on the mat, it was over. I was strong but at barely six feet, he'd have me pinned in under a minute.

I struck first, popping him in the nose to blur his vision. He stumbled and I took advantage. The big man yielded. My kicks had broken at least two ribs and he could barely breathe.

The Alpha nodded. "Yield accepted. The challenge is won by Lucas Benelli."

A second wolf stepped forward immediately. He was a wiry blond with crystal blue eyes that spit sparks of hate.

Don't look into the crowd. Nobody matters but her.

"Aaron, are you ready?" The blond never took his eyes from mine as he nodded to his Alpha. He was the one who had wanted to fight at the sports bar and the same one I had fought at the base.

"Lucas?"

"I am ready, sir."

This wolf was dangerous and skilled. He feigned left and struck right. We were about the same height, our reach equal, and he hated me.

This challenge went on and on until we were both near exhaustion. I had a split lip and swollen eye, but I managed a sleeper hold. In under a minute the bout was over, the wiry blond passing out from lack of oxygen. As soon as he went limp, I released my hold. He was doing what he thought was necessary to protect Breanna. I respected that.

"Challenge won by Lucas Benelli due to Aaron's inability to continue."

A quiet murmur filtered through the spectators. Tristyn stood in the corner, keeping a wary eye on the crowd. He was watching my back like he had so many times before. He knew, without saying a word, how hard this type of situation was for me. The room was small, there was only one way out, and werewolves surrounded me.

Breanna.

Another challenger stepped forward. He looked familiar but not friendly. The top of my head reached his nose. I allowed my wolf to surge. A deep breath cleared my head.

"Ordy, are you sure you want to do this?" Alpha McGregor asked the dark-haired werewolf standing before me. I didn't hear his answer before his fist connected with my jaw. The room began to tilt as another punch ripped into my tender ribs.

My opponent lunged forward and I went for his legs. He leaped sideways, but not before I swiped his knee. He roared in pain and thudded to the floor. I went for his ribs, hoping to pound the breath from his lungs. He scissor-kicked me across the room and climbed to his feet.

I circled, my motion keeping him off balance. I got in a few good punches before he sent me flying into the wall with a massive uppercut. I jumped to the side as he charged. The floor shook from the force of him hitting the wall. My vision was blurry, three images of my attacker dancing before my eyes.

The mountainous werewolf was much quicker than I had originally thought and he managed to get a hold of my arm and slam me into the mat. I rolled as his crushing elbow missed my head by a few millimeters. There was no air left in my lungs and the rib that had cracked earlier snapped.

I kept rolling but stopped before getting too close to the cheering crowd. The jeering males infuriated my wolf. If my wolf took over, Galen would end the challenges and I'd lose my chance to see Breanna. Every survival instinct inside me cried that I get away from this place. Too many werewolves, too many male werewolves, too much anger to fight. My wolf demanded to take charge, but I fought him.

Pain exploded across my face as the mountain's fist connected with my cheek, my vision darkened from the impact. I stumbled back and fell against Tristyn. He caught me and helped me to my feet.

"Luc, are you sure about this?" he asked in Italian.

I pushed my wolf down and focused on my attacker. I was fighting my wolf and this giant who wanted to break me into pieces. Panic lanced through my muddled mind. My hands trembled, my wolf begging, pleading to take control, to save me from this fate.

The panic faded as the mountain charged and I shoved Tristyn toward the wall. Tree trunk arms jerked me into a bear hug and snatched me off the ground. With every breath I took, his arms tightened and the room got darker.

Chapter 15

Breanna

The grout was smooth and I was trimming the edges of the corner tiles when fists pounded on my front door. The nippers slipped and took a chunk out of my finger.

"Damn it." Blood splattered all over my fresh white grout.

"Breanna. Open the door!"

"Simon?" He was always so polite, the only person who actually used my doorbell. I tripped over the grout bucket on my way to the door.

"What's wrong?" I asked, wrapping a paper towel around my bleeding finger.

"What the hell were you doing?" He wrinkled his handsome face in disgust.

"Grouting. Why are you banging on my door?"

"Grouting? What is--oh, never mind. There is more pressing business for you. We need to go to Galen McGregor's home."

"Galen's house? Why?" I didn't have time for any stupid werewolf crap.

"Get your coat. We need to go now."

My entire team had lost their minds. "No, not until I know why. Is Aaron in trouble again?"

"Your wolf," Simon stopped mid-sentence and checked his phone before hurling a string of French profanities. "Get in the car, Breanna."

I didn't know whether to be angry or afraid. Simon was never like this. "Sime, what were you saying about a wolf?"

He looked at me, his eyes deadly serious. "Lucas is at Galen's house."

My heart dropped to my stomach.

Simon grabbed my arm and escorted me to the car. "We need to go now."

Lucas had come to see me. He had really come. I was so happy I could do a Snoopy Dance, but Simon was freaking me out. He was upset Lucas was at Galen's house, but Lucas was only following werewolf protocol for visiting out-of-pack territory.

The forty-five minute drive took twenty. Simon was talking on his Bluetooth the whole trip, while Celeste sat quietly in the front seat monitoring text messages. I sat in the back and tried to do something with my hair. With a stained t-shirt and filthy jeans, I looked like a homeless person. I should have grabbed a jacket.

Simon peered into the rearview mirror. "The wolves will try to interfere but you need to get inside."

"Is Lucas all right?"

Simon glanced at the cellphone screen. "I don't know. He's presently engaged in a challenge with Theodore."

"What? Why the hell is he fighting Ordy?"

"They challenged him and Lucas accepted their challenges. He has to win the challenges in order to stay in the territory."

"Challenges? Why did they challenge him?" Somebody's ass was so mine.

"They want to protect you."

My intestines double-knotted. "Protect me? Protect me from what?"

"They believe he is a threat to you."

"They'll kill him."

"That is a possibility," Simon replied.

"Not what I wanted to hear, Sime. Stop the damn car and let me out. I can fly from here."

The BMW slid to a stop and I hopped out, shifted on the spot and took to the air. I flew over the guards and landed outside the massive front door of Galen's estate.

Lydia, a werewolf I knew from the diner, was standing at the door. I shifted to human and reached for the knob.

"I'm here for Lucas."

The bushy-haired brunette nodded. "The Italian? He's inside, getting his ass handed to him."

"Where are they?"

She crossed her arms and blocked my path. "I can't let you in, Bre. This is werewolf-- Uck."

I punched her in the nose and she fell against the wall, her hands flying to her bloody face. Silver flakes appeared in her eyes as she lunged.

I sidestepped her attack and followed up with a leaping roundhouse. Lydia stumbled headfirst into a tree and cursed a blue streak.

"Lydia, I don't want to fight you but I'm going in this house."

"I have my orders," she mumbled around bloody teeth.

"Sorry." I kicked her in the face and she dropped like a sack of potatoes, not even grunting as she hit the ground.

I pushed open the latch and slipped inside the massive oak door. Galen's house was magnificent, everything screaming power and control. Damn, his foyer was bigger than my living room and that coat rack in the corner would cost me six months' salary.

The raw smell of musk was so heavy it took my breath. Muted sounds of a crowd drifted from an open door leading to a basement. I'd been to Galen's house a few times, but never inside. This was one big-ass house.

I snuck past a group of werewolves leaning along the step railing and made my way into a shadowy corner of the basement. At some point the wolves would pick up my scent, but for now the fight was all they cared about.

The scene was like something out of a movie. Werewolves, all in human form, gathered in the basement. Blood-splattered mats covered the floor and the stench of sweat, blood, and musk hung in the air. The crowd cheered, shouting encouragement to one of their own as he threw another werewolf onto the mat.

I recognized Ordy's hulking, shirtless form immediately, his eyes fully silver, blood flowing from his mouth and eye. He was breathing heavily and intently watching his opponent. I'd seen Ordy fight and rarely did he need more than a couple minutes to dispatch any opponent. From the heave of his shoulders, he'd been at it for quite a while.

Lucas. Damn it. He was fighting Lucas.

Lucas looked much worse than Ordy but was holding his own. His face was bloody and swollen, one of his eyes almost completely closed. His silver eyes locked onto his opponent, his hair matted with sweat and blood, knuckles dripping with blood. His ribs were already black and blue and splattered with blood. He rolled to his side and quickly sprang to his feet.

Holy shit, he's gorgeous.

Ordy charged, his signature move to force an opponent to submit, but Lucas was quicker and side-stepped the attack. A sickening crunch resounded in the room as Lucas nailed Ordy in the gut with a wicked snap-kick. Ordy dropped to a knee and Lucas struck again, a crushing elbow to the back of his head.

I'd never seen another wolf take Ordy down. The crowd went completely silent as Ordy fell toward the padded training floor. Lucas stumbled backward and pitched into a corner. He was sucking air and fighting to get back to his feet when Galen stepped onto the mat.

"I've seen enough. I declare this challenge a draw."

A devastatingly handsome blue-eyed blond vampire emerged from the shadows and knelt beside Lucas. The Alpha looked over to the battered Italian werewolf. "Do you wish to continue?"

Lucas whispered to the vampire as the crowd waited. The vampire frowned as he answered. "He will fight the next challenge."

Damn, how many challenges did he have?

Mikalev Sherposki stomped onto the mat. "I'm next," he snarled as he closed in on Lucas, who had yet to regain his feet.

Do something, Welker.

The need to protect Lucas tore through me. Rage at his pain pushed my magic forward, my fingertips itching to fire up anyone responsible for hurting him.

"Don't touch him, Mik." I pushed past the outer wall of werewolves and stepped onto the mat. The werewolves parted and allowed me free access to the ring. Mik wasn't happy to see me. Oh well.

"Not your concern, Bre," Mikalev said. "Pizza Boy wanted a fight and we're gonna give it to him."

"Yeah, real fair fight, Mik. How many of you guys has he fought already?" I didn't stop until I was in the middle of the ring between Mikalev and Lucas. "And his name is Lucas, not Pizza Boy."

"Hello, Breanna. I wondered when you'd show up," the salt-and-pepper-haired Galen said solemnly as he joined me on the mat. I'd always liked Galen. He really cared about his wolves and did his best to keep the peace. He hadn't been exactly friendly when I first arrived in Bravo, but after an incident in which I'd rescued three werewolves who would have otherwise drowned, Galen had seemed to accept me. Some days I even thought he liked me. Today wasn't one of them.

"Alpha McGregor, what's going on here?"

Galen swept his hand toward Lucas and the vampire. "Lucas Benelli, a member of the Italian Pack, has requested to be in Wisconsin Pack territory. Challenges have been lodged by members of my pack regarding his request."

"Why?"

A soft murmur filtered through the room. Maybe questioning an Alpha wasn't exactly the best decision I could have made.

Galen looked annoyed. "Why what?"

I was annoyed but tried not to roll my eyes. "Why did they challenge him? Out-of-territory wolves visit here all the time and I don't ever remember them being challenged."

A bloody-shirted Aaron nudged forward. "They weren't here for you."

A wave of dominance washed through the room. Galen's head slowly swiveled toward Lucas, who was glaring, silver-eyed, at Aaron.

"I would never hurt her," Lucas answered in a voice much too deep and gravelly to be human.

I think Galen said something, but I didn't catch it. My heart thundered in my ears, drowning out everything around me. Lucas was here, mere feet away, and all I could think about was running my fingers through his hair, feeling those muscles along his chest ripple under my hands, tracing that line of dark hair that disappeared under the waist of his sweats. Oh, and killing anyone who threatened him again.

"Breanna?" Galen asked.

Damn, he'd asked me something. "Oh, I'm sorry, Alpha. What did you say?"

A second murmur floated through the crowd and Galen looked perplexed. I guess he wasn't used to repeating himself. "I said the Italian wolf has asked to be in our territory so he may speak with you."

I made a point to look Galen in the eye. Every wolf in the room could hear my pounding heart. "I'd like to see him."

The wolves murmured again. That was really getting on my nerves. "Something to say?" I asked the churning group. "Something I need to be aware of here?"

I was directly challenging the group and every wolf there knew it. Galen cocked an eyebrow but otherwise didn't react.

Mikalev took a step toward Lucas and I blocked his path. "Leave him be, Mik."

"He took the challenge, Bre. He has to fight me."

I stepped toe-to-toe with Mik and looked up. "Then I challenge you for the right to challenge him." I glared at the familiar faces. "And anyone else who wants a piece of me can take a number and step right up."

"What? You can't do that." Mikalev looked at Galen. "She can't do that, can she?"

The big Alpha huffed. "Actually, she can. Do you want to fight her, Mik?"

"Oh, hell no."

"I will." Zeke Trenton shoved aside the wolves around the mat. "I will take the witch's challenge. It would be my pleasure to put her in her place."

A wave of anger raced through the room, sending me to my knees. Lucas leaped over me and had Trenton by the neck.

"Do not threaten her," Lucas growled, tightening his fingers around the major's throat.

Zeke kicked and clawed but Lucas had him pinned off the ground, against the wall. He held the formidable Trenton easily by one hand. All I could do was gape. Holy cow, nobody did that to Zeke Trenton.

"Lucas, do not kill him," Galen ordered.

Lucas blinked at the Alpha's command. Dominance and compulsion choked the room, but Lucas didn't let go. He bared his teeth at the struggling wolf. "No one threatens her."

Everyone saw the shock on Galen's face when Lucas's grip didn't loosen. An Alpha wolf always maintained control. Galen laid a hand on Lucas's shoulder and I sprang forward, ready to step in if the Alpha attacked. Trenton was purple.

"Wolf, I am the Alpha of this territory and you will not kill one of mine."

Lucas flinched under Galen's touch. I ducked and came up between Lucas and Trenton.

"Easy, Wolf, it's okay."

Eyes that were totally silver peered at me. His grip on Trenton tightened.

"Wolf, if you kill Trenton, the Alpha will kill you and then I'll have to kill the Alpha and this will all get very messy."

Maybe Galen didn't hear that.

Lucas looked down at Galen's hand on his shoulder and back at me. With a deep sigh, he dropped his hand from Trenton's throat and closed his eyes. Trenton fell in a heap. Galen closed his eyes and the dominance in the room increased. Every werewolf in the room, except Lucas, dropped to the floor. Lucas squeezed his eyes shut and bowed his head.

I'd never seen anything like what was going on between Galen and Lucas. I was afraid Galen may retaliate against the defenseless Lucas, who was now standing with his shoulders sagging and his fists clenched at his sides.

Galen laid a second hand on Lucas and watched as Lucas dropped to his knees. The room was absolutely still, the other wolves in some sort of trance. Slowly, deliberately, Lucas turned his head to the side and exposed his throat, the sign of submission among wolves. I shoved the Alpha but he didn't budge.

"Don't hurt him, Galen," I said, touching the top of Lucas's head. "He was protecting me."

"I know," the Alpha acknowledged. Galen didn't sound angry, but there was huskiness in his usually perfectly controlled demeanor.

Lucas drew in several deep breaths, as if he was struggling to breathe. I dropped to my knees beside him.

"Lucas?"

He opened his eyes and smiled at me. The smile faded when he realized the other werewolves were behind me. He grabbed my arm and pulled me to his chest, his wolf surging. His heart pounded, the pulse in his throat clearly visible.

"It's okay, Wolf," I whispered in his ear, but it wasn't okay. He wasn't okay. There should have been growling and snarling, but Lucas was doing neither. He was holding me as if my life was in danger. I tried to pull back and look at his face but his arms locked around me in a grip a bear couldn't break.

Someone brushed against my back and a growl rumbled deep in Lucas's chest. Dominance and power slammed into me as Galen came closer.

No words were exchanged, but something happened between Galen and Lucas because Lucas collapsed in my arms, his eyes clenched shut.

"Damn it, Galen, you said you wouldn't hurt him," I yelled as I eased Lucas onto the mat. He was breathing normally and appeared to be unconscious.

Galen leaned forward and I called up a ring of flames to prevent him from coming closer. Lucas was out cold and I'd be damned if I'd let anyone hurt him.

The Alpha jumped as the flames leaped and licked toward the ceiling. They weren't real, just an illusion to keep the Alpha back, but they looked and felt real.

"Lucas? Hey? Can you hear me?"

Nothing. Nada.

I looked around for somebody to trust, but found nobody. I stroked his hair and gingerly touched the bruises on his face. Lucas had taken a much worse beating tonight than at Ederle but once again, he'd held his own. There was lots of blood on the mat, not all of it his.

The flames danced and I held Lucas. I knew every wolf in this room but right now, there wasn't an ally among them. They were pack wolves and would always follow Galen's orders.

The blue-eyed vampire had left his shadowy waiting place and was in deep conversation with Galen. Geez, he must have been crazy or maybe he wasn't as good a friend as I'd thought.

How would I get Lucas out? I couldn't carry him and it didn't look like he was going to wake up in the next few minutes. I could take him to my house and ward the door so nobody could come in. Okay, think, Welker. How the hell to get him out of this basement?

The pack wolves remained in whatever type of trance Galen had put them in and Lucas wouldn't wake up. Now what to do? Okay, worse case, I could call Christopher and Simon, but the vampires generally stayed clear of pack crap. Guess they were smarter than me.

The blond vampire looked through my flames. He didn't seem concerned about angry werewolves surrounding him. His gaze drifted from me to the flames and a tiny smile played on his lips before he stepped through my fake flames and knelt beside Lucas.

I shielded Lucas with my body. "Do not touch him."

The vampire nodded and placed his hands on his thighs. "You must be Breanna. He's talked about you non-stop since the night on the mountain road."

Ah, classic technique of trying to make me feel comfortable. This vampire was good.

"And you would be?"

His smile would have been charming under normal circumstances but now it didn't faze me. "I'm Tristyn Ziccardi, Lucas's best friend." The smile faded. "My mate is the witch representative to the Divine Council."

This was the guy Christopher talked about. This seemed legit.

"How many did he fight?"

Tristyn sobered. "Three. This last one was tough. I wasn't sure how it would turn out."

He could have died tonight because of me.

"He's okay, Breanna," the vampire said as he nodded toward Lucas. "He needs rest. Galen has given us use of his guesthouse for the night."

I wanted to believe him. All my senses said the vampire was telling the truth, but if I was wrong, Lucas would be in danger.

"If you'll allow me, I'll carry him out of here."

I swallowed hard and looked down at the helpless wolf on my lap. "If you hurt him, I will kill you."

The vampire acknowledged my threat and slipped his arms under Lucas's legs and shoulders. He stood in one fluid motion and carried Lucas toward the stairway. I broke my fire illusion and walked behind the vampire as the wolves began to stir. All this musk and dominance was giving me a headache.

Galen watched as we climbed out of the basement. I was halfway up the steps when I wheeled around and went to Galen.

"What did you do to him?"

The Alpha looked me dead in the eyes. "You aren't the only one who can speak to wolves, Breanna."

It wasn't surprising an Alpha could talk to a wolf directly, but I'd never heard any of the guys say that had happened to them. Maybe that was part of the Alpha mojo magic thing that allowed Galen to control his wolves.

But Lucas wasn't his wolf.

"He will be fine after he rests and I give my word my wolves will not go near Lucas or Tristyn." The green eyes twinkled. "You, however, have some things to work out with my pack."

I did not take orders from Alphas. "Excuse me?"

Galen nodded toward Aaron and Ordy. "They felt the need to protect you. That's why they challenged him."

I snorted. "I told both of them I wanted to see Lucas and they did this territorial bullshit anyway."

Aaron and Ordy were bloody and bruised. The two were the strongest combat fighters we had, but apparently Lucas had bested them. The pack wolves moved around the basement. They all looked dazed.

"Anyone who goes after Lucas will deal with me."

Galen watched the vampire climb the final steps leading to the foyer. "You would do best to go home tonight. Lucas needs to heal and he will need to deal with his emotions. Tristyn will look after him."

"What the hell does that mean? His emotions for what?"

Galen leveled a glare and I was almost intimidated. Almost.

"When he is ready, Lucas will tell you." The Alpha put his hands on my upper arms. "Be patient with him, Breanna. Life has not always been kind to Lucas."

Chapter 16

Lucas

I took a breath and opened my eyes. Nothing looked familiar. Nothing smelled familiar. Nothing sounded familiar.

Fuzzy memories of a big wolf charging toward Breanna came to mind. I shook my pounding head and rolled to the side. "Breanna?" Where the hell was she? What had happened?

I was dressed in gray sweatpants and a gray sweatshirt that smelled much too strongly of musk. My heart stuttered. The bed creaked. "Breanna?"

Blood stained the shirt. My knuckles looked like hamburger. My jaw rebelled at opening and my ribs hurt like hell.

"Hey, little brother," Tristyn called from the doorway. He was leaning against the frame.

"Where is she?" I yelled. How could he just stand there like nothing was wrong?

"Calm down, Lucas. Breanna is fine."

"I have to find her."

He tossed a phone in my direction. "I promised you would call as soon as you woke up."

"I have to go."

Tristyn shoved me back onto the bed and my wolf surged.

"Don't," I warned. He knew not to push me when my wolf was ascending.

"Call the witch before she comes over here and kicks my ass."

"What?"

Trist grumbled under his breath as he glanced at his watch. "Just call her, Lucas. I'll explain later."

My best friend looked genuinely alarmed. Tristyn was the calm one, the level head in tough situations. If he was worried, things were bad.

I called and Breanna answered before the end of the first ring. She sounded tired and concerned but said she could get a little sleep now that she knew I was okay.

It was four in the morning when I hung up. She gave me directions and I promised I see her around noon for lunch.

"She's okay," I said to Tristyn as I shuffled stiffly out of the bedroom. "Where the hell are we, anyway?"

"Galen's guesthouse."

I had been so worried about Breanna, I'd forgotten about the Wisconsin Pack and the challenges. I'd only fought three. There were supposed to be ten.

"I told her I'd meet her for lunch." Maybe we could meet somewhere on the way out of town. If it had been just my ass on the line, I'd take a chance, but I wouldn't endanger Tristyn.

Tristyn's forehead wrinkled. "We can stay through Tuesday. You won your challenges last night. We have to meet with Galen today when you get cleaned up."

Maybe the other challengers bowed out.

I tried stretching to relieve the stiffness in my back. "I remember a wolf threatening Breanna and then everything goes black. What happened?"

Tristyn looked startled before tossing a bottle of water in my direction. "You don't remember what happened with Galen? You submitted to him."

"I did what?"

Trist settled into the opposing recliner. "On your knees, head back, throat exposed, eyes closed."

I had never submitted to anyone, even my father. Tristyn knew that.

For a werewolf, submission was a way of life. It was a way to avoid fights and recognize the dominance of another wolf. Wolves submitted to those who were more dominant as a matter of respect. My wolf had never met another wolf dominant enough to require submission.

I vaguely remembered having my hand around a wolf's neck and the Alpha demanding I not kill. My wolf wanted the blood of the wolf who had threatened Breanna.

"Did Breanna see it?"

Tristyn nodded. "Yep, she went after Galen as soon as you collapsed."

"Went after him?"

"Shoved him away and told him not to hurt you. Hell, she said she'd kill me if I hurt you."

"She went after an Alpha werewolf?" Nobody challenged Alphas unless they had a death wish.

"She summoned a ring of fire and backed him off when he was checking on you. I tell you, Luc, you know how to pick 'em. She was ready to take on the whole pack, the Alpha, and me if that's what it took to protect you. The girl is fearless."

My head was thumping like a tuba was inside my brain. "I collapsed? How did I get here?"

"I carried you."

Oh for the love of all that was holy. She was fearless and I couldn't even stay on my feet. First she found me bleeding beside the road and now she'd watched as I passed out and got carried around by a vampire. Great.

"What happened between you and Galen?" Tristyn asked.

"I have no idea. I don't remember anything."

Trist leaned forward. "That means your wolf was in charge, right?"

My wolf must have been totally in charge because everything was black between trying to kill the wolf who'd threatened Breanna and waking up here. It was rare for my wolf to completely take over. I usually had at least a clue what was going on.

"You sure you've never met Galen before?" Tristyn asked.

"Yeah, I'm sure. Why?"

He shrugged. "I don't know, just that you acted different around him." "Different?"

"Don't take this the wrong way, Luc, but it was like your wolf respected him. I've never seen you react to anyone like that."

Because it was the first time my wolf not only acknowledged an Alpha, but responded to one. Maybe it was because of Breanna, my wolf needing to protect her.

Whatever the reason, I hoped Galen didn't mention it to my father. We had enough issues without him knowing I'd submitted to another Alpha.

"Galen said we could meet him for breakfast at six if you were up."

It was a few minutes before six when we arrived at the Alpha's main house. My gut clenched at the sight of so many werewolves, but they stayed away from us. I kept my head up and beckoned my wolf to be on alert. Normally he was surging, trying to take over anytime I was this close to a pack. Today he felt calm. That made me nervous.

"Good morning, Lucas," a female werewolf said as she led us to the dining room. "Our Alpha is expecting you." She looked me up and down and then turned her attention to Tristyn, who, of course, smiled at her.

I slammed on the brakes as we entered the massive dining area. Several dozen werewolves sat around a long table and all looked up when we walked in the room. Tristyn, unaware I had stopped, knocked me unceremoniously into the room. I spun on my heel to leave when Tristyn grabbed my arm.

"What are you doing?" he whispered.

There was no way I could go in there.

Tristyn's fingers tightened on my arm. "Luc, buddy, come on. You can do this."

My heart thundered in my throat. My wolf was surging. I clenched my eyes and tried to breathe. No luck.

"Think about Breanna."

My stomach somersaulted and the room tilted. Black spots danced in the corners.

"Can you see her, Luc? Her hair? Her eyes? The way her skin felt against yours?"

The panic subsided and my breathing slowly returned to normal. My heart remained in overdrive, but my wolf settled. Beads of sweat rolled down my face and neck. I wiped my sleeve along my forehead and nodded.

"I'm okay."

Tristyn didn't say a word as he released my arm and squeezed my shoulder. He never did. He knew packs sent me into full-blown panic attacks, the remnants of a childhood I couldn't seem to shake. I'd tried. God knew I'd tried.

"Lucas, Tristyn, come in," Galen called from his chair at the far end of the table. "We have plenty. You boys do like pancakes, don't you?"

My stomach rumbled even though this room was the last place I wanted to be. I opened my mouth to decline when Tristyn pushed past me.

"Breakfast would be nice. Thank you, Alpha McGregor," my vampire friend answered confidently, looking over his shoulder at me.

There were several single chairs but no chairs side by side. That meant I would have to sit between two pack wolves. My intestines knotted.

Hold it together, Benelli.

"You have to do this for Breanna," Tristyn whispered.

He was right but that didn't make this any easier. Only the thought of her would get me through this.

"C'mon, little brother. You can do this."

We found seats near the middle of the table. When Tristyn covertly gave me the spot between two attractive women I wasn't interested in the least. However, the women were not as unnerving as the men.

I summoned my wolf and allowed my natural dominance to flow. Forks dropped and the eating stopped. From the end of the table, Galen spoke.

"Nobody here means any threat, Lucas. We're only eating breakfast."

I stared at my empty plate. My stomach roared, demanding attention. The woman to my left passed a plate full of pancakes.

"Did you call Breanna?" she asked as I took the plate.

"This morning, before we came over here," I stuttered. My wolf retreated.

The pretty brunette sighed. "Good. She was not happy to leave you last night, but it was the only way the pack would settle."

Someone across the table growled. I looked over and found livid blue eyes.

"Aaron," Galen called. "Why don't you get Lucas a glass of milk?"

The compulsion of the Alpha swept through the room, touching a nerve inside me and forcing me to look away from Aaron stomping toward the kitchen.

"Alpha McGregor, these pancakes are spectacular," Tristyn said. "Thank you for having us."

I continued to stare at my empty plate even under the weight of the Alpha's gaze. The brunette flipped a stack of pancakes onto my plate.

"Syrup?" she asked.

"Uh, sure."

She poured the maple syrup over my pancakes. My head spun. It was hard to breathe. All the wolves watched me and heard my galloping heart.

"How was Breanna this morning, Lucas?"

I met Galen's eyes and quickly looked back at my plate. This was all so new to me, the compulsion was strangling. Galen wasn't asking me to do anything. Should I eat? What should I be looking at? Why wouldn't my heart slow down?

"She's fine," I mumbled.

"What was that?" Galen asked more loudly than necessary.

Breathe, Benelli.

"She's fine, Alpha McGregor. We are meeting for lunch."

"Good," the Alpha answered around a mouthful of pancakes. "She loves Steak and Bake if you're looking for somewhere to take her."

A glass slammed onto the table, the milk spilling onto the tablecloth. Aaron growled. I shoved my chair back, ready to respond.

"Boys, there will be none of that this fine morning," Galen said from the head of the table. The power and authority resonated in the rich timbre of his voice. My wolf relaxed. I panicked. What the hell was wrong with me?

The meal seemed to drag on forever. I methodically chewed my pancakes and made a conscious effort not to choke. My throat kept closing every time someone passed behind me.

The buzz of conversation was intriguing. What was going on at work, who was dating whom, how the weather would affect activities later tonight, things normal people talked about. They were relaxed, like a real family. The woman beside me, Lydia, tried to carry on a conversation. I wasn't much for talking. I'd probably say something stupid anyway.

Tristyn was talking to the Alpha like they were old friends. He could talk to anybody. I, however, had the social graces of a grizzly bear. The woman to the left of me casually brushed my arm and I almost jumped out of my chair. She raised her eyebrows like I was a moron. I mouthed an apology and went back to staring at my plate.

The Alpha rose and walked toward me. He paused behind my chair and placed a hand on my shoulder. His power coursed through my veins. My wolf should have responded, but he remained quiet. My heart galloped along, skipping a few beats as the Alpha stood over me.

"Come with me."

I bit my lip and looked at Tristyn, who was in a laughing conversation with the Alpha's second-in-command. Even the pack wolves I fought last night were happily chatting away. Everybody loved Tristyn.

Push the chair back. Stand up. Breathe.

The wolves watched as I followed the Alpha into his study. It was an enormous room filled with rows and rows of leather-bound books. It smelled dusty and old, much better than the musk-filled dining room.

"Have a seat, Lucas." The Alpha motioned toward a heavy leather couch and closed the door. He sat on the edge of his desk. "You fought well last night. Did your father teach you to fight?"

"No, sir," I answered. The Alpha waited, expecting more of an answer. "Tristyn's father worked with me for several years."

"Ah, that explains it. You fight like a vampire. Perhaps you would teach some of my younger wolves? They do not have the strength to fight against the older wolves in true werewolf style."

I nodded and shrugged. "I'm not much of a teacher."

Galen eased off the desk and onto the far end of the couch. I was as close to the other end as I could get. "Do you know how to get to Breanna's house?" he asked.

"She gave me directions this morning." My mouth was dry and I kept swallowing to keep from choking. My wolf was being calm and I didn't have a clue why. I usually had to fight for control when another werewolf, particularly a male werewolf, was this close.

"You are welcome to use the guesthouse during your visit here. My wolves will not challenge you again and of course Tristyn is also invited."

"Thank you, Alpha McGregor."

The Alpha took a deep breath and exhaled slowly. His wolf was restless and my wolf was apparently on hiatus. The silence shredded my nerves.

Galen reached into his pocket and withdrew a business card. "You can call anytime. The number on the back is my personal cell."

I took his card and tucked it in my shirt pocket. I wanted out of here. Everything was so weird. I didn't have control and didn't understand what was happening. The more I fought, the worse it seemed to be.

"Have you spoken with Josef?"

"No, sir, I have not." That was one conversation I was not looking forward to having.

"Why didn't you tell him you were coming here, to another pack's territory?"

I licked my lips, trying to find the right way to tell him my father would have forbidden my visit. Protocol dictated my Alpha request permission for my presence here. Galen McGregor could have, under werewolf law, had me killed the moment I stepped onto his territory.

A knock on the door startled me.

Galen growled before jerking open the door. "Zeke, what is so important you left the pack breakfast?"

This was the wolf who had threatened Breanna. I stood to face him.

"I wanted to speak to the Italian."

"About what?" Galen asked.

The werewolf lowered his eyes. Galen glanced at me before focusing on the wolf at the door. "Zeke, you weren't thinking of challenging Lucas again, were you?"

Zeke's Adam's apple bobbed as he swallowed. "He got a lucky jump on me, Alpha, and I wanted a chance to fight him fair."

Galen considered the werewolf's request for a moment before answering. "Lucas will not be challenged again during his stay. He has earned the right to be in my territory."

Zeke kept his opinion to himself and sulked away. I was more than willing to fight him.

Galen closed the door. "Tristyn would like to visit with some of the local vampires. I'll call Simon DuChard and have him come by so you can meet him as well."

I gave him a weak smile. Why did he think I would want to meet a vampire? Had he heard the rumors, too?

"Major DuChard commands the Recon Unit of Bravo."

I'd met him in Italy. He was her boss.

"He is Breanna's commanding officer and thinks of her as a daughter."

"Oh." A vampire thinking of a witch as a daughter was as strange as me and Trist being best friends.

Galen extended his hand and I looked at it suspiciously. I never touched male werewolves, but he was the Alpha and my wolf wanted to please him. I wanted his approval.

I forced my hand forward. The Alpha's power sizzled through me. A strangled cry escaped my lips as I grabbed the couch with my free hand. Whatever he did hurt like hell. It also was soothing, like he was cauterizing a wound. He didn't let go as I went to my knees. He didn't let go as I went flat to the floor and was pinned to the wood.

Images of the holding cell in my father's basement clawed to the surface. I tried to slam the door shut. Stephano's hand over my mouth, the look on my father's face as he walked away, crying myself to sleep at night in boarding school.

A hand brushed through my hair. Galen would force my head back and expose my throat as my father had done with so many of his pack wolves. It was a display of total dominance and one my father often practiced with wolves new to his pack. He had tried it once with me when I was sixteen and I had thrown him across the room.

The hand on my head slid down my face along my jaw and grasped my chin. He urged my face up and looked into my eyes. I tried to turn away but he would not allow it. Forceful yet gentle, Galen prevented my escape.

More memories surfaced. Father-son banquets alone, the pillow over my head as Stephano ripped my clothes, the smell of blood on the silver dagger.

I gasped for air as Galen's hand moved down my throat. My wolf surged and retreated, leaving me completely alone. I fought to stand, to pull away from Galen, but I couldn't move. He had me and there was nothing I could do.

My heart stuttered as the memories of being pinned to the floor came into the light. The strangled cry of a child begging his father for help escaped my lips. I was ten again. Stephano had snuck into my room. I tried to scream as he covered my mouth. I searched for the pack bond, the one guaranteed way to reach my father. There was nothing. Nobody heard me.

And then it was over. Galen was gone and the door to his study was open. I was flat on the floor, my face wet with tears, my hair drenched with sweat.

I sat in the study, trying to pull myself together. My hands were trembling, my knees knocking, my heart racing. Galen knew. He'd seen it all and there wasn't a thing I could do about it. At least he'd left without letting me see the look of disgust on his face.

Chapter 17

Breanna

I changed clothes four times and forgot to brush my hair. Dashing around the house like a madwoman with a toothbrush in my mouth, I froze when the doorbell rang. Lucas had called a little while ago and I told him to come on over. His voice sounded strained and I wondered if the wolves had been giving him a hard time. Galen promised they wouldn't, but something was definitely wrong.

I sprinted to the door and almost yanked it open with a toothbrush still in. Not wanting to keep him waiting, I tossed the toothbrush behind the bookcase. I'd tried to find a dress in my closet, or at least a skirt. Nada. Celeste had made a frantic clothes run with me and helped me pick out a nicely tailored black pantsuit. It made my butt look good and Celeste said it set off my eyes.

With one last deep breath, I reached for the door.

"Hi," I said as the old oak door swung open.

"Hey, Bre, what's up?" Aaron asked nonchalantly.

Lucas was supposed to be here at ten hundred and it was presently nine forty-five. Could I kill Aaron and dispose of his body in fifteen minutes?

"Why are you here?"

Aaron strolled past me and sank into my recliner. I closed my gaping mouth before catching any flies. "Aaron Justin Miller, get out of my house this instant."

Aaron rolled his eyes at my three-naming. I looked around for something to kill him with without damaging my house. The hammer under the kitchen sink was calling my name.

"Get out of my house now."

He grinned and flipped the footrest out. "Why? Afraid I'll interrupt something?"

"I'm going to interrupt your breathing pattern if you don't get your ass out of my house."

He chuckled, which infuriated me.

"Out!" I grabbed his hair and tried to drag him from the chair. He shook me off and seized my wrist. With one jerk, he pulled me over the back of the chair and into his lap.

"Hi there," Aaron said suavely, his nose inches from mine. I punched him in the face.

"Ow, damn, Bre. I was only trying to be nice."

I stormed to my feet. "Get your ass out of my house." I glanced at my watch. Lucas would be here in ten minutes and my house would reek of Aaron. Ug.

"Aaron, so help me, if you aren't out of my house in the next ten seconds I will neuter you."

A horrified look trailed across his face as he instinctively covered his privates. "Ouch, Bre."

"Seven seconds." I reached for a butcher knife on the bar that separated the kitchen from the living room.

"Bre," Aaron said shakily as he climbed out of my recliner. "I was just checking up on you. Don't get all mad."

"Three seconds."

Aaron scrambled for the door as my internal timer hit zero. I was two steps behind him when he cleared the couch and zipped out the front door. He leaped the porch in one bound and I was hot on his trail, knife in hand.

Aaron slid across the hood of his black Camaro and snatched open the driver's side door. I stopped mid-way through the yard, holding the knife like the Statue of Liberty. A big whiff of Lucas-scented air reached my nose and my womanly parts woke up abruptly.

My face was burning before I turned around. It didn't matter how much he'd seen or heard, since I was standing in my yard with my hair in a crooked ponytail and a butcher knife in my hand. So much for making a good feminine impression.

"Hello," I called cheerfully. Lucas was standing on my porch, just to the side of the front door, holding a beautiful bouquet of flowers. A soft pink ribbon fluttered in the breeze.

"Hi," he answered as he descended the steps toward me. I stared at the brown remnants of my yard while his musk and leather scent enveloped me. His black leather boots soon entered my field of vision. Geez, I loved a man in boots, especially when he looked so good in a denim jacket and jeans.

The warmth of his body surrounded me and somewhere deep inside my mind, a tiny door opened. I looked up and found him smiling. He was absolutely irresistible.

"You're pretty brave, coming near a crazy woman," I mumbled.

"Sounded like you were defending your territory," he answered. "These are for you."

Our fingers brushed when I took the flowers. "Thank you."

"Were you really going to neuter him?"

I loved the naughty little sparkle in his eyes and who could resist those damn dimples?

"Not with this knife," I retorted. "I was thinking more about using a spoon."

"Oh, ow." He backed away a half step. "I promise I'll be on my best behavior."

Much to my relief, Lucas accepted my invitation to come inside. I fished around in the cabinet and found something to hold the flowers. They were too pretty to be in an orange juice jar. The only other choice was a Big Gulp cup.

"Did you have any trouble finding my house?"

He shook his adorable head. "No, your directions were dead-on."

This was awkward. We didn't actually know one another and here he was in the middle of my living room. But I wanted him in my living room. The need to close the door on the world and protect him consumed me.

He's really here.

His face showed only a hint of the fighting from last night, a little cut above his eye, some bruising along his jaw. His ribs were probably sore, though he showed no signs of it.

He rescued me from the uncomfortable silence. "Are you hungry?"

"Starved." Breakfast hadn't happened, since I'd been running around trying to make myself presentable.

A glimpse of my reflection in the microwave door reminded me how ridiculous my hair looked. "Would you mind if I brushed my hair before we left? It won't take a sec."

"Sure," he answered quickly. "Take your time."

I hurried down the hall and ran a comb through my hair. When I returned to the dining room, Lucas was gone.

Damn. Did my hair look that bad?

"Lucas?"

Noise from the opposite end of the house got my attention. I tiptoed down the hall and found Lucas kneeling in the bathroom. The grout from yesterday wasn't completely dry.

"Who did your tile work?" he asked without looking up.

"I did."

His smile sent my heart into arrhythmia. "Nicely done."

"The corners aren't flat." I knelt beside him and pointed to the row along the tub. "The grout wouldn't smooth out here."

He leaned forward onto his hands. He was pure power, masculine and strong, and parts of me that had been dead for a long time were suddenly very much alive. I swallowed hard as his arm brushed mine. Damn, what was wrong with me? Just being near him made my hormones explode.

"You have to change the pattern when you get near a hard corner like the tub bottom." He looked back at me with a wink. "How about we pick up a fresh container of grout while we're out and we'll come back and fix this?"

Oh holy hell, was it possible to fall in love this fast? A werewolf who actually knew what grout was? "I'll buy lunch."

He rocked back on his toes, his tan hands resting on heavily muscled thighs. "Lunch is on me, but you can buy ice cream afterward."

"Deal."

Lucas stood and followed me up the hall. I felt like a prey animal.

And I'd made fun of Flopsy. Shame on me.

It was a short ride to the Steak and Bake Diner, my favorite place to eat. We found a booth tucked into the corner and split a basket of cheesy fries while waiting for our food.

"Do your ribs hurt much?" I asked before washing down my fries with cold chocolate milk.

"They're a little sore."

Wow. Not too proud to admit pain. I love that.

He reached across the table for my hand. I met him halfway.

At that moment every ounce of air in my lungs left. Gently, ever so softly, his fingers traced little circles on the back of my hand.

If this is a dream, don't wake me up.

Lydia arrived with our food and Lucas released my hand. Immediately I missed the warmth of his touch and intentionally left my hand on the table, praying he would reach for it a second time.

I hope Lydia hadn't spit in our food after the wallop I'd laid on her last night.

We inhaled the food and ordered seconds. Lydia kept our fry basket full and brought us a double serving of apple pie for dessert.

"I'm sorry the wolves went after you last night," I said over a spoonful of vanilla ice cream.

"They were protecting you."

"I don't need their protection."

Lucas looked over his bowl at me and smiled. "I've noticed."

He and Galen were the only werewolves I'd ever seen with dimples. The spoon slipped through the ice cream and banged onto the bowl bottom. "I told them I wanted to see you."

"You did?"

Tongue-tied, awkward moment. "Yes." Hot face. Hot face. Hot face.

"I couldn't wait to see you again. I wanted to be there when you got off the plane, but with work and having to go through Alpha McGregor, I couldn't arrange it."

Holy hell. He was so damn sweet I felt bad for ever doubting he'd come see me.

"I know what it's like to come home to an empty house all the time. I thought the flowers would make you smile after being gone for so long."

If I was the crying type, I'd be bawling right now.

Lucas left a twelve-dollar tip for Lydia. I wasn't sure if he was always a big tipper or if he was trying to make friends with one of Galen's pack. We waited patiently at the register while a new human girl struggled with the computer keys. She flashed smiles at Lucas.

Touch him and I'll rip out your bottle-blond hair.

A couple of Galen's pack came through while we were stuck at the front. They all spoke to me and gave Lucas cold yet respectful looks. If it bothered him, he didn't show it, though I did feel his surge of dominance when one wolf came a little too close.

Our quick trip to the hardware store turned into a three-hour trek. Lucas knew all about laying tile, painting, plumbing, and anything else I asked about fixing my house. He was better than my *Home Improvement for Dummies* book and a whole lot more helpful than the clerks at the store.

By the time we reached my house again, it was almost fifteen hundred hours. We were carrying in the plastic tub of grout and a few new tools when his phone vibrated. He checked the screen and frowned. "I forgot about Tristyn."

"Do you need to go?" Damn, damn, damn.

"I told Tristyn I'd pick him up after lunch. He's waiting for me at the Divine Council offices."

I could throw him on the couch and put him out with a sleeper hold to make him stay longer. "I understand. Maybe we can get together some other time."

He dropped the bags and pulled me to his chest. Normally such a display of force would offend me, but from him, I liked it.

"Maybe?" he asked with a twinkle in his dark brown eyes.

I tried to look away. He would have none of that. He tipped my chin and looked into my eyes. I swear he saw everything, even the parts I tried to hide. It was intoxicating and, at the same time, terrifying how easily he took control of me. It wasn't compulsion, but there was something magical about him, something I couldn't fight.

"How about I pick up dinner tonight and we'll work on your floor?"

Could he have been any more perfect? "Okay, that sounds good. I'll make something for dessert. What do you like?"

The dimples appeared and my knees went weak. "I'm a wolf. I'll eat anything." His eyes sparkled as his grip tightened. That feeling of being a prey animal returned. Now I understood the glassy-eyed look the rabbits had when I caught them.

"Would six o'clock be too early?" he asked as I reveled in the musk and leather scent.

"Um, no, that's fine. You can bring Tristyn if you like." I really hoped he would come alone, but it seemed rude not to invite his friend.

For a fleeting second Lucas looked hurt. "He's busy."

Oh, that didn't come out like I had intended. "Okay, I just thought if you weren't comfortable leaving him with all that's going on with the pack."

I swear he stood a little taller. "That's very thoughtful. He'll want to spend a few hours on the computer." He ran a finger along my jaw and my body threatened to spontaneously combust. "Trist isn't much into house repair."

"Whatever you think."

He traced a white-hot path along my neck with his fingers. His breath caressed my face. He smelled so warm, so masculine. I wanted to throw him on the carpet and attack him. A mischievous smile and twinkling brown eyes were the first things I saw when I pried my eyelids open. He scented my arousal and I definitely felt his. Denim jeans hid nothing.

His phone vibrated a second time. "Damn." He leaned his forehead on my shoulder. My arms, with no instruction from me, went around his waist. A sound resembling a growl rattled in his throat when I laid my head on his shoulder. "God, this feels good," he whispered in my ear.

He nuzzled my hair, his lips brushing along the top of my head. A shiver ran up my spine when his breath tickled my ear. A calm so palpable I could taste it settled over me as his rough breathing hypnotized what little rational mind I had left.

"I've dreamed about holding you," he rasped as he held me tighter against his chest. "Since that night when you found me, I haven't stopped thinking about you."

I buried my head in the soft curls resting along his collar. My dreams had been of him, too, and now, having him here in my arms, I was afraid to wake up and find only a stale Pluto pillowcase.

"I'm glad you're here," I managed to say just before his lips covered mine in a gentle yet aggressive kiss. His tongue danced along, asking for entrance, while subtly demanding compliance. He made me feel safe.

The phone vibrated a third time and he growled.

I laughed. "You'd better go."

He tucked a stray hair behind my ear. "I'll be back by six." He kissed my forehead. "What would you like for dinner?"

"Whatever is convenient will work," I answered as he backed toward the door while still holding my hand. "I'm not picky."

He grinned and pulled me toward him in a move reminiscent of a ballroom dancer. "Do you like lobster?"

I shrugged. "I'll eat about anything."

His dimples were shining. "Like a wolf, huh?"

"Well, I'm a little pickier. I do like my food cooked."

* * * *

It was exactly two minutes before six when the black Suburban rolled into my drive. I opened the door and trotted out to help Lucas with dinner. Knowing werewolves, there would be a whole lot of food.

"Glad you made it back."

He set down the bags and welcomed me into a big hug. I hesitated for one billionth of a second before stepping into arms so thick with muscles they could break me into pieces. His chest was hard and warm, his bristly chin rubbing along my cheek. I liked that.

"I missed you," he whispered.

"I didn't know if you'd make it. How many first dates have taken you to the hardware store?"

He pressed a kiss to my forehead. "I've never had a date who knew what a hardware store was."

An involuntary shiver ran up my spine as he slid his hands along my sides and settled around my waist.

He pulled back and looked at me curiously. "Ticklish?"

I wasn't. "No, it's a little chilly out here."

The look in his eyes said he didn't believe my lame explanation, but he was gentleman enough to let it go. "I'll grab the food if you'll get the door," he said.

Lucas retrieved our dinner, carrying so many bags he couldn't see where he was walking. I acted as his scout, making sure he didn't trip on the steps or run into the doorframe.

I took the bags from the top of the pile and set them gingerly onto the bar. "Smells great," I said, pulling Styrofoam plates from the paper bags. "What did you get?"

He waggled his eyebrows like a fiend. "Lobster, shrimp, steak, and hot dogs."

"Hot dogs?"

His smile made my heart somersault. "I was hungry on the way so I grabbed a snack. I left one for you."

Werewolves. Always hungry. "I'm not starting with a hotdog when there's all this real food."

"Eat whatever you like. I'll go get more if we need it." He winked as he popped the cork on a bottle of champagne. "Can you grab a couple of glasses?"

My Mickey Mouse glasses didn't seem appropriate for champagne. The other options were little jelly jar glasses or the plastic cups I'd gotten with my last burger. I opted for Mickey and Minnie.

Lucas looked a little puzzled at my glass selection but didn't say anything as he poured the bubbly. He offered me Minnie. "I'd like to propose a toast," he said gallantly.

I giggled at the formal nature of a toast with Mickey and Minnie, holding my glass alongside his.

"To the most beautiful woman in the world."

"Where is she?"

Tiny silver flecks shone in his eyes. "Right here."

He tipped my glass with his and my face felt extraordinarily hot. I watched the bubbles float to the top of champagne.

He came closer, his scent enthralling. His scratchy beard met my cheek. "I'm sorry if I make you uncomfortable," he whispered. "I'm new to all this."

My heart fluttered. "I'm not used to someone being so nice to me."

His eyebrows knitted. "You're kidding, right?"

My first reaction was to shove him away for making fun of me, but the sincerity in his eyes hit home. "I don't date much." My face got hot again.

He smiled and then ducked his head, crimson staining his cheeks. "Me neither."

"What?" I asked. "I don't believe that. A guy like you must have women lined up."

The crimson darkened. "No, this is all very new. I've never met anybody like you."

"You mean a witch surrounded by crazy werewolves who all act like my older brothers?"

His laugh was light but real. "Well, yeah, there is that. I was thinking more along the lines of meeting somebody I wanted to get to know." He lifted his chin and stared into my eyes. "Somebody special."

Goner. Toast. History. Done. He had me.

He leaned forward and pressed a kiss to my forehead. "Am I coming on too strong? Tell me if I'm pushing too much." He nibbled his bottom lip like he was expecting me to reject him.

I wrapped my fingers in his hair and pulled him close. "I'm really, really glad you came."

His smile could have lit up the world. It did light up mine. "You're all I've thought about since I crashed my bike."

"You didn't crash it. The Malandanti ran you off the road." Of all those heartfelt words he'd just shared, leave it to me to latch onto the Malandanti.

He caressed my cheek with the back of his hand. "I have never felt like-- What did you say?" The gentleness was gone from his voice and a surge of power filled the room.

"About what?"

He shook his head like it was full of cobwebs. "Malandanti?"

Oh shit. *Way to ruin the moment, Welker.* "Yeah, on the mountain road that night. That was Malandanti activity."

He sat heavily in my cheap wooden kitchen chair and rubbed his temples. It was a safe bet he hadn't heard anything about the Malandanti activity. Simon had spoken with the Italian Alpha, who apparently didn't think that tidbit of info important enough to share with his pack.

All the sparkle was gone from Lucas's eyes. "How do you know it was Malandanti?"

"I'm a recon soldier. We gather intel on all supernaturals and I can feel black magic before the wolves or vampires smell it."

"Why would they be after me?"

I took his hand. "Sacrifices are the way they strengthen their magic. An Alpha's son would make a powerful offering."

He looked at me, his face etched with pain and anger. "My brother disappeared a year ago."

Chapter 18

Lucas

My father had known about possible Malandanti sightings yet hadn't mentioned it. Why the hell would he not share information like that with his pack? Or if not the pack, at least with me? My mother would need to be protected, the Divine Council notified. There were so many things that needed doing, yet he had done nothing. Even if he had chosen not to believe Major DuChard's information, my father should have told Mom and me.

If that wasn't bad enough, I only had three days left with Breanna. The thought of not seeing her made me sick. What had I been thinking coming here? She was everything I'd ever wanted and everything I couldn't have. She had a life, a career, and though not blood-related, Bravo was her family. More importantly, she was happy here. She had everything she needed without me coming along and screwing up her life. She'd already had several run-ins with her fellow soldiers because of me. That couldn't be good for her safety when they were on missions.

I tried to be quiet while stepping through the front door of Galen's guesthouse. It was about three in the morning and Trist would be asleep.

"Hey, buddy, how'd it go?" Tristyn called over the chatter of the television.

"Why are you still up?"

Tristyn held up a phone. "Your girl called. She was worried about you, said you weren't answering your phone."

My phone was in my jacket pocket. "My father kept texting, so I turned it off when we were working on her floor."

"While you were doing what?"

I snatched a beer from the fridge and collapsed into the recliner. Trist stretched on the couch, watching a hockey game.

"We laid tile in her bathroom."

"That was one hell of a romantic first date. What's tomorrow? Plumbing the kitchen?"

I took a slug of beer. "If that's what she wants to do."

Trist crinkled his forehead. "Why are you in a foul mood? I thought you'd come back floating."

I shrugged. I didn't want to talk about it. She was perfect and I was an idiot. What was I thinking? I had permission to visit, but couldn't stay in another pack's territory. This couldn't be permanent.

The phone hit my lap. "You need to call her," Tristyn said, sounding annoyed.

I snarled at his toss. "Yeah, I will."

"Now," Tristyn insisted. "She'll be over here if she doesn't hear from you."

I stared at the phone. "It was a mistake for me to come here."

Trist looked at me like I had three heads. "What the hell is wrong with you? I thought you had a great time with Breanna."

"I did."

"So what's the mistake?"

"It can't work between us."

"Why?"

I threw the phone across the room. "Because I'm a damn pack wolf and can't live here."

"Galen likes you. Why couldn't you live here?"

"My father will never release me to join the Wisconsin Pack. He would rather I go lone wolf and get killed than join another pack."

Tristyn retrieved the phone from the corner. "Fine. She can live in Italy. I know it isn't as safe for a witch, but she's more than capable of taking care of herself and, with you, she'd be fine."

"That would take her away from her career. Bravo is her family and I wouldn't ask her to choose me over them."

Tristyn made a sarcastic face. "That's very unselfish of you, little brother, but don't you think she should have some say in this? And while we are on this topic, isn't it a little early in your relationship to be deciding your future living arrangements?"

"She's the one."

Instead of a snappy comeback, Tristyn sat in the recliner beside me. "You know that already?"

I did. She was the one I had been searching for my whole life. I had known the first night I saw her. The way she touched me, the way she looked at me. She was the one. It was crazy how everything happened so fast and now it was clear how cruel fate could be. I'd finally found her and I couldn't have her.

Tristyn bumped my knee with the phone. "I'll do some research and find a way around your dad. Do you think Galen would let you stay in his territory as a lone wolf?"

"Maybe, but that wouldn't be fair to ask. My father would shit a brick and I don't want to cause problems for Galen. I can't even go lone wolf unless I'm released from the Italian Pack."

"You could challenge Josef."

"One of us would die."

Tristyn let out a breath. "Give it some time. Things will work out. Hell, look what Alexandria and I went through to be together. If it wasn't for you, we would have never made it. There's a way for you to be with Breanna. We'll find it." He tossed the phone in my lap. "Call her."

Breanna didn't answer. I stepped onto the porch and called her again. The phone went to voicemail. I fumbled around for the keys to the SUV and headed back to her house. The Suburban's accelerator was on the floor while the knot in my stomach tightened.

Everything was dark. All seemed quiet. Four miles from Breanna's house, the urge to turn down an unnamed side road was overwhelming. Immediately the glare of my headlights fell upon a kneeling form in the middle of the road.

I knew it was her without seeing her face. My wolf knew. A wolf would always recognize his mate.

Breanna shielded her eyes from the light. When she realized I was driving, she dashed to the driver's door.

"We gotta get him to Galen. He's hurt."

I jumped out the door and followed her to the whimpering wolf. From the looks of it, he'd run out in front of a car. Blood trickled from his mouth. His eyes were glassy. If this was a pack wolf, Galen would already know he was hurt and should have been on his way.

Breanna was stroking the wolf's fur as if he were a harmless pet. I knelt beside her and the wolf growled, his lips pulled back, showing shiny white teeth.

"Calm down. This is Lucas. You remember me telling you about him?"

Silver-green eyes flickered toward me before settling on her. My wolf growled at the gentleness with which she touched the injured one. She should not have been touching another wolf. She was mine.

A sharp slap on my arm startled both me and my wolf. "Don't scare him, Lucas. He's just a kid. Help me get him in the truck. I've called Galen. He's not answering."

Get him in the truck? I didn't help other wolves and I definitely didn't touch them.

"Have you got a blanket or anything in that monster vehicle?" she asked as she adjusted a homemade splint on the injured wolf's leg.

"Uh, no I don't think so," I stammered.

She made an annoyed face. "Fine, we'll make do." She whipped off her jacket to reveal the most incredible arms. They were long and smooth, muscled and tan. I'd never really noticed a woman's arms. Breanna's were magnificent. She had a small tattoo of two crossed swords surrounded by a ring of fire. It was the same tattoo I'd seen on the wolves during the challenges.

"Lucas?"

I was staring. "How are we going to get him in the back?" I wasn't touching him.

She looked at me like I was a fruit bat. "You can pick him up."

"He's a pack wolf," I choked as Breanna stared at me with those mesmerizing amber eyes.

"No, he's not. He's newly turned and new here. Now get over here and help me get him in the truck. I'll hold his head."

I swallowed my protests and scooped the wolf into my arms. He rumbled. I ignored it, instead focusing on the beautiful woman at his head as she talked to the injured wolf in a low, soothing voice.

I laid him in the cargo compartment and Breanna hopped onto the tailgate.

"What are you doing?"

"Riding with him," she snapped. "Let's go. I'll call Galen again."

She eased the wolf's head onto her leg and I slammed the tailgate closed. Her hands on another wolf drove me mad. I couldn't look at her touching him without wanting to rip his head off. I focused on the road as we sped toward Galen's house.

Mine. Mine. Mine.

The steering wheel cracked in my hands. The drive to Galen's seemed much longer than it should have. Maybe I missed a turn?

Breanna's head was down, her face turned toward the wolf lying on her jacket. The messy way her hair spilled around her face was mind-numbing and those perfect lips would feel so good against mine.

The "thwack" sound of the tires running off the road jerked me back to the reality of the situation. She was chattering to Galen.

"Galen's calling you," she yelled from the back.

Sure enough, Galen's call came through within seconds. His voice was crisp and clear as he gave directions to the medical containment area on his property.

We arrived in ten minutes and Galen was pacing outside the cement building. Several pack wolves, some of whom I recognized from the pack breakfast, were leaning against the wall waiting for our arrival.

Breanna had the window down and the tailgate dropped before I got out of the driver seat. She barked orders at the approaching wolves as Galen placed his hands on the injured wolf. They used a backboard and eased the black wolf out of the cargo compartment and into the building. Breanna was beside Galen, the eyes of the injured wolf locked onto her.

She belongs here. She loves them.

I slammed the tailgate closed. My wolf rumbled and the werewolves standing outside looked over at me. Galen wouldn't be out for a while and, in all likelihood, neither would Breanna. I ran my hand through my hair and took a frustrated swing at a nearby oak tree. Shards of pain quickly spread across my knuckles and up my arm, but it was a welcome distraction from the knots in my stomach and the pounding in my head.

"You're a piece of work, Benelli." The werewolf with the hateful blue eyes strode out of the darkness toward me. "Leave it to Bre to find someone so fucked up."

Aaron. The fast one who had caught me in the face with a wicked kick and the one who had tried to challenge over a glass of milk at breakfast. He stopped a few feet short and extended his hand.

"If she likes you, I guess we'll have to give you a chance. I'm Aaron Miller."

I looked at his hand and then back to his eyes. Surprisingly there was no silver.

He shrugged and dropped his hand. "Yep, you are one fucked-up werewolf." He took a step closer. My wolf surged as his anger flooded my nostrils. "Don't hurt her or we will kill you."

Two other werewolves, including the mountain I had fought during the challenges, ambled toward us. I was the dominant wolf but they were a pack. They took care of one another. If one fought, the others watched his back. It was the way of werewolves--well, except for me.

The pack wolves fanned out in front of me. I crossed my arms and leaned against the tree. They didn't want me here. I didn't want to be here, but Breanna was inside and I would not leave without her.

Tristyn called and offered to come over and wait with me. I needed to do this alone. How would I ever be with Breanna if I couldn't deal with the soldiers in her unit? They were not threatening. Actually, they were trying to talk to me. One asked about the size of the Italian Pack while another wanted to know what Italian pizza was like. The drum of my heartbeat drowned out most of their words. I shoved my hands behind my back so they wouldn't see the tremors in my body. These wolves were too close. It was hard to breathe.

The door rattled open and a wolf I'd never seen stepped into the light. He wasn't much taller than me and had the same build as Galen. The wolves dipped their heads as he walked out. I took a couple of steps away from the tree.

"Kid's gonna be fine thanks to Breanna," the sandy-haired thirty-something werewolf said. "A few broken bones but nothing vital. Dad's staying with him tonight. Everyone else can go home."

The man came toward me. I met his eyes. He kept walking until he was only a few feet in front of me. "Breanna will be out in a couple of minutes. She's getting Levi to change to human form for Dad and then she'll be here. She wanted me to let you know."

"Thanks," I managed to grind out in spite of his proximity.

"I'm Cody McGregor." The lanky werewolf nodded politely. "Welcome to Wisconsin Pack Territory."

"Lucas Benelli."

Cody raised an eyebrow. My dominance was flooding him and it was taking all my concentration not to hyperventilate. My wolf was on full alert. I balled my fists and slammed them into my jacket pockets.

"If you need anything while you're here, give me a call. Bre has my number."

Why did she have his number? Had he been out with her? Had he touched her? Did she have feelings for him? I hated the ease with which this other wolf had used her name. Breanna was mine.

The wolf nodded and went back inside. I stayed against the tree, mulling his words and fighting with my wolf. The smell of musk was like a cattle prod, every whiff making me jump. More and more wolves were arriving and I was gnawing on my fist to keep control.

When I was about to lose it and dash into the darkness, the door cracked open and Breanna slipped out. My wolf wanted to howl.

"Hey you," she called softly as she closed the door behind her. Then a miracle happened. She walked past the wolves straight into my arms. It was like they weren't there. She was looking for me.

"Thanks for waiting for me." She pressed a kiss against my cheek. "I'm sorry I snapped at you earlier. Levi's a special case. He's the wolf we found in Paraguay."

The wolves against the wall were staring at us. I met their eyes and dared them to come closer.

Mine.

She smiled shyly and my knees turned to jelly. "Levi's a kid and when he gets scared, his wolf takes over. I never did figure out why he was out by himself."

She snuggled into my chest, the hint of strawberries tickling my nose. God, she was beautiful. "Is he going to be okay?"

Her cheek rubbed against my chest as her head bobbed. "Yep, just needs rest and some attention from Galen."

She cupped my jaw gently. "Are you all right?"

I brushed a kiss onto the top of her head. "I am now."

Her arms tightened around me and my wolf settled. I couldn't live without this, without her. Whatever it took, I'd make it work. I pulled her against my chest and closed my eyes. I'd found heaven.

"Do you want to stay in the guesthouse tonight? There's plenty of room." She looked tired. "I'll sleep on the couch," I offered, not wanting to offend her.

She smiled and curled her fingers in my hair. "I'd better go home. If I'm here, the wolves will sleep on your porch."

Oh yeah, forgot about that pack thing. "I'll drive you home."

We held hands on the drive home and I escorted her to her door. My wolf was already fuming about leaving. Maybe I could sleep on her porch.

"If I didn't have to go to work tomorrow, I'd invite you in."

She caressed my jaw and I think I purred. She looked into my eyes and I swear she could see everything I thought.

"Will you call when you have a break?" Even with dark circles forming under her eyes, she was still stunning.

"It will probably be well after lunch. We've got New Recruit Day and usually work through lunch."

I tried not to show how disappointed I was at not having breakfast and lunch with her. She had a career. I had to respect that.

"We'll do dinner," I said as she unlocked her door. "By the way, how did you find that wolf in the road?"

She looked over her shoulder and her cheeks were pink. "I, was, um, well, I was going to check on you."

I grinned. She'd been checking on me? "Think I got lost?" I asked as her face got redder.

"I don't want anything to happen to you."

With those soft words, she ripped away all my defenses. I pulled her into my arms and allowed my wolf to surge as she melted against me and held on.

"I'm glad you're here," she whispered. "I really like you."

"I really like you, too," I answered without letting go.

My heart stopped as I tucked her hair behind her ear. There was no judgment, no accusation, no disdain from her. *Please, God, don't let this be a dream. Please let her be real.*

"Thank you for coming here," she whispered.

I cupped her jaw and she pressed a kiss into my palm. I couldn't form a coherent sentence. All I could do was hold on to the most precious thing I'd ever known.

It was hard to say goodbye but the sun was sneaking over the horizon and she needed to rest. I trudged to the truck and waved as she closed her door. It was a forty-five minute drive to Galen's, but it took me over an hour. When I arrived at the guesthouse, Galen was sitting on the porch steps, watching the sunrise.

"Good morning, Lucas."

"Good morning, Alpha," I answered with my eyes down. His dominance was stifling, even outdoors.

Galen placed a hand on my shoulder and it took everything I had not to drop to my knees.

"Thank you for helping the youngster last night. He wouldn't have made it had you not brought him to me."

"Breanna told me what to do."

Galen let out a belly laugh and slapped me on the back. "Oh dear, my boy. You have no idea what you're getting into, do you?"

"She's a witch. I know that."

Galen gave me one look and I instantly regretted my tone. "She's not just a witch, Lucas. That woman can command an army with a flick of her finger. Every wolf in Bravo would die for her."

"I meant no disrespect, Alpha McGregor." Could I not do anything right?

"Why don't you get some rest and we'll go watch the new recruits try out for Bravo?" Galen was asking. As usual, it wasn't really a question.

"Breanna said she wouldn't be able to have lunch today anyway."

Galen guffawed and started to walk away. "I'll be back around eleven. Tristyn is welcome to come along if he wants." The Alpha stopped and looked over his shoulder. "You met Cody last night?"

I nodded, keeping my head down. I felt like the most submissive wolf on the planet when I was around Galen. That pissed me off.

"He thought he offended you. Something about Breanna having his number?"

I didn't respond. What could I say? Cody was the Alpha's son and I was nobody. And only an idiot lied to a werewolf.

Galen watched intently, one eyebrow cocked. "Did Cody offend you?"

My wolf rumbled as I met Galen's eyes. "Yes."

The eyebrow went higher.

Chapter 19

Breanna

The screeching Donald Duck alarm clock meant it was time to tug on my fatigues. I was due on base at zero nine hundred for New Recruit Day, the day when all the supernaturals who want to join Bravo Company came for tryouts.

The newbies separated into two groups. Simon and I each took a group and went toe-to-toe with the wannabes. Later, we compared notes and evaluated the potential of each candidate. The majority of new recruits were werewolves. There were usually a few vampires. I was the only non-werewolf or non-vamp who had ever tried out. Simon had added an "other" category to the sign-up sheets because of me.

"Hey, Bre," Aaron called as I strolled through the groups of new recruits. Musk was heavy in the oversized gym, as was the smell of hot, sweaty bodies. The testosterone could have choked a moose.

I ignored Aaron and made my way to Simon. A few of the recruits growled as I passed. They all liked to talk about what they would do to the witch and none of their suggestions involved dinner and a movie. In the past, the comments would infuriate me. Now I just smiled. I'd do my talking in a few minutes.

"Oh, Bre, I said hello," Aaron snipped as he loped alongside me.

"Go away."

He didn't. "Where's the pizza maker?"

WTF? "Aaron, get away from me or I'll kick your ass in front of everyone," I snarled low enough only he could hear.

Aaron cocked his head. "Yeah, right."

I turned and he scurried toward Ordy, who was putting the recruits into groups.

"Greetings, my dear," Simon called suavely. "I trust your evening went well?"

"I need to talk to you about that." I had jotted down some notes when Lucas was going over his brother's disappearance and wanted to run the intel by Simon.

"Your evening was not pleasant?" Simon asked, looking very confused.

"Oh, yeah, Lucas was, um, well, he was great. I mean we had a good time." I shook my head, realizing what my words sounded like. "Oh, no, not like that kind of good time, I mean we spent time on my floor."

Simon arched an eyebrow. Oh damn.

"No, not like that. I mean, he was helping fix the tile in the bathroom." Simon tilted his head. "He worked on your floor?"

Oh, geez, this was not the conversation I wanted to be having before I squared off with werewolves who thought I was a squeaky toy. "I'll explain later, all right? Just tell me which group I have."

"Two."

Simon introduced me and the whistles abounded. A few of them came from the newbies but most came from my unit. They knew how much that ticked me off. A particularly mouthy and large wolf from the first group complained about the unfairness of having to fight Simon while his friend got a free pass because he was in my group.

"Hey, you," I called to the obnoxious wolf. Behind me, my unit whooped. "What's your name?"

He bared his teeth. My unit went wild, whooping and clapping when the idiot took a step toward me in a pathetic attempt to intimidate. Dumbass thought the cheering was for him.

"As your ranking superior, I expect your respect and compliance."

He rolled his eyes.

Oh, how I hated the eye roll. I looked at Simon and he nodded slightly.

I looked at the wolf's name patch and then straight into his hazel eyes. "Let's go, Edmondson. If you can take me, you're in Bravo."

He scoffed. "Yeah, right."

"She's right, Edmondson. If you can take her, you're in," Ordy echoed as he closed the distance between us. "That's how I got in."

Ordy winked at me. Yep, he had challenged me and my first roundhouse kick had sent him flying over the ropes and into the crowd. He didn't tell Edmonson that part.

I leaped into the ring and held the ropes. Edmondson bounded over the corner post like it was nothing, apparently insulted by my offer to hold the ropes for him. He bounced, aching to engage what he mistakenly believed was a weaker adversary. He was about to learn a life lesson.

Edmondson made a kissy face at me. I laughed. My unit catcalled. The new recruits let out howls of support for their comrade, who stood directly across from me. The dull gray room was electric and I loved it.

I bowed to Simon, nodded to Ordy, and patted my chest twice over my heart as a salute to my unit. A big "*bu yah*" echoed throughout the training area as Bravo Company responded to my acknowledgement.

The power of an Alpha surged through the room, Galen undoubtedly hiding somewhere in the dark seats. He often came and watched New Recruit Day. It was like a scouting report for him, checking out potential new pack members before he had to deal with them one on one.

Edmondson was bouncing on the balls of his feet, his eyes flaked with silver. He was a big wolf, standing a formidable six-three and weighing around two-forty-five. He dwarfed my five-eleven frame but I was faster and, though he didn't believe it yet, a hell of a lot better trained.

Chants of "Bre, Bre, Bre," rose from the rafters as Edmonson and I began to circle. He was predictable and typical werewolf, relied too much on his size and strength. He dove, I darted. He lunged, I sidestepped. Simon tapped his watch and I took control, three spinning whipkicks followed by a groin shot and a nasty uppercut.

Edmondson hit the mat like an oak. I straightened my hair and leaped over the ropes. When he woke, Edmondson would have a headache the size of Texas and he'd have to take a lot of ribbing from his buddies, but unless Simon overrode me, I'd let the brawny werewolf into Bravo. He was arrogant and cocky. He was also strong and, with the right training, he'd make a good addition to our already extremely cocky and arrogant group of werewolf soldiers. Every one of our present soldiers had challenged me when they tried out for Bravo. Once they'd had their heads handed to them like I'd just done to Edmondson, they'd been more than ready to buy into our rather unorthodox regime.

My guys whooped and yelled, chants of "witch" filling the air. The new recruits sat in stunned silence.

"Anyone else doubt Master Sergeant Welker?" Simon asked the group of newbies.

I waited, hands on my hips, for any of them to step up. Nobody took the challenge.

I gave a little bow to my commanding officer once again before taking my group of recruits to the far corner of the training area. Celeste arrived to tend to the groggy Edmondson.

As my group meandered toward our ring, I looked into the high seats and tried to find Galen. He had an uncanny ability to hide in plain view, an Alpha mojo magic thing I guess. I wouldn't see him unless he wanted to be seen.

It was almost sixteen thirty before our day with the recruits was done. I'd taken a couple of shots and would have some bruises, but none of my blood stained the mats. I considered it a good day.

The day would be better once I talked to Lucas. I'd missed hearing his voice today.

I was sitting cross-legged on the mat, putting the finishing touches on my reports, when a surge of power washed over me. It felt like Galen, sorta. More like Galen on steroids.

"Hi, beautiful," he said in a lyrical voice thick with Italian accent. Sparkling brown eyes flaked with a tiny bit of silver met mine as I looked up to find Galen, Lucas, and Tristyn approaching.

"Hi, handsome," I responded, my heart rate tripling as I jumped to my feet. He swallowed me in a hug and gingerly touched my bruised cheek.

"Ouch," he empathized as his fingers brushed the red skin under my eye. His arm tightened as he whispered in my ear. "You were amazing." He lifted me slightly off the floor.

When my feet touched the floor, I let out a breath. "How long have you been here?"

He nuzzled my hair and my hormones started to fire. "Since about noon. Galen invited us to come along and watch the new recruits."

Galen laughed good-naturedly. "I told Lucas he needed to know what he was getting into." My face got hot--really, really hot--as Galen continued. "When that first wolf went after you, Lucas wanted to go down and save you. I told him you wouldn't appreciate his interference, but it still took both Tristyn and me to stop him."

That explained the silver flakes in Lucas's eyes. "So, you saw all of it?" I asked, realizing there was no hope of convincing him I was Barbie in camo.

Tristyn grinned. "Galen's not kidding about it taking all of us to hold him back. He was ready to kill that first wolf who took a swing at you."

Lucas snorted, his breath tickling against my ear. I closed my eyes and drew in a deep whiff of musk and leather. The countdown to me pulling him onto the floor and ripping his clothes off began.

The moment ended when Lucas tensed, a growl rumbling in his chest. I didn't need to open my eyes to know it was Aaron. Lucas tightened his arms around me, his wolf surging in a blatant display of possessiveness. Countdown aborted--or at least delayed.

"Shhh, he's no threat," I said softly, hoping the others wouldn't hear. Lucas's breathing was ragged, almost panting, as Aaron came closer. Lucas murmured something in Italian.

Galen intervened. "Aaron, don't you have somewhere to be other than here?"

"Yes, he does," Simon bellowed. "Miller, to the range."

Aaron didn't flinch. Lucas postured, every cell in his body poised for a fight. Tristyn stepped between the two wolves to break the intense eye contact. Galen placed a hand on Aaron's shoulder. Lucky thing, I was about to stomp Aaron into the floor myself.

"Easy, Wolf." Lucas lowered his head until his forehead rested against mine. "Shh, that's good," I said as his body relaxed and his breathing slowed. His wolf was fearless, quick to fight, and difficult to control. Lucas and his wolf had only threads of an uneasy truce. Neither totally trusted the other. I'd never felt this kind of struggle in a werewolf before.

Ordy marched over and grabbed Aaron by the arm. Galen nodded his approval. Ordy didn't look at Lucas or me when he retrieved Aaron and led him to the double glass doors that opened onto the firing range.

"Bonjour, Ambassador Ziccardi, Alpha McGregor, and Monsieur Benelli." Simon nodded in his typical eloquent greeting.

"Bonjour, Master DuChard," Tristyn responded quickly with a nodding flourish of his own. "Please, call me Tristyn."

Lucas was best buddies with an Ambassador. Damn, I felt out of place. "Hey, Simon," Galen said. "What'd you think of this crew of recruits?"

Galen and Simon discussed the newbies as the five of us walked up the hall toward the offices. Lucas had a death grip on my hand as we passed multiple groups of werewolves. They all gave us a wide berth and none made eye contact with Lucas. A muscle ticked in his jaw as we passed a laughing group of my guys.

Tristyn walked casually beside Lucas, either unaware or unfazed by the hostility his buddy was giving off. Tristyn leaned forward to see me around Lucas's broad chest. "Your combat skills are quite impressive, Breanna. You're not only quick, but your accuracy is amazing."

"Thanks. I learned from the best."

Lucas stopped glaring at the passing wolves long enough to question me. "And who would that be?"

He was cute when he was jealous. "Simon," I answered. "I trained with him over a year before I made it into Bravo Company and then it took another seven before I was good enough to be promoted to a lead combat instructor."

"Oh," he groused before resuming the uber-dominant "don't come near my woman" looks.

"So Lucas tells me you are an earth witch?" Tristyn asked politely as we turned the corner toward Simon's office.

I nodded. "And you are an Ambassador?"

His face lit up. "Yes. I work for the Divine Council as the Ambassador for Supernatural Relations."

Well, that sounded important. "Supernatural Relations?"

Lucas chuckled. His steel-trap grip on my hand had loosened since we left the training area. "He talks to everyone."

Tristyn frowned at his friend. "I address issues, prevent various factions from killing one another, settle disagreements, and whatever else arises. Lucas and I were both agents until a little over a year ago. I took the ambassadorship and he stayed in the field until he was needed in Italy."

I tugged on his hand. "Why did you leave the Divine Council?"

He shrugged and dropped my hand. "Does it matter? I'm not an agent anymore."

If there hadn't been the hint of sadness in his voice, the bluntness would have bothered me. I had obviously hit a nerve.

"Do you have time to talk to Simon about your brother?" I asked as we stepped through the open office door.

Lucas drew in a ragged breath before slowly agreeing. He unclenched his fist and reached for my hand. I met him halfway, slipping my fingers through his.

"I didn't mean to snap at you," he whispered. "I'm just not accustomed to--"

"I know," I interrupted. "Me neither." He smiled but there was sadness in his eyes. "You can trust Simon and if there's anyone who can help us find your brother, it's him."

His arms slipped around my waist and I found the curls brushing his collar. "Us?" he breathed in my ear. "That's the best thing I've heard in a long time."

I planted a kiss on the end of his nose. I really liked "us," too.

We talked to Simon for over an hour before heading out in search of food. After grabbing a couple burgers and shakes, we dropped by my house for me to take a shower and change clothes.

"What did you want to do tonight?" he asked when I emerged squeaky clean and dressed in jeans and a sweatshirt.

One look at him sent my heart into overdrive. His nostrils flared slightly, no doubt scenting my arousal. Embarrassed enough to want to bury my head in the sand, I chose that moment to rearrange the flowers he bought for me.

I chewed my lip. "There's no hockey tonight. How about we rent a movie or something?"

He crossed the room and placed his hands on my hips, his chest pressing against my back. "What would you like to see?"

Oh, hell, that was one loaded question.

If it was possible to die of embarrassment, I was about to do it. "*Transformers*," I blurted out, snatching the flowers around.

"Cool. I loved the first one. Have you seen the second one?" he asked. "I haven't."

"The second one would be great. There's one of those box things down at the corner. I'll run down there and get it."

I whirled away and grabbed my wallet from the bar. As I reached for the door, I glimpsed the confused look on his face.

"I'm pushing you, aren't I?"

My heart threatened to break into a thousand pieces. He had that scared kid look again.

"No, you aren't pushing me," I answered, my hand falling from the knob to hang limply at my side. "I react so strongly to you and, to be honest, it scares me a little."

"I'm sorry," he said, stepping away. "I didn't mean to upset you."

I clenched my eyes closed, wishing I was better in situations like this. I wasn't sure how to act, what to say, what to do. Hell, I wasn't even sure how I should be feeling.

"Do you want me to go?" Lucas asked tentatively.

A walk to the box to get the movie would be good for both of us. "That would be great."

He nodded curtly, grabbed his coat, and brushed past me. I darted out the door and ducked in behind him. He strode toward his truck and I skidded to a halt.

"It isn't that far. I thought we'd walk."

Lucas looked at me like I was a psycho with an ax. "What?"

"To get the movie."

His forehead crinkled. "I thought you wanted me to leave."

I opened and closed my mouth like a puppet. "No, no, no, I meant go with me to get the movie. Not go as in go away." My face began to burn as I realized how poor my communication skills really were. "I'm sorry, Lucas. I don't want you to go."

His eyebrows rose, his face a mask of confusion.

I banged my hand on my forehead. "Away. I don't want you to go away."

I felt about three inches tall. Lucas closed the distance between us and took my hand as his warm breath tickled my face. "That's good to hear, because I didn't really want to leave."

His smile was genuine and kind in the face of my blunder. I swallowed hard, gathered my courage and looked into his eyes. "I'm not so good at this kind of thing."

"At what?" The back of his hand brushed along my jaw and I shivered. My damn chin would not stop trembling. "Feelings crap."

"Me neither."

Lost, totally and completely lost in his eyes, I didn't try to speak. What was there to say?

"You are so beautiful," he murmured. The warmth of his body blanketed me, the gentleness of his touch raising goosebumps along my arms. His hands drifted along my back, caressing, pulling me closer.

My knees turned to jelly when our lips met, his mouth covering mine with tenderness and wanting. My fingers curled in his shirt, urging him closer, needing to feel the hardness of his chest against mine.

"We'll go slow, okay?" he whispered, pulling back to look into my face.

Slow was about the last thing my body wanted right now. I buried my face in his neck, the scent of musky male mixed with leather igniting the slow burn spreading through my body.

I tangled my hands in his hair and tugged his lips to mine. He growled, scooping me into his arms and carrying me toward the front porch. I should have objected to the manhandling, but everything in me wanted him, craved him, needed him.

And it felt really good to be held without worrying about name, rank, and serial number.

Chapter 20

Lucas

We were five steps from the porch when the sound of a car engine broke the stillness. Two steps from the front door, her arms tightened around my neck.

I didn't make it inside before they called to her.

"Hey, Breanna! Can we talk to you a minute?"

I froze, my back to whoever had ruined this magical, perfect moment. I tried not to growl, holding her tighter, unwilling to share.

"Not now, fellas," Breanna snipped, burying her head in my neck.

Footsteps pattered up the sidewalk toward us. My muscles bunched, prepared to defend against an attack that never came.

"Actually, we wanted to speak to the Italian."

Her head never moved from my shoulder. "Too bad. He's mine tonight. You can talk to him tomorrow."

Her words almost brought me to my knees. She wanted me.

The footsteps came closer and she stiffened. My wolf roared to life, the need to protect my mate overwhelming.

Mate?

"Towsky, you guys need to go away. I'm not in the mood to play your stupid reindeer games tonight," Breanna said over my shoulder. "Lucas is mine." She leaned up and glared at the werewolves behind me. "Leave."

I was hers?

More footsteps approached. Breanna took a big breath and I set her gingerly on her feet. "I am so gonna kill somebody tonight," she said low enough only I could hear.

Had a group of six werewolves not been closing in on us, her comment would have been amusing. There was no fear on her part, the scent of her anger filling the crisp night air.

"They are part of Trenton's unit," she bit out. "This is not a social visit."

I allowed my wolf to surge, my dominance stopping the approaching wolves in their tracks. Breanna nodded her approval before addressing the group.

"What the hell do you want?" she asked the apparent leader of the group. His gaze landed squarely on me.

"We want to talk to him."

Breanna's head tilted. "Why?"

"Werewolf business."

The werewolf probably had no idea how bad an answer he had given. Breanna's sharp intake of breath was the only physical indication she was about to make these werewolves very sorry for their actions.

She glared at the group. "Galen said Lucas was to be left alone, that he had earned the right to be in this territory. Leave now and nobody gets hurt."

A smaller wolf in the back let a chuckle slip. Bad, bad idea.

The fire in her fingertips scorched my skin. She dropped my hand and took a single step toward the group. They parted, except the chuckler, who apparently was not familiar with Breanna's powers.

"Wolf nuts roasting on an open fire," she said in an icy voice. "Witch sparks nipping at your nose."

The werewolf wasn't laughing anymore. He looked left and right, noticed his fellow soldiers had backed away from him, then squared his shoulders and took a step toward Breanna. A fireball landed at his feet and he yelped. He leaped sideways, roared a curse, and charged.

The world lost its color, turning to shades of black and gray as my wolf responded to the attack. Breanna braced for the charging wolf but I met him first, grabbing his shirt and tossing him to the side.

The air exploded as the remaining five wolves attacked. With Breanna at my side, the attacking wolves didn't stand a chance. The fire I expected to see flare from her fingers never materialized--instead she became a whirling combat machine with kicks and punches coming faster than the wolves could counteract.

I took out three while she easily handled the other two. By the time the air settled, I had a bloody lip, she had a bruise on her cheek, and the wolves were all down for the count.

"Assholes," she snarled as the last wolf rolled away, grimacing in pain.

"What did they want?"

She shrugged. "Probably Trenton's doing. He's never liked me."

"Why?" I asked, brushing my hand across her hair. All the wolves seem so dedicated to her.

She sucked in a big breath. Apprehension rolled from her in waves. "I killed his brother."

There was no way I was going to ask her to explain.

She tightened her grip on my waist and rubbed her cheek against my chest. "I tried to get to him," she said, her voice breaking. "The Humvee was sinking and I got the guys in the back seat but the current was too strong." Her body went boneless in my arms. "By the time I made it back down, both of the werewolves in the front seat were dead. Trenton's brother, Isaac, was driving. He was a recon specialist, like me."

"You did all you could." She would have fallen had I let go. "You didn't kill him."

"I wasn't strong enough," she said hoarsely. "I tried to get back to him." Her voice muffled against my chest. "I swear I tried."

We stood in the yard for a long time, holding one another. A few snowflakes dusted her hair. She shuddered a few times and held on like her life depended on it. I'd never felt so helpless. Unable to do anything except hold her close and allow her emotions to run their course, I kept a watchful eye on the six wolves as they climbed to their feet and struggled back to their truck.

"You can't keep beating yourself up about this, Breanna," I offered softly when she began to stir in my arms. "You did your best."

"It wasn't good enough." The self-loathing in her voice was so out of character for the confident woman I had grown accustomed to.

"Could anyone else have saved him?"

"Doesn't matter what anyone else would have done. I'm the one who surfaced with a dead recon soldier."

A rustle in the bushes had us both leaping to our feet. Galen pushed aside the boxwoods and nodded a greeting. His power hit me when his eyes met mine.

"Isaac wasn't your fault, Breanna. Had he not disobeyed orders and driven on that road, none of them would have needed saving." Galen's voice resonated with the authority of an Alpha, though there was an edge of understanding, of kindness.

The vulnerability Breanna had shown was gone, the cool facade of an elite soldier now in place. She stood tall beside me, her grip on my hand strong. A part of me wanted to send her inside and deal with the Alpha on my own, but that would be wrong. She was at my side, where a mate should be.

And I hadn't had a panic attack when the werewolves surrounded me.

"What happened here?" Galen asked, looking directly at me.

My wolf settled, leaving me stammering for words. "Six wolves attacked us."

Galen's eyebrows shot up. "Unprovoked?"

Breanna kicked an imaginary rock. "I started it."

The big Alpha didn't believe her. "How did you start a fight, Breanna?"

"I threatened his nuts," she answered. "And he took offense."

Galen laughed heartily and clapped a gloved hand on my shoulder. I held my breath as his power coursed through my body. "From what I gathered, they were here to stir up trouble with Lucas. Your actions were acceptable given the circumstances."

"Circumstances?" I asked.

He looked at Breanna for a few seconds before turning back to me. The slight upturn of his lips made me uncomfortable. "I'll leave you two alone." He patted me on the shoulder again. "If you need me, either of you, don't hesitate to call."

Galen disappeared into the hedges, leaving Breanna and me sitting on the steps.

"Sorry I lost it," she muttered. "I hadn't thought about that night in a long time."

I draped my arm around her shoulders and pulled her close. "No need to apologize. That's what friends are for, to listen."

Her amber eyes sparkled. "Friends?"

I touched the silky soft skin along her neck. "Everybody needs somebody to listen. Somebody to trust."

Her cheeks went pink. "I can field strip an AK-47 with my eyes closed, can take down the meanest supernatural you put in front of me, but I don't know shit about relationships. I'm not exactly a princess."

"You're an angel."

She laughed to herself. "You must have recurring post-concussion syndrome from that motorcycle wreck."

How someone so beautiful could be so modest dumbfounded me.

And made me love her more.

Our shoulders bumped, her strawberry scent tickling my nose. I had never felt anything like this. I wanted her beside me for the rest of my life. My throat was tight, my heart hammering as my brain tried to find the right words to say.

"Want to go get that movie?" she asked with a half smile.

I took her hand and kissed her fingers. "Honestly?"

She nodded.

"No."

I stared into her eyes, praying I had not pushed her away. After an eternity of silence, she squeezed my hand and stood, tugging me up along with her.

"Me neither," she whispered as she led me toward the front door.

Chapter 21

Breanna

At any moment spontaneous combustion would occur. Everywhere Lucas touched me sizzled, his hands working me into a frenzy. The warmth of his body seeped into mine, the tenderness of his lips igniting inescapable need.

It didn't matter that I was a master sergeant or that I was a witch. Nothing mattered as he tugged my sweatshirt over my head and tossed it into the corner. Nothing mattered as I unbuttoned his shirt and ran my hands along the granite muscles of his chest.

Except Lucas.

His tongue danced with mine as he pulled me onto the bed beside him. A hot tingling between my legs turned to a slow burn as his fingers slid along my stomach. My hands trailed along the rippling muscles in his back and captured the firmness of the most incredible ass ever created.

He is so perfect.

The pressure of his body against mine was sinfully good, the feel of male desire sending my own need into the red zone. I now understood the stuff of romance novels. Hells bells, this was good.

Lucas growled when I grabbed his hair and pulled him toward me. He was gentle. I wanted wild, feral. Now.

My nails raking along his back made him tremble as he nipped the "send Breanna into orbit" place behind my ear. My hips arced toward him, demanding, pleading. The primal need to feel him inside me was out of control. I was out of control.

"Lucas," I cried, my body stretching to accept him, to consume him. He ground slowly against me, whispering my name as he surrendered to the passion of the moment. Throaty growls and the power of Alpha male sent me to oblivion.

The connection between us spiraled higher until we panted for breath, out bodies covered in sheens of well-earned sweat. I buried my head in his chest, the security of his arms the most blissful thing I'd ever felt. He brushed a kiss on the top of my head.

"Amazing," he said softly. "You are amazing."

"You're pretty damn amazing yourself," I mumbled into the ripped muscles of his chest.

His fingers found my chin and tipped my face toward him. "You are so beautiful." His fingers travelled along my neck. "An angel."

Before I could respond, his finger covered my lips. "And no, I did not hit my head again."

Lucas spooned around me, his chest pressed to my back. His leg rested possessively over mine, our interlocked hands curled against my chest. The feel of him made my soul happy. He wanted me. Me. And I wanted him. All of him.

He can't stay in Wisconsin. The son of an Alpha must remain with his pack.

I tucked our hands tighter against my chest. My heart wanted to feel him, as if holding him would make the real world go away. For now, the real world didn't matter. Lucas was in my bed, his head resting against my Pluto pillow. Everything was perfect.

* * * *

The annoyingly happy singing of an idiot bird perched on the windowsill woke me.

"Can it, Tweety," I muttered, rolling over to find the warmth of my wolf.

The only thing there was a cold spot.

"Lucas?"

Pluto grinned at me. I punched him.

I tucked the sheet around me and padded into the bathroom. Lucas had showered and was gone, long gone from the lack of steam on the mirror. At least he'd hung the damp towels back on the rack and not tossed them in the corner.

I prayed for some sound from the other side of the closed bedroom door, anything, a clink of a glass or the scrape of a fork. Hell, the stupid TV blathering would have been good, but there was nothing.

"Damn it." My heart did a nosedive. If I'd fallen for a one-and-done kind of guy, I would kick my own ass. Stupidly feeling the need to be quiet, I snuck into the hall toward the kitchen.

The constant tick of the cuckoo clock echoed from the hall.

"Oh, for the love of Mother Earth, please be here somewhere."

Nobody answered. No toe-curling Italian accent, no drop-dead sexy werewolf, no brown eyes that made me melt, nothing but the cuckoo clock and the steady hum of the refrigerator.

With the Pluto sheet dragging behind me, I trudged to the recliner, a big hole gaping in my chest. Anger would have been easier.

Sinking into the recliner and pulling my feet off the chilly floor, I buried my head against my knees. His lonely lost little boy look had done a number on me.

And I had fallen for it.

"Stupid, idiot, moron, dumbass." The damn cuckoo clock laughed at me.

I grabbed my phone from the bar. Should I call him? Would that be groveling? I did have my pride, though right now I'd trade every shred of it for a call from Lucas. Had I really been that wrong about him?

The cuckoo clock shrieked from the hall and I couldn't take it anymore.

Chapter 22

Lucas

My trip to find breakfast had taken longer than expected--however, I had real strawberries and pancakes. Breanna loved strawberries.

Watching her sleep, holding her, feeling her breath against my arm, all things I never thought possible for somebody like me, a screwed-up werewolf who couldn't feel pack bonds.

Boldly affectionate and fearlessly demanding, Breanna had taken me on the ride of my life last night. She wanted me. Me. And I could not live without her. The way it felt to have her arms wrapped around me. I could have lain in that bed forever if my stomach hadn't roared so loudly she rolled over.

As I pulled into her drive, a strange sensation crawled up my spine. Uneasiness, sadness, anger. My wolf stirred.

Breanna. Something was wrong.

The front door was ajar. My trip had taken almost an hour, and she had been sleeping peacefully when I left. A Pluto sheet pooled on the floor beside the recliner. The cuckoo clock lay in pieces on the hall floor. Picture frames hung crooked on the walls.

My heart pounded. The only scent was Breanna's, but she wasn't here. The doorknob crumbled in my hands as I plowed into the bedroom, yelling for her.

There were no sounds anywhere, her clothes tossed in the corner just as they had been when I left. The Pluto pillow was across the room. The nightstand lay on its side. Her phone was in three parts by the wall.

There was no blood, no fresh scent. My wolf surged as I ran room to room, praying she would answer. She didn't.

I ran around outside, looking for footprints or any sign of what may have happened. There was nothing out of place other than the slightly open front door. My phone shook as I called Tristyn.

"Is Breanna there?" Maybe she'd gone looking for me at the guesthouse. Why hadn't she called?

"No. Haven't seen her."

"Damn." My heart jumped to my throat.

"Luc, what's wrong?"

Tristyn listened while I relived the nightmare. By the time we hung up, I was pulling into Galen's drive. There were lots of cars in the parking area, but Galen's SUV was missing. The front door opened and Cody McGregor stepped into the light.

"Good morning, Lucas. Come for breakfast?"

Food was the last thing on my mind. "Is Breanna here?"

"No."

I swiped a hand through my hair. This could not be happening. More wolves spilled from the house and my stomach wretched. My already racing heart tried to beat out of my chest. Now was not the time for a panic attack. I backed toward the Suburban before turning quickly and jerking open the door.

The smell of musk intensified. "Hey, Lucas?"

The door handle crunched in my hand. "What?"

Cody pulled open the passenger side door. "I'll help you look for Breanna."

My wolf surged. "I don't need any help." Other werewolves didn't help me.

He acted like he didn't hear me. "I know the area."

There wasn't time to argue and he was more familiar with the area. My gut clenched at the thought of being so close to him inside the Suburban. Sitting as close to the door as I could, I turned the key and waited while he made a phone call.

"Let's go," he said, slamming the door. "She was on base an hour ago."

We checked the base. Breanna was gone. Her scent lingered strongest in the training area. The heavy aroma of musk and sweaty bodies kept my wolf on edge. Cody spoke with several werewolves while I talked to the vampires. They remembered seeing her earlier, but had no idea where she may have gone.

I walked around the base and picked up a faint whiff of strawberries. Getting down on my hands and knees, I followed the scent to a sidewalk leading off base. Satisfied the scent was Breanna's, I started walking.

Cody ran across the road and caught up with me. The startled look on his face meant he'd caught her scent also.

"I got it," I said with more of a growl than voice.

"Yeah, but you might need backup if something's wrong. I'll go with you."

What the hell? "Why?" My wolf surged.

"Damn, man, I'm just trying to help. Calm your ass down."

Help? He was trying to help? Nobody helped me.

Cody fell into step beside me. "This is the way Breanna walks home. Have you tried calling her?"

"Not since I got to Galen's."

Cody snorted. "Well, shit, check your phone. Maybe she's called or something. I tried, but got her voicemail."

I cut my eyes at him before jerking the phone out of my pocket. Cody looked back at me and nodded. "We'll find her."

The uneasy truce between my wolf and me settled. Cody wasn't threatening. Actually, there was a familiarity to him, like our paths had crossed at some point. His wolf was not as dominant as mine, but Cody was no submissive. He was, like me, the son of an Alpha, and it showed.

My phone displayed the missed calls. No Breanna.

"She hasn't called," I said, stopping in front a row of oak trees.

The squalling of tires, a Camaro barreling toward us, drowned out Cody's answer. I shoved Cody and jumped onto the hood just before the car slammed into the oaks.

"Holy shit," Cody exclaimed as he rolled to his feet. "Lucas, you all right?"

I landed on the hood, rolled over the roof, and splatted on the pavement behind the still-running car. I couldn't catch my breath and my clothes were torn. Nothing felt broken except my head.

I was shaking the cobwebs out when a military boot crushed my hand.

"I told you I'd kill you if you hurt her. You were warned."

The boot caught me under my chin before I could roll out of range. Stars and dots danced in front of my eyes as I tried to scramble away from the blows pummeling my head.

The hits stopped abruptly. "Aaron, what the hell is wrong with you?" Cody demanded. I managed to crawl toward the idling car.

Blood gushed from my nose and onto the pavement as the boots advanced toward me. I pulled myself up by the bumper and faced my attacker. His eyes were fully silver, his scent reeking of rage and musk. Aaron's wolf had fully ascended and he was coming after me.

My wolf surged, his anger and power whipping through me. This time I would kill Aaron.

"Aaron, stop." Cody's voice carried the authority of the Alpha.

"He hurt Breanna." Aaron glowered at me.

I readied for a charge, but Cody held out a hand for me to stay back. I considered pushing Cody out of the way and finishing the battle, but my wolf was willing to give the Wisconsin second-in-command a chance to handle the issue. Aaron belonged to him.

"Lucas?" Cody said without taking his eyes from Aaron. "Did you hurt Breanna?"

"No."

Cody put both his hands on Aaron's shoulders. Dominance filled the air. Aaron dropped to his knees and lifted his chin in submission. Slowly the silver diminished and Aaron closed his eyes.

"Aaron?" Cody urged him to stand.

Aaron bowed his head. "I did not mean to endanger you, Second."

Cody looked over at me. "Why do you think Lucas harmed Breanna?"

Aaron's eyes remained down. "When I saw her earlier, she was crying." He lifted his head and glared at me. "Breanna never cries."

Chapter 23

Breanna

I walked home. Alone. Past the cozy cottages and playing children, one foot in front of the other. With my pity party in full swing, I rounded the corner and walked headlong into the memory of my first bouquet of flowers. God, how did people live through things like this? I'd been shot, stabbed, choked, and fried with magic, and all that was nothing compared to this. I couldn't breathe without consciously thinking about it.

The front door was slightly open, as I'd left it when I flew out.

Hard to turn a doorknob with nothing but feathers.

Of course there was nobody inside. Why would there be? He was gone, probably already on a plane back to Italy. I'd made an absolute fool out of myself over him.

Suck it up, buttercup.

The door clicked closed behind me as I made my way toward the fridge. A grocery bag peeked from behind the bar.

"What the hell?"

I retrieved the bag and found three Styrofoam plates of pancakes and two containers of strawberries. A note waved at me from the fridge door.

Hey Babe,
Gone to get breakfast. Be right back.
L

If I'd been a screamer, I would have belted one. Why hadn't I seen this note before? I banged my head against the fridge.

Because I'd been busy pouting in the recliner.

Cursing at my own stupidity and clutching his note, I sprinted to the bedroom for my phone. The parts went back together, sorta. Lucas didn't answer.

"Damn it, damn it, damn it." I kicked my pile of clothes in the corner. Lucas must have thought I was the world's biggest bitch to run out on him after he'd left a note. I tried Galen. His phone went straight to voicemail.

My knuckles were bloody and bruised from the pounding I had laid on the heavy bag on base. I had spent hours flying around and beating a bag senseless because I thought Lucas was a one-night stand. The words on his note blurred as more tears fell. What the hell had I done?

Dashing out the door with phone in hand, I stopped at the end of my walkway. Where to go? Left would take me back to base. Right would take me to Galen's. Would either take me to Lucas?

"Oh shit, what if he's gone?" I didn't have Tristyn's number. Simon didn't answer. Lucas's phone went to voicemail. Galen's phone went to voicemail again.

Running out of options, I called Cody. He answered immediately.

"Cody, have you seen Lucas?" I asked.

Please say yes. Please say yes.

"Hold on a sec, Bre."

"Hold on?" He was putting me on hold? What the hell?

"Breanna?"

Oh God, it was Lucas. "Where are you?"

His breathing sounded labored and ragged. "Billingham Street."

"Stay there."

I turned left and sprinted toward the intersection three blocks away.

Blue police lights were flashing as I rounded the corner onto Billingham. A Camaro had plowed into the row of oaks surrounding Dorchester Pond. The human police officers were talking to Cody. The knot in my stomach tightened. Where was Lucas?

"Breanna?"

Lucas was standing behind an elm tree less than twenty yards away. I ran and leaped into his arms. Every muscle in my body constricted around him.

"Are you okay?" he asked.

"Uh huh."

His fingers trailed through my hair. God, I loved him. His scent, his body, his voice, everything about him. Everything.

"Where were you?" he asked. "I came back with breakfast, but you were gone."

No words formed yet. The oxygen hadn't reached my brain. He was here, really here, and I was the biggest idiot on the planet. How the hell would I explain this without sounding like a pathetic stupipod?

I am a stupipod.

He loosened his arms to allow me to slide to my feet. I held on tighter. It was immature, but I wasn't ready to admit my screw up. What the hell was wrong with me? I had no control around him. It was like a foreign Breanna took over and the real Breanna went away to a "special place." *WTF?*

"Baby, what is it?" He nuzzled my hair. I squeezed my eyes shut. Damn it, no more crying.

Between sniffles, I realized the crumpled Camaro belonged to Aaron. Cody was talking to a uniformed police officer while Aaron inspected the damage.

Lucas's stomach roared. His breakfast was on the floor in my kitchen. *Selfish, pathetic stupipod.*

"Let's get something to eat," I managed to sputter. Werewolves hated being hungry.

"My truck is on base," Lucas said as he helped me regain my footing.

I wiped my eyes with the heel of my hand. "Why are Aaron and Cody here?"

His face hardened for a moment, eyes flashing silver. "We were all looking for you."

On the ride to IHOP, Lucas listened quietly to my pitiful explanation of what had happened.

"It's okay," he said after I finished.

I let out a deep breath. "I'm an idiot."

He tenderly caressed my cheek. "You are the most beautiful thing in my life."

"You need to get out more." I chewed my lip.

IHOP had all-you-can-eat pancakes. Big mistake when there's a hungry werewolf at the table. We shared a bench in a booth. His leg bumped mine as we ate, my free hand resting on his thigh. I was feeding him a forkful of strawberry waffle when the thrum of Alpha power washed over us.

Chapter 24

Lucas

Breanna's hand tightened on my leg. We were in a corner booth far from the door, but the power of the Alpha touched us.

"What the hell does he want?" Breanna mumbled.

"Lucas, Breanna, may we join you?" Galen asked as he and Cody strode toward us. It wasn't really a question.

Breanna stiffened beside me, her strawberry scent tainted with uneasiness. I took her hand while Galen and Cody slid onto the bench across from us. Neither werewolf smelled angry, but Alphas could hide their true emotions.

"Alpha McGregor," I said with my eyes down. Breanna squeezed my hand.

"So tell me about the incident this morning," Galen said. His voice gave away nothing.

Breanna scooted closer. "Incident?"

My wolf was uneasy with her so close to the werewolves across the table.

Galen leaned forward, resting on his elbows. "Perhaps I should start." The big Alpha focused on me. "Thank you for saving my son this morning."

Breanna bumped my shoulder. "You didn't tell me anything happened."

It hadn't seemed important to tell her about Aaron trying to run over me. She would have only been upset.

"What would you have me do with Aaron?" Galen asked.

"Aaron?" Breanna croaked. "What does this have to do with--oh, damn, his car this morning? I thought he was helping look for me."

Cody snorted. "Yeah, you could say that."

Galen's eyes hadn't left me. "Lucas? What is your answer?"

"That is your decision, Alpha. I am not of your pack."

Galen tented his hands. "If you were, what would you ask of me?"

"Somebody tell me what happened this morning," Breanna demanded.

Cody explained Aaron's attempt to skewer me with his car. Breanna's scent changed to a mix of anger and fear as the conversation came full circle.

"Lucas? You are a future Alpha. How would you handle this?" Galen asked after the waitress took his order.

My wolf rumbled but the power of the Alpha kept him in check. "I am not a future Alpha," I answered through gritted teeth.

"You're the Alpha's son," Cody answered. "You have to be."

"No, I do not."

Cody opened his mouth to argue but Galen intervened. "Josef says you are his Second."

I swallowed hard. I hated these conversations. "I am not involved with the Italian Pack."

"What?" Cody asked. "How can you not be involved with the pack when your father is the Alpha? Don't you care about the other werewolves?"

"No."

Cody sat back. "You have to care about your pack. You're a wolf. That's what we do. We care about our own."

Normal werewolves cared. I was not normal. A normal werewolf would feel the bonds of his pack, the bond to his father. I was broken.

Galen's forehead wrinkled. "If you care so little for the Italian Pack, why do remain with them?"

Breanna's fingers tightened around mine.

"My father will not release me."

The air around the table was heavy. Galen's eyes were on me. I chose to avoid his glare, hoping he wouldn't ask the dreaded question. He did.

"What of Breanna?"

"What about me?" Breanna asked. "What does Lucas being in the Italian Pack have to do with me?"

"A wolf needs to be with his mate and he can't stay here with you." Galen's words fell like a hammer.

"Mate?" Cody asked as he leaned forward. "You two are mates? Cool."

I glanced at Breanna before addressing Galen. "I will not ask anything that may put you in a position of poor favor with my father, Alpha McGregor."

"What?" Cody and Breanna asked in unison.

My stomach was threatening to expel the pancakes. This was not where I wanted to discuss the delicacy of the situation. I couldn't leave the Italian Pack, she couldn't leave America, and I had no idea what to do about it.

Galen broke the silence. "Lucas won't ask me to allow him to stay in Wisconsin Pack territory."

"What if he did?" Breanna asked.

"He would not," Galen replied.

"Would not what?" Breanna asked. "Would not ask or would not be allowed to stay?"

"Both."

Remaining in Wisconsin had never been an option, but hearing Galen saying it so definitively was like having a door slammed in my face.

"That's stupid," Breanna snapped. "Why the hell can't he stay here?"

"Werewolf law," the three of us answered in unison. Luckily no humans were sitting close enough to hear our conversation.

"Yeah, well, that's stupid, too. Do you want to stay here?" she asked.

She had no idea how much I wanted to wake up beside her every morning for the rest of my life, but staying here was not an option. If I didn't leave, Galen would forcefully remove me. Breanna didn't need to see that.

I looked into her eyes. "I can't, Bre."

"That is not what I asked."

God I loved her tenacity. "Yes, I want to stay, but--"

"There," she said to Galen. "How can we make this happen? There has to be some way around this ridiculous law."

Galen's eyes hooded. "Lucas could challenge the Italian Alpha."

"Does Lucas have to kill him to win?" she asked.

A knife jabbed my heart. I knew the answer before Galen said anything.

"Yes, he would need to kill Josef and then Lucas would be the new Alpha of the Italian Pack."

Breanna slammed her hand on the tabletop hard enough humans turned around to stare. "He doesn't want to be the Alpha. Can't Lucas just maim the Alpha enough that he says uncle?"

Galen almost smiled. "No. The Alpha would never concede. However, Lucas is strong enough to defeat Josef."

My chest tightened. Alpha werewolves never encouraged challenges.

"Why do you say that?" Cody asked.

Breanna was uncomfortably quiet, though her hand never left mine.

"Their wolves hate each other," Galen answered solemnly.

Gunshot wounds hurt less than hearing another Alpha say my father hated me.

"Lucas, let's go," Breanna said, abruptly sliding out the booth.

I didn't understand why she was angry. Protocol dictated I not leave without Galen's permission, but my wolf demanded I stay close to my mate.

"You didn't finish your breakfast," Cody responded. "And we weren't done talking yet."

"Eat it," Brenna snapped. "I lost my appetite."

She was treading dangerously close to offending the Alpha.

"Why is that, Breanna?" Galen asked with no hint of emotion.

She lasered him with amber eyes. "Don't start your bullshit with me, Galen. I'm no wolf."

Silver flickered in Galen's eyes and my wolf surged. Breanna threw a five-dollar bill on the table and met the Alpha's gaze. I slid out quickly and tucked her behind me.

"Alpha McGregor, with your permission I will remain in your territory two more days. My plane leaves at seven-fifteen Tuesday evening."

Galen stood and Breanna pushed around me. I was trying to block her when Galen extended his hand.

"Lucas, you are a good man and I wish I could help, but you understand I cannot violate werewolf law?"

I shook his hand. The power coursing through me was more bearable than a few days earlier. However, my teeth still clenched. Inside, my wolf rumbled. Breanna was much too close to a potentially dangerous situation.

"Yes, sir," I answered while Breanna muttered a string of profanity. "Thank you, Alpha."

Chapter 25

Breanna

We arrived at my house, cleaned up the pancakes from earlier, and settled onto the couch.

"So, what's the deal with your father? Why won't he release you?"

Lucas put his arm around my shoulders. "I'm his only son."

"So what you want isn't important?"

His chest rose and fell. "The pack is important. He feels it is my duty to be the next Alpha."

I bit my lip so I wouldn't stick my foot in my mouth. I hated shit like this. "The fact you have no desire to be the Alpha doesn't matter?"

He shook his head. "Tristyn is trying to find another legal way for me to get out of the pack."

I couldn't stop myself. "Why don't you fight him? Galen said you could beat him. You could become Alpha long enough to release yourself and then he could have it back."

Lucas leaned his head against mine. "I can't fight my father. One of us would die."

"And you don't want to kill him?"

Lucas took a long deep breath. "He's my father."

The pain in his voice made me swallow my sarcastic reply. From what I'd heard, Josef Benelli was a first class asshole, particularly to Lucas.

"The Divine Council can't intervene on your behalf? How did you get away with going to college in America and being an agent?"

A muscle in his jaw ticked. I had hit that nerve again. "Nic was around then. Josef didn't really care what I did."

"Has he ever cared what you did?"

Lucas clenched his jaw. "He's my father, Bre. I can't kill him."

Smartass reply aborted. No need to add to the pile of shit already on his shoulders.

"What about your mom? Can't she talk to him?"

"She says I'm being selfish by not wanting to be the next Alpha."

Good God, his entire family was loco. "That's ridiculous."

He sighed and looked at the ceiling. It was scary how much he reminded me of Galen when he did that. "She's right, Bre. Look at what's going on here."

"What the hell are you talking about?"

"I'm creating problems for you here."

Oh, for God's sake. "No, you aren't."

"Did you fight with the wolves in your unit before I came along?"

He had no idea. "Constantly."

"Really?"

"They're like my brothers. Of course we fight. Every day."

He looked surprised. "What about Cody?"

"What about him?"

"Do you fight with him?"

Was he jealous of Cody? "I don't talk to Cody much. He isn't in Bravo. I call him when one of the pack wolves is in trouble and I can't get Galen. He's the Wisconsin Second."

Brown eyes bored into mine. "He likes you."

"He's not my type."

Lucas's eyebrows knitted.

I caressed his jaw. "I like dark eyes, a bit of beard stubble, broad chests, strong hands, and Italian accents."

He grinned.

"I like a man who knows how to sweep me off my feet while at the same time realizing I'm no helpless female."

He growled.

"I like a man who is secure enough to let me be on top."

The growl got louder.

"A man who will let me have my way with him."

In a blur, he carried me into the bedroom. Lucas sank beside me and put his hands above his head in mock surrender.

I crawled on top and kissed him. His hands rubbed along my legs until I caught them and placed them back above his head.

"Stay."

His grin was devilish. "Yes, ma'am."

I slowly unbuttoned his shirt and ran my fingernails along his chest. He writhed on the bed. Power filled the air as he moaned softly. Following the path of dark hair that disappeared beneath the waistband of his pants, I nipped the top of his jeans.

His breaths came in short pants as I pulled his pants to his knees.

No underwear. Yummy.

I fondled his sac until he was ripping the sheets from the bed.

"Oh God, Breanna. I can't, I can't, I can't wait."

My hips moved against him, my heart pounding. His eyes were bright, heated with passion as he cried my name over and over, his body convulsing in time with mine.

The colorful bursts of stars slowly receded until I found myself staring at the sweaty, chiseled chest of my werewolf.

He rolled onto his side so our noses were inches apart. "I'll kill my father if that's what it takes to be with you."

"You don't want to do that."

"If that's the only way, I'll do whatever it takes."

He meant it. Every word of it. I could see it in his eyes. "What if I come to Italy?"

He kissed my forehead. "Italy isn't safe. Italian Pack territory has an open-kill policy on witches. Besides, you can't leave Bravo."

Actually, he was sort of right. I had just re-upped for five more years for Uncle Sam and the Divine Council. Those contracts were ironclad.

"I thought the Divine Council had outlawed open-kill policies."

He bowed his head. "The Council discourages it, but werewolves set their own laws within their territories."

"What about Tristyn's mate? She's a witch."

"When they come to the Italian Pack territory, it is usually straight to my house. My father has forbidden the Italian wolves from engaging Tristyn or Alexandria."

"He did that for you?" Wow, maybe the ole asshole wasn't as bad as I thought.

"Tristyn's father threatened a war between vampires and werewolves in Italy unless the Italian Pack agreed to leave Tristyn and Alex in peace."

Nope, I was right. Josef Benelli was a total asshole.

"You don't think if we explained the situation, your father would give me the same protection?"

Lucas bit is lower lip again. "Honestly? No. I think he would send the wolves after you because of me. He has a chosen group of women from whom he thinks I should pick my mate."

I bumped his nose with mine. "Are they prettier than me?"

His fingers trailed along my jaw. "No one is prettier than you."

Chapter 26

Lucas

I was staring at the phone screen when the faint smell of strawberries tickled my nose. I'd tried to call my father. He didn't answer. My plane left in a little less than three hours and we would be leaving for the airport in a few minutes. Tristyn had left a few days earlier, flying out to Bulgaria to help Alexandria with some type of witch issue.

"What's up?" Breanna asked as her hand trailed along my shoulders.

"I was calling my father to tell him I wouldn't be home until the weekend."

She half scowled before kneeling in front of me. "Lucas, baby, we've talked about this. I'll be there in ten days. If you stay here, you'll only make him angry and that's not something we need."

She was right. That didn't make it any easier. Wolves didn't leave their mates and my wolf was roaring.

"I'm thinking about going lone wolf."

She didn't bat an eyelash. "No, you aren't."

"Yes, I am."

She scowled. "And where would we live, Antarctica? Even I know lone wolves can't live in pack territory."

This situation seemed impossible. "I'll talk to Galen about joining the Wisconsin Pack."

"And you are getting out of the Italian Pack how?"

"I'll fight my father."

"And how will you live with the guilt of killing him? And who will take over the Italian Pack? Under werewolf law, if you defeat the Alpha, you must take over leadership of the pack. Is that what you want?"

My wolf rumbled impatiently. She was all I wanted. I wanted to wake up beside her and go to sleep with her curled next to me. Was that really too much to ask?

"I could resign from Bravo and we could live in Italy," she said with a completely emotionless voice.

"I can't let you do that."

That was not the right thing to say. Her eyes flashed and her face went fire truck red. "Let me?"

I banged my head on the chair. "I didn't mean it like that."

"Exactly how did you mean it?"

"I'm not making you choose between Bravo and me."

"You think I'd pick Bravo over you?"

"You've built a great career here. Bravo is your family. I know that."

I didn't think her face could get any redder. I was wrong. She balled her fists and stormed into the bedroom. The house shook with the force of the slammed door. I swore under my breath and retrieved the recently repaired cuckoo clock that had fallen.

Before I could go after her, Breanna reappeared, her face a stone facade. "We need to get to the airport so you can get through security."

When I reached for her hand I saw the faint pink streaks on her cheeks. "I'm sorry," I said as I pulled her into my arms.

"I'm fine," she mumbled into my shirt. "Allergies."

I stroked her hair and held her. Leaving her was the hardest thing I'd ever done, and I wasn't the only one struggling. She was much better at hiding the hurt than I was.

"I could tell him my flight got cancelled," I said, only half joking.

She shook her head and reminded me of a schoolteacher chastising a child. "I'll be there in ten days and we'll deal with your father together."

Every time she talked about us doing something together, my wolf wanted to howl with pride. Not only had I found my mate, but she would fight with me.

Mates were not common in the world of werewolves and even if a wolf did find his or her mate, there was no guarantee the mating would be a happy one. Most werewolf couples weren't actual mates, just couples. Mates, once bonded through blood, linked life forces. It was the ultimate act of sacrifice and gave each mate the ability to pull energy from the other.

I'd never heard of a werewolf mating with any species other than werewolf, but I wasn't exactly up on the social etiquette of werewolf mating practices.

"I have something for you," Breanna said as she reached behind her neck and unclasped a necklace. "It's a guardian stone. Some people call them witches' stones. It will get hot in the presence of black magic, so if you feel it getting warm, you need to get the hell away from wherever you are."

She placed it around my neck and fastened the clasp. I touched the cool green oblong stone. "It gets warm?"

Her soft fingers covered mine. "Yes, in the presence of black magic. If it gets hot, you are in big trouble."

"Big trouble?"

She nodded and her ponytail bobbed adorably. "Yes, heapum big trouble, kimosabe."

"Where did it come from?"

Her smile faded. "My grandmother gave it to me just before she died."

"Baby, I can't take this. It must mean the world to you if it came from your grandmother."

She lifted a hand to touch my cheek. "You mean the world to me. I can feel the black magic. You can't. If there are Malandanti anywhere nearby, this stone will let you know soon enough you can get away from them."

To see this incredible woman here before me offering something so precious because she wanted me to be safe was a defining moment in my life. My father be damned if he wouldn't accept her.

"Thank you," I whispered as I nuzzled her hair. "I'll keep it safe until you get to Italy."

She bumped her head against my shoulder. "You keep you safe until I get to Italy. I refuse to share my wolf with anybody, especially Malandanti." She rose and pulled me up toward her. "C'mon. We gotta go if you're going to make your flight."

The flight was uneventful. I would never forget the image of Breanna standing at the window waving and then the owl on the wing of the plane. She'd been stronger than me, forcing on a happy face and urging me to think about what we'd do when she arrived in Italy rather than the seemingly eternal ten days it would be before I could hold her again.

We were spending Christmas together. I didn't know much about Christmas traditions other than a big meal and presents. Breanna mentioned always wanting a Christmas tree. This year she would have one and I'd pull it up by the roots if that was what she wanted.

Simon had filed the paperwork giving Breanna three weeks of leave starting in ten days. I wanted to take her someplace special while she was in Italy. Euro Disney wasn't so far away and she loved that silly mouse. I made a mental note to call a travel agent.

The plane landed and everyone hurried toward the baggage claim. My bag appeared and I grabbed it before rushing for the pretty blond customs agent.

I was on the escalator when the smell of musk slammed into me like a freight train. My father knew I was coming back tonight, and that wasn't him coming toward me.

When the escalator lifted, four Italian Pack werewolves milled about near the newsstand. I bit my lip and allowed my wolf to surge. They weren't here to give me a group hug and tell me how much they'd missed me.

I made eye contact with the four werewolves as they turned to face me. The looks on their faces told me they felt my displeasure.

"Lucas?"

I kept walking as Ernesto Tandolinni fell into step beside me. He was a big wolf, standing a good six inches taller than me, and the informal leader of this greeting party.

"What?" I snapped.

"I need to talk to you."

I gave him my most disinterested glare. "About what?"

He reached out and touched my arm. I whirled and pushed him to the wall. "Do not touch me."

"Sorry," he muttered with his eyes dropped. I quickly stepped back so as not to attract any more human attention. "I need you to listen to me."

I sucked in a deep breath. "What?"

"It's about Tessa."

"What about her?" I asked, more annoyed than anything. I hadn't had a chance to call Breanna yet and was dying to hear her voice.

"I want to challenge you for her," Ernesto said with forced boldness.

"Fine. Challenge won. She's yours."

He was very confused by my answer. "You can't do that. We have to fight."

"Why do I have to fight? If you want her, she's all yours."

Ernesto shook his head. "No, the Alpha said I had to formally challenge you and we would have to fight the formal challenge before the pack."

"Fine, whatever. When do you want to do it?"

"The rules are there has to be a full pack meeting and then we fight the challenge. The next pack meeting is Saturday night."

I bit my lip. I hated pack meetings. "Fine, whatever. I'll be there for the challenge."

The other wolves were mumbling behind us. "Got something to say?" I growled at them. They backed away and averted their eyes.

"Did my father approve your challenge of me?"

"Yes, he told us you would be arriving tonight."

Wow, thanks for the heads up. The wolves were still there. "Anything else?"

"I love her, Lucas. I want to be with her. You swear you'll take this challenge?" Ernesto had never said more than two words to me and I had no ill will toward him other than he was a member of the pack. I understood the raw emotion in his voice and the desperation in his eyes.

"I will be there and I have no interest in her."

I started away and he grabbed my arm. My wolf surged and I shoved Ernesto. "I told you not to touch me."

Ernesto's eyes flashed silver and that sent my wolf into a rage. I fought to control the rage before I made a scene in the middle of the airport. Ernesto realized the danger and backed away. "I just want your word you'll be there."

I glared at him rather than speaking. He moved to the side to let me pass. I needed to get out of here now, before airport security came scurrying.

The group wisely decided to go the opposite direction. I found my parked SUV and quickly climbed inside the cold, dark interior. My wolf and I needed time alone, time to calm down, and time to call my mate.

I had to wait fifteen minutes before my hands quit shaking enough to punch the buttons to call her. I had no personal issue with Ernesto's challenge, but any time a wolf called me out, my wolf responded tenfold. It was the way of the wolf world--survival of the fittest, the strong prevail.

Breanna answered on the first ring. Her voice was salve for my soul.

"Hey, baby, everything okay?" she asked. She should have been asleep, though she sounded fully awake.

"Everything's fine. I got through customs without much hassle."

She took a deep breath before responding. "What happened?"

"Not much, the bags were a little slow coming down but I knew the customs agent."

"Lucas. Tell me what happened."

I fidgeted with the steering wheel, trying to decide if I should tell her about the challenge. I didn't want to upset her, nor did I want to make her think there was more to this challenge than there really was.

"Lucas," she said. "If we are going to make this relationship work, you have to trust me to handle the truth about whatever happens. No sugar-coating and no leaving stuff out. Now, what the hell happened?"

I told her and she listened to every word. I thought she might be upset or angry. She stayed cool and calm.

"Are you all right with the pack meeting before the challenge? I can hop a transport tonight and watch your back if you need me."

My mate was fearless. "I hate pack meetings but they aren't dangerous."

"Are you going to fight that wolf?"

"No. I'll show up and yield to him. He wants Tessa and he can have her."

"And what's your father going to say?"

"Nothing I care to repeat in the presence of a lady."

She laughed. "That's fine, but you can tell me. We both know my vocabulary."

I caught myself smiling. "It won't be good. He'll say I'm being a coward, that the son of an Alpha should take every challenge seriously, yadda, yadda, yadda."

"Hmm, I guess the yadda, yadda, yadda part is the Italian cussing, huh?"

Some of the tension left my body and my wolf calmed during my conversation with her.

"How did you know something happened?" I'd been wondering about that since she first asked what had happened.

I could hear her smiling. "Gut feeling. Maybe it's that mate thing settling in?"

Something was settling in, that was sure. Just hearing her voice soothed my otherwise impossible wolf. "Probably. The mate bond does take some time to click into place, or at least that's what I've heard."

* * * *

"What do you mean you aren't going to fight him?" my father roared through the phone. "You've been challenged and you will fight."

"Fine, whatever," I mumbled in response. There was no need to argue. He wouldn't listen to anything I said.

"You'll be attending the pack meeting?"

"Yes, I'll be there."

"Good. There are rumors of Malandanti activity in the area and I want the pack to be aware of the danger."

I stopped working on the purchase order on my desk and stared out the window. "Yeah, about that. Breanna thinks there might be a link between Niccoli's disappearance and the Malandanti."

"Breanna who?"

"Master Sergeant Breanna Welker from Bravo Company."

"The witch?" Josef huffed. "What the hell would she know about that?"

"I talked to her and she had some ideas about finding Nic."

My father ground his teeth. "Why would you be talking to a witch about pack affairs? You know better than that."

The phone slammed in my ear and it didn't take a rocket scientist to know my father was on his way over. I glanced at the clock. Maybe if the traffic slowed him, it would take forty-five minutes for him to leave his office and reach mine.

I smelled the musk and my stomach sank. My father had been in the building when he called.

The door to my office shuddered as the hulking form of my father filled the doorway. He was taller than me and dark-haired, with piercing blue eyes. Now his eyes were completely silver and my wolf went on full alert.

"What the hell is wrong with you?" he demanded as he swiped the papers from my desk. My wolf surged and I held my ground, meeting the silver-eyed glare of my father.

"Don't," I warned as he came around my desk toward me.

The last thing I remembered was him grabbing my shirt.

By the time I pushed my wolf down, I found myself in Clara's office. She was huddled in the corner, her head turned away from me.

"Clara?" I called softly.

Slowly she looked at me, her eyes wide with fear.

"What happened?" I asked. My head thumped.

She didn't say anything, just looked toward my office. Papers were scattered in the doorway and a broken chair lay in the middle of the floor. As I entered my office, my father leaned heavily against the wall near the window. Blood was freely flowing from his mouth and eye.

"Father?" He didn't answer and I stepped cautiously into the room. "Father?"

"Stay away from me, Lucas."

I stopped in the doorway, the flow of my Alpha's dominance washing over me. My wolf didn't like it. He wanted to go toward the smell of blood. My father was injured and vulnerable, a perfect time to attack.

I fought my wolf and backed into Clara's office. I didn't want this. I had attacked my father. What to do, what to say? How badly he was hurt? Exactly what had happened?

The fear on Clara's face was more than I could take. What had I done?

My foot caught on the corner of the desk and I fell backward onto the floor. I leaped to my feet just as my father stumbled to the doorway of my office.

"I'm sorry. I didn't mean--"

"I'm fine."

He brushed past me without making eye contact. The smell of his blood excited my wolf.

"Alpha?"

He walked slowly down the hall with only a hint of a limp. For him to show any sign of weakness meant he was in excruciating pain. This was exactly what I hadn't wanted to happen.

The office looked like a disaster area. My desk splintered, all the chairs broken, papers strewn over the floor and two fist-sized holes in the wall. I pushed the heels of my hands into my eyeballs to displace a thundering headache.

I had attacked my father. I had attacked my Alpha. The worst part was I didn't remember it. My wolf had taken over and acted. Under werewolf law, I should be dead now. Wolves didn't attack Alphas and live. They finished the job and took over the pack or the Alpha killed them. The fact the Alpha was my father made it worse. Scarier still was my wolf had taken over. Total loss of control was a death sentence.

I sank into the corner and looked around at the disaster that used to be my office. I pulled my legs to my chest and laid my head on my knees. I felt like a child again, the child who had attacked a packmate and was awaiting the wrath of his father.

My phone vibrated in my pocket and I ignored it. Two minutes later the text message alert beeped.

Do u need me?

Everything inside me was raw. I did need her, but I didn't want her to see me like this. Besides, she was across the ocean and safe from the bullshit going on here in Italy. She was coming in eight days. I could hold on until then.

I took a deep breath and called her. She answered within half a ring. I told her everything I remembered, which was, in truth, not much. Our conversation was short. Too short.

"Mr. Benelli?" Clara called cautiously from the cracked doorframe.

The sunlight pouring through the window made my head throb even more. "Yeah, Clara?" I answered without lifting my head. I didn't want to see the disgusted look on her face.

"Are you all right?"

I swallowed hard. "I'm fine, thanks. I didn't hurt you, did I?"

"No, sir, I'm all right. I'll clean up this mess."

"You don't have to do that," I answered, finally summoning the courage to look at her face.

She looked around before answering. "I don't mind and it would do you good to go for a run. You've had a rough day."

The purchase order I hadn't finished was on the floor, splattered with blood. "I need to finish the paperwork for the Silverstein job."

She eased into the office, carefully staying against the far wall. "I can do that for you. Go on, I'll look after the office."

"Thank you, Clara." I did need to get out of the office and a run would clear my head. My wolf was still pushing for me to go after my father. I didn't really understand why my wolf had always been so aggressive toward my father. It couldn't be normal for a wolf to hate his creator so much.

I headed out to the pack grounds and found my favorite boulder. I liked to come here and sit. The wind in the trees helped me think.

Chapter 27

Breanna

"Damn cargo planes," I muttered as I readjusted the pile of parachutes acting as my makeshift bunk. This was the first transport to Europe I could find.

When Lucas had called earlier this morning, I had been on my way to the base. I felt his rage and his fear and later so much sadness I had to slip into the forest and take a few minutes to gather my wits. I couldn't see or feel what had happened to upset him, but he was in danger and I was on my way.

I probably should have told him I was coming, at least given him a heads-up, but he would have insisted he was fine and told me not to come. Yeah, well, that wasn't happening. He was my mate and I would not let anything happen to him.

Galen was standing at my office door when I finally got to work. His face was ashen as I told him I was heading to Italy. He agreed with my decision and gave me three hundred dollars in Italian currency he had picked up on his way to see me.

Being on the same wavelength as an Alpha werewolf was scary. I'd asked how he knew Lucas was in trouble and Galen gave me the patented "Alphas know all" look and disappeared out the door without a word. Damn werewolves.

I e-filed a request for emergency leave. The request was denied. I called Simon and he re-filed the request. Denied again. I submitted my resignation. Simon went nuts and started calling everyone he knew. My resignation wasn't worth the paper it was written on. As of ten-fifteen this morning, I was AWOL.

Absent Without Leave. Criminal. Fugitive.

Now I was somewhere over the Atlantic Ocean on a cargo plane bound for Germany. From there I could catch a plane or a train or a bus or something to Italy. I'd steal a Jeep if that was what it took. Simon wouldn't have reported me yet.

He won't report me. He'll do some paperwork and make some phone calls to make all this legal 'cause that's what Simon does.

The mate bond thing was messing with my head. I wondered if Lucas could feel it as strongly as I did or if being a witch magnified the emotions. I hoped so because if that rush of sadness I felt earlier was real, my poor wolf was in bad trouble.

I couldn't sleep on the cold lumpy parachutes so I looked over the intel report on the Italian supernatural population. There were almost two hundred werewolves in Italy led by Josef Benelli. There were sixty-four known vampires, a handful of fae, a couple of trolls, three dark witches who hadn't been seen in thirty years, a white witch, seventeen shapeshifters, and three miscellaneous.

What the hell is a miscellaneous?

The intel had been gathered almost ten years ago so the numbers probably weren't accurate. It was, however, a clear picture of who ruled Italy. Two hundred werewolves was one hell of a pack and Josef Benelli must have been one hell of a strong Alpha to handle that many wolves. Galen's Wisconsin pack only had thirty-three members and that was counting the newly indoctrinated Levi.

And the Europeans so love witches. Not.

A little deeper into the intel I found a few old--as in seventeen-hundreds--reports of Malandanti activity. Simon had added the notations for my sightings along with the attack on Lucas, though he had left it as "suspected Malandanti attack on lone werewolf." Yep, almost three hundred years since the word Malandanti had even been uttered. No wonder nobody believed me.

Finally the plane descended and landed at Ramstein. I harassed the cargo guys until they found me a flight to Ederle. I'd be in Italy by tonight. I'd call Simon when I landed and then I'd go find Lucas. I hadn't felt any more big surges of emotions from him in the past twenty-four hours, but he hadn't responded to any of my texts either. It was eight in the evening so maybe he could have been out running. I didn't feel he was in danger so it was okay to wait a couple hours for the transport to arrive rather than illegally commandeering some other mode of transportation.

I headed off to the mess hall and scrounged something that resembled a broccoli casserole.

I checked my phone again. No Lucas. Celeste called and asked about my trip. She said Simon had placed Bravo on alert and he had somehow managed to get paperwork filed making my "trip" legal. Simon was awesome like that.

The second transport plane was a smaller one and the ride was rough. The pilots were a couple of Minnesota boys so we talked about hockey the whole ten-hour trip to Ederle. When we landed, my bloodstream was all caffeine and sugar. Twenty-four hours with no sleep was not good for me.

I was three steps onto the tarmac when a searing pain in my right side sent me to my knees. It felt like a red-hot poker stuffed against my rib cage. I jerked up my shirt to find what the hell was wrong.

My skin was its usual color with no indication of a bite. A wave of rage roared through me, followed by tingling of fear and sorrow.

Lucas.

Chapter 28

Lucas

The silver blade slipped between my ribs before I could knock it from Stephano's hand. Ten wolves had surrounded me as I left the pack meeting. I'd yielded to Ernesto, just as I'd promised, and headed home. Stephano's group came out of nowhere and blocked my path. We were two miles from my father's house and another ten miles from mine. I'd taken the opportunity to run to the pack meeting, hoping the exertion would make my wolf stay calm. That had worked. I managed to make it through the meeting and the challenge. Things had gone well until now.

The silver was wreaking havoc with my senses and my ability to fight. My wolf struggled, the silver a deadly toxin to us both. I'd killed three of the wolves and seriously injured two more, but I hadn't seen Stephano until it was too late.

One of the wolves caught me and pinned my hands behind my back. I roared and snapped my foot into his stomach before jerking the knife from my side. The silver burned my hands. It felt as though my insides were cooking and something was hot against my chest.

Breanna's stone. What had she said? It would get hot in the presence of black magic?

Stephano charged and I braced for his impact. I punched him in the face and caught him in the stomach with a good kick. Another of his cronies slammed a fist into my injured side. I couldn't breathe.

I tried to cover my head as the group kicked me across the rocky path. Rolling into the stream and struggling to my feet, I grabbed the wolf closest to me and snapped his neck. The next wolf jumped on my back and I crashed into a boulder before pulling him over my head and bashing his face into the giant rock.

Five wolves were dead and Stephano was circling me. I could ignore the pain from the stab wound, but with the silver was in my bloodstream, I saw three of him.

"Silver hurts, don't it, boy?" Stephano taunted. "I remember it well, thanks to you."

I didn't say anything, refusing to waste energy by engaging in dialog with the one wolf I hated more than anyone else on the planet.

He held open his jacket and showed off two more silver daggers. "Like them? Had those special made for you, I hoped we could relive a few happier times before I killed you, but I guess not."

Images of a fifteen-year-old Stephano sneaking into my room clouded my mind. My wolf finally surged and I lunged for Stephano's throat. He laughed and kicked me in the side. I fell and he jumped on my back and pinned me to the ground. With his free hand he snatched my hair and bared my throat.

"I should have done this years ago," he snarled.

I was going to die. The blurry glint of the silver blade flashed before my eyes.

Stephano's blood-curdling laugh echoed in my ears just as it had when I was a child. I didn't want to leave Breanna like this.

"What the fuck?" Stephano yelled, flinging me to the side.

All I saw was bright lights and then heard the roar of a motor. I choked on blood and the world was very out of focus.

"I'll kill you," Breanna said in a voice so cold it was acidic. "Nobody hurts my mate."

"Your mate?" Stephano laughed.

Her eyes blazed. My cousin stepped toward her. I crawled to my knees.

"I had him first," Stephano sneered. "And he begged for more."

I died inside when she cocked her head at his words. "What?"

Stephano bared his teeth, his eyes flashing silver. "His ass belonged to me many, many times."

Breanna appeared totally disinterested in the secret that ripped my world apart. My wolf tried desperately to surge, but the silver prevented any change.

"Lucas is mine now and I'd appreciate you moving so I don't spatter your blood all over him."

Stephano laughed again. However, this time there was a hint of nervousness. "You're a fucking witch."

"Yep. And you are fucking dead."

I didn't see her move, but the next second Stephano was on the ground, grasping his throat.

"Hurts, don't it, asshole? Yeah, collapsed tracheas are a bitch, but that won't kill you."

Stephano rolled away, trying to get to his feet. Two more wolves emerged from the darkness. I clawed at the rocks, desperate to get to my feet. A wave of strength hit me and my body responded to the renewed energy. Had that been from my father?

Fire flared from Breanna's fingertips and suddenly the trees went up in flames. The other wolves ran, leaving only Stephano behind to deal with one very pissed-off witch. I'd seen Breanna use some of her magic in Wisconsin, but this was amazing. I'd heard stories about the power of witches, but nothing could have prepared me for the intensity in her eyes. Lightning strikes shook the ground and the wind howled as her chants grew louder.

Stephano was on his back, cowering in fear. "I am a pack wolf," he whimpered. "My Alpha will protect me."

A tree toppled beside Stephano. The ground shook.

"Your Alpha ain't got shit on me, asshole. You'd better be begging Lucas to save your worthless life, 'cause he's the only hope you got."

I had no doubt Breanna would kill Stephano if I gave her the word. I wanted him dead a hundred times over, but if Breanna killed him, my father would come after her with a vengeance.

"Lucas, what do you want me to do with him?"

"We should leave that to the Alpha to decide," I said, stepping closer to her.

"Are you sure?"

I took her hand. It was like grabbing a live electrical wire. "Yes. Because he is a pack wolf, Stephano's life belongs to the Alpha. We do not have the right to take it without permission."

She narrowed her eyes and a lightning bolt struck within inches of Stephano's groin. He screamed like a child and curled into a fetal position. When she looked at me, her eyes were still glowing. "Are you sure?"

I nodded and she sighed.

"Fine. I won't kill him this time."

"Lucas!" My father burst from the woods with two dozen wolves at his side.

Breanna threw a line of flames to stop their progress. My father ranted and Breanna increased the intensity of the flames so the crackling drowned out his words. She didn't bat an eye at his anger.

"I'm guessing that's the Alpha over there about to have a coronary."

"That would be him."

She bit her lip. "Not exactly the way I'd planned to meet your father."

She doused the flames and stood tall as Josef stormed toward us. My wolf tried to surge again and I pulled her to my side.

"Don't touch her."

Much to my relief, my father stopped in his tracks. "What is this?" he demanded. "Why did this witch attack my wolves?"

"She didn't attack them. They attacked me."

The silver was starting to burn again as my father bellowed, "Why did they attack you?"

"It's Stephano and some of his friends. They surrounded me here. Stephano was going to kill me until Breanna showed up."

She was meeting my father's livid glare square on. "That asshole has fae silver daggers in his coat and he had one at Lucas's throat when I got here," she said, nodding toward the cowering Stephano.

"*Merda di toro!*" my father retorted.

"It's not bullshit," Breanna muttered as she marched toward Stephano.

Stephano's eyes widened as Breanna reached inside his coat and pulled out the two silver daggers. "You want to hold these?" she asked Josef.

My father looked disbelievingly at the daggers. "You planted those."

Her shoulders slumped. "Oh for shit's sake, will you get your head out of your ass? Either kill this piece of shit or I will."

"No one kills my pack wolves."

"Yeah, well, you should tell that to him, because he tried to kill your son. Why don't you grow a pair and do something to help Lucas?"

Josef stood with his mouth hanging open. Nobody ever talked to him like that. Breanna didn't care.

"Wolves, leave us," Josef demanded.

"What about dickless over there?" Breanna asked, inclining her head toward Stephano.

"Dominic, see that Stephano is placed in the holding cell," Josef ordered one of the wolves by his side.

The pack separated, leaving Josef intently watching Breanna. She turned to me the moment the pack disappeared and began checking the stab wound in my side.

"That's pretty deep. We need to get the silver out."

"It's in my bloodstream," I answered, feeling very dizzy. She eased me onto a boulder and placed her hand on my side. The waves of strength I had been feeling had stopped when my father arrived.

"This might hurt a little, but it will get the silver out."

"Do not touch him!" Josef roared as he ran toward us.

A blue-white shield of flames appeared and the world around us disappeared.

"I trust you," I said when she raised her eyebrows.

She half smiled before turning her attention to my side. Her chants were like whispers. My side warmed and was soon burning intensely. I tried not to squirm as she moved her hands back and forth over the open wound.

"You don't look anything like your father," she said.

My chuckle hurt like hell. "My brother looked just like him. I'm the reject of the family."

"Bullshit," she snapped. "There's nothing wrong with you."

Just when I thought the wound couldn't get any hotter, it did. I hissed as the heat consumed my whole side. A cloud of silvery dust tinged with blood floated above Breanna's hand. I felt stronger with every passing second as the silver left my body.

"Better?" she asked as the last remnants of the toxic dust came toward her outstretched hand.

I nodded and looked into her eyes. "Thank you."

She ran a hand along my jaw. "We'll talk about all this later. How about we get somewhere I can take a shower? I'm feeling rather funky."

She must have been on a plane for hours. There were dark circles under her eyes and her hair was a mess, but she was the most beautiful woman in the world.

"When did you get here?"

"About twenty minutes ago," she said with a scowl. "If I'd been a little earlier maybe you wouldn't be hurt."

"How did you know?"

She took my hand and placed in over her heart. "I felt it. I felt the knife. I felt the silver. I felt your rage." Her eyes softened. "I felt it all and I got here as fast as I could."

I pulled her to my chest and rested my chin on her head. She was everything. I took her hand and led her toward my father, who was watching us warily.

"Alpha, this is Breanna Welker."

I couldn't read my father. His face was stone as he nodded in greeting.

"Sorry about the fire," Breanna said with a shrug.

"You would have killed Stephano?" Josef asked stoically.

"He tried to kill Lucas so, yes, I would have killed him and never given it a second thought."

A muscle ticked in the Alpha's jaw. "Stephano is a pack wolf."

"So is Lucas."

"This is none of your concern," Josef replied.

Breanna tilted her head and met his gaze. "My mate is most certainly my concern."

Josef looked from Breanna to me. "Your what?"

This was not the way I had envisioned telling my father.

"Breanna is my mate," I answered.

"You can't be mated to a witch. You are a werewolf, son of an Alpha."

I was so sure he'd see, just like Galen, we were mates. I put my arm around Breanna's waist. "She is my mate."

My father hesitated before speaking. "Bonded?"

Breanna answered first. "Not yet but we will be as soon as you give us your blessing."

The woman had balls of steel. My father looked shocked.

"You expect my blessing?" he asked. "You want me to approve of my only son taking a witch as a mate?"

Breanna stepped toward him. "I would defend him with my last breath. For that I ask your blessing."

Josef met my eyes. "This is why you were in McGregor's territory?"

"Yes."

Breanna offered her hand and Josef looked at her like she was a leper.

"We will be together with or without your blessing, Alpha Benelli. I have no wish to create more issues within your pack and, for Lucas's sake, I hope you will try to be open-minded about me. I am a soldier dedicated to supporting the causes of the Divine Council and I do not practice any type of sacrificial magic."

Breanna whipped her head around toward the trees. I didn't scent anything unusual, but something certainly had her attention.

"Is your stone warm?" she whispered.

Now that I thought about it, the stone was warm. I rolled the blue-green rock in my fingers and the heat increased.

"Black magic." She tugged me away from the clearing.

"More of my pack is arriving," Josef answered defensively. "There is no black magic here."

"Yes, there is," Breanna answered. "It isn't strong, mainly residual stuff, but it's here."

My mom and Tessa, along with ten other werewolves, pushed through the bushes and into the clearing.

"Josef, is everything all right?" Mom asked.

"No, not exactly," my father answered, cocking an eyebrow at Breanna.

"Lucas, honey, are you-- Why is there a witch here?"

My mom's peaceful brown eyes flashed silver as I drew Breanna beside me. "Mom, I want you to meet Breanna."

Mom looked at Breanna like she had the plague. "Why are you touching a witch, Lucas?"

"Breanna is my mate."

My mother's face turned blood red. "Josef, please end this charade now and destroy this parasite."

I jerked forward. Breanna caught me and pulled back. "Don't," she said softly. You'll only regret it later."

"Mom, Breanna is my mate and you will speak to her respectfully or not at all."

She glared at Breanna and then turned to Josef. "Are you not going to kill her? I thought you had a zero-tolerance policy on witches in our territory."

Josef's eyes rested on my and Breanna's intertwined fingers. "The witch averted a catastrophe tonight. She lives."

My mother exploded, hurling insults at everyone. I hoped Breanna's Italian wasn't good enough she understood everything my mother was saying.

The Alpha watched as his wife stormed into the woods. The wolves who had arrived with her watched as she tore through the brush.

"Go with Gemma," Josef ordered. "She is angry and sometimes has poor judgment when she is angry."

The wolves glanced at Breanna before following my mother's path through the darkened trees. Breanna was watching the wolves suspiciously. As they left, the stone she had given me cooled.

"Do you want to talk to your father alone?" Breanna asked when it was just the three of us. "I really need to make a couple of phone calls anyway."

My father continued watching Breanna like she was a circus freak. She kissed me on the cheek, shifted to her owl form, and flew into the darkness.

"She can shapeshift?"

I smiled as the beautiful owl landed soundlessly in the trees across the clearing. "Yeah, owls and wolves are her kindreds."

"Kindreds?"

"The animals she is tied to through Mother Nature. Breanna is an earth witch, not a black or white witch. All her magic is based on her connection to the earth."

He shook his head in disbelief. "I've never heard of an earth witch."

This was going better than I had expected. "Neither had I. Alexandria said the earth witches were very rare. Most have been killed because their magic isn't strong compared to other magical races."

He huffed. "Looked fierce to me."

"She's a soldier in Bravo. She's tough." I'd always respected females who were serious about their careers, but I was especially proud of Breanna's role in combat training her recon unit.

For the first time in many years, my father actually smiled at me. "You truly believe she is your mate?"

"I know she is."

He clasped his hands behind his back, a very un-Alphalike gesture. "Are you sure she hasn't put you under a spell? She is a witch."

"My wolf claims her. No spell could make that happen."

My father nodded. "How did you meet her?"

"She's the one who found me the night I crashed my bike."

"The night the Malandanti supposedly attacked?" He scowled and paced. "I don't like any of this, Lucas, but I can't deny the witch did save your life tonight. It was pure luck I found you."

"Luck? That wasn't luck. You came when you felt my call."

My father dipped his head. "I felt Stephano's fear."

"I felt you. Your strength helped me when Stephano's wolves were attacking."

My father looked away. "That was not me, Lucas. I felt a disturbance in the pack, but nothing from you." Josef bowed his head and the scent of his sadness touched me. "I must see to the pack and Stephano. I will give the order the witch is to be left in peace."

"Thank you."

"Why is the witch here?"

"She came to check on me."

He scowled. "She must leave immediately."

"She's spending Christmas with me."

"She can't stay, Lucas. I will not tolerate a witch in my territory. How long is this visit?"

"She has three weeks of leave and then she has to return to Wisconsin."

My father didn't say anything, only stared at the moon.

"I am formally requesting to be released from the Italian Pack."

"Absolutely not."

I ignored his response. "We both know things aren't working here. The pack hates me. We fight all the time. I could live in Wisconsin as part of Alpha McGregor's pack. Breanna is safe there."

Dominance choked the crisp night air. "I'm sure McGregor would indulge your desire to join his pack. He would take great pride declaring you submissive to him." My father threw up his hands. "He would kill you as sure as you stand before me with these ridiculous requests. I will not release you from this pack. You will not travel to Wisconsin again and that witch will be out of my territory within three days."

My wolf surged at the threat. "Stay away from Breanna."

"You forget your place, Lucas. You are strong, but I am the Alpha. Your life is mine to do with as I wish. You are my son and I have given you far more second chances than you deserve. This is my final warning. You will take your place as a rightful member of the Italian Pack."

"Or what?"

My father sighed heavily and disappeared into the darkness. He didn't have to say he would kill me.

An owl flew silently into the clearing and transformed into my beautiful mate in a dull flash of blue light.

"Everything okay?" she asked as she looked toward the path my father had taken.

"It is now."

"Where's your father?"

"Gone to see to the pack."

She let out a whistle as she slid onto the rock next to me. "Not exactly the way I had hoped to meet your parents."

I reached for her hand. "The Alpha declared you must leave in three days."

"Humph," she grunted.

"It's not safe for you here."

"We got three days before he's sending the wolves after me? Then we'll worry about what we are going to do in two and a half." She tugged my hand as she spoke. "I called Simon and he's got some things in the works, so stop worrying and let's find a shower."

Chapter 29

Breanna

It wasn't unusual for a hot shower to feel so good, but it was unusual for someone else to lather fruity shampoo through my hair. Lucas had given me the most seductive soaping and now his fingers were working the tension out of my neck and shoulders.

"You smell good enough to eat," he murmured in my ear.

I turned and every hormone in my body went ballistic. The soap was trailing down his chest and outlining the eight-pack abs. He closed his eyes and rumbled deep in his chest as I helped the soap reach the areas farther south.

I wrapped my arms around his neck and pulled his lips to mine. As long as we had hot water, we would be the only two people on the planet.

His hands set me on fire as he pinned me against the wall. My body craved him and burst into a breath-stealing orgasm before I could even get my fingers in his hair. I purred and moaned as he ground against me, the water and his body contrasting the cool tile wall.

He increased his pace and I bit my lip to keep from screaming his name to the heavens. I couldn't get close enough to him, couldn't hold him tight enough as his rhythm worked me into a frenzy of heat and lust. We reached our pinnacles simultaneously, panting each other's names over and over as the hot water showered us.

After quickly toweling off he carried me to the bed. I'd never felt more wanted than I did at this moment. His gentle caresses, the way he whispered my name, the way he looked into my eyes as he made love to me. I had been right to make this trip. Lucas needed me as much as I needed him.

* * * *

The first thing I noticed was the rise and fall of his chest. The second thing I noticed was how tightly his arms wrapped around my body. The third thing was, unfortunately, I really, really had to pee.

I tried to shrug from under his arms. That was impossible so I tried blowing on his chin. He rubbed his head against the pillow and pulled me tighter. Oh damn, my bladder did not like that.

"Lucas, baby, I need to get up."

"Huh? No, it's not time to get up," he answered sleepily.

Damn, he was cute, but that did not matter to my bladder. "I gotta go to the head, sweets."

"What's wrong with your head?" he asked as he jerked upright. "Did you get hurt last night?"

If my bladder hadn't been moments from exploding, I would have laughed. His hair was standing straight up. "I need to go to the bathroom."

He crinkled his forehead and cocked his head before my statement trickled through his sleep-induced haze. "Oh, oh, yeah, um, yeah, sorry," he said as he whipped the cover back so I could escape the warm comfort of his bed.

I kissed him on the nose. "Don't leave."

It was almost one in the afternoon when we finally left the bed and padded into the kitchen. His house was just like him, quietly powerful and earthy. Hues of deep browns and greens accentuated the heavy wooden furniture scattered throughout the three-bedroom, three-bath home.

The single-story brick house was nestled on twenty fenced acres just outside of Vicenza. It was an expensive piece of property, peaceful, with natural landscaping and plenty of room for a solitary wolf to chase rabbits and mice.

"I've got bread, eggs and milk. How does French toast sound?" he asked without pulling his head out of the refrigerator.

I was busy ogling his fine posterior when he looked over his shoulder and caught me. "French toast is fine," I said quickly as my face got hot.

He flashed a purely masculine grin and wriggled his butt. I growled and pretended to be reading the ingredients on a can of mixed nuts.

We played around in the kitchen while he fixed breakfast. It was like some kind of fairy tale. I wrapped my arms around his waist and pressed my cheek against the muscles in his back while he pulled the last toast from the pan and plopped it onto a plate.

"Milk okay?" he asked.

"Sure, that's fine. Where'd you learn to cook?"

He shrugged. "I got tired of eating Rice Krispies so I bought a couple books and watched some of the cooking shows."

The thought of Lucas sitting in front of the television watching Julia Child was enough to make me giggle out loud. He gave me a confused look but didn't ask.

"So, how did you swing the time off to get here?" His cheeks blossomed. "I'm not complaining, just curious," he added cautiously.

I put the forks on the table beside the plates. "I requested leave."

His nostrils flared at the scent of my mistruth.

"I did request leave," I reiterated. "It was denied."

He froze in place, the frying pan in one hand, spatula in the other. "And?"

I rearranged the silverware. "I re-filed."

His shoulders slumped. "And?"

"It was denied, so, I, uh, well, I left."

Lucas returned the pan to the stove and tossed the spatula in the sink. "Does Simon know where you are?"

"Uh huh." I rearranged the silverware again.

He slid onto a chair and stared at me. "Are you in trouble?"

I did my best to explain what had happened. Lucas didn't say much, worry etched his face.

"It'll work out, Lucas. Simon was gonna make some calls and get everything legal."

"Legal?"

Damn. Bad choice of words.

"Are you illegal now?" he asked incredulously. "You're in trouble, aren't you? You're in trouble because of me." He ran a hand through his hair.

"Not in trouble, per se. More like walking a fine line."

He didn't go for it. "You're AWOL?"

I grimaced. Not what I wanted to discuss. "Technically, but Simon knows what's going on and he's dealing with the paperwork."

Lucas slammed his hand on the table. "This is exactly what I didn't want to happen. You're ruining your career because of me."

I snorted. He had no idea how much trouble I'd caused during my seventeen-year military career. "My career isn't ruined. I'm just taking leave a little early."

"Without permission," he snarled under his breath. He looked up, his handsome face bruised from the night before. "Because of me."

Ninety-nine times out of a hundred, this type of discussion would have made me angry enough to spit. With Lucas, it was unsettling. He wasn't upset with me, which I could have handled. Instead he felt responsible, angry with himself for creating a hardship for me, and that was much harder to handle.

I cupped his face in my hands. His eyes so filled with dejection my breath caught. "I would give up everything for you." He started to argue so I put a finger to his lips. "However, this is but a typical day in the life of Master Sergeant Breanna Welker. I have gone AWOL more times than either Simon or I can remember and he always fixes the paperwork. Yeah, this time it was for you, but it wasn't the first and certainly won't be the last time I left without going through the proper channels."

He didn't look convinced.

"I love Bravo but nothing, nothing, is more important than you."

It was an awkward moment, one in which neither of us spoke as my words hung heavy in the air. His eyes were wide, staring into mine as if seeking the real truth. His fingers glided along my jaw.

"You would leave Bravo? For me?"

The disbelief on his face took me off-guard. "Well, yeah," I answered, trying to hide the impatience welling inside me. "I mean I'd rather not have to choose, but if I do, then it's definitely you."

The disbelief slowly faded to uncertainty. "I won't let you do that."

He kissed the top of my head and walked into the den without a word. I followed him.

"Lucas?"

"If you want to walk away, Bre, I won't stop you."

"What?" What the hell?

He stared at the empty fireplace.

I exploded. "You think I would walk away because things are tough? You think I'm too weak for this, or have you changed your mind? Maybe having a witch for a mate isn't so convenient."

I don't know what he said because the door slammed too loudly behind me. I hit the front porch and shifted without bothering to check if anyone was around. I left before the waterworks started because I'd be damned if I would cry after what he said.

* * * *

It was a little after four in the morning when I landed in the tree outside of Lucas's house. Lights were on inside. I didn't see any movement, the silence punctuated by the occasional ting of something hitting metal.

I'd been flying around Vicenza for hours and was exhausted and cold. I wanted the warm, strong arms of my wolf. I didn't want to fight. I didn't want to cry. I wanted feel his breath in my hair. None of this was his fault any more than it was mine. It just sucked.

The metallic tings came about every ten seconds. It was an odd sound, especially given the stillness of the night.

I hopped to the ground and shifted to human. I'd give up Bravo, my career, hell, I'd never do magic again if that would keep him safe. We could run away together, like they did in the movies.

Dream on, girlfriend.

Werewolves weren't exactly incognito and with the amount of dominance Lucas threw around, we couldn't hide anywhere. A witch and a werewolf would attract attention, no matter where we landed. Supernaturals were everywhere.

The tinging stopped for about a minute before resuming. The sound was coming from the laundry room so I took the stairs.

I was sure he would scent me first, but he was so engaged in what he was doing he hadn't noticed I was ten feet behind him. The sight of him made me pause. Dressed only in sweat pants and ripped to the hilt, Lucas was more gorgeous every time I saw him. Sweat glistened on his back as he lifted a hockey stick and slammed a puck into the open door of his dryer. The puck clanged against the back of the dryer drum before coming to rest.

"Nice shot."

He whirled, hockey stick held high in the air. The tenderness in his eyes brought tears to mine. He dropped the stick and rushed toward me.

"I'm sorry, I'm so sorry," he breathed into my ear.

Damn, how could I have been so selfish to leave him alone like this? "I'm sorry for leaving. I just needed to get away."

Lucas pulled back. "I tried to find you but you disappeared."

"I know how to fight, Lucas, but I'm not very good with relationship stuff. When you said I could leave, I thought you meant you didn't want me."

His breathing was ragged. "I didn't mean I didn't want you. I meant if you have changed your mind about being with me I would not force you to stay."

"We have to work together to figure this shit out."

He let out a long deep breath and pulled my hand to his lips. "I'm not very good at this relationship stuff either."

Something sarcastic almost escaped before I slammed my lips closed. Lucas was the most sincere man I'd ever met and didn't deserve smart-ass comments.

I kissed his nose. "We're a weird pair, huh?"

He grinned and tucked my hair behind my ear. "A pack of two."

Chapter 30

Lucas

Breanna curled next to me on the sofa, the morning sun making her auburn hair shine like spun gold. We'd spent the last few hours talking about possible solutions to our problem and didn't have a workable plan yet.

"There's something wrong here, Lucas. I felt black magic last night and I felt it when I was here before. While you were talking to your father, I called Simon. Bravo will be here as soon as they can. They've been dispatched to somewhere in Canada to round up a couple of kid-eating trolls and then they are catching a transport to Ederle."

"They're giving up their holiday?"

"Yeah, I felt bad about it, but I need help with the Malandanti issue and whatever else is going on with this pack. Besides, they'll be pissed if I didn't call them for backup in this kind of situation."

"The issues within this pack have been there for a long, long time. They have nothing to do with the Malandanti," I practically snarled at her.

She touched my cheek. "Okay, so why don't you tell me about those issues?"

A door slammed in my mind. "I don't want to talk about it."

"Why? Don't think I'll understand?"

I stormed out of the room and into my backyard. I couldn't tell her. She'd never look at me the same if she knew.

She followed me outside. I couldn't breathe and couldn't make my hands stop shaking.

Her fingertips brushed against my back. "Lucas, I've seen a lot of wolves fight, but I've never seen anything like you did last night. Ten on one and you were holding your own, even with silver in your blood. You have the strongest wolf I've ever felt and believe me, I've been around a hell of a lot of wolves." She brushed her hand through my hair. "Things that don't kill you make you stronger. What happened?"

"I'm not that strong, Breanna. If I were, it would have never happened."

"What would have never happened?"

There was a crack in the wall holding those memories I'd worked so hard to bury. "Stephano."

"The one who stabbed you? Damn, I knew I should have killed that asshole. Next time I won't ask."

I jerked away from her. "When I was nine, Stephano's family moved in with us. His mom is my mom's sister. At first it was great. Stephano was fifteen. We'd play games and build models, stuff me and Nic did before Josef decided Nic needed to spend more time learning pack business and less time playing."

I pinched the bridge of my nose and willed my stomach to settle. I wanted to vomit.

"Stephano started coming into my room at night when I turned ten. My wolf was beginning to show, but werewolves don't have their first change until their sixteenth birthday. Father thought I was exaggerating about my wolf but I wasn't."

I grabbed a tree for support. "My wolf didn't like Stephano. I didn't understand what was happening. When you're young and a natural-born wolf, things don't always make sense. That's why I tried to talk to my father, but he was always busy with Nic going through his first changes. Josef thought I was jealous because Nicolli was turning into a real werewolf and I wasn't. What he didn't realize was my wolf was surging and I didn't know how to stop it."

I took a swing at the tree and rewarded myself with bloody knuckles and flying wood splinters. Breanna grabbed my hand before I could swing again. My stomach lurched.

"Stephano would touch me and I thought that was what wolves did. He kept telling me how much he liked me and he just wanted to be my friend. He would hold me down on the bed and do things to me." I took a breath, but didn't look at her. "One night he really hurt me and I ran into my parents' room. My father was so angry because he thought I was making everything up. If anything was wrong, he would have felt it through our pack ties and he didn't feel anything."

Breanna took my hand. My wolf settled even as my heart raced. Sweat poured down my face as the memories of Stephano roared to life.

"I tried not to go to sleep at night and my grades went down. My mom had conferences with my human teachers and they kept telling her my attitude was bad and I was acting out. Everyone assumed it was a jealousy thing between me and Nic, but it wasn't."

She leaned against my shoulder without saying a word.

"I couldn't take it anymore so I stole a silver dagger from Josef's study and snuck into Stephano's room one night while he was asleep. I stabbed him in the chest, but wasn't strong enough to make the knife go through his ribs. His screaming woke up the whole house."

I tried to swallow away the cottony feeling in my mouth. "My father was furious but, worse, he was ashamed. Stephano told my father I had snuck into his room, that I wanted him to do things to me. He said he refused and I got angry and stabbed him."

"Did nobody believe you?" Breanna asked softly.

I shook my head and tried to make hands stop shaking.

"Father arranged for me to go away to a private boarding school in France so I would be away from the pack. Mom said it was to protect me. It was really because he didn't want me around."

And still doesn't, but I'm all he has left.

"Son of a bitch," Breanna snarled under her breath.

"I was the youngest kid at L'Ermitage. The headmaster was a werewolf. The other kids were human. They didn't have much to do with me and I didn't try very hard to make friends. I wanted to go home."

"Even baby wolves need their packs," Breanna whispered.

"I'd been at L'Ermitage for three months and nobody came to visit. Mom called. My father never did. One day I got in a fight when some of the other boys tried to steal my lunch. Headmaster Dampier called me into his office and gave me ten lashes for fighting."

I slammed my hand on the table. "He locked me in a closet without anything to eat or drink." God, it had been so dark in that closet. "He said if he heard me crying, he'd give me ten more. Sometime during the night, a couple of slices of bread slid under the door. At first I was too scared to take them, but I was so hungry I ate them anyway.

"The next day, after Dampier let me out, I was sitting by myself in the library. I'd missed breakfast and lunch. A blond kid I'd never seen before came over and sat with me. He didn't ask, just took the chair across the table. When he was sure nobody was watching, he pulled a sandwich and a bottle of water out of his backpack and gave it to me."

"Tristyn?"

"Tristyn and I became friends and I finally told him everything that had happened. He was the first person and the only person who ever believed me."

He'd never said a word, just sat there and listened. He saved my life.

"I believe you."

I stared into the darkness. "I'm not so good with werewolves, Breanna. My wolf surges when I get around them, particularly males. I don't always know how to pull him back so we end up fighting a lot."

Fucked up and broken.

She lifted my fingers to her lips. "Your wolf is trying to protect you, just like when you were a kid."

"I know, but that makes pack meetings really difficult for me. Hell, I don't even like female werewolves. The pack never understood what happened. They think I snapped and tried to kill a packmate. Josef never told anyone my side of the story."

He never even asked me what happened.

"Your wolf stays defensive and that's why the other wolves stay away from you?"

"I can't stop it. My wolf is always angry, always ready to fight whenever I'm around other wolves."

Fucked up and broken.

She leaned against my shoulder and her touch quieted my mind.

"With you, my wolf is calm. My world is right side up instead of upside down like it usually is."

"Oh, so I'm your personal source of Zen, huh?"

"Maybe that's why I could do the pack meeting. It was the first time I've been to a pack meeting since I went away to college."

My last pack meeting had been a disaster also. I'd spent the whole time in the corner trying not to throw up. Nic had laughed at me.

Breanna leaned against the wall. "Do you think it was a setup?"

"Maybe, probably, no, I don't know." The pack hated me.

"You need to get out of this pack."

"It isn't that easy. I'm the Alpha's only remaining son. Alpha's sons don't walk away from their packs."

"This isn't your pack."

"By birth it is, whether I want it or not."

"Your father is an ass who has done nothing to deserve your loyalty."

I rubbed my temples, hoping to alleviate some of the pounding. "He's the Alpha of the largest pack in the world. He does what he thinks is best for his pack."

"What about what's best for his son?" Breanna demanded.

"There's something wrong with me, Bre. If I was normal, Stephano would have never come after me."

She stomped her foot. "Stephano needs to be hung up by his balls in a swamp somewhere. That shit he did had nothing to do with something being wrong with you."

She was trying to make me feel better, but I knew the truth. "I've never fit with the pack. My father and I fight constantly. I have a difficult time controlling my wolf. I've disappointed my parents with almost every decision I've ever made and now I'm ruining your life."

"Ruining my life? Really? Aren't you being just a touch melodramatic?"

"Aaron was right about me. I'm fucked up and you deserve better."

Her face went red as she stormed around the room. "Aaron? Aaron said that to you? The same Aaron who went goo-goo over a vampire who used him as a Slurpee and Bravo had to go rescue him? Aaron who can't keep his mouth shut? I will kick his ass all over Wisconsin when I see him."

Her tirade made me smile.

"We're mates, Lucas, and like it or not, you are stuck with me. Unlike the rest of your fucked-up family, I will not walk away from you, nor will I send you away. I'm here for the good and the bad so you may as well get used to it and get over the attitude. If I deserve better, then you'd better step it up and be whatever it is you think I deserve because, baby, you're mine, I'm yours, and that's the way it is."

She leaned against the tree and crossed her arms.

"And for the record, you didn't do anything wrong," she added sternly.

"What?"

"When you were a kid and all that shit happened, your father should have protected you, not sent you away."

The little pieces of wall that held back my feelings washed away as she touched my jaw and turned my face to her.

"Not. Your. Fault."

I'd have given my soul to hear that when I was a kid.

"You're in my world now and I promise you'll always have somebody on your side."

Her words slowly seeped into my emotionally mushy brain. "I'm sorry about earlier."

She planted a kiss on my lips. "Forgiven and forgotten. Got any ice cream?"

* * * *

I left her with a kiss on the cheek and a promise I'd call later. Breanna was going back to Ederle to return the Humvee and do paperwork while I headed to the office to finish the purchase orders before the Christmas holiday.

"Hi, Clara," I said, hurrying into my office.

"Good morning, Mr. Benelli," she answered in her usual chipper voice.

My office looked like nothing had happened. A new desk sat in the place of the splintered one, the holes in the walls repaired, and all the scattered papers stacked neatly on the desk.

I leaned against the doorframe. "Thank you, Clara."

The lady werewolf was labeling file folders. "You're welcome, Mr. Benelli," she said with a smile. "It was good to see you at the pack meeting Saturday night."

"Probably my last one for a while."

"I heard about Stephano."

I could have gone all day and not heard that name.

Clara slammed a filing cabinet drawer. "You should have let the witch have him."

"You know about that?"

Clara shuffled the papers on her desk. "The Alpha forbade any wolf to attack her or you. He was very upset about the incident involving Stephano." She looked at me. "He realized how close he came to losing you."

I bowed my head. I hadn't called or anything since that night. "How was my mother?"

"Humph. Gemma was fine other than being angry with your father. She thought he should have killed the witch and believed Stephano only attacked because he was under the witch's spell."

"What? Breanna saved my life. Stephano wasn't under any kind of spell."

Clara rearranged the stacks of papers on her desk. "The Alpha agrees. However, your mother was livid with his decision to spare the witch's life."

I never in a million years would have thought my father would be more accepting than my mother.

"What happened to Stephano?"

"I'm not sure. He was taken to the holding cell in the Alpha's basement and nothing more was mentioned about him."

A tremor jolted my body. I'd spent time in that dank, dreary cell as a child after I'd attacked Stephano. I'd begged my father not to lock me away by myself in the darkness, but he dragged me down the stairs by my arm and tossed me inside. I remember crying until I made myself sick. To this day I didn't sleep in total darkness.

It was almost time to go home when the smell of feminine musk and the slamming of doors announced the presence of my mother.

"Lucas," she huffed as she entered my office without a glance at Clara. "I need you to come with me tonight."

"Sorry, Mom, I promised Breanna I'd be home for dinner."

"What? Don't tell me you plan to see that witch again. For God's sake, Lucas, what are you doing? Your father has Stephano locked in the basement because of what that witch forced him to do."

"Breanna had nothing to do with Stephano attacking me and you know it. That's old, unfinished business. Breanna saved my life."

Her deep brown eyes flashed silver. "Could you for once doing something right and stop this nonsense? That witch is creating a rift within the pack. She is using you to get to the Alpha so she can destroy us."

My wolf was rumbling. "Breanna isn't using me for anything."

My mother cackled--a terrible, evil sound. "You are a fool."

I don't know what stunned me more, the iciness of her voice or her actual words.

"Gemma, there is a call for you on line one," Clara called calmly from her desk.

"Who is it?" my mother snapped.

Clara never met my mother's silver-flaked glare. "The Alpha."

Gemma snatched the phone from Clara's hand. Whatever Josef said made my mother livid. She slammed the phone on Clara's desk and left without another word. I was speechless.

Clara inspected the injured phone and tossed it in the garbage.

"Clara, why did my father call on the office line?"

Clara winked at me. "He didn't. I called him."

"Thanks, Clara."

She smiled politely and returned to her work as I headed out the door. My truck was out back in the employee parking area. I'd never gotten into using the VIP parking at the front of Benelli Enterprises. I left that parking area for my parents.

I'd only taken a few steps into the parking lot when the presence of another being set off my wolf. There was no musk so it wasn't a werewolf. I checked the stone Breanna had given me. It was cool to the touch, though there was a red mark on my chest where the stone had been resting.

"Ciao, Lucas."

Istagio Serendelli stepped into the dim light of the parking lot. Istagio was, as always, impeccably dressed. Tonight his dark eyes were troubled, his forehead wrinkled in concern.

"What's up, Istagio?"

"There is a situation I wish to discuss with you. Is there somewhere we can speak in private?"

I motioned to my truck and unlocked the doors. Istagio felt we needed to drive and not idle in the parking lot. He was as paranoid as every other vampire I knew. When we were several blocks from Benelli Enterprises, he broke his silence.

"Talia is missing."

"When?" Another disappearance wasn't a good sign.

"I haven't heard from her in almost three days. She went to visit a friend in Marseille, but never arrived."

"A friend?" I asked skeptically. Talia wasn't exactly Miss Congeniality.

Istagio shrugged off my skepticism. "Yes, another vampire she had spent time with many years ago. The two normally visit once a month and it was Talia's turn to go to France."

I glanced at my watch. Breanna would wonder where I was. "Do you want me to call Tristyn and have him check into her disappearance?"

Istagio watched the passing traffic. "Yes, I would appreciate his assistance."

"What else is going on?"

Istagio leaned his head back on the seat. "Have you had any indication of a witch being in Vicenza?"

Oh shit. No need to lie. Eventually the vampires would sense Breanna's presence and vampires hated witches.

"I know of an earth witch, but she is of no threat."

"I know of only one earth witch and she is most definitely a threat to her enemies. No, I am referring to black witches. I have felt the vibrations of dark magic in the air."

I was relieved the conversation turned away from Breanna. At least Istagio knew about earth witches. Unlike the werewolves, the vampires tended to try to learn about their enemies rather than just killing them on sight.

"There have been more rumors about Malandanti."

Istagio flinched at the mention of the dreaded dark witches. We weren't friends, but he was someone I preferred to have on my side.

"I hoped we killed them all three hundred years ago. It was a horrific battle and many of my kind lost their lives."

I'd heard the Malandanti wars had been equally brutal for werewolves. The dark witches had sacrificed my father's mother and his older sister, which helped explain his zero-tolerance policy toward witches.

Istagio squinted as the bright lights of an oncoming tractor-trailer flashed in his face. "Have you spoken to Tristyn about the rumors?"

"A little. I know the military is on its way."

Istagio arched a brow. "Bravo is coming to Italy?"

"They were here about three months ago and are scheduled to return sometime during the holidays."

The funny little smile returned to Istagio's face. "Ah, good. It has been too long." He shook off the distant look and resumed our conversation. "I will contact a few of my allies and determine the vampire course of action. Would you please keep me advised of any actions the werewolves may be taking?"

Werewolves and vampires generally didn't work together. Sharing a common enemy as powerful as the Malandanti, werewolves would be stupid not to pool the resources. However, the werewolves would never publically acknowledge any help from the vampires and the vampires were equally stubborn. It was another old-world belief system that vampires and werewolves were mortal enemies.

"I'll call as soon as I know anything." We'd made a big circle around the block and I was pulling back into the Benelli Enterprises parking area. "If the vampires come up with any ideas, will you let me know?"

Istagio inclined his head. "Absolutely. Our kinds will need to work together if the rumors of the Malandanti return are true. There would have been much less bloodshed three hundred years ago had we trusted one another." He extended an icy hand. "Please let me know when Bravo arrives."

With a quick goodbye Istagio disappeared into the darkness, leaving me to ponder the weirdness that seemed to be coming from all directions.

I'd never come home to a meal waiting. The food smelled great, but everything in my body was hungry for the woman waiting at the door. I was instantly hard at the sight of her in sexy black jeans and one of my Boston Bruins t-shirts.

I tugged at the hem of the shirt. "Hmm, looks better on you."

Her cheeks turned the cutest shade of pink. "I missed you."

If she had any idea how much I liked seeing her in my clothes, she didn't let on. Knowing my scent was drenched all over her body was satisfying to me and my wolf. I really wanted to lay her down and rub my body all over hers, but she'd worked so hard to make a great dinner, I didn't want to insult her by having the dessert first.

"How was your day?" she asked, placing a whole turkey on the table.

"Okay. My mom came by and had a tantrum. How about you?"

"Well," she started as she placed a plate of dinner rolls beside me. "I spent most of the day at Ederle speaking with General Armfield, the base CO."

Hmm, that sounded important. "And what did General Armfield have to say to my most beautiful mate?"

Her cheeks flushed pink as she poured glasses of milk. "He offered me a job."

My fork clattered onto my plate. "What?"

She smiled apprehensively. "It's a new position."

"This position, would it be based at Ederle?"

She nodded and I couldn't stop myself from leaning over the turkey and kissing her. She was going to be here, in Italy, with me. Then it hit me.

"Does this mean you're leaving Bravo?"

She shrugged half-heartedly. "Yeah."

I took her hand and pulled her over onto my lap. "You don't want that."

"No, but I'll be with you."

Taking her away from the people she loves? Selfish bastard.

I wrapped my arms around her. "You don't want to leave them."

"No, and I won't leave you either. There're too many enemies here, too many lies and secrets. My gut says you need someone you can trust here. If I'm assigned to Ederle, your father can't come after me. The Divine Council will support my right to be here."

"I wish I could just fight him and get it over with."

She rocked back to look into my eyes. "You think you'll kill him?"

"Our wolves hate each other."

She narrowed her eyes. "No offense, but is that normal for a father and son? The only ones I know are Cody and Galen and they get along great."

Nic and my father had been so close they could read each other's minds. In my father's eyes, Nic was the sun. I was more like mud. "We've never been close, even before everything happened."

"I still say he's an asshole," she snipped.

"He's my father, asshole or not." I should have been at least a little angry at her insults about my father. I wasn't.

"Since I would be employed by the military, the Italian Pack would have to deal with my presence."

"What would you be doing at Ederle?"

"Paperwork, mostly. It would be an on-base position." The hint of sadness in her voice punctured my heart.

"If I can work things out with my father and get released, could you rejoin Bravo?"

She took a deep breath and bit her lip. "I could try out again if a spot was available and if the higher-ups approve my request." She shrugged like she was trying to convince herself she spoke the truth. "Bravo will be fine. Simon can handle the wolves and Ordy has always wanted my position. Levi needs a place of his own, so I'll offer him my house. He doesn't have any money, but Galen will loan it to him."

"Will you be all right?"

Her lip quivered. "I'll be with you. I'll be fine."

"This isn't fair to you."

She snorted softly. "Most of life isn't. What's your point?"

I leaned my head against her shoulder. "Bravo is your family."

Her eyes suddenly sparkled mischievously. "What's wrong, wolf? Afraid I'll cramp your bachelor pad style?" She asked as she nibbled my ear.

The food would have to wait. I carried her into the bedroom and tossed her onto the bed. "I'm a mated wolf now, baby. My bachelor days are over."

She wriggled to the top of the bed. "Yeah, so how many women have you taken in this bed?"

"None," I answered truthfully.

She wrinkled her nose. "What? I don't believe that. A stud like you? Women must be lining up down the street."

I took my shirt off and she made the cutest growling noise. "No, I've never had another woman in this house other than my mother and if you are going to be the mate of a werewolf, you must learn the nuances of growling."

She sat up and glared at me. "And what is wrong with my growls?"

I nipped the skin along her neck. Heavens, she smelled good. "You sound like a cat."

A sharp slap across the back of my head interrupted my exploration of her neck.

"I do not sound like a cat."

I nibbled her earlobe and she purred like a kitten. "Okay, babe, whatever you say."

Chapter 31

Breanna

It had been days since I'd seen my unit and, damn, I missed their smelly asses. The first one to scent me was Aaron and he dashed across the tarmac and scooped me into a big wolf hug. The others soon followed, a sea of musk swallowing me. I was used to it since the werewolves were so openly affectionate, even with each other. They loved high-fiving, hugging, slapping each other on the back, or just bumping shoulders. It was a wolf thing, always craving physical interaction.

Damn, I'm gonna miss this.

"Hey, Bre, it ain't true about you taking that post at Ederle, is it?" Ordy asked.

I figured Simon would have told them. "Yep, I had to do it, Ordy. There's some heavy shit going down over here and we need somebody on top of it."

Bravo will come to visit. I'll see them.

He scowled. "Then let's send Aaron's scrawny ass over here. At least we could all get some sleep without having to listen to his stories about women."

I can make new friends and Simon will take care of Bravo.

Aaron leaped into the conversation. "Oh, go ahead and tell him the real reason you're taking it, Bre. It's that fucked-up Italian wolf."

I punched him in the shoulder. "Hey! Don't say that about Lucas." I owed him an ass kicking anyway.

Aaron rolled his eyes and I punched him again. "Truth is truth, Bre. You're leaving us and throwing away your career for a loser."

"Go to hell, Aaron." I headed toward Celeste. I needed her perpetual happiness and pointless chatter.

Camp Ederle. No elves. No vampires. No werewolves. Just humans.

"Oh, Breanna," she chirped, "I've missed you so much!"

I could pick her up she was so tiny. "I missed you, too, Cee. Everything going okay for you?"

She filled me in on the latest happenings and gave a great rundown about the progress Levi was making with his young wolf education.

Celeste finally stopped and took a breath. "Now, tell me about you and Lucas."

It was fun talking girl stuff with Cee and I knew she would be happy for me. She giggled and jumped up and down when I got to the story about picking out an ugly Christmas tree and clapped at my tales of cooking dinner. Cec, more than anyone, understood my limited domestic abilities.

"Ah, Breanna, my dear, it is good to see you," Simon said as he pulled me into a hug and kissed the top of my head. *This is a no-tears-allowed zone. Suck it up.*

After a quick debriefing, the Bravo wolves disappeared into the mess hall. The Bravo vampires disappeared to the busy city district. Both groups were hungry for dinner and needed to be satisfied before the big meeting tonight.

The Divine Council had called a Gathering, a meeting of the Council and the supernatural leadership of the area. There would be lots of werewolves and vampires. Bravo would also be there.

This will be my last formal duty with Bravo. Damn.

Simon and Celeste agreed to have dinner with Lucas and me before the Gathering. I wanted Simon's opinion on how we should handle the Gathering. Lucas wanted us to go together or at least sit together. I thought we would be better to go separately and remain as such during the meeting.

Lucas was worried about me. I kept telling him I had lots of guys in camo watching my back. I was worried about him, specifically about his father. The Alpha didn't like me, yeah, big surprise, and I didn't like the way he treated Lucas. For an Alpha, Josef Benelli didn't seem very protective of his wolves, especially his only son.

The restaurant was a short drive and Lucas was waiting by the door when we arrived. It felt like I hadn't seen him for days even though it had been fewer than four hours.

"Hey, baby," Lucas whispered as he nipped my ear. "You smell like ten different wolves." There was a little irritation in his voice, more from his wolf than him.

I nuzzled his neck. "Hmm, more like fifteen, but who's counting?"

A growl rumbled deep in his chest so I left out the part about five vampires.

We made our way to our table and ordered. Simon and Celeste opted to share a dinner since he would not be eating anyway. Lucas and I didn't share. He wanted his rare steak and I wanted a big veggie stromboli.

Dinner was over much too quickly. Simon agreed with my take on attending the Gathering. Lucas reluctantly agreed to go with his father while I would lead the second line of Bravo. It made sense even though my mate did not approve. I didn't want to tell Lucas how much I wanted to march in with Bravo. It was my duty.

Not that I liked the idea of Lucas sitting with a group of pack wolves who cared nothing about him, but the other wolves were not nearly as likely to harass him if he was beside his father. I had complete faith Lucas could best any wolf who would challenge him, but even he was no match for a group attack.

"Will the Ambassador be attending the Gathering tonight?" Simon asked as he held the door for all of us.

Lucas sighed. "No, Tristyn and Alex are in South Africa trying to head off a vampire war." From the heave of his shoulders, Lucas would have felt better having his friend at the Gathering. I would have felt better, too, and it would have been nice to have another witch in the building, if only for moral support.

"Breanna, the CO at Ederle was quite impressed with you and has called three times asking if you had made a decision," Simon said as he pretended to sip a glass of red wine. "Have you made a decision?"

I glanced at Lucas. "I'm gonna take it."

Simon nodded slowly. "I will call Ederle tomorrow." He let out a breath, something vampires rarely did since they didn't need to breathe. "Are you sure?"

"Yes."

It hurt to answer his question when I wanted to shout no, no, no. It was so stupid, really, the whole pack and territory thing. I'd bet Galen would let Lucas stay with me regardless of pack affiliation. Josef Benelli's head would pop off and spin around if that happened. Ordinarily I wouldn't give a happy damn what someone like Josef Benelli thought, but he held power over Lucas and I would have to play nice. Well, sorta, anyway.

"When do you report to Ederle?" Celeste asked as she snuggled under Simon's arm.

"January first." Lucas squeezed my hand. I smiled at him. He was so excited about me staying in Italy and I was, too, for the most part.

We said goodnight to Simon and Celeste and headed home. Lucas tucked me under his arm as we trekked into the blustery December night. Shoppers scurrying to finish their Christmas shopping crowded the streets.

"I thought after the Gathering we could go out if you wanted, dancing or something." He tried so hard to act nonchalant about this Gathering.

"All I want to do is go home with you where we can be by ourselves."

Tonight would be hard for both of us for different reasons. He hated pack things, which now I understood. I hated meetings like this because my guys were always on edge out of concern for me. I also despised the attitude some of the Divine Council members had toward Bravo Company. The ones who had never gotten their hands dirty a day in their supernatural lives loved to pass judgment on us.

Most of all, I hated the thought of Lucas surrounded by the Italian Pack. They didn't care about him at all and, frankly, I didn't have much faith his father would help him if he needed it. Lucas, however, was loyal to his father and would at least hold up the image of a united Italian Pack at the Gathering.

Damn, this was so complicated. If Lucas was the son of any other werewolf, we wouldn't be having this discussion. Being the son of the Alpha made it difficult. Stupid bullshit.

I slid my arms around his waist and leaned against his chest, the steady beat of his heart thumping in my ear. "Keep a check on that stone I gave you."

His breath tickled the top of my head. "We'll be all right. We can get through this and then I'll talk to my father again." His chest rose and fell with a deep breath before he pulled back to look at me. "Are you sure you want to take the position at Ederle?"

No, but what choice did I have? "It's the best move for now."

He trailed a finger along my jaw. "Is it really best for you?"

"Being with you is what's best for me and if this is the way we have to do it, then so be it. I'm not gonna lie to you and pretend this is all great. I want to go back to America to be with Bravo, but if I have to make sacrifices to be with you, then I will."

His arms tightened around me as he nuzzled my hair. "We can buy a new house if you like, something closer to Ederle."

"I don't need a new house to make me happy, Lucas."

He bit his lower lip and sighed. I laid my head against his chest and listened to the steady beat of his heart.

Chapter 32

Lucas

My father was pacing by his study window when I arrived a little before midnight. The Gathering was a very big deal, full of posturing and pretension. I had only attended one as a Divine Council agent and hated it. Tonight would be worse.

"Where's Mom?" I expected her to meet me at the door and fly into another one of her rages about Stephano.

"Downstairs," my father mumbled without turning around.

"Is she riding with us?"

Josef stopped his pacing. "Us?"

I took a deep breath and pushed my wolf back. "Don't you think it's best if we arrive together and show a unified front for the Italian Pack?"

Josef's eyebrows rose. "Yes, I do think that is best, but did not expect you to share my view."

To be honest, I didn't share his view--however, I was his second-in-command even if I didn't want to be. Any sign of weakness at a time like this could lead to a disaster. Breanna was right, but that didn't mean I liked being here.

"How many wolves are you taking?" I asked, not really caring.

Gatherings like these were tricky. Show up with too many wolves and your pack would look insecure. Show up with too few and your pack would look weak. The Italian Pack was easily the largest pack in all of Europe and with the meeting on Italian soil, the image my father's pack projected would be under scrutiny.

"Twelve, counting the two of us."

"And Mom?"

Josef shrugged, his face blank. "She will be there, but not sitting with me."

For the life of me, I didn't understand how my mother could be taking Stephano's side in all this. She ranted to anyone who would listen that Breanna was the cause of all of the Italian Pack's problems. Though they were not mates, my parents had been together over one hundred years. For her not to be by Father's side could send the wrong message to the other packs and that hurt my father deeply.

"Where is the witch?" Josef asked as he looked toward the open study door.

"Breanna is with her unit. We will not be together during the meeting."

He narrowed his eyes. I took a deep breath and prepared for his rant.

"And why is that?" Josef asked sarcastically. "She change her mind about being with you?"

The venom in his words stung. "No, she felt it would be best for your pack if the two of us did not draw attention. She felt the issues at hand were of such importance that we should not distract anyone from working together in order to defeat the Malandanti."

He looked stunned by my answer. My mother stomped up the steps from the basement and we braced for Hurricane Gemma.

"Lucas," she said, entering the study. "Go downstairs and apologize to your cousin. He is miserable without his pack."

Unless it was snowing in hell, there would be no apology from me. I looked at the woman who appeared to be my mother and tried to discern what on earth was wrong with her. My father's disappointment in me wasn't unusual, but my mother had never acted this way, no matter how many times I screwed up. It made no sense she would so staunchly back Stephano when multiple wolves had come forth to speak of his plan to kill me.

Stephano had known Ernesto was not a real threat to me, but had not expected me to yield and walk away. Stephano's plan had been to attack after the challenge because he thought the fight would have weakened me. When the fight didn't happen, he recruited six more wolves to help him attack after I left the sanctity of my father's land.

The one who had suffered most was Ernesto. The moment I yielded, Tessa shrieked and stormed out of the challenge area. She'd never cared for Ernesto and had led him along for weeks. It had all been a ploy between her and Stephano to get to me. She'd told Ernesto in front of the entire pack she didn't want him. Ernesto disappeared that night.

Alpha power filled the room. "Lucas and I are riding to the Gathering together. Do you wish to ride with us?"

"Where is the witch?" she snarled, her eyes flashing silver.

I didn't know who this woman was. She could not be my mother.

"Not here," Josef answered with an impatient sigh. "Are you riding with us or will you be taking another car?"

"Tessa and I will be going together. Lucas should ride with us."

My father jumped in before I could answer. "Lucas will be riding with me. Let's go, son."

It was a tiny moment, just three little letters, but it meant the world to me. He hadn't called me "son" in years.

The ride to the Gathering was quiet for me since Josef spent the entire twenty-minute trip on his phone. He was shoring up old alliances and calling in favors. The politics had already begun and we hadn't even gotten through the doors yet.

Gatherings of supernatural force always took place in large, old structures on the outskirts of town. The Divine Council employed sorcerers, who were responsible for ensuring the secrecy of these meetings. To the human eye, the building would look deserted, no cars in the parking lots, no lights burning inside. However, the inside would be teeming with the energies of hundreds of werewolves and vampires along with whatever other supernatural might have been invited.

The stench of musk took my breath when I stepped from the vehicle. Josef was wrapping up a phone conversation with an Alpha from France and I'd heard the word "witch" mentioned more times than I liked.

I walked a step behind my father, a sign of respect for my Alpha. The other members of the pack, including my mother, fell into step behind me. When Josef pulled open the door, it took every ounce of strength I had to keep my wolf at bay. This was my worst nightmare, a room full of Alphas and Alpha wannabes, and they were all staring at us.

I clenched my teeth and focused my attention on the back of my father's head. If I made eye contact, my wolf would surge and nothing good could come from that. The whispers were rampant as we took our seats near the front of the meeting area. The vampires congregated to the right of the building while the werewolves were to the left. Bravo Company would occupy the middle section.

I had hoped Bravo would already be in place, but they had yet to arrive. It was going to be tough watching Breanna from so far away.

"Bonjour, Josef," one of the four French Alphas said as he closed the distance between himself and my father. "I received your message and will do as you asked. I consider my debt to you paid and am no longer at your beckon."

My father extended his hand. "Terms agreed."

The two shook hands and the French Alpha disappeared into the mass of churning werewolf bodies. Before I could ask my father what the Frenchman meant, a Lithuanian werewolf approached.

"Alpha Benelli?"

My father looked at the young Lithuanian like he was worthless. "What?"

The youngster bowed his head. "My Alpha sends his regards and says he will support your position."

Josef nodded curtly. "Give him my regards."

The Lithuanian kept his head bowed as he backed away from my father. Josef Benelli was the most powerful Alpha in this building and he was putting out enough dominance to choke a bear. My wolf was edgy, the walls of the massive building closing in. I forced my thoughts to another time, to the night Breanna and I picked out a Christmas tree.

I'd gone to the biggest, proudest tree on the lot. It was magnificent as it towered over all the other trees. My mate, however, found a smaller, less perfect tree on the wreath lot.

"How much is this one?" she'd asked in broken Italian.

The weathered old man smiled at her attempt to speak the language. "You don't want that one, *tesorina mia*. That one will be used to make wreaths."

"Why?" she asked as she fingered the branches.

The old man pulled the tree forward and spun it around to show a damaged area. "It was on the bottom of the pile during shipment and is not perfect. No one will want it."

She had looked over at me, her eyes determined. "We want it."

"Why would you want this ugly tree?"

She reached for my hand. "Because you don't have to be perfect to be wanted."

I pulled her into my arms in the middle of a snowy, deserted Christmas tree lot while the little old man bundled our ugly tree. I'd offered to pay. He declined, saying being around someone as beautiful as Breanna was payment enough.

A door slammed open and I returned from my mental hiatus. The Divine Council was entering the room, led by the Elvin leader, Shalamon Lisel. The tall, thin elf was ancient and had been the Divine Council leader for nearly one hundred years. It had been his prophecy that foretold of Tristyn's existence, a living vampire who would help bring peace to the supernatural world. As typical of elves, Shalamon had golden blond hair and fair blue eyes. He was a gifted psychic and, as he entered the room, his presence was a wave of calm.

The Council members took their seats as the wooden floor vibrated, the members of Bravo Company marching in. They were dressed in battle fatigues, shiny black boots, and each member packed a sidearm and at least one knife. Simon led the group and I scanned the faces for my mate.

She marched through the door and a murmur washed through the crowd. My groin tightened at the sight of her. Dressed in baggy camo, she was still beautiful.

Her eyes, just like those of every other Bravo member, were straight ahead and her face was stone. She was the only witch in a room full of supernaturals, and if she was the least bit intimidated, it didn't show. She was power, she was grace, and she was mine.

I choked back a growl as she passed French Pack wolves and they made obscene gestures toward her. Several of the members of Bravo placed a hand on their sidearms but made no eye contact.

A muscle ticked in her jaw, but her eyes remained straight ahead as she passed the Italian Pack. A derisive hiss came from someone nearby. She didn't flinch.

Once Bravo had taken their seats, the meeting began. The Council spoke of alliances between packs and a few points of political business among the vampire factions. The master vampires were not really territorial, but they were protective of members of their lines, those vampires they had created. The werewolves were extremely territorial and an innocent mistake like crossing territory lines usually ended in a killing.

I was only half listening as the orders of business continued. I couldn't take my eyes off Breanna. She, along with the other members of Bravo, was sitting at relaxed attention, very aware of every motion around her. Her auburn hair, pulled back into a tight braid, stopped at her shoulders.

"Alpha Benelli, you have indicated you wish to address the Council," Shalamon Lisel said. The Elvin leader's voice was celestial. Everyone in the building could hear him, though he barely spoke above a whisper.

My father stood and I rose to my feet behind him. It was a show of a united pack and though pack politics were pointless to me, I did enjoy the feeling that for once my father and I were on the same side.

"Leader Lisel, I have spoken to many Alphas and we are all greatly concerned about the possible return of the Malandanti. I, on behalf of the Italian Pack, petition the Council to support open pack hunts for witches."

It was as if a giant foot had kicked me in the stomach. Open pack hunts were opportunities for werewolf packs to hunt and kill witches on sight.

Hundreds if not thousands of witches had been torn to bits by wolf packs all over Europe. The packs never stopped to determine the nature of the witch, so innocent white witches were destroyed along with the much more sinister black witches.

I drew in a ragged breath, which won me a wicked look from my father. I met his eyes and then turned my attention to Breanna. She hadn't moved a muscle, though her jaw did look clenched tighter than before.

I grabbed the chair in front of me and engaged in out-and-out battle with my wolf. He wanted my father's blood for threatening Breanna.

I was losing my fight to my wolf when a calm voice spoke to me. "Do not fear, Lucas. Your mate knows you do not support your father's stance."

I looked around. There was nobody speaking to me.

"Remain at your father's side and I will deal with this issue."

Shalamon Lisel watched me intently. He gave the tiniest smile before turning his attention back to my father.

"Alpha Benelli, you say you have spoken to the other Alphas. Who here supports the open pack hunt proposal?"

All around the room Alpha werewolves stood. The Elvin leader looked across the room with his eyes narrowed.

"Vampires, do you support Alpha Benelli's proposal?"

A blond master vampire from France addressed the Council. "I speak only for myself and my lines, but we do not support the genocide of another supernatural race. There are peaceful witches who do not deserve to be hunted like animals simply because they are magical."

Shalamon Lisel nodded and said nothing. Another master vampire from Spain did support my father's proposal and that created a furor of conversation. The members of Bravo continued to stare straight ahead. A few seated on the ends did sneak peeks at the areas making the most noise.

With a wave of his hand Shalamon Lisel quieted the crowd. "Major DuChard, do you believe open pack hunts are a plausible solution to the threat of the Malandanti?"

Simon stood and bowed to the Council. "No, sir, I do not."

The elf was scrutinizing Breanna as Simon spoke.

"What is your opinion, Master Sergeant Welker?" Shalamon Lisel asked with his hands tented.

Breanna stood and the murmurs began again. She waited for silence before speaking.

"Leader Lisel, with all due respect, sir, I am a soldier. I have no opinion on Divine Council policy. I follow the orders of my commanding officer."

She nodded to Simon and retook her seat. The room was eerily silent.

A Swiss werewolf member of the Divine Council addressed Simon. "Major DuChard, how many witches has Bravo Company encountered in the last ten years?"

Simon stood at rapt attention. "Twenty-seven, sir."

"And the nature of these witches?"

"Fifteen were black witches, seven were gray, four were white witches, and one was an earth witch."

"Were any of these witches Malandanti?"

"No, sir."

The Swiss werewolf leaned back in his chair. "What is the status of those witches?"

"The black witches were killed during combat, three of the gray were executed on orders from the Divine Council while the other four were disciplined and released. The four white witches were left in peace, though two later died from wounds they received during an unprovoked werewolf attack. The earth witch is my second-in-command."

A Russian wood fae member of the Divine Council tilted her head. "Who among you was responsible for the executions?"

Simon blinked once. "Master Sergeant Welker and myself, ma'am."

The wood fae looked at Breanna. "Master Sergeant Welker, how do you feel about killing your own kind?"

Breanna's shoulders heaved as she popped to her feet. I had thought this meeting was going to be difficult for me, but what I was dealing with was nothing compared to what she getting.

"Ma'am, I am a soldier. I follow the orders of my commanding officer. It is my duty to protect the members of my unit, the members of the supernatural world, and the occupants of the human realm with diligence. I take no pleasure in killing any being, regardless of the supernatural race. However, I will do whatever I must to ensure the safety of my fellow soldiers."

A German vampire Divine Council member looked amused. "Have you killed vampires, Master Sergeant Welker?"

"Yes, sir."

A Czech werewolf Divine Council member leaned forward, his eyes flickering silver. "Have you killed werewolves?"

"Yes, sir."

The werewolves did not like that answer. Breanna held fast. A brash member of the Belgian werewolves lurched forward.

"That witch killed my cousin," the red-haired Belgian bellowed. "I demand vengeance."

Growls and cheers of support abounded. I was seconds from leaping across the aisle and choking the idiot when Shalamon Lisel's voice echoed in my head.

"She is safe, young Benelli. Your actions will not help. She will jump to your defense and endanger herself to be by your side."

The Czech werewolf nodded his head. "Yes, I have heard of that killing. What does the witch have to say about that?"

Simon rose to Breanna's side. "I would request Master Sergeant Welker be treated with the respect a soldier of her rank deserves or Bravo Company will not take part in this Gathering."

The Belgian werewolves were agitated and yelling threats. The chaotic energy increased in the room and even the vampires were edging forward. The members of Bravo Company took protective positions around Breanna while she stood firm beside Simon.

Shalamon Lisel stood and silence engulfed the room. "Master Sergeant Welker, please accept my apologies for the disrespect of some members of this Divine Council. Your service and dedication to Bravo Company is above reproach."

She nodded stoically. "Thank you, sir."

I'd never realized until that moment how difficult it was for her to serve. She risked her life to keep the supernatural world safe and this was the payment she received.

Simon addressed the German werewolves. "Your cousin had attacked, killed, and eaten three humans by the time we caught up with him. Master Sergeant Welker was trying to talk him down, but he charged and she had no choice but to kill him. He had injured four members of Bravo and was out of control. It was a justified measure and, for his crimes, much quicker and humane than a man-killer deserves."

Ordy turned to the Czech werewolf Divine Council member. "Master Sergeant Welker has saved every werewolf in this unit at one time or another from certain death. She jumped into a freezing river to pull me out of a truck when a bunch of trolls we were chasing blew up a bridge. Sir, threaten her and you threaten all of us and believe me, boy, you don't want us coming after your ass."

Christopher stood beside Breanna. He faced the vampire Divine Council Representative. "Master Sergeant Welker is an asset to this company and not one among us would hesitate giving up our lives to protect her."

The silence was deafening. A werewolf threatening other werewolves and vampires threatening vampires in the name of a witch was unheard of and, if you believed what my father was muttering, unnatural.

"The witch has cursed them, she has them under her control," my mother screeched.

Breanna turned to see who was screaming and sadness flickered in her eyes before the stoic look returned. She glanced in my direction.

My father would never forgive me but I smiled at her. I had not supported hunting witches before I met Breanna and certainly would not now.

"Someone kill that witch. She is bespelling the son of the Alpha," the high-pitched, squeaky voice of my mother rang out. "She is evil."

I glared at my mother and she settled back into her chair. Tessa was shooting daggers at me with her eyes as she took her seat.

"Alpha Benelli," the Divine Council werewolf representative asked, "do you believe the witch is bespelling your son?"

Breanna resumed her stoic stare even in the midst of the ridiculous accusations. My father lifted his chin.

"No, my son is much too strong for that."

I tried not to let my reaction show. My father had called me many things. Strong was never one of them. Maybe he was playing the game of perceptions because we were at a gathering of Alphas, but his words made me stand a little taller.

"And he is to be mated to one of the women in my pack. That alone would prevent bespelling by a witch."

If it was possible to break a jawbone by clenching too tightly, I was about to find out. I looked up to see Breanna staring ahead, her chin trembling slightly. I'd explained my father's desire for me to mate with Tessa and thought, after the challenge with Ernesto, Josef would drop it. So did Breanna.

Shalamon Lisel cocked a single brow and looked to Breanna. She nodded ever so slightly before her chin lifted and her shoulders squared.

The chair I was leaning on splintered in my hands as my father rambled on about dates and details of my supposed mating with Tessa. When Tessa leaned over and wrapped her arm around mine, it took all my strength not to slam her into the floor. This was all a show and more about hurting Breanna than about what the other Alphas saw.

The Council members finally decided to decline my father's request for open pack hunts, though the opposition to their decision was boisterously boasting about their plans. I watched with my heart in my throat as Bravo Company marched out the door. Breanna didn't glance my way as she passed.

When the Council formally ended the meeting, I leaped the row of chairs between me and the door. My father yelled, but I ignored him and headed toward the wolves in camouflage. I had to get to Breanna before she left.

Vampires and werewolves milled about within the ranks of Bravo, but there didn't seem to be anything going on other than friendly exchanges. I scanned the group. She wasn't there. Most of the faces weren't friendly. I couldn't blame them. They knew Breanna was leaving them to be with me.

"She's gone, Lucas." Simon stood a few feet behind me, his hands clasped behind his back. "She needed time to herself."

I panicked at the thought of her alone in hostile territory. The Council may not have condoned pack kills on witches, but that didn't mean they wouldn't happen.

"She's in owl form and wanted me to tell you she'd see you later tonight at home."

I bit my lip and dropped my head. What had I done?

"She's okay, Lucas. The talk about you having another mate upset her so much she wanted to formally challenge the woman from your pack. I did not think that would be a good idea given the hostility of this environment so I suggested she take the scenic route back to your home."

He sounded positive she would be going to my house. I wasn't so sure. What if I had upset her to the point she didn't want to see me again?

"She made me promise I would assure you she was coming back tonight. She needed to get her thoughts clear and felt you may have pack issues to deal with as well. Gatherings such as these are very stressful for Breanna. She is always concerned one of the other soldiers will get himself into trouble on her behalf."

And I hadn't helped her at all. I'd stood by my father as he basically asked for permission to hunt and kill my mate and anyone like her.

Yeah, I was a great mate. Way to stand up for your woman, Benelli.

"She loves you, Lucas. I've never seen her so happy and I know it is because of you. Things are complicated now but don't lose heart. She will stand by you through the storms of hell and I can assure you we will always have her back."

"Major DuChard, may I ask a question and you give me an honest answer?"

"Of course. What is on your mind?"

I glanced around to make sure no one was eavesdropping, though with werewolf hearing, they could all hear our conversation.

"About the position at Ederle." I bit my lip as I struggled to find the words. She was giving up her military family for me and that wasn't right. She shouldn't have to give up the people she loved for me. Hell, it was dangerous for her on a good day and with things like they were now, it was only a matter of time until things boiled over. "Is that a bad move for her in terms of her career?"

Simon pondered my question for a few moments before responding. "It is a lower pay grade and she is leaving Bravo so, yes, it is a terrible career move."

"If I wasn't involved, would she take it?"

Simon didn't hesitate. "No."

I let out a breath at the decisiveness in his voice. None of this was right. She had worked so hard to get where she was and now she was going backward because of me.

"I can't let her do it."

Simon smirked. "Have you not learned, my dear boy, that once the beautiful Breanna makes up her mind, nothing can deter her?"

"Oh yeah. I've noticed."

"Lucas, you should know she was AWOL the day she left Wisconsin." Simon walked toward the darkened tree line and I followed. "Breanna came to me insisting she needed to go to Italy immediately, that you were in danger. The chain of command was not willing to grant her request, regardless of how we phrased it, so she stormed out the door, making her absent without leave. I called Ederle and arranged the interview to give her a legitimate reason, on paper, to be in Italy. I suspected the situation may come to this."

My mother was right. I was selfish. "She shouldn't have to choose."

"I agree. However, it is the nature of the situation at hand. She will never leave you, not with the threat of Malandanti in the area, but at least she will maintain her connection to the military, thus preventing other supernaturals from blatantly attacking her."

I snapped my fist against the closest tree. The only way out of this dilemma was for my father to release me from the Italian Pack. He'd denied my request again tonight when I'd asked just before we'd left his house. I could petition the Divine Council. Even if they approved, I would have to fight my father. That was the only reason I hadn't spoken to Breanna about completing our mate bond. The bond would link our life forces. If my father killed me during the challenge, and there was a good chance he would with the power of the pack behind him, Breanna would die as well. That was a risk I wasn't willing to take. I wasn't afraid of dying, but she didn't deserve any of this bullshit.

Simon watched me curiously. "I assume your father denied your request to leave the Italian pack?"

"Four times in the last two weeks," I answered.

"If you fight him, one of you will die?"

"Probably."

"And you do not relish the idea of killing your father, though your wolf hates him."

"Breanna tell you that?"

Simon smiled sadly. "No, she would never betray your trust. I have my sources."

I stopped punching the tree and looked at him. "You checked on me?"

His face turned to stone. "Breanna is a daughter to me. Yes, I have been checking on you since the night she risked her life to see you safely to the hospital. You think I would allow you near her without knowing who you really are?"

The smell of the vampire's anger was strong enough to make the wolves at the corner of the clearing look in our direction.

Simon turned his back to me. "Did she tell you how she made it into Bravo?"

"Not really. I know she was seventeen when she joined the Army and it took her several tries to make it into Bravo." She had never talked much about her past. I knew her parents died when she was young and her grandmother in North Carolina raised her. Anytime the topic came up, Breanna seemed so sad I didn't push her.

"She had been assigned to an all-human unit in Alaska. When government budget cuts closed the base, she transferred to another all-human unit in Alabama. The area was the territory of a small, hostile group of werewolves. One night they found her in the forest and did their best to kill her. She managed to get away and called the officer who recruited her."

"The recruiter was a vampire?" I remembered her telling me that.

"Yes. The recruiter called me because he didn't know what else to do. There is no protocol for dealing with a wounded witch. I went to that dreadful place and to this day I cannot get the image of her out of my mind. She was battered, bruised, cut, and bitten but she snapped to attention and saluted when I walked into her room."

"Breanna told me it took her several years to break into Bravo."

Simon stared into the darkness. "She was so determined. I'd never seen anything like her. Positively fearless and bitterly loyal, there was no way I was going to let her be reassigned to a desolate location where she could mysteriously disappear."

He shook his head and smiled. "She never used her magic when she was trying out for Bravo. She'd go into the ring and battle toe-to-toe with me or whoever was up at the time. The wolves called her names, the vampires shunned her, and no one would train with her."

"Breanna told me you taught her how to fight."

"Yes, and she was the best student I've ever had. Whatever I said, she would do. I'd find her practicing long after everyone else was gone, over and over, until her technique was perfect. She wanted into Bravo so badly and I wasn't going to deny her."

It was all getting clearer now. "That's not what you were supposed to do, was it? That's why you are here, commanding Bravo Company rather than a general somewhere. You helped her and it hurt your career."

The vampire shrugged and his face softened. "Taking an elf maiden as my mate didn't help my career either but you are correct, Breanna was not supposed to become a member of Bravo."

"They love her, every one of those wolves adores her. I saw it in their eyes tonight when they surrounded her. How did you do that, get them to accept her?"

"Ah, yes, that is another story. Once Breanna did make it into Bravo, the soldiers rebelled, led by one Ezekiel Trenton."

"He's in the Wisconsin Pack, isn't he?"

Simon nodded. "Yes, he is the one who threatened her and you attacked."

Oh yeah, the night my wolf took over. I remembered Trenton now. "He had a brother."

Simon bit his lip. "That wasn't Breanna's fault. She almost drowned herself trying to save those werewolves. I told Isaac not to drive on that bridge but he would not take orders from a vampire."

Simon took a few seconds and regained his composure.

"That was the beginning of the Combat Unit. Technically they are a part of Bravo, though they don't claim the affiliation to us. All the werewolves joined the Combat Unit and the two vampires left the military altogether. Breanna and I were able to rebuild Bravo to what it is today."

Simon tipped his head to the sky. "As to your question, they love her because she loves them. She has proven herself so many times, they would gladly lay down their lives for her just as she's done for them."

I shoved my hands in my pockets. I wasn't worthy of this woman. "Has she ever saved you?"

"Once, several years ago. A group of witches had taken my precious Celeste." A faraway look clouded the vampire's face before he continued. "Breanna almost died that night. None of us knew one of her powers was the ability to absorb black magic. She tried to shield the wolves from the spells, but her magic wasn't strong enough so she dropped her defenses and took the magic into her body."

Simon turned away, his voice cracking.

"She was so sick, bleeding profusely from her nose and mouth, and unconscious by the time it was over. She spent a week in the hospital on fluids to regain her strength, never complaining or asking for anything other than cheesy fries from Steak and Bake."

I laughed softly. She loved her cheesy fries.

"I understand the situation with your father is delicate and so does Breanna. She will never push you to leave your family, but you must know it is in her best interest for the two of you to live in America."

"I know. I've requested release from the Italian Pack. My father won't budge and going lone wolf is too dangerous for Breanna."

"She'll do whatever it takes to protect the ones she loves. Never forget that, Wolf. Never underestimate what Breanna will do."

Chapter 33

Breanna

The leaf burst into flames. *Good. Die.* I needed to burn something and the leaf was the least-living combustible thing I could find. How dare that blond bimbo bitch of a werewolf put her hands on Lucas?

Another leaf met an ashy demise. I'd wanted to stomp her ass there in the parking lot but Simon said no. He was worried about public perception.

"Public perception, my ass." I wanted it very clear to her and anyone else that Lucas belonged to me. Guess the werewolves weren't the only territorial supernaturals.

The worst part was I didn't want to leave Bravo. I loved the guys, loved being a part of something so important, and loved the adrenaline rush of tackling danger head-on.

"Stupid werewolf bullshit," I snarled as I fried more leaves. It shouldn't have been this hard. Lucas should be able to live with me in America. He didn't want to be in Italy any more than I did. Backward-ass werewolf law screwed up everything.

I loved him. I knew that, but did I love him enough not to hate him in a few years when I was going insane without Bravo? None of this was his fault, yet he'd be the one I blamed. I knew how I was. Forgiveness was not my strongpoint.

I leaped off my rock and quickly stomped the decent-size brush fire. A little rainstorm might be needed one to take care of the last few embers.

"Damn it, damn it, damn it." I kicked the pile to make sure I'd killed all the sparks.

"Hello, Breanna."

Damn vampire, sneaking up on people. "Stagi, that better be you 'cause I'm in the mood to kill something."

Istagio Serendelli appeared from the darkness. Handsome as ever, the master vampire had long had a thing for me. At one time I'd had a thing for him too. Now the sight of his ultra-magnificent self didn't stir a single hormone.

"You follow me?"

He smiled his most sexy, seductive smile. A few months ago that smile would have made me think seriously how luscious he was beneath his finely tailored suit. Tonight I only noticed how starkly white his teeth were.

"I wanted to speak with you after the Gathering but you rushed away." He stepped soundlessly toward me.

I shrugged and took a step back. I might not have wanted to jump his bones anymore, but that didn't mean I wanted him up close and personal either. He didn't take the hint. Actually he seemed to take my shuffle backward as a challenge.

"I have heard rumors your heart now belongs to a werewolf?"

Yep. He'd taken it as a challenge. "Who told you that? Simon?"

Istagio crinkled his nose. He and Simon weren't exactly best friends. Stagi and I had dated a few times and Simon, who generally did not get involved in my business, had not approved and had voiced his concern.

"No. Major DuChard barely acknowledges me. It was Christopher LeCavalier who shared this information."

Istagio was inches from my face before I could blink. Damn, I wished I could move like the vampires. That would have been so helpful in the field.

I met Istagio's eyes. "Lucas Benelli is my mate."

Istagio traced a finger along my jaw and my body betrayed me by shivering. "Your mate?"

"Yeah. My mate. Got a problem with it?"

He smiled and showed his fangs. "Are you sure he is your mate? I find it difficult to believe anyone could claim you." I really wished he would stop touching my cheek so softly.

Cold lips crushed against mine. Istagio pulled me toward his chest and deepened the kiss. His tongue slid along my lips, his hands locked around my waist. Before Lucas, Stagi was the only supernatural I had ever considered stripping and taking to bed.

Now there was nothing. No heat. No desire. Nothing.

Istagio leaned his head away from mine and stared into my eyes. "You love him?"

"Yeah, Stagi. I do."

Istagio released my waist. "Lucas is a good man, though I do not see the attraction you would have to the stench and dirt of a werewolf."

Arrogant vampire. "He is my mate, Stagi."

"You are giving up your career for him? He made you choose?"

Jerk. "No, Lucas did not make me choose. There just aren't a lot of options."

"Ah, Josef is preventing Lucas from leaving Italy?"

I swallowed the lump in my throat. "He won't release Lucas from his pack ties."

Istagio smiled broadly. "Another reason you should chose a vampire over a wretched werewolf. I would follow you to the ends of the world."

"What-ev-er, Stagi. Get over yourself."

The vampire inclined his head. "Have you met Gemma?"

"Oh yeah. She's thrilled about me, too."

There was no humor on Istagio's face. "Did you get a strange sense about her?"

I snorted. "You mean other than the waves of hate and rage directed in my direction?"

"Actually I was referring to black magic."

The night in the clearing, when Lucas had been under attack by Stephano, I had felt residual black magic as the pack arrived. "Now that you mention it, I did feel something weird around her."

Istagio nodded ever so slightly. "You know Lucas's brother disappeared under strange circumstances."

"You think the Malandanti took him?"

"Perhaps." Istagio knew more than he was letting on.

"Spill it, Stagi. What do you know?"

A sly smile spread across his face. "I know Lucas is an honorable man."

"And?"

"He has been grossly mistreated and unfairly maligned for things he did not do."

"And?"

"There are issues within the Italian Pack, issues of which Lucas may not be aware."

Why couldn't vampires just answer a damn question like normal people? "Are you saying his mom is practicing black magic?"

"No," Istagio answered, his eyes hooded. "But she has changed much in the last year."

Chapter 34

Lucas

Breanna had been gone almost five hours. I'd played so many rounds of dryer hockey, my stick needed retaping. I'd tried her phone at least a dozen times. It went straight to voicemail.

I sat on my front steps and dug the heels of my hands into my forehead. It was time to challenge my father. Breanna throwing away her career because of me wasn't right. She deserved better than that.

I considered packing a bag and disappearing. I'd leave a note and she could get on with her life, but I couldn't do that to her.

An Alpha's son gone lone wolf probably wouldn't last more than a few months at best. I'd end up dead somewhere. She'd give up everything to come find me. Simon's talk reminded me how powerful Breanna's feelings really were. She was the real deal. No faking and no pretending. Breanna loved with all her heart and no form of hell would stop her from coming after me. I couldn't let her take that risk. At least if my father killed me, she would know I was dead and wouldn't put herself in danger trying to find me.

Werewolves like me weren't supposed to live. I didn't submit to the dominance of my Alpha. My wolf wanted to kill everyone, especially my father, and I didn't feel any pack ties. When I was a kid, I would try so hard to send a message to my father, like I was tugging on the pack bonds, so he would come and make Stephano or Dampier stop hurting me.

He never came.

I took one last long look out at the dark tree line before heading back inside. I needed to leave Breanna a note.

The pen was poised over a blank piece of paper when Breanna burst through my front door.

"I want you and I will do whatever it takes to be with you." She strode across the room and put her arms around me. I dropped the pen and held her.

"I want to be with you, too." My throat was desert dry.

She wriggled in my arms and I loosened my grip. "What were you writing?"

I opened and closed my mouth like a dying fish. She saw right through me. "You were going to fight your father, weren't you? That was going to be a goodbye note?"

Her words were more of an accusation than a question. I stayed away from words and just nodded.

Breanna pushed me away. "No."

I didn't understand her reaction. "No?"

She grabbed the top of my pants and jerked me toward her. "You're doing it for me, because you don't want me to have to give up Bravo to be with you."

"Is that such a bad thing?"

"It is if he kills you. And what if you win? You'll have to live with knowing you killed your own father *and* who the hell will lead the Italian Pack? Under werewolf law, if you kill him you have to do it. You don't want that and there's probably some other dumbass werewolf law that says an Alpha can't be mated to a witch."

I wasn't expecting that argument. She had a valid point about werewolf law and witches as mates. "Besides," she said as she unzipped my pants, "you haven't talked this over with me. I thought we made a pact to always discuss the things that would impact us both."

My jaw moved but there were no sounds. She was unbuttoning my pants with one hand and fondling my balls in the other. I clenched my hands into fists and forced my lungs to take air.

"I choose you, Lucas Benelli. I want you in every possible way, including some that are probably illegal in fifteen states."

My eyes crossed when she pushed my pants down and dropped to her knees.

"My choice and I choose you."

She took me in her mouth and I'm pretty sure I whimpered.

Chapter 35

Breanna

I awoke to the smell of bacon and eggs. There were voices in the next room. I sat up and caught sight of my hair in the mirror. Ug, that wasn't a pretty picture.

With the sheet around me, I padded to the door. Eavesdropping was rude. Oh well.

The rich, lyrical voice of my wolf was the first I heard. "There is a lot of support for his idea."

The responding voice was deep and vaguely familiar. "Vampire and werewolf?"

The sound of eggs scraped out of the frying pan. "More werewolves of course but there were some vampires."

A soft, feminine voice surprised me. "How did Breanna do?"

"She was awesome even when the Council was rude to her. She kept her head up and didn't back down to anyone." There was a pause as liquid poured into glasses. "I was so proud of her."

The feminine voice responded. "I can't wait to meet her."

"I'll go check on her in a few minutes. She was out late last night after the Gathering."

The male laughed. "Uh huh, I'm sure that's why she's sleeping in this morning."

My face got hot as the group laughed and joked about Lucas's eggs and a few other things I didn't want to discuss. A strange vibration made its way through the door. It was definitely magic. White magic.

I skipped to the bathroom as footsteps came toward the bedroom. Lucas didn't need to know I was eavesdropping and I really needed to pee.

The door opened and clicked closed. "Hey, babe, you're awake?"

I tried to make my voice sound sleepy. "Just got up."

I finished my duty and entered the bedroom to find my wolf waiting for me. Dressed in a black pair of jeans, a white t-shirt, and barefoot, he looked good enough to eat. Hell, who needed breakfast when I had this?

He wrapped me in his arms and kissed the top of my head. "Good morning, beautiful."

"Right back at you, my studly wolf."

He laughed softly. "Tristyn and Alexandria are here. They stopped by to see how things went at the Gathering."

I yawned. "Do they normally show up so early?"

Lucas tucked my hair behind my ear. "It's almost noon."

"Oh." Guess I was more tired than I'd realized, but then again we hadn't actually made it to the sleep part of being in bed until the sun was coming up. "I'll be out in a couple minutes, okay?"

He kissed me on the cheek and returned to the kitchen. I pulled on a pair of jeans and one of Lucas's t-shirts before taking a deep breath. Alexandria was the most powerful white witch on the planet and she worked for the Divine Council. From what Lucas had said, the leader of the Divine Council had prophesized Alexandria's existence along with Tristyn's.

Lucas was scrambling another pan of eggs and his guests sat around the kitchen table. I met Tristyn's crystal blue eyes immediately. He stood and smiled at me.

"Good morning, Breanna," he said politely. "This is my mate, Alexandria."

I walked toward the table and offered my hand. "It is an honor to meet you, Alexandria."

The petite brunette smiled and took my hand. "The honor is mine, Breanna. I have never encountered an earth witch."

"Yeah, me neither."

Everyone laughed and I took a seat at the end of the table. Lucas winked at me before piling the steaming eggs onto my plate. I smiled at him and he grinned.

"Wow, it's really true," Alexandria said.

"What?" Lucas asked.

"You two are crazy about each other."

I met Lucas's gaze across the kitchen. Yes, I was crazy about him. He was gorgeous, sweet, sexy as hell, and he let me be me. I never had to pretend around Lucas and for that alone I was head over heels in love with him.

The conversation soon turned to the events at the Gathering. I finished my eggs and listened as Tristyn explained some of the finer points of Divine Council policy. Alexandria was very unhappy about the Italian Pack's proposal for open witch-hunts. I reached out and took Lucas's hand as he bowed his head.

"I should have voiced opposition to the proposal," he mumbled.

"No, you shouldn't. Your father would have stroked out there in the Gathering and, well, ug, that wouldn't be good."

He squeezed my hand. "I let you down last night."

"No, you did not," I said, vehemently slamming my milk glass. There was no way I was going to let him feel guilty about what had happened. It was not his fault. "If you had done anything other than stand beside your father, you would have created a scene and that's the last thing either one of us needed. It was bad enough when that bitch's hands were on you. Anything more than that and there would have been blood."

I noticed then all eyes were on me. Slamming my milk glass probably hadn't been a good idea but, damn it, the situation wasn't his fault any more than it was mine. It was what it was and right now, it seriously sucked for both of us.

"What bitch?" Alexandria asked with her brows raised.

"Tessa," Tristyn and Lucas answered in unison.

I tossed my napkin on the table. "She ever lays a hand on you again and I'll knock the blond out of her hair."

"Oh my," Alexandria said under her breath.

Lucas broke into a big grin. "Wow, I might go hug her just so I could see you do that."

I gave him my best glare. "Not a good idea, Wolf. I do not play well with others."

Lucas raised his hands in mock surrender and smiled at Alexandria. "My mate is vicious."

We all laughed and the fellows headed off to the basement for a round of dryer hockey, leaving Alex and me to talk.

"I've only read about earth witches," she said. "Lucas says your magic is grounded in nature?"

"Yeah I can't do the cool stuff like some of you white witches, but I'm pretty good with fire and I can summon animals if I need help. I've been working on controlling the weather. I can call up a good gust of wind and am fairly accurate with lightning. My rainclouds and hailstorms need work."

Her bright smile was contagious. As was true of every white witch I'd ever met, Alexandria was beautiful. "My fire magic isn't very good. I almost burned down our house one night trying to light the fireplace while I was cooking dinner."

"I wish I could do all that protection stuff you guys can do," I lamented. "I have a few shielding spells but that's about it." Protection spells would be so helpful for the guys when we were under attack. Oh, damn. I guess I didn't have to worry about that anymore.

She scrunched her face. "Maybe we could help each other. I'm good at protection spells and you're good with fire. I don't know if our magic is interchangeable but it's worth a try."

Cool. I'd never practiced magic with anybody before. This was gonna be fun.

By the time the guys came back, we had been quite successful. I learned a simple protection spell that would enable me to control who could come through a door. Alex was getting better at summoning fireballs, though she had made the table cloth a little toasty a couple of times.

"We'll have to do this again," she chirped. "I haven't had anyone to practice with in a very long time. Hey, Lucas said you could do some really cool stuff with silver. Would you show me that next time?"

"Sure, and maybe you can teach me how to ward something big, like a building."

We fist-bumped. "Deal."

Chapter 36

Lucas

"I think Rudolph is a witch," Breanna said as she leaned over me to retrieve her cup of hot chocolate. "This whole flying reindeer thing is some sort of supernatural and I vote witch."

"But what about the red nose?"

She took a sip from her recently acquired Minnie Mouse mug. "A curse. Probably pissed off a sorcerer or something."

She set the cup back on the table beside my Mickey Mouse mug as I enjoyed the feel of her body against mine. "And they completely got the elves wrong. Those look more like trolls."

We watched a few more minutes of the movie in companionable silence. She was snuggled against me on the couch, the light of the Christmas tree dancing across her face.

Best. Christmas. Ever.

As the credits rolled on screen, I retrieved a small gold box I'd hidden in the drawer of the coffee table.

"Merry Christmas, baby."

She stared at the box. "It's not Christmas yet. We aren't supposed to open presents until tomorrow."

There were plenty of brightly wrapped packages under our scrawny tree for Christmas morning.

"I know, but I really want you to open this one tonight. Please?"

She took the box delicately and then tore into the paper like a kid. When she flipped open the lid, she took a sharp breath.

I'd gone through this moment in my head for over a week. She was supposed to open the box, squeal how great the wolf head silhouette necklace was, and then wrap her arms around me.

Instead she just sat there, staring at the open box. When she finally looked up at me, there were tears in her eyes.

I felt like a moron. She didn't like it.

"I can take it back. We can find something else you like." I reached for the box.

She snatched it away. "You will not take it back."

The diamond eyes of the wolf glinted in the dim light. I commissioned the piece especially for her as soon as she decided to stay through the holidays. The werewolf jeweler even said the necklace resembled my wolf form. His assistant raved about how beautiful it was.

Apparently not, because Breanna didn't like it.

"It's okay, Bre. Really. I can take it back."

The tears streamed down her face. "You had this made for me?"

I nodded slightly, the lump in my throat growing painfully large.

"I've never seen anything so beautiful."

With trembling hands, she lifted the necklace from its black silk bed. She held it up, the light from the Christmas tree creating a myriad of colors.

"Will you help me put it on?"

Our fingers brushed as I took the necklace. She lifted her hair and bundled it on top of her head. I fastened the chain around her neck.

"Thank you," she said softly, fingering the wolf head. "I will never take it off."

The phone rang as I cradled her face. At that moment, nobody else mattered but her.

"Do you really like it?" I wasn't convinced.

The tears glistened in her eyes. "It is the most incredible gift anyone has ever given me. I can't believe you went to all the trouble to have it custom made." She blushed. "It's really too pretty for me."

The phone rang again. With a snarl, I checked the number. My father.

Ignoring the ringing, I took Breanna's hands in mine. It was time to tell her, to admit out loud how much I loved her.

The phone shrilled again. Text messages. Voice mails. Could the man not take a hint?

"Maybe you should answer that."

I didn't want to talk to my father. He'd ruin this beautiful moment.

"It's my father," I mumbled.

She cupped my jaw. "Then you should definitely answer."

"Why?"

She smiled sadly. "If I'm going to stay here, we need to try to make nice. No sense making things worse by ignoring him." She leaned her head against my shoulder. "He'll just show up over here anyway, so why not talk to him on the phone and get it over with?"

"I'll call him after we watch *The Island of Misfit Toys*."

She kissed the back of my hand. "Go on and call him. I've got a couple of texts I need to check on my phone."

She disappeared into the bedroom while I scrolled through my father's messages. They were all the same. Call him immediately.

He answered on the first ring and promptly yelled at me for taking so long to return his call. After his tirade, he got down to business.

"You need to go to Ferrara tonight and attend to the worksite. The police called earlier and said there had been a break-in."

I pinched the bridge of my nose and tried to play nice, as Breanna had suggested. "You expect me to drive two and a half hours in a snowstorm on Christmas Eve because someone might have stolen some drywall?"

"Yes," he answered emphatically. "Or come here and oversee the pack meeting."

Breanna came back into the room, her bright smile slipping a bit when she looked at me.

"Fine," I growled. "I'll leave in a few minutes." I hung up the phone without waiting for his response.

"What's up?" Bre asked.

I explained about the burglary and my father's demands.

"Oh, okay. I'll let Simon know we can't make it."

"Can't make what?"

"Some members of Bravo are here for the holidays. He suggested we get together tonight for a drink." She ducked her head. "Might be awhile before I see them again."

Leave it to my father to screw up Christmas Eve. I wondered if there really was a break-in or if he was just jerking me around.

"Why don't you go ahead and meet Simon and I'll drive down to Ferrara? I should be back around midnight and then we can open more presents because it will be Christmas."

She crinkled her forehead. "The weather isn't very good. I don't like the idea of you driving that far by yourself."

I kissed her cheek. She was so awesome. "I'll be fine. It's an easy drive and the main road will be clear. I've got four-wheel drive if I need it. Go on. Have fun. I'll see you back here."

"Call me when you're on the way home?"

I planted a kiss on the end of her adorable nose. "Promise."

The roads were not great and the heavy holiday traffic made my two-hour trip closer to three. When I pulled into the worksite, nothing was out of the ordinary and I certainly didn't see any law enforcement officers.

I parked under the lights and walked around to the back of the construction area. Nothing looked out of place. All the temporary utility buildings were locked, the scaffolding secure, and from what I could see, all was well.

What the hell?

The receptionist at the Ferrara Police Department had no idea what I was talking about. I called my father. No answer. I gritted my teeth and called my mother. No answer.

Breanna's phone rang and rang. The voicemail never clicked on. My chest tightened. I tried Tristyn. He and Alex were flying out to California sometime today and were most likely in the air over the Atlantic Ocean. I scrolled through my list of contacts and found Simon's number. No answer, no voicemail.

My foot leveled on the accelerator when I hit the autostrade. I tried Breanna again and again. Something was very wrong.

Open witch-hunts.

Thoughts of Breanna being in danger consumed my mind. I had no idea how fast I was going, but the lights along the roadside became one big blur. The steering wheel cracked under the pressure of my hands.

"Please let her be all right," I prayed as the SUV neared triple digits. I tried her again. Nothing. Nothing from my father. Nothing from my mother. No answer from anyone I called. It was as if everyone had fallen off the planet.

I made it back to the city limits of Vicenza in two hours flat. The smell of smoke and burning wood filled the SUV. A bright orange glow lit the otherwise dark night sky and the glow was getting brighter the closer I got to my home.

Less than a half mile from my house, I passed rows of emergency vehicles. I tried Breanna again. Nothing. A quarter mile from my drive the police formed a blockade. I skidded to a halt and yelled to the uniformed officer that I lived in the house around the curve. He radioed ahead and waved me through.

My heart dropped and my wolf surged when I turned down my drive. All I could see were flashing lights and humans until I looked past the fire trucks.

My house was gone, replaced by a huge pile of cinder and ash.

"Breanna!" I yelled as I leaped from the truck and dashed toward the rubble. "Breanna! Breanna!"

Four firemen tried to stop me. I shrugged them off. There was nothing left, nothing at all, but none of that mattered. What mattered was Breanna.

"Mr. Benelli?" a kindly old man wearing a CHIEF hat said. "I am sorry we could not save your home."

"Breanna? Where's Breanna?" I roared at him. Damn the house. I pushed past him and ran to the waiting ambulance. Maybe she was hurt and they were taking her to the hospital.

The world stopped when a gurney carrying a black body bag rolled past. I couldn't breathe. I couldn't think. That couldn't be her.

"Mr. Benelli, who was in the house?" the human in the CHIEF hat asked.

"My...my..." A human wouldn't understand the idea of a mate. "My girlfriend, Breanna."

He placed a hand lightly on my shoulder and I didn't have the strength to move away from him. I couldn't take my eyes off the gurney. That couldn't be her. She was a witch, a combat-trained soldier, that couldn't be.

"We found one body inside, too badly burned for any type of identification."

Some sort of sound came out of my throat as I shuffled closer to the gurney. I didn't know who was in that bag but it could not be Breanna. It couldn't be.

A deep breath revealed nothing except the smells of burnt flesh and wood.

"We found this on the body."

He held up a sooty necklace and my heart cracked. It was the wolf. I pulled the necklace from the human and dropped to my knees. It couldn't be true. Breanna couldn't be gone, not like this. There must have been some mistake.

I tried to touch the body bag. My hands wouldn't move. Nothing would move. Her face flashed through my mind over and over. I kept expecting to wake up and find her safe beside me in our bed.

"We aren't sure what caused the fire but it appears to have been some sort of gas explosion." I kept seeing Breanna's face, her beautiful smile as she kissed me before I drove away, the way she waved when I backed out the driveway.

Inside me something broke. None of this could be happening. I'd only been gone a few hours and she'd been perfectly fine when I left.

The sights and sounds all blended together as the world became hollow. Someone was trying to talk to me but all I heard was the mournful cry of my wolf. Our mate was gone, taken, dead.

I dashed around the scene, frantically calling to her. Maybe they were wrong and she had gotten out of the house and was lying in the bushes.

Who was in the body bag?

I roared her name, begging her to come out as I ran through the dark forest. The sounds of the firemen quieted as I ran farther. Oh God, what could have happened? *Please let this not be real. She's okay. She's alive. I feel it. I feel her.*

How did that person get her necklace?

I fell to my knees and clawed at the dirt. *No. No. No.* She couldn't be gone. She was alive. She was strong. She promised she wouldn't leave me. *No. No. No.*

I'd killed her.

Images of her tortured my overwhelmed brain. Over and over I saw her waving goodbye, saw her fingering the necklace, saw the body bag rolling past.

I couldn't stop the shaking. The forest beckoned. People called to me but they didn't matter. Nothing mattered. I ran until the voices were quiet. My wolf finally won and I lay in a thicket for the change. I had no strength left to fight, no will left to live. My world was ashes.

My wolf demanded vengeance. Breanna had not died in a freak accident.

She was dead because of me.

Chapter 37

Breanna

The sound of dripping water was getting on my last nerve. Wasn't that a form of ancient Chinese torture? When I'd forced my eyes open a couple minutes ago, I had no idea where I was. With some sort of collar around my neck, I could barely move my head and the rope biting into my wrists didn't help. At least my hands were in the front and not the back. Whoever had me was not a professional or they would have known better than to leave my hands so useful.

My head pounded and every muscle in my body was angry. "Must be the drugs."

One minute I'd been standing on the porch of Lucas's house, getting ready to go meet Simon, and the next I'd felt a sharp jab of pain in my neck. I'd caught a whiff of musk before I dropped like a rock. Whatever they'd used had knocked my ass out cold.

Now I was in a small, drab room with no window and a flimsy wooden door. The bed smelled of musk, sex, and blood and I slid to the floor as soon as my muscles agreed to work. I didn't know what had been occurring on this bed and didn't want any part of it.

Damn, it had been years since an enemy had captured me, yet here I was. Careless, Welker. Way too careless.

"It's Christmas. I should be on the couch with Lucas or better yet in bed with him. What the hell is going on here?" I mumbled, squirming my way toward the wall. I wanted to scream for someone to tell me where I was but decided the brash, no-fear approach might not be the most effective in getting me the hell out of this situation.

Aaron would have called this a SNAFU. Situation Normal All Fucked Up.

My stomach churned, threatening to hurl its measly contents. Anger tried to consume me. I refused to give in.

Angry witches made stupid decisions.

Outside the flimsy door, someone was speaking. My Italian was terrible. From the whiff of musk, they must have been werewolves. I wasn't picking up any magic right now, but didn't know exactly how much this damn collar interfered. We used something similar when we captured witches and sorcerers to prevent them from accessing their magic and, at the moment, I couldn't make an ant-size fireball.

Footsteps grew louder and the hushed speaking quieted as another wave of musk rushed into the room. This one carried an Alphalike sense of dominance. It wasn't as strong as Lucas, though it was substantial.

The door opened and the silver-flaked eyes of a tall, dark-haired werewolf stared down at me. His features were hawkishly handsome in a *GQ* kind of way. I got nothing off him that would make me afraid, but did get the sense intimidation was his primary operating procedure. Fine. I could work with that.

I pushed back into the corner and huddled like a terrified child. I thought back to the time Celeste had almost died and just the memory was enough to send shock waves through my body. Those thoughts of fear would make my body react with a cold rush of adrenaline. The wolf would think the smell of fear was for him.

I forced my chin to tremble when he entered the room. Damn, I hated to play the pathetic female routine, but it worked so well with overconfident asshole types.

The *GQ* werewolf strode across the room. I wanted to kick the shit out of him. Better to play it safe and scared since I didn't know what was outside the door.

"So you are the one who has been creating havoc with my plans. Hmm, you're not so bad for a witch."

I bit my lip and counted the pairs of shoes on the floor behind him. Nine wolves flanked him. That was too many for me to get through without my magic. *Okay, find another way.*

The *GQ* wolf touched my chin with his finger and I worked hard to react like a scared child rather than a combat-trained soldier. With one move I could snap his neck but the part after that was a bit of a concern. I was pretty sure the other wolves would return the favor.

I refused to meet his eyes. Submission, weakness, fear, all the things that sent a wolf into prey mode were oozing from me. His nostrils flared as he cupped my face. I found my trembly voice.

"What do you want from me?"

He snorted and leaned closer to get a bigger whiff of my scent. The bulge in his jeans grew as he growled and grabbed a fistful of my hair. The *GQ* wolf looked over his shoulder. "Leave us."

The others quickly departed, leaving only the two of us in the dimly lit room. He pulled me roughly to my feet and slammed me against his body. I tried to look wild-eyed and terrified. It must have worked because the *GQ* wolf's eyes were full of silver.

He shoved me to the bed and reached for the button on his jeans. "I am Nicolli Benelli, the true heir to the Pack of Italy."

Lucas's brother? All righty, that was not what I'd expected and he sounded like he'd been watching way too many John Wayne movies. Maybe that was how he had been killing time this last year since he'd disappeared.

Unlike Lucas, Nicolli looked exactly like Josef Benelli.

Damn, it was hard keeping up the terrified witchy routine. "You're Lucas's brother?" What an asshole. "He said you went missing. He looked for you." Dickhead.

The evil cackle reminded me of Gemma. "I heard. He always was licking my father's boots for a scrap of recognition."

"Why are you doing this?" Hey, I was getting pretty good at the girly-voice stuff.

"Mom talked Lucas into coming back to Italy after I disappeared." He finger-quoted the word 'disappeared'. "I knew Lucas and our father would never get along."

"So why," I began before quickly switching to trembly voice, "why involve Lucas? He didn't want to be here."

Nicolli slowly unbuttoned his shirt. "I want to be Alpha now. The pack needs me. My father is old, his ideas outdated, but with the power of the pack behind him, he is almost impossible to defeat in a challenge. The only one strong enough is Lucas and even if the challenge ended with my father killing Lucas, the Alpha would be sufficiently weakened that I could finish the job."

Nicolli ran his hands along my back and grabbed my butt. Damn, I wanted drag his nuts through his nose. "Lucas would never kill his father."

A wicked smile. "Yes, he will."

Oh hell.

Nicolli spun me around and pulled my back to his chest. "The firemen found the charred remains of a body inside Lucas's house. Poor thing was burned beyond recognition but there was a necklace burned into her skin."

I glanced down at the bare spot where my wolf silhouette should have been.

"Lucas left last night," I answered with a real trembly voice this time. "We had a fight."

It was stupid to lie to a werewolf. He'd sense my dishonesty. Desperate times called for desperate actions.

"No, my dear, I believe he went to check a burgled worksite while you joined your friends for a drink." Nicolli's lips grazed my ear and I tried not to puke. "They say he fell to his knees when the body bag went by."

I forced myself not to move as his hands trailed down the front of my shirt and across my chest. If I could only get out of this collar I'd roast his nuts.

"Lucas loved you. Why are you doing this to him?"

Nicolli tore open my shirt and I almost nailed him in the balls. "Lucas was a mistake that should have never been allowed to live. He has never been a real werewolf any more than he's ever been a real man. He is nothing."

And to think Lucas had wasted time looking for this asshole.

"Soon my dear brother will find a scent trail leading away from his once-happy love nest straight to Josef's house." Nicolli's eyes sparkled wickedly. "Consumed by grief, Lucas will attack the Alpha and kill him, or at the very least weaken him enough I can finish the deed."

"Sorry son of a bitch," I snarled before crushing an elbow into Nicolli's ribcage. The corresponding crunch of bone made me smile. A little pain in his side for what Lucas was going through didn't seem quite fair, but it was the best I could do right now. I tried for a swift kick in the groin. Asshole brother was too quick and bounced just out of reach.

"You fucking bitch," Nicolli sneered with teeth bared. He lunged and I ducked enough to send him flipping into a corner. My hands were tied, otherwise I would have followed and beat the shit out of him.

I bounced on the balls of my feet, ready for a headlong rush. Nicolli stood calmly and brushed the dust from his pants.

"It was difficult at first, convincing the Malandanti to help me. I travelled the world to find the information necessary to form an alliance with them."

That explained the Paraguay witches' stories about Levi being payment for their information. What a piece of shit.

"The Malandanti have been very helpful with all of this. With their assistance I was able to coerce a few loyal wolves into helping me, but when you came along, things got a bit trickier. Seems your bear routine a few months back, the night they were going to bring Lucas to me, unnerved the Malandanti. The plan was to offer Lucas as a sacrifice and that in turn would give me the power to defeat Josef in a formal challenge but oh, no, the little earth witch had to step in and screw it all up."

This wolf was completely *loco*. "Why are you doing this? Lucas is your brother. He wants nothing to do with this pack. He's only here to help his father with the company."

Nicolli guffawed and I wanted to rip his eyeballs out of his head and shove them down his throat. "And the pack has no interest in him. That's why my plan will work. No one will rush to his aid when my wolves and I arrive, particularly when the pack sees the Malandanti working with me." Nicolli glanced at his watch. "Hmm, by now I suppose Lucas has wandered out of the woods and started sniffing around the rubble. Everything will be over soon, little witch, and I will be the new Alpha of the Italian pack."

I scanned the room quickly for a weapon. There was nothing unless I could suffocate him with a dingy mattress. With no magic and limited fighting ability, this was not my finest hour.

"You haven't asked the magic question," Nicolli said as he straightened the front of his shirt. "What am I going to do with you?"

Eat shit and die, asshole.

He took a deep breath as if my dilemma actually troubled him.

"I thought the Malandanti would take you, at least as a sacrifice, but they want nothing to do with you. I tried to convince them. They declined my offer. I did find a vampire who was interested in purchasing you as his personal companion."

Simon once told me the blood of a witch was like a drug to some vampires, addicting and intoxicating. Witches taken by vampires rarely lived more than a day before the vampire, so consumed with need, drained the witch dry.

Great, that sounded peachy. This day kept getting better and better.

That shitty grin appeared on Nicolli's face again. "Does the name Spiro Devereaux sound familiar?"

I swallowed the lump in my throat. Spiro Devereaux was a French master vampire who absolutely hated Bravo and most especially me. Celeste had belonged to Spiro before Bravo stormed his hokey castle and rescued her and ten other elves he kept imprisoned in his basement. Spiro wouldn't kill me. He'd drain me almost dry and make me live for another day of hell.

Oh joy.

Nicolli whistled and the goon wolves flanking him earlier rushed into the room. I got off a couple of whip kicks before ending up face-first into a wall. When the stars stopped flashing and the room quit spinning, my hands were tied behind my back.

The air around us took on a slight vibration, the power of a master vampire slowly filling room. Ug, not good. My nose was bleeding and my lip cut. Great, I already looked like an appetizer.

The musky mountain werewolf pushed me through the door and a bright light punctured my eyes. What the hell time was it anyway? That couldn't be sunlight, way too bright, and a master vampire wouldn't be bopping around in the middle of the day unless he absolutely had to.

"Satisfied?" Nicolli asked. I tried to find who he was talking to, but my eyeballs hadn't adjusted yet. That must be a flashlight in my eyes. The vampire vibration was getting stronger and I pushed back against the mountain. Damn mountain didn't budge.

A rush of cold air made the hair on my arm stand up as a blindfold covered my eyes. Panic crept into my mind as the rising tide of claustrophobia grew. Without warning a cold hand grasped my hair and forced my head back. It was a classic move for a vampire to feed and I bucked against the mountain in a futile attempt to stay away from the fangs. The collar covered most of my neck, though he could easily reach my jugular.

"Don't," Devereaux warned in a low voice. I gulped as the cold breath fell on my exposed neck. My heart pounded as adrenaline coursed through my body. I tried to focus on my training, to calm my runaway fear. My muscles constricted when fangs scraped along my neck.

Something like a whimper slipped from my lips and my knees buckled. There was only a sliver of pain before I was floating.

* * * *

Everything was dark. I was bound hands to feet and the damn blindfold was still in place. I shifted, trying to roll onto my back until something hard stopped my motion. Apparently the vampire hadn't taken all my blood, but he had taken enough to make me pass out and now I was rolling around like a blob in what felt like the trunk of a car.

A vampire had never bitten me. I'd always heard it could be as painful or as pleasurable as the vampire chose. The more venom used in the bite, the less pain the victim felt. I hadn't felt much pain and that didn't make sense. Spiro Devereaux hated the air I breathed.

The sounds of cars passing and rubber on asphalt confirmed my thought and reminded me of my ridiculous claustrophobia. In spite of my best efforts, my heart raced and my breaths came in short shallow bursts. Great, keep it up and I'd suffocate before Spiro Devereaux had a chance to drain me again.

When the engine slowed and the car turned off the road, I tried to force my fear-soaked brain to come up with an escape plan. Even if I managed to get in a well-timed head butt, that probably wouldn't do any damage to the master vampire and my mode of escape didn't look too promising at the moment.

Gravel crunched under the tires and then the engine purred to a stop. I took a deep breath and thought about Lucas. Whatever it took, I would see him again.

Soft footsteps shuffled alongside the car. A key slipped into the latch. I gritted my teeth to stop my chin from trembling.

"Breanna?"

That didn't sound like Devereaux. Cold hands brushed my arms and I jumped.

"Breanna, it's okay. It's Christopher."

The blindfold fell my head and the bright blue eyes of Christopher LeCavalier stared back at me.

"Chris? What the hell?"

He quickly sliced the rope bonds from my wrists and ankles. "The real Spiro Devereaux was unavoidably detained after word got out he was about to purchase his own personal witch." His blue eyes sparkled mischievously. "Master Devereaux should be more careful to whom he brags. Word got back to Simon."

I wrapped my arms around Christopher's cold granite body. "Thanks for coming for me."

He chuckled. "For the record, you are delicious."

"That was you?"

He winked. "Simon told me you wouldn't deal well with the car ride in the trunk so he suggested I take enough blood to help you sleep until we were far enough away I could set you free." The handsome vampire's forehead creased. "I didn't hurt you, did I?"

I wasn't about to tell him the bite actually felt good. "Nah, I'm fine, but no more snacking. Where's Bravo?"

He held up a phone. "At Ederle, waiting for your call."

I snatched the phone and leaped into the car. "Take me to Josef Benelli's house."

Chris bowed his head. "We haven't seen Lucas since the fire, Breanna. Nobody knows where he is. Istagio said Lucas lost it when he saw the body bag being hauled away."

"You didn't tell him you were coming after me?" How could they not tell him?

Christopher's eyes never left the road. "After the fire we were all upset. Simon went to the morgue to identify the body. He knew it wasn't you on that slab but he didn't want word to get out until he knew where you were. Simon did try to call Lucas. Nobody, not even Tristyn, knows where he is."

My magic rushed around now that the collar was off and I felt lightheaded. Worse than the lightheadedness was the sinking feeling in the pit of my stomach. Lucas was out there and he thought he was alone. If Nicolli had been telling the truth about Josef's scent, there was no doubt where Lucas would go. The only question was what would happen.

Chapter 38

Lucas

The sickening crunch of bone snapping echoed through the clearing outside my father's home. We had been fighting almost an hour and Josef wasn't dead. Yet.

That was my goal, to kill him for what he had done. When I pulled myself together and returned to my house, I'd found a scent trail leading directly here. The heaviest scent belonged to my father and my wolf demanded vengeance.

"Why did you kill her?" I kept asking.

"I don't know what you're talking about," he kept answering.

And we continued to battle. This fight would not stop until one of us was dead." I was stronger but my father had the power of the pack behind him. He'd tossed me into the cement picnic table and my spine cracked. A surge of strength repaired the break before my father got to me.

Now his leg was injured and from the way the wolves were stumbling, he was pulling power from his pack. I got to him first and wrapped my hands around his throat. The tiniest hint of fear flickered briefly before he stopped fighting.

"Lucas, I swear to you I did not kill the witch."

I threw him against the brick steps. My mother screamed and ran toward my father's broken form.

"Lucas, stop it!" she yelled before one of the pack wolves pulled her away. No one would interfere with this challenge and my wolf wanted blood.

I stood over my father and looked down at his bloodied face. He was heaving and had no defense against me.

"Why did you have to kill her? I loved her!"

He shook his head. "I did not kill her."

I raised my fist to deliver the deathblow and hesitated. This would not bring Breanna back and he was my father. Whatever was wrong with me, why ever I couldn't feel the bonds of the pack, this was my father.

I wanted to hear him admit he had taken the woman I loved. It would be so easy to kill him, to rip his throat out, but that wouldn't take away the hole in my heart. Nothing would ever fix that. She was gone.

I stumbled backward and stared at the blood on my hands. I had killed her. She was here in Italy because of me. If she had stayed in America, she would have still been safe. She would have been alive.

I turned away from my father and buried my head in my hands. It was my fault, all of it, and I deserved to die.

My wolf took over and spun as the same silver dagger I had used to stab Stephano sliced the air beside my head. I knocked the knife from my father's hand as his other hand closed around my throat. With the power of the pack, he slowly constricted my trachea until my vision darkened.

The smell of silver surrounded me. I hoped he would slice quickly and deeply even though I did deserve to suffer.

His hand fell away. There were grunts and groans as air rushed into my lungs.

"Lucas?"

The faint hint of strawberry reached my nose. My mind was playing tricks on me or perhaps my father had killed me and I didn't know I was dead.

"Lucas?"

The smell of fire replaced the strawberry. Warm soft hands on either side of my face caused me to open my eyes.

"Breanna?"

Bruises and blood covered the beautiful tear-streaked face of my mate. I reached for her cheek, unwilling to breathe until I was sure she was real.

Her fingers brushed my chin and I pulled her to my chest. "How? I thought--"

"I know," she rasped. "I'm okay. Are you all right?"

I looked past Breanna and saw my father watching intently from behind a wall of flames. My wolf roared to life. She must have sensed my wolf because she wheeled in my arms.

"Alpha Benelli, your son Nicolli is to blame for this shit."

We both climbed to our feet and I tugged her behind me as my father scrutinized her. Typical Breanna refused to stand behind me, opting instead to remain at my side. She laced her fingers through mine and met my father's stunned gaze.

"Nicolli is dead," he answered with eyes blazing.

"Uh, no, he isn't, and I've got the bruises to prove it."

Gemma went berserk. My father grabbed her before she could make it to Breanna. I wasn't sure what to say myself, but did catch an inkling of scent on Breanna's skin that reminded me of my brother.

"What proof do you have?" Josef asked suspiciously.

"I spoke to him," Christopher replied, striding into the midst of the gaping werewolves. "He thought I was there to purchase the earth witch for my own uses."

"Who the hell are you?" Josef demanded.

The vampire stopped beside Breanna. She nodded to him. "This is Lieutenant Christopher LeCavalier of Bravo Company," she answered loudly enough for all the wolves to hear.

"Alpha Benelli," Christopher began with a slight nod of respect, "Master Sergeant Welker speaks the truth. Bravo Company is on its way here and by our intel, so is your son."

"Shit," Breanna muttered. "He's got Malandanti magic."

I studied my father's face as he listened to the vampire's account of what had taken place. Nicolli, alive and well, was on his way here to kill my father.

"You're lying," Gemma snarled and pointed at Breanna. "That witch is doing all of this."

Breanna shook her head in disbelief. "You have one seriously fucked-up family, my wolf."

In the midst of one of the worst days of my life, she could make me laugh. I squeezed her hand to make sure she was really there.

"How do you know it was Nicolli?" Josef asked the vampire.

Christopher squared his chin. "He bore a striking resemblance to the photo we have on file for Nicolli Benelli. He was a powerful werewolf and had a loyal following of at least forty wolves."

Breanna edged forward. "He is working with the Malandanti. That's why Lucas thought you were responsible for the fire. The Malandanti used their magic to create a scent trail leading Lucas to you."

Josef didn't believe her, I could see it in his eyes. "Why? Why, if this person is truly my son Nicolli, would he do these things?"

"He wants the pack."

"The pack was to be his. He knew this." Josef turned away, shaking his head. "No, none of this makes sense. I don't believe Nicolli would do the things you say. He is my son. He would never betray his Alpha or his pack."

Breanna rolled her eyes and shook her head. She was battered, blood dried on her lips and cheek, but it was the bruising on her neck that looked the most painful.

"Bravo will be here any minute. If you won't listen to me, maybe you'll listen to my CO," she bit out, amber eyes blazing with fury. God, I loved this woman.

A sharp pain in my lower back made my knees buckle. The pain stole my breath as I tried to climb to my feet. Something was very wrong. It felt as though my insides were frying, the coppery taste of blood caught in my mouth.

Breanna's hand snatched from mine and the ground rushed quickly toward my face. Her blurry feet disappeared and I clawed at the dirt. I tried to call her name but only managed garbles and blood.

Something wet and sticky touched my fingers. Breanna? Where was Breanna? I needed to help her. She was in danger. What the hell was in my back? The searing heat had spread and my wolf was struggling to ascend. I didn't want to change here, not now.

"Lucas, can you hear me?" Soft hands gently eased me onto my side. My stomach retched and more blood filled my mouth. I couldn't breathe, couldn't move. I was dying.

"Hold on, baby, I'll get that shit out of you, just hold on, okay?"

I would fight for her. A surge of power raced through my body, temporarily halting the scalding heat. The putrid smell of black magic and fear hung thick in the air. Breanna called for someone to help her and nobody responded. I tried to lift up onto my elbows. The surge from earlier was gone and the flames inside me increased again.

Voices faded in and out. Breanna was beside me and I think her hand was on my back. She barked orders at someone and then her gaze turned to me.

She whispered something. The shouting was loud, the roaring in my head deafening. I wanted to tell her I loved her, but blood clogged my throat.

"It's a spell," Breanna yelled. "I can reverse it if you'll watch my back."

"Gotcha, Bre. Do what you need to do, we got you covered," an American man answered from somewhere above me.

"Thanks, Aaron."

She pressed her hand into mine and the searing pain in my back doubled, then tripled. More blood emptied from my mouth. It felt like all my organs were sliding up my esophagus and then, as abruptly as it started, the pain stopped.

I gasped for air and squeezed Breanna's hand. She was sitting cross-legged on the ground, watching me intently. Fresh blood trickled from her nose and mouth and her eyes looked very tired.

"Better?" she mumbled.

I slowly sat up beside her. A wall of soldiers surrounded us. Members of Bravo fought with members of the Italian Pack. What the hell was going on? I looked over my shoulder and saw my father under attack by two pack wolves.

She noticed my father's dilemma. "C'mon. We'll help him." She swiped at the blood on her face before tossing a fireball at one of the attacking wolves. "Hey, asshole, come get some of this."

The wolf bared his teeth and charged her. He met my fist as it crashed through his nose. The second wolf had my father pinned against the steps until Breanna raked her nails across the wolf's eyes. He bellowed in pain and lunged for her but she darted to the side and decked him with one hell of a spinning whip kick.

She winked at me. "He's the one who threw me into the wall," she said, pointing to the bruise blossoming under her left eye. What had she been through?

The wolves retreated into the trees and Simon called for Bravo to give chase.

"No," Breanna argued. "It's a trap. They've got Malandanti help."

Simon retracted his order and called his soldiers into my father's courtyard. Josef was taking care of an injured pack wolf and flashed a look of displeasure toward the milling soldiers. He hated uninvited strangers in his territory.

Breanna started toward the group, pulling my hand to follow. "I am not leaving you again," she said firmly.

I wasn't about to let her get out of my sight either. "Bre, I need to talk to my father."

"Not right now," she answered quickly. "He's got some heavy shit on his mind."

"Well, yeah, and we've been fighting for the last hour so I'm part of that heavy shit."

She snorted. "You thought he was responsible for my death. In the last twenty minutes, you found out I wasn't dead and your long lost asshole brother is not only alive but trying to kill you and your father. I'd say that gives you a free pass to do things you wouldn't ordinarily do."

Her smile quickly faded. I shook her arm. "Bre, what's wrong?"

She squeezed her eyes closed. "Damn, damn, shit, shit."

"What?" I looked around but didn't see anything.

Simon stormed toward us. "Lucas, we need the Italian Pack to get inside your father's home."

I nodded and dashed toward my father with Breanna in tow.

A fresh wave of guilt ran through me when he turned. "Alpha," I said, purposefully lowering my eyes. "Bravo has requested you move all your wolves inside."

"Why?" Josef demanded.

"Because the Malandanti are here," Breanna answered impatiently.

"My wolves will fight. We will not hide."

"Your wolves will get slammed by their black magic and Bravo will have to fight twice as hard. Get your asses inside and let us do our job."

Josef's eyes flickered to silver. "You forget your place, witch."

A little fire broke out around my father's feet as Breanna glared at him.

We returned to the soldiers, all the way Breanna muttering something about my father being the world's biggest shithead.

"All right, what's the plan?" Breanna barked as we neared the group.

Simon motioned toward the trees. "They are less than a mile away. What kind of magic do you feel, Breanna?"

She crinkled her forehead. "I don't know numbers. The magic is strong."

"Can you shield us?"

"If you stay together. If the group splits, I'm not sure I'll have enough juice to go around."

Simon launched into military speak and I didn't have a clue what he was saying.

"What can I do?" I asked Breanna when Simon had finished.

"Stay with me, watch my back," she answered. "It will take a load off my guys and let me focus on my magic."

I nodded. "Done."

She planted a kiss on my cheek and the hint of strawberries teased my nose. Would this day ever end?

A few minutes later Breanna and I had climbed to the roof of my father's house. She felt it would give her the best view and make it harder for the Malandanti to get to us.

"The Malandanti aren't fighters," she explained. "They've got some potent binding spells and the silver poisoning cast like they hit you with earlier. Get through their magic, they ain't got shit. I have to hold off the magic and Bravo will take care of the rest."

"Why did they just go after to me?" I asked, rubbing my lower back.

She took a deep breath. "That was a teaser from a forward scout group. They knew I'd protect you. It was a ploy to see if I was here yet. The wolves were under orders from Nicolli to determine the strength of your father."

"Do you think my brother is with them?" I believed Breanna's account of what happened with Nicolli, but there was a small part of me hoping somehow all of this was a big mistake.

"Yes. He's the leader. He'll be there somewhere. The bigger question is how many of the wolves inside your father's house are going to be loyal and how many will follow Nicolli?" Breanna wrapped her arms around me and I welcomed her warmth. "Once Bravo has a fix on the Malandanti, we'll leave the roof and get to your father," she said softly. "I give my word I'll do what I can to protect him."

After all she had been through, after the way my father had treated her, she was willing to try to keep him safe. I didn't have a clue what to say so I hugged her.

Chapter 39

Breanna

The tendrils of black magic seeped into the estate. I was ready. With Lucas at my back, I didn't have to worry about any of Nicolli's wolves sneaking up the trellis and interrupting my chants.

I dropped to my knees and asked the Great Mother for her blessing. I would need her help to pull this off. As I began my chants, my magic swirled like a great wind. My mind cleared and the power of Mother Nature filled me.

The cloak-clad Malandanti topped the hill. Gun-toting werewolves surrounded them. I didn't see Nicolli yet.

"Here they come," I yelled to the Bravo guys. I glanced over my shoulder and saw Lucas scanning the area immediately around the house. Everyone's lives depended on me being able to stop the Malandanti.

I chanted my shielding spell and a blue-green light glowed above the Benelli house. I repeated the ancient words over and over, louder and louder, until the radiance encompassed the entire courtyard. Everyone within that glow would be safe from the spells of the Malandanti. Now I just had to hang on and hope Bravo got it done before I hit empty on my magic tanks.

The sounds of fighting erupted behind me, but I couldn't lose focus. Lucas would take care of whatever came onto the roof and Bravo was depending on me. The black magic pushed against my shield. I held onto my faith. I'd chanted this shielding spell hundreds of times. This time I surrendered my body completely to my magic and allowed Mother Nature to flow with all her might.

Time had no meaning as the light grew brighter. The more intense the light, the more powerful the shield would be. I heard shouting, screaming, groans of pain, and gunfire all around, but it was the voice of my mate that gave me hope.

"Hold on, Bre, they've almost got them all."

The magic tank was depleting quickly. I leaned against a massive brick chimney and willed the light to continue burning. The last vapors of my magic emptied into the shield.

"It's over, baby. They got 'em," Lucas called to me from across the shingled roof.

The blue-green light flickered before disappearing with a pop. I'd never worked so hard to maintain a shield and my body was exhausted. I rocked back and plopped my butt onto the roof. Damn, I was tired.

Lucas knelt in front of me. "You okay?"

I nodded and my brain slopped back and forth in my head. "I just need to sit a couple of minutes and recharge. Why don't you go on with the guys and check on your father?"

His jaw clenched. "I'm not leaving you."

I wasn't about to argue with him and it felt good leaning my head against his chest. A few of the Bravo guys yelled up to make sure we were okay and Simon waved from across the clearing. After about ten minutes, Lucas and I climbed carefully down the trellis and headed toward the captured werewolves and the pile of dead Malandanti.

"Gonna burn them?" I asked Simon.

He nodded suavely. "Yes, as soon as the Divine Council confirms my request."

It was customary to burn the bodies of witches to ensure no other magical beings could use the bodies for rituals.

Lucas helped me sit on the remnants of a cracked cement picnic table on the far side of the courtyard.

"Give me a couple more minutes and I'll provide the spark for that fire."

Simon relaxed enough to smile. "As you wish, my dear," he said as he returned to the business of securing the captured werewolves.

Lucas was resting his chin on his hand and staring at me. He had fresh bruises on his face and his knuckles were bloody but he was smiling.

"Just when I think I know you, you do something absolutely amazing," he said.

My grin ended up a grimace as my split lip protested my smile. "So how many wolves did you kick the shit out of?"

He chuckled and took my hand. "Lost count after twelve."

I was going to kid him about his lack of counting ability when a strangling sense of black magic grabbed my lungs. Panic flashed in

Lucas's eyes before he glanced down at the guardian stone I had given him.

"Get Simon and tell him more are coming."

Lucas nodded and dashed across the clearing toward Bravo. He reached Simon, who looked over his shoulder in alarm.

I choked on another blast of black magic and grabbed the edge of the broken table to keep from falling over. I'd used all my magic to shield Bravo from the first wave and now a second wave was on its way. Shit. Not good.

The spells descended like a curtain from the sky. I called up a few vapors of magic and kept the evil at bay. I didn't have enough to shield everyone. The Malandanti stood at the top of the clearing with a second, larger force of werewolves surrounding them. The first wave had depleted me and the Malandanti knew it.

"Lucas? Bring our father to me and I will let you live."

Lucas tried to run toward me but a Malandanti energy bolt slammed into him and dropped him in his tracks. I lurched to my feet and ran to my wolf.

A hideous laugh filled the air. Lucas was writhing in pain when Josef Benelli stepped from his home.

"Nicolli?" the Alpha called. "What are you doing?"

A second bolt flew toward Bravo. The guys scattered, ducking behind whatever they could find to use as protection.

Nicolli Benelli brazenly marched forward. Without the Malandanti he wouldn't stand a chance, but with their magic backing him, there wasn't much we could do.

Josef Benelli's face turned purple as he stumbled toward us. A Malandanti binding spell, like a boa constrictor, slowly squeezed the life from his body. Lucas reached out for his fallen father and the two grasped hands.

"Lucas, I'm sorry," Josef murmured.

The wolves of Bravo shouted. The Bravo vampires were bursting into flames, another damn Malandanti spell. Simon was strong enough to resist. The others couldn't. The wolves were helping put out the flames when they clutched their throats and stumbled to their knees.

All around me, the ones I cared about were dying. The tendrils of magic made my chest hurt but I wasn't the target. The Malandanti wanted me to watch.

Nicolli laughed as Lucas tried to shield his father. It was a laugh I would never forget and never forgive.

I knelt and took a handful of dirt, a connection to the one who gave me strength. Tears spilled down my face as I watched the struggles of the wolves and listened to the screams of the vampires. Lucas cradled his father, pain coursing through their bodies.

"Bring it," I said before dropping the last of my defenses. The magic rushed toward me like I was a vacuum. For a few seconds I could hear the Bravo guys yelling to one another. They would know to attack the Malandanti and kill them where they stood. Hopefully the Italian Pack would rush in and help with Nicolli's wolves. I would handle the magic. It was up to them to do the rest.

Chapter 40

Lucas

My father drew in a huge breath, the color of his face looking less purple by the second. On the hilltop, the soldiers of Bravo Company hacked away at the dark witches, who were no longer very effective.

Nicolli ran toward us, his wolves flanking and attacking the rushing pack wolves spilling from the house. My father was weak, both from the Malandanti spell and the fight with me. Nicolli headed straight for us.

Breanna was literally glowing. She was on her knees looking up at the sky. I couldn't get close to her--whatever spell she was using putting off enough heat to scorch the dirt around her.

My brother's scent grew stronger and I stood to meet him.

Nic stopped a few feet in front of us and eyed Breanna. "Hmm, guess I underestimated her." He tipped his head and smiled at me. "Oh, Mother, why don't you come out?"

My father growled and tried to stand. Nic smirked at my father's efforts as my mother burst out of the house and rushed to Josef's side.

"Nicolli, what are you doing? You were only supposed to take Lucas and the witch. You didn't say anything about harming your father." Tears streamed down my mom's face as she knelt beside my father.

Josef jerked his head toward Gemma. "What do you mean, take Lucas? What is going on here, Gemma?"

She sobbed uncontrollably, her words coming out as senseless babble.

Nic shook his head. "You can leave now, Lucas. You don't want any part of the pack and that's all I want. Hell, you can even take your witch and go in peace."

I glanced over at Breanna, now completely consumed by a blue-black light. At my feet my father held my mother, who seemed inconsolable.

"No, Nic. I will not allow you to kill my father."

My brother half chuckled. "I expected as much. You always were the trooper, trying to make Father like you even when he couldn't stand the sight of you."

I don't know where the sudden surge of strength came from, but I seized the opportunity and decked my brother. Blood burst from his face and I went after him. Nicolli was no match for me and he knew it. He tried to scramble away. I grabbed him by the feet and dragged him back in front of my father.

I let loose the fury I had held in for over twenty years. Nic tried to fight back. I hit him harder. I beat him to a bloody pulp and pulled him up by his scruff. I should have killed him for what he had put us through, for what he had done to Breanna, but ultimately his fate was the Alpha's decision.

"Lucas?" Breanna called softly.

She was falling to the side, her face covered in blood. I threw my brother into the dirt and ran to catch her before she hit the ground. I cradled her in my arms as tremors shook her body. Her eyes were barely open and her breathing labored.

"Bre, baby, I'm right here."

She coughed and blood seeped from her lips. The guardian stone she had given me was blazing hot. I yelled for Simon and he was there in seconds.

"She absorbed the magic of the Malandanti. We must get her to the hospital now," he said.

Breanna gagged on more blood and went limp in my arms.

"Bre? Breanna?" I cried, shaking her. "Baby, wake up, you gotta stay with me."

A single long breath escaped her lips and I felt her soul pulling away.

"No, no, no," I bellowed. I snatched a knife from Simon's belt and slashed my palm and then Breanna's. With our palms pressed together, our blood mixed, allowing the mate bond to take hold.

The air rushed from my lungs as Breanna's soul returned to her body. Bonded. Our lives intertwined. She could use my energy to heal herself. She could use my energy to live.

"Lucas, what have you done?" my father rasped from behind me.

I would not survive without her. I held her close, begging her to come back, desperate to see her open her eyes.

"Lucas, we must get her to medical care immediately," Simon insisted. "Your bonding will only hold her for so long."

I scooped Breanna into my arms and followed Simon. She gasped for breath and her face was almost gray. I'd never been so helpless in my life.

"Bre, baby, can you hear me?" I asked, climbing into the Humvee.

Several of the Bravo wolves leaped into the backseat. "We'll watch your back, Lucas."

I nodded to them and saw the fear in their eyes, too. None of us could live without her. I smoothed her hair and wiped the blood from her face.

She lay motionless all the way to the hospital. Simon slid the Humvee into the emergency room entrance and called immediately for the special religions team. Dozens of elf doctors and nurses, some of whom had helped me, surrounded the vehicle. When Simon yanked the door open and the nurses saw I was holding a witch, the motion all stopped.

"We do not treat witches," one of the nurses snipped.

"You will treat her or you will deal with me," I answered, releasing every ounce of dominance I could summon.

One of the doctors pushed forward and took Breanna's vitals. "What happened?"

Simon laid a hand on Breanna's forehead. "She absorbed a great deal of black magic in order to save--" He choked on his words. "In order to save us."

They wheeled out a stretcher and I laid her onto it as gently as I could. She wasn't conscious and blood streamed from her nose and mouth. Her body felt cool to the touch, but she was using our bond to stay alive. I stumbled and Aaron put out a hand to help me.

"She's pulling energy from you?" he asked quietly.

I nodded and grabbed the side of her stretcher. She could take everything I had if that was what she needed to survive.

The nurses wheeled the gurney into the brightly lit hospital and down the hall. I stayed at her side until we reached the big wooden double doors of the operating room. The Elvin doctor who had taken Breanna's vitals turned to me.

"We have to take her into surgery to repair whatever internal damage the magic has done," he said quietly.

She looked so fragile lying on the crisp white sheets.

"We're bonded," I whispered, pulling her fingers to my lips.

The doctor nodded sympathetically. "We will do what we can for her. You should rest, have some food. You will need to keep yourself strong for her." He took a heavy, deep breath. "Perhaps speak with your Alpha about using the pack bonds to give her more strength." He bowed his head. "It will take more than the strength of a single wolf to pull her through this."

I kissed her softly on the forehead.

The elf team disappeared with my mate behind the double doors. I stared at the solid doors. I couldn't move, couldn't function.

The wolves and vampires of Bravo Company spread out among the chairs in the tiny waiting area. Their faces were pinched with worry, most of them still covered in blood from the fight with the Malandanti.

For the first time in my life, I wasn't upset about werewolves surrounding me. Their hearts were heavy like mine. We were all lost.

Another yank on my energy forced me to settle into the closest chair. Celeste, Breanna's little elf friend, moved to sit by me. Her tiny, waiflike hand gripped mine as tears flowed down her cheeks.

"She loves you so much. She'll fight for you."

I nodded and fought back a rising tide of emotion. Breanna needed me to be strong.

The power of an Alpha touched the hospital almost an hour after Breanna went into surgery. None of the other wolves acknowledged my father as he came toward me.

"Lucas? Are you all right?"

I felt like a paper mache version of myself. "I'm fine."

He placed a hand on my shoulder and I flinched. There was no energy left to fight him anymore.

"She is taking your strength?"

"Yes, but the doctor says it won't be enough." I looked up at him. "He said I should talk to you about using the power of the pack to save her."

The shock in his eyes was real. "Use the pack bonds to save a witch? That would mean opening the pack to her. I can't do that."

"Do it for me. Save her for me. I'll do whatever you want. I'll be your future Alpha. I'll submit on my hands and knees in front of the entire pack. I'll do anything, just please don't let her die."

I had no pride left. Everything inside me was broken.

"I'm sorry, son. I cannot risk the pack for her. If she truly loves you, she will sever your bond, accept death on her terms and leave you to live your life."

My heart almost stopped beating at the thought of her breaking our bond. I looked at my father and saw the pain in his eyes. He didn't mean to be cruel, but his pack always came first.

I shuffled away from my father as Simon closed in on him. Voices raised in anger from both Simon and my father. I stared out the window.

I was getting weaker and weaker and that wasn't a good sign. If Breanna was pulling on me this hard, she must have been dying.

An eternity later the Elvin doctor emerged from the double doors. He pulled his surgical mask over his head and wiped his face with a green hospital towel.

I held onto the doorframe and braced for whatever he might say.

"She is out of surgery and we've moved her to a room." The doctor paused, his sad blue eyes falling to me. "There is much internal damage. We did what we could, but her body is slowly shutting down."

Celeste wailed and flung herself at Simon. Tears shone brightly in the eyes of the Bravo soldiers. I leaned against the wall. Otherwise I would have fallen.

"Can I see her?"

"She will not regain consciousness."

My hands were shaking. "Can I see her?"

The Elvin doctor looked around uncomfortably at the scene before him. The room was full of vampires, werewolves, and one hysterical little elf, all grieving for a witch.

"Come with me."

I didn't look at faces as I made my way to the double doors. It was hard enough to put one foot in front of the other at this point. The doctor led me down a hall and into a sterile, whitewashed room. The sharp smells of antiseptic attacked my nose, but it was the beeping of the monitors that rattled my brain most.

We stopped outside the door. "I don't mean to sound cold, Mr. Benelli, but I would suggest you say your goodbyes to her."

With those words he walked away and left me in the hall alone, my hand resting on the door handle.

Nothing could have prepared me for the sight of her surrounded by machines, tubes in her mouth and nose. A respirator pumped beside her bed, three IV lines connected to her arms.

I pulled a chair beside her bed and delicately clutched her hand in mine. There were no words I could say, nothing. I pressed her hand to my face, silently pleading with her to open her eyes just once. There was no motion, no movement, nothing except the sounds of machines forcing air into her lungs.

The reality of the situation slammed into me like a ton of bricks. I wasn't feeling her pull anymore. She was slipping away, slowly releasing our bond.

"Breanna, no, please don't," I sobbed. "Please don't leave me."

* * * *

I'd felt a little tap but there had been no pull on our mate bond in hours. If the heart monitor stopped beeping, I would crumble into a million pieces.

Galen sat beside me now. Simon had visited for a few minutes. Aaron and Christopher had also stuck their heads in the door but didn't stay. Nobody was used to seeing Breanna weak. She was the rock all of us leaned on and now she was here, dying, because of us, because of me.

"How's she doing?"

I bit my lip and tried to hold back the seemingly endless tears. "Not good." My voice broke and I choked on the words. This couldn't be happening.

Galen leaned closer and placed his hand over mine. "There are things you need to know."

"What?" What could be so important now? Breanna was dying. What else mattered?

"We need to speak to Josef and to--" He paused before adding, "And Gemma."

I had no idea who was in the waiting room. I hadn't left Breanna's side for three days. "I don't know where they are," I mumbled. My father had dropped by several times. My mother had not.

"I called them when my plane landed. They're both in the waiting room."

I pressed my lips to Breanna's cold hand. "I can't leave her. I don't want her to be alone."

Galen squeezed my hand. "This is important, Lucas, for both of you."

"We will sit with her while you attend to these matters." Simon said, standing with Celeste in the doorway.

I didn't want to let go of her hand. I was afraid if I let go, she would slip away, but Galen was persistent. I pushed aside a tube and kissed her on the cheek. "I'll be right back. Please don't leave."

I swiped at the tears and followed Galen into the waiting area. My mother and father were against the far wall and my mother looked like she'd seen a ghost when Galen faced her.

"McGregor, this is a foolhardy time to make a play," my father growled.

Galen leveled a glare at my mother. "Gemma? You need to tell him the truth."

Josef stepped nose-to-nose with Galen. "You will not address my mate in that tone."

Galen never blinked. "Josef, we both know she isn't your mate. Your chosen wife, perhaps, but not a bonded mate."

The room was getting tipsy. One of the vampires offered a chair and I took it gladly.

"Tell him, Gemma. Tell your husband the truth about Lucas."

"What the hell are you rambling about, McGregor?" my father roared.

There was a heavy silence in the air before Galen spoke. "Lucas is my son."

My lungs imploded. My father launched himself toward Galen. My mother screamed. The wolves and vampires rushed in to separate the two big men. I slipped away from the chaos and went back to Breanna's room. I didn't understand what was going on, why Galen would think I was his son, or what the hell my mother was screaming. All I knew was that my world was slowly crumbling.

Celeste placed Breanna's hand into mine before she and Simon quietly left us alone. I laid my head onto the bedside and tucked her hand under my chin.

"If you must go, take me with you," I whispered. "I will not live without you." I'd never meant anything more in my life. "Don't break our bond."

The door opened and the rush of Alpha dominance filled the room. Galen sat beside me and placed a hand on my shoulder. "I know this is a bad time for all this to come up, but you need to know the truth."

I rubbed Breanna's fingers along my cheek, wishing I was really feeling her touch. Never in my life had anything hurt as much as watching my mate slowly dying.

"Do you remember the night you defended Breanna and I stepped in to keep you from killing Zeke?"

I stared at her fingers. The world had gone black that night. My wolf had ascended and taken complete control.

"That was your wolf acknowledging mine. A son meeting his father. Have you felt surges of power these last few hours?"

I had. Those surges had saved my life a couple of times.

"Those were from me. How did I know you and Breanna were mated?"

I choked back a sob as I remembered that day. She had been so beautiful.

"I should have told you then, but I couldn't risk a pack war with Josef without being completely sure. I'm sorry for everything you've gone through, but I can help now if you'll trust me."

This was all too much for me to take in. None of it mattered anyway.

"The wolf doesn't lie, Lucas, and your wolf has known you were not Josef's son just as Josef's wolf has known it. That is why the two of you fight."

Galen squeezed my shoulder. "I met your mother at a Gathering in Switzerland. I had no idea she was Josef Benelli's wife. We spent the weekend together and I never saw her again. I'd felt tugs on my wolf for years, but every time I'd check, Cody was fine. Now I understand. It was you. You were reaching out for help, for your father. Josef didn't feel it because you have no bond to him. You are bonded to me, as my son."

"So?"

Galen's power flashed through me. "The doctors say the power of a pack can save her."

Breanna's hand felt colder.

"I can help you save her."

I looked into his eyes and saw he spoke the truth. "How? How can you do that? She isn't a part of your pack."

"As my son, we share a bond. If you will lower your defenses and accept my pack, they will give you their strength as brothers. Because you are her mate, you can give that strength to her."

"Josef hasn't released me. I can't join another pack."

"You've never been a part of the Italian Pack. He doesn't have to release you. You have no bond to him and you have never been accepted by the pack."

"Your pack doesn't want me."

He tilted his head. "They don't know you. You have kept so much hidden, so much pain buried. That is not natural for a wolf. A wolf should share his pain with his pack. You have never had that chance, but I am offering it to you now."

"Why would they help me?"

He smiled sadly. "Because they love her."

This could be it, a way to save her, a way to save us.

"What do I have to do?"

"Join my pack. Enough pack members are in the waiting room that we can perform the ritual there. You will need to submit to me as your Alpha and allow the pack into your soul."

My breath caught in my throat.

"Yes, they will see everything that happened to you. They will see what you endured as a child. They will feel that pain just as you did, but it will help you heal. Once you have fully accepted them, their strength will flow through you and into Breanna."

Simon and Celeste stayed with Breanna while I followed Galen into the waiting area. The pack had closed the doors and the members were shoulder to shoulder in a circle. Josef and Gemma were gone.

Galen led me to the center of the circle and I kneeled before him. He moved around behind me and placed his hands on my shoulders. His power crashed through me as he lifted my chin. I saw the glint of a knife blade. This was a blood rite. He would cut my throat and heal me with the power of the pack before I bled out. It was an act of total submission and complete trust. If I did not allow the pack into my soul, I would die.

I drew in a sharp breath as he pulled my hands behind my back and secured them with silver cuffs. The silver would prevent my body from healing itself. It would also drain what little strength I had left.

The pack wolves surrounded me. I didn't have the energy to panic. All I could think about was Breanna.

"I'm sorry, son, but this is the way it must be," Galen rasped in my ear. I leaned against his legs so I wouldn't topple over onto the floor. "If there was more time, I would do this more gently."

I closed my eyes and swallowed hard. "I submit to you, my Alpha."

The knife burned. Memories raced to the surface--dark pictures of Stephano, of the cell, of the headmaster, of Josef's disappointment. Other images, foreign ones, flooded my mind as the pack bonds reached out. My memories belonged to them and their memories belonged to me.

Fire ripped through me, the pain almost unbearable. No air reached my lungs, my heart stuttered. The smell of my own blood enraged my wolf, but the silver kept him in check.

Breanna.

Icy coldness replaced the fire. My body convulsed, my wolf fighting to ascend. More voices floated through my head. The voices united into a chorus calling to me, pleading with me to find them.

Air rushed into chest. My stomach wretched, emptying my breakfast onto the floor.

"Lucas?"

Far away, Galen called to me, to my wolf. I wanted to go to him. He would make the world right. My Alpha. My father.

"Lucas? Son?"

Galen was closer now. I could feel him. All I could see was empty blackness, but he was there, waiting. Others were there, too. For the first time in my life, acceptance surrounded me, a cocoon of serenity. Strength flooded my body. Precious warmth flowed through my veins. It felt like dozens of hands reached for me, pulling me out of the darkness toward my Alpha.

My pack.

My eyelids fluttered open, the light painfully bright. I faltered, hurdling face-first toward the floor, but the hands once again reached for me, held me, helped me.

My brothers.

The silver cuffs clattered away from my wrists.

"Lucas, take my hand."

My muscles were mush. The simplest motion impossible.

The world came into focus. The pack wolves surrounded me, their heads bowed as they gently urged me to my feet. More strength poured through my body, pushing away the insecurities and doubts that had so long plagued my mind. I was stronger than ever before.

My brain function resumed, my muscles recognizing the signals to move.

I reached for Galen's hand. The pack wolves steadied me until Galen's fingers grasped mine.

"Welcome, my son."

The surge of emotion surprised me. I blinked at him, unable to put into words the powerful feelings of acceptance.

He placed a hand behind my head and pulled me close.

"Go to your mate, Lucas," he whispered. "We'll be here waiting for you."

Every step toward her room was a feat in concentration. My muscles and brain were not fully communicating yet, but each time I felt myself falling, another wave of strength pushed me forward. The pack bonds were like hundreds of tiny fingers tapping on my skull, demanding acknowledgement. Another wave of strength, this one much more powerful than the rest, quieted the barrage of noise.

My Alpha.

I pushed open her door, praying she would be sitting up in bed, smiling as I walked in.

Simon and Celeste rose from their chairs.

"Did she wake up?"

Tears flowed freely down Celeste's cheeks. "She hasn't moved since you left."

I sank onto the chair. Breanna should have been awake by now. Galen had promised the pack bonds would help.

Alphas kept their promises.

I tucked her hand against chin and willed her to feel the strength of the pack. Power ebbed and flowed through my body. I clenched my eyes closed and concentrated on the feel of her skin against mine. To my last breath, I would give everything to save her.

Her fingers twitched. It was a tiny movement, nothing more than a brush of butterfly wings, but I felt it. I pressed her hand to my lips.

"Please, Breanna. Please come back."

The incessant beeping of the heart monitor increased. I panicked.

"Bre? You feel that, don't you? Those are pack bonds. Our pack, baby. We're all waiting for you to come back to us. We all need you. I need you."

My voice cracked. The monitor leveled off and the beeping resumed its former steady rhythm.

"I'm a Wisconsin Pack wolf now. There's so much I want to tell you, but you need to wake up. Find your way back here. Do whatever it takes, but please come back."

Her fingers did not move again. I laid my head on the mattress and pressed her hand against my cheek. I would not go on without her. There was not enough power in the pack to make my life worth living without her.

The beeping monitor sped up again. I squeezed her fingers, doing everything I could to hold her in this world. I would not let her go without a fight.

The doctor came in and sat in the chair beside me. I'd never been around many elves, but the bitter scent of sadness clung to him.

"We've done all we can do. It's time to let her go."

My heart shattered.

The doctor thinned his lips. "I'm sorry, Lucas. I wish there was more we could do, but the damage was too extensive for us to repair. The kindest thing we can do now is let her go peacefully."

"Breanna is a fighter," I rasped, staring into her face. I'd do anything for her to open her eyes and give this doctor a piece of her mind for giving up on her.

"She was a fighter, but this was a fight she could not win. We need to take her off the respirator and allow nature to take its course. That is what Breanna would have wanted."

The Elvin doctor had no idea how close he was to being ripped to pieces. He did not know her and had no right to tell me anything about what she would want.

"She hasn't given up. Neither have I."

"At least allow me to remove the feeding tube. It is irritating her throat tissue. We can keep the IVs and supply her body with nutrients."

I wasn't ready to let her go, but what if the doctor was right? Was I being selfish in keeping her here, trapped in a body ravaged by pain?

"If I remove the tube from her throat, she will be able to talk if she wakes."

The tone of his voice made it clear the doctor had no hope Breanna would ever wake up. He did not know her.

I talked to Simon and Celeste before finally agreeing with the doctor's request. They both felt Breanna would not want to live like this, bedridden and machine dependent. They hadn't completely given up hope, but they heard the doctor's spiel about the chances of brain damage and regaining consciousness.

Breanna was strong. She would come back.

I scarcely breathed when the respirator was unplugged. The heart monitor never lost its rhythm. The doctor had the decency to look mildly surprised.

The hours blurred together. The only sound in my world was the beeping. Pack wolves came and went. Celeste and Simon ventured in and out. Galen tried to get me to go eat, but I would not leave her.

My body gave in to sleep at some point. I woke with a start, terrified by the silence in the room.

No beeping.

"Hey, handsome? You're breaking my fingers."

I jerked my head up and found myself staring into the most incredible amber eyes.

"Breanna?"

"Expecting somebody else?" she asked with a weak smile. "That beeping was getting on my nerves and you needed to sleep so I hit the mute button."

My chin trembled as I pressed my lips to her wrist.

"I feel like I got hit by a truck." She brushed her fingers along my jaw. "And you look like hell. You've been here the whole time, haven't you?"

I cupped her hand in mine. I would never let her go again. "The doctor didn't think you'd make it."

Her eyelids fluttered and she scowled. "Stupid elves. Cee's the only one I ever met with the sense to come in out of the rain." She frowned. "Well, except for Lisel, but I'm not convinced he's one-hundred-percent elf. Lot of magic around him."

"I love you," I choked. I'd been waiting to say the words until I could look into her eyes. She looked startled at first, but quickly recovered.

"I love you, too." Her cheeks turned pink. Her fingers traced my jawbone. "I didn't want to leave you. Maybe one day I can explain everything that happened, but right now I'm too tired to do much of anything but lie here and look at you."

I loved her so much it hurt.

"Now explain why the hell I feel like my entire unit of werewolves is in my head."

"Pack bonds."

"Pack bonds? Did you? Are you? What happened?"

I kissed her on the cheek. "Let's just say I can stay in Wisconsin and help finish that resurrection project you call a house."

Meet the Author

Jacky Russell is married to a non-werewolf and lives in North Carolina on a farm that serves as a halfway house for demon dogs and other animals who have lost their way. When not hard at work on the next adventures of Bravo Company and the Wisconsin Werewolf Pack, Jacky is a vocal fan of the Carolina Hurricanes hockey team. She also enjoys competitive dog sports and lemon meringue pie.

www.ingramcontent.com/pod-product-compliance
Lightning Source LLC
Chambersburg PA
CBHW020741250626
47155CB00003B/860

* 9 7 8 1 6 1 6 5 0 9 0 3 3 *